THE OUTLAW FROM NEWVILLE

A Game Warden Henry Glance Novel
Book 2

STEVEN T. CALLAN

coffeetown**press**

Kenmore, WA

coffeetownpress

A Coffeetown Press book published by Epicenter Press

Epicenter Press
6524 NE 181st St.
Suite 2
Kenmore, WA 98028

For more information go to:
www.Camelpress.com
www.Coffeetownpress.com
www.Epicenterpress.com
www.steventcallan.com

This is a work of fiction. Names, characters, places, brands, media, and incidents are either the product of the author's imagination or are used fictitiously.

Cover photo and back-cover photo by Steven T. Callan
Design by Melissa Vail Coffman

The Outlaw from Newville
Copyright © 2025 by Steven T. Callan

Library of Congress Control Number: 2024952546

ISBN: 978-1-68492-312-0 (Trade Paper)
ISBN: 978-1-68492-313-7 (eBook)

For my mother

Doris Louise Callan

1928 - 2021

Acknowledgments

Writing my second novel about California Fish and Game Warden Henry Glance was like reconnecting with an old friend, reliving decades of life experiences, researching another college term paper, and at times, sweating blood. I wouldn't trade the experience for the world and would like to thank three very important people for helping to make it possible.

I'm forever grateful to Phil Garrett, at Epicenter Press, and Jennifer McCord, at Coffeetown Press, for supporting my writing for the last twelve years.

To Kathy Callan, my loving wife and partner for life, I can't thank you enough for your unwavering encouragement, your invaluable advice, and the endless hours you've spent editing since this adventure began.

PART ONE
Willie Radcliff
Henry Glance

1912 - 1973

ONE

PRESTON EARL RADCLIFF, THE TALL, HANDSOME, ruggedly built son of a wealthy Chicago cattle buyer, was twenty-two years old in 1912 when his father died of a heart attack and left him six and a half million dollars. Three months before receiving his degree in agriculture from the University of Illinois, Preston was reading the *Chicago Tribune* on a bench in the university's student commissary.

"Preston," said Bill Akers, a longtime friend and fellow student, "I'm so sorry to hear about your father."

"Thank you, Bill. It was unexpected."

"How old was he?"

"Fifty-nine."

"That's awfully young. How are you getting along?"

"It was rough for a while, and I've had a lot to take care of, but things are getting better."

"That's good. The three of us are going to grab a table. Would you like to join us?"

Radcliff was about to decline when he spotted an attractive young lady standing behind Akers. She was wearing a white, cotton dress, and her long, auburn hair was wrapped in one of the Edwardian styles of the day. "Sure," he said, flashing a smile. "My next class doesn't start for another hour."

"I'd like you to meet Molly Bryer," said Akers. "I think you already know Ralph Jenkins."

"I just realized where I've seen you before," said Radcliff, lightly squeezing Miss Bryer's offered right hand. "You sit in the front row of my animal husbandry class." Radcliff had never seen her in a dress before. She usually showed up for class wearing Levi jeans, a long-sleeved denim shirt, and a pair of Red Wing work boots splattered with cow manure.

"I can see why you might recognize her," said Akers. "Molly is the only female student in the entire Agriculture Department."

Everyone chuckled, except Jenkins, who was waiting for Preston to release his girlfriend's hand.

"What are you going to do when you graduate?" said Akers, looking across the table at Radcliff. "Do you have anything in mind?"

"The first thing I'm going to do is sell my father's house."

"What about your mother?" said Molly. "Where will she live?"

"Preston's mother is no longer with us," said Akers.

"I'm so sorry. I didn't know."

"It's okay," said Radcliff. "I was six years old when she died and don't remember much."

"You should see his father's house," said Akers, purposely changing the subject. "It's in Forest Glen, one of the classiest neighborhoods in Chicago."

"I'm sure it's beautiful," said Molly.

"I'll say!" said Akers. "Three stories, a wraparound covered porch, and a front lawn that could pass for the University of Illinois football field. The surrounding property is forested with red oak and sugar maple, just like it was in Abe Lincoln's day."

"Bill, maybe I should hire you as my real-estate agent," said Radcliff. "I loved growing up in that house, but it's way too big for one person to wander around in."

"You could always get married and have children," said Molly, again drawing Jenkins's ire.

"I'll probably do that someday, Miss Bryer, but right now I have something else in mind."

"What's that?" said Akers.

"As soon as I graduate and sell the house, I'm moving out to California."

"What are you going to do in California?" said Akers.

"I'm going to buy fifteen hundred acres of rangeland and raise cattle."

"Where is this rangeland?" said Molly.

"It's in the northwest corner of the Sacramento Valley, near a tiny speck on the map called Newville."

"What does this rangeland look like?"

"I haven't seen it yet, but according to the written description I received from my agent, it's an emerald-green land of rolling hills, clear-running streams, and grass-covered valleys. His letter said it's ideal for raising cattle."

"How did you hear about this place?" said Jenkins.

"I first read about it in the *Tribune*. My agent and I have been writing back and forth for a couple months now."

"It sounds like some kind of swindle, if you ask me," said Jenkins.

"Nobody asked you, Ralph," said Molly, reaching across the table and lightly touching Preston's right hand. "It could be the beginning of a wonderful adventure, and I think Preston should follow his dream."

"Maybe if you ask him nicely, Preston will take you along with him," said Jenkins, standing up from the table, gathering his books, and storming out the door.

PRESTON RADCLIFF AND MOLLY BRYER WERE married on Tuesday morning, June 25, 1912, in Sacramento, California. When the brief ceremony was over, the happy couple climbed into the Model T Ford Preston had purchased in San Francisco and steered north toward the small Sacramento Valley farm town of Orland. Arriving in Orland, they headed west for twenty-two miles on a narrow dirt road. Crossing over Stony Creek, they wound through the foothills of Glenn County, and as the sun dipped below the mountains to the west, arrived in the tiny, picturesque hamlet of Newville.

"I love it!" said Molly. "Living in a quiet little town like this is what I've always dreamed of."

"It's a far cry from Chicago," said Preston. "Let's see if we can find ourselves a place to sleep tonight."

Preston and Molly putted past a two-story dwelling that looked like a hotel, but two boys were batting rocks with a stick nearby and Molly was looking for something a little more romantic. Pushing onward, the newlyweds came to a row of clapboard buildings—two stores, several more dwellings, a doctor's office, a dance hall, and a butcher shop—before coming to a rustic inn with a wooden walkway and a bench out front.

"This isn't exactly what I had in mind, but it will have to do," said Molly.

"Good decision!" said Preston, exhausted and eager to settle in for the night.

The couple awakened at 6:00 the next morning to the clanging of hammer against anvil. "What's that noise?" said Molly, peeking over the covers at the stark, dimly lit room.

Preston raised the window shade to find a buckskin horse tied to the hitching post next door. The sign on the building read BLACKSMITH. "It's the sound of our new home," he said. "I guess we'd better get used to it."

Preston and Molly were waiting on the bench in front of the hotel when a Pierce-Arrow Model 66, five-passenger touring car pulled up. The middle-aged driver was so slender, he made the wrinkled sack suit he wore look two sizes too big.

"I'm Melvin Pendergast," the man said, removing his straw boater and exposing his thinning gray hair. "May I assume you are Mr. and Mrs. Preston Radcliff?"

"You may," said Molly, extending her hand. "Do you live here in Newville, Mr. Pendergast?"

"Please call me Mel. I actually live in Chico, a little over forty miles east of here."

"You've come a long way," said Preston, making a mental note of Pendergast's firm, confident grip. "How long have you been in the real-estate business?"

"I was an accountant in Sacramento for fifteen years before dabbling in real estate about five years ago. After collecting a handsome commission on my first big sale, I said, 'This is the business for me!' I sold my house, moved to Chico, and have done quite well ever since."

"I can see that," said Preston, looking down from the porch at Pendergast's shiny, maroon-colored automobile.

"If you folks would like to take a ride, we'll drive out to the property we've been corresponding about for the last three months."

Molly rode up front with Pendergast, and Preston sprawled out in back. The trio putted west across a dry streambed, entering a vast landscape of rolling hills, rocky outcroppings, and a sea of amber grass studded with majestic blue oaks.

When the tour was over and Pendergast had returned Preston and Molly to the hotel, he asked if they had any questions or concerns.

"I have one concern," said Preston. "In one of the letters you sent me, you described the property as an emerald-green land of rolling hills, clear-running streams, and grass-covered valleys. The land we saw today was as brown as that horse over there, and all of the streams we crossed were bone dry."

Pendergast smiled. "Glenn County's abundant rangelands were emerald green at the time I wrote the letter. The Sacramento Valley is blessed with a Mediterranean climate."

"Please explain what you mean by a Mediterranean climate," said Molly.

"It means the rangelands of Glenn County are generally green from the first of November, when the grass begins to grow, until the first week in May, when the rain stops, the weather warms, and the grass turns golden brown."

"What about the streams?" said Preston.

"Most of the streams in this part of the country are seasonal. That means they run during the rainy season and go dry or below ground during the summer months. The only streams around here that generally run year-round are Grindstone Creek and Stony Creek. Grindstone Creek is four or five miles south of here, and you crossed the main branch of Stony Creek about eight miles west of Orland."

MOLLY HAD FALLEN IN LOVE WITH the quiet, small-town atmosphere of Newville. Between business ventures, Preston hired a local carpenter to build his bride a modest home northwest of town, with the white picket fence she had always wanted.

As the weeks and months went by, Preston became increasingly impressed by Mel Pendergast's sincerity, knowledge of the area, and salesmanship—so much so that he asked him to become his business partner. Taking advantage of Preston Radcliff's capital and Melvin Pendergast's expertise, the two entrepreneurs began leasing grazing rights and buying up large tracts of fertile farmland all over Glenn and Butte counties.

THE RADCLIFFS' ONLY CHILD WAS BORN on a hot July afternoon in 1916. They named their son William Lawson Radcliff, but from the day William was born, everyone called him Willie. Throughout his early childhood, Willie was large for his age, rambunctious, and too much for his mother to handle. If he was playing with any of the younger children in town, someone always ended up crying.

Preston Radcliff was consumed by his prospering business and had little or no time for his growing son. To make up for it, he gave Willie everything he asked for. That included the Winchester Model 56 bolt-action .22-caliber rifle, with a five-round clip, that Willie received for his eleventh birthday.

One week later, while Preston was away on business, Willie ran out the back door of the house carrying his rifle and a box of .22 long-rifle cartridges. "Don't shoot anything you're not supposed to," shouted Molly, scrubbing the kitchen sink.

"I won't," Willie shouted back.

Ten minutes had gone by when Molly heard the sharp crack of her son's rifle going off near the neighbors' place. Thinking Willie had rid the neighborhood of another pesky ground squirrel, she shook her head and went back to her housework. Molly was running her carpet sweeper across the living-room rug when she heard heavy boots stomping up the back steps and a hard *KNOCK-KNOCK-KNOCK* on the door.

"Molly, it's Norvell Trucks. I need to talk to you." *KNOCK-KNOCK-KNOCK.*

"Hold your horses, Norvell," said Molly, removing her apron and adjusting her hair. "I'm coming."

Molly opened the back door to find her closest neighbor with a scowl on his face and a Rhode Island red lying limp in his left hand.

"That kid of yours just shot Matilda, my best laying hen."

"I'm so sorry, Norvell. His father and I will be happy to pay you for it."

"This ain't the half of it, Molly. Besides Matilda, Willie has killed one of George Cooper's white Pekin ducks and the widow Rigsby's guard goose."

"What's a guard goose?" said Molly.

"They're better than any watchdog. If anyone approached Agnes Rigsby's property, that gander of hers would start honking ta beat the band. Yesterday afternoon, while Agnes was in Orland visiting her sister,

Gus Willard heard the usual ruckus coming from the old lady's house. He figured it musta been Agnes coming home early, until he heard a rifle shot and the honking stopped. A few minutes later, Gus saw Willie and another kid slinking through the trees on the other side of the creek. Willie was carrying a rifle."

"Is Mr. Willard sure it was Willie?"

"He's sure, all right. Ain't no mistaking an eleven-year-old that big."

"I'll make sure Preston has a talk with him as soon as he returns from his business trip."

"When will that be?"

"Early next week."

"I wasn't gonna mention this, but now I think I'd better."

"Mention what, Norvell?"

"Abe Kinsel thinks Willie shot one of his goats. He saw it limping around this morning after hearing a .22-rifle shot coming from behind his barn last night."

Molly didn't respond. She remembered having told Willie he could stay out after dark playing kick the can but he had to leave his rifle at home.

"Molly, did you hear what I said?"

"I'm sorry, Norvell. I don't know what to say."

"Say you and your husband are gonna do something about it. Ever since Preston gave Willie that rifle, your son has become the worst outlaw in Newville."

TWO

JUST BEFORE DAYLIGHT ON SUNDAY, MAY 21, 1972, California Fish and Game Warden Henry Glance kissed his wife on the cheek and quietly slipped out the bedroom door of their rented 1930s-era farmhouse west of Gridley.

Henry Glance and Anne Sharp had first met in February 1968, on the Chico State College campus. Henry was a junior transfer from Riverside City College, majoring in biology, and Anne was a freshman in the Chico State teaching program. It hadn't taken Henry long to fall in love: Anne was beautiful inside and out, passionate about nature, and everything he'd always dreamed of in a life partner. They began a three-year courtship, culminating in their wedding on the banks of Big Chico Creek nearly a year ago.

"Where are you going?" said Anne, opening her eyes.

"I was hoping not to wake you," said Henry, reentering the room. "That telephone call last night was from our dispatcher in Sacramento. She gave me some information about a possible violation near Bangor. I'm going to drive up there and check it out."

"Your captain was right, Henry. You never know when to quit."

"Do you remember when I told you I didn't want to just take up space—I wanted my time on Earth to have meaning?"

"I do."

"I love nature almost as much as I love you, Sweetheart. This job provides me with a way to make a difference in the world."

"I understand," said Anne, smiling and reaching for her husband's hand. "Have you eaten anything?"

"I ate a bowl of granola and a banana out on the front porch."

"Did your girlfriend come down to join you?"

Henry chuckled. "Rosie came trotting up the steps a few minutes after Glen Darby's barn lights came on. When I finished eating, I gave her a dog biscuit and sent her home."

"Please be careful," said Anne, rolling over and attempting to fall back to sleep.

"I will. Love you!"

"I love you too."

Henry walked down the hallway to the spacious farmhouse kitchen, headed out the back door, and followed a well-worn path to the old hay barn where he kept his patrol truck. He had just swung open the barn doors when the familiar crow of a rooster pheasant captured his attention. Turning eastward, in the direction of the neighbors' alfalfa field, he stood in awe of the brilliant, early-morning sun peeking over the horizon. *How could it get any better than this?* he thought.

He hopped into his 1971, forest-green Dodge Power Wagon and drove outside. After closing the barn doors, he slid back into the driver's seat, opened the wooden box next to him, and made sure everything he'd need for the day's investigation was inside: the *California Fish and Game Code*, Title 14 of the *California Administrative Code*, the *California Penal Code*, Title 50 of the *Code of Federal Regulations*, and field guides to every bird, mammal, fish, reptile, amphibian, insect, and wild-growing plant in California.

Glance drove out the gravel driveway to the county road, crossed over the Feather River, and passed miles and miles of three-foot-high grass transitioning from the emerald greens of spring to the grays, yellows, and golden browns of the long, hot summer to come. Heading east on La Porte Road, he stopped at the Bangor Store to meet with the informant who'd telephoned Sacramento dispatch the previous evening.

"Good morning," said the middle-aged female clerk.

"Good morning," said Glance. "How are you dealing with this weather?"

"It's good for business. We're having a hard time keeping beer and ice in the store. Say, aren't you the young game warden who tracked down that no-good skunk who murdered Norm Bettis?"

"What made you ask that?"

"We saw your picture in the paper a couple weeks ago. My husband, Chester, and I read that you were assigned to Norm's old warden's district. The author of the story said you made it your personal goal to find the missing game warden and solve the mystery of his disappearance."

Glance chuckled. "Those were the reporter's words, but I did feel like I owed it to my predecessor to find out what happened to him."

"Hadn't it been something like thirteen years since Norm disappeared?"

"Yes. Thirteen years by the time I started working the case."

"Norm used to come in at least once a week during the summertime. He'd head straight for that cooler by the door and pull an Orange Nehi out of the ice-cold water. 'I've been looking forward to this all day,' he'd say."

"That's a great story. I learned a lot about Warden Bettis during my investigation. He was very well-liked and respected in the community."

"He sure was. They broke the mold when they created Norm Bettis."

"By the way, my name is Hank Glance. I'm sorry I haven't dropped in to say hello before this."

"It's good to meet you, Hank. I'm Irene Carter. My husband, Chet, is the one who called Fish and Game yesterday. I bet that's why you're here."

Glance nodded. "Is your husband around?"

"He was out back telling the truck driver where to stack the cases of beer. Here he comes now. Chet, this is Warden Hank Glance, the young man who cracked the Norm Bettis murder case."

"It's a pleasure to meet you," said Carter, shaking Glance's hand. "Come on back to my office." Carter led Glance across the creaking wood-slat floor, through a pair of swinging doors, to a tiny desk next to the walk-in meat locker. "Have a seat. I'll find another chair."

Glance pulled out the information he'd received from the Sacramento dispatcher and began reviewing it.

"This is the first time I've had the opportunity to meet you, Hank. How long have you been working for the Department of Fish and Game?"

"Three years, Mr. Carter."

"Please call me Chet."

"Chet, I'm eager to hear about the peregrine-falcon aerie and what happened yesterday."

"I'm what you might call a bird enthusiast."

"Nothing wrong with that. So am I."

"When I'm not running the store, I'm usually out looking at birds through the lens of my spotting scope. For at least the last two years, there's been a pair of peregrine falcons nesting in a canyon near here."

"Really!" said Glance. "Peregrines were placed on the U.S. and California endangered-species lists a couple years ago. At that time, there were only five recorded nesting pairs in the whole state."

"I don't know if this nest has been recorded. I've never told anybody about it."

"Please tell me why you think someone may have robbed it."

"Last Sunday, Irene and I took a drive into the canyon I just told you about. There's a beautiful little stream at the bottom, so we thought we'd make a day of it and have a picnic. When we reached the rocky cliffs about halfway down the canyon, I directed my spotting scope on the nest site."

"Is it difficult to find?"

"Not if you know where to look. There's plenty of whitewash on the rocks below the nest."

"What did you see?"

"Four peregrine fledglings were huddled at the edge of a small cave on the side of the rock cliff. I've been checking on these birds since they were hatched."

"How far along were they?"

"They had most of their feathers, but I could still see patches of white down here and there. Based on what I saw last year at this time, they were a week or so away from fledging."

"And what happened yesterday morning?"

"A little after 9:00, two men walked into the store. Both of them looked like they were about thirty years old. The taller of the two was thin, with long, reddish hair tied in a ponytail. 'What happened to you?' I said, looking at the ugly, three-inch gash on the right side of his neck. He ignored my question, handed me a twenty-dollar bill, and said they needed gas."

"What did the other man look like?"

"He was shorter, with a little more meat on his bones. I remember him having long, dark hair. He wore black horn-rimmed glasses held together with white adhesive tape. I was about to walk outside and turn on the gas pump when this character took a Snickers off the rack and dropped it on the counter."

"At least he had good taste in candy bars," said Glance, chuckling.

"I'll give him that," said Carter, "but when I asked the sonofabitch if he wanted anything else, he pulled a quarter out of his pocket and flipped it at me. The quarter bounced off my hand and onto the floor. As I bent down to pick it up, he grabbed the candy bar and followed his buddy out the door."

"They don't sound very friendly. What were these two driving?"

"It was a faded-blue Jeep Wagoneer. When I walked outside to turn on the gas pump, I noticed that the back of the Jeep was filled with rock-climbing equipment."

"What do you mean by rock-climbing equipment?"

"You know—ropes, harnesses, helmets, shoes, and carabiners."

"Sounds like you know something about rock climbing."

"During my college years down in Southern California, I worked part time in a sporting-goods store that sold climbing equipment."

"Did you see anything else in the Jeep that looked suspicious?"

"I saw a large, rectangular-shaped object in the back seat. It was covered by a blanket."

"Could the rectangular-shaped object have been a dog carrier?"

"Yes, but the shrieking sound I heard coming from it wasn't made by any dog. It was the same sound I had heard coming from the falcon nest the week before."

"Please tell me you wrote down their license number."

"I did," said Carter, handing Glance a sheet of scratch paper with the license number R25743 written on it.

"Was this a California plate? It doesn't look quite right."

"It was blue, with white lettering. I think it might have been a Nevada license plate, but I was concentrating on the number and trying not to let them see me looking at it."

"Excuse me while I radio our dispatcher and ask her to run this."

Glance returned a few minutes later.

"The license number came back to a 1969 Chevrolet Camaro," he said. "The Camaro was reported out of service in 1970. The registered owner at that time was Honest John's Used Car Rentals, Fallon, Nevada."

"What do you think happened?" said Carter.

"If I had to guess, I'd say the Camaro was totaled in a car accident and towed to an auto-wrecking yard. Our boys may have jumped the fence and removed the license plates."

"So, the license number I gave you was no good?"

"Not necessarily. If nothing else, it gives me a place to begin my investigation. I'd like to run up to the nest site and see if any of the fledglings are missing. Are you able to get away for a couple hours?"

"You bet. Let me run in and tell Irene she's gonna have to mind the store until I get back."

Warden Glance and Chet Carter headed northeast out of Bangor for twenty-three miles before turning north onto a narrow dirt road that led into the canyon Carter had described. The first mile was an easement through private property owned by a ninety-two-year-old gentleman named Homer Sug. Everything beyond that belonged to the Bureau of Land Management and was open to the public. Sug lived in a dilapidated farmhouse that hadn't seen a coat of paint since Teddy Roosevelt was president.

"Pull in here," said Carter. "We'll ask Homer if he saw those guys go by yesterday."

"You mean somebody actually lives in that house?"

"Homer has lived there since the day he was born."

"Can we get to the front door without forcing our way through those blackberry vines?"

"We won't have to. Homer's walking this way from the barn."

"Hello, Chet," said Sug. "What brings you out this way?"

"Homer, I'd like you to meet Warden Hank Glance."

"How do you do," said Sug, shaking Glance's hand.

"Very nice to meet you, Mr. Sug. Did you happen to see anyone come by the house yesterday morning?"

"Sure did. They drove by before daylight, headin' into the canyon. It was too dark to see who it was. That same rig came back out about three hours later."

"How do you know it was the same rig?" said Carter.

"Same squeaky wheels."

"Could you tell us what the car looked like?" said Glance.

"It was one of those Jeep station wagons. I think it was blue, but it was covered with dust, so I couldn't be sure."

"How many people were in it?"

"Two. I yelled at 'em to slow down. The dust cloud they left behind was as high as my house."

"Would you please call me if you see them again?" said Glance, handing Sug his business card.

"I'd be happy to, but I don't have a phone."

Glance and Carter thanked the old gentleman for the information and followed the road for another ten minutes before dropping into the canyon. "It gets pretty rough from here," said Carter. "It's a good thing you're driving this four-wheel-drive pickup and not a sedan like the one Norm Bettis used to patrol in."

"How far to the cliffs?"

"You'll be able to see them when we round this next bend. Stay as far to the left as possible. It's a long way down if we stray too far to the right."

As they rounded the bend, Carter pointed to the rock cliffs. "The best place to view the nest is next to that tall pine up ahead."

"I see the whitewash," said Glance, coming to the pine tree Carter had mentioned. "That would be a tough climb, even for an experienced rock climber. It's straight up."

Glance and Carter stepped out of the truck and were greeted by the piercing call of one of the adult birds soaring above the nest site. "That's the tiercel," said Carter.

"I'm impressed," said Glance, recognizing the term Carter had used for an adult male falcon.

Carter smiled. "The female may be on the nest. She's much larger."

"I see her now." Glance peered through his spotting scope while leaning across the hood of his pickup.

"That's a great idea—mounting your scope on a rifle stock."

"It saves me time and effort not having to mount it on the window or set up a tripod," said Glance. "I see the fledglings. It looks like there's only two. Would you like to see?"

"Sure," said Carter, taking the scope from Glance. "There's only two, all right. The hen just took off. Do you hear her calling?"

"I do. She's disturbed by our being here. After what happened yester-day, I can't say that I blame her."

"Come and look at this," said Carter. "Follow the cliff downward from the nest and tell me what you see."

"Metal pegs," said Glance. "I see one . . . two . . . three . . . four of them."

"Pitons like that are pounded into cracks in the rocks so carabiners and climbing ropes can be attached to them," said Carter.

"That clinches it!" said Glance. "The two men who came into your store yesterday stole two fledgling peregrines from that nest up there. They probably discovered the nest site some time ago and installed the metal pegs during the off-season, when the birds weren't around."

"I think you're right, Hank. The mistake they made was stopping at my store."

"Let's hope so. I'm going to walk up to the base of the rocks. We'll see if they were careless enough to leave footprints."

"I'll go with you."

Glance and Carter traversed the side of the mountain until they came to the base of the rock cliff. The farther they climbed, the more the adult peregrines protested. At one point, the tiercel swooped within two feet of Chet Carter's head.

"Wow!" said Glance. "It's amazing how protective they are. That explains the gash you saw on the taller man's neck. If he hadn't been wearing a hel-met, he might have lost an eye."

"It would have served him right," said Carter. "Look at this. It must be where they laid their ropes down. I also see footprints."

Glance photographed and measured two sets of prints. "This set looks like tennis shoes," he said.

"I wouldn't swear to it," said Carter, "but I think the guy who bought the candy bar was wearing high-top, black-and-white tennis shoes. These other prints are partially smeared, but they could be from rock-climbing shoes."

"Here's the way I see it," said Glance. "The man with the gash on his neck did the climbing. He snatched two of the fledglings, put them in a bag, and lowered them down to his buddy who was wearing the tennis shoes."

Glance didn't care how much overtime he had on the books. Peregrines were dangerously close to becoming extinct. He would track down the people responsible for taking those fledgling falcons or die trying.

While dropping Chet Carter off at the Bangor store, Glance asked if he could use his telephone. "I'd like to call Honest John's Used Car Rentals in Fallon, Nevada," he said. "I'll reimburse you for the long-distance charge."

"Of course you can use the phone," said Carter. "Don't worry about the long-distance charge. I want to catch those two falcon thieves as much as you do."

"Thanks so much, Chet."

"Honest John's," said the voice on the other end of the line. "John speaking."

"This is Fred Mitchell, at Fred's Garage in Sparks. I want to have a car hauled away. Can you recommend an auto wrecker in Fallon?"

"Don't you have any auto wreckers in Reno or Sparks?"

"There's a couple, but I'd just as soon not do business with them."

"The only one in Fallon is Luke's Auto Dismantling. It's off Highway 95, north of town."

"Is that where you have your cars towed?"

"If we need to have a car towed to an auto wrecker, that's usually where it ends up."

"HOW WAS WORK TODAY?" SAID HENRY, walking through the back door, finding Anne at the kitchen stove, and kissing her on the lips.

"It went well. We're preparing for the field trip to Gray Lodge Wildlife Area tomorrow, and I had to make sure we still have enough parents on board to help with the transportation."

"I'd be happy to help if I didn't have to drive to Fallon, Nevada, tomorrow."

"I know you would, Sweetheart. The kids always get excited when you show up at my classroom. They're still talking about that injured owl you brought in a couple weeks ago. How many tacos would you like?"

"Four, please. I didn't have a chance to eat lunch today."

"That reminds me: What was the report you had to check out?"

"Someone ripped off a peregrine-falcon nest and took two of the fledglings."

"That's terrible, Henry. Do you know who did it?"

"I have a description of a couple suspects and the car they were driving."

"Knowing you, you'll figure out a way to catch them. As soon as you wash up, we'll eat."

After dinner, Henry telephoned Captain Chuck Odom and asked for permission to drive the undercover Bronco to Fallon, Nevada. Odom always kept it at his home in Paradise, twenty-two miles up the mountain from Chico.

"I'll give you three good reasons why I shouldn't let you drive the state undercover rig seventy-five miles into Nevada," said Odom. "One, you already have way too much overtime on the books. Two, your trip to Fallon sounds like a boondoggle. And three, Nevada is out of our jurisdiction."

"Nevada *is* out of our jurisdiction, but we're federally deputized," said Glance. "That deputization authorizes us to enforce Title 50 of the *Code of Federal Regulations* in states bordering California."

"I can't get anything past you, can I Hank? That federal deputization is intended to be used only on special occasions when a federal agent or a warden from the other state isn't available. It's not intended for routine fishing expeditions like the one you're talking about. If this is so important, why haven't you contacted U.S. Fish and Wildlife or one of the Nevada wardens?"

"I have, Chuck. The Chico federal agent's position has been vacant since Bob Northrup retired. The Nevada warden who covers Fallon is off with an injured back, and Rex Parker, the Reno Fish and Wildlife agent, is in Alaska on assignment. The case I'm working needs to be investigated now or the fledgling peregrines that were ripped off could end up in Saudi Arabia."

"I told you what I think, and I'm not going to change my mind, Hank."

"Thanks anyway, Chuck. I'll try to figure something else out."

"What the hell is that supposed to mean?"

"Tomorrow is my day off. I'll take my personal car and go on my own time."

"Remember this, Warden Glance. If you get yourself into a jackpot, don't call me to get you out."

"I understand, Chuck. Good night."

THREE

Most of Newville burned to the ground in 1929, prompting Preston and Molly Radcliff to build the new home they'd been talking about since the birth of their son. Two years earlier, Preston had purchased 2,000 acres of riparian forest on the east bank of the Sacramento River, nine miles west of Chico. Using plans he'd saved from his father's Chicago mansion, Preston hired a Chico contractor to build what became known as Radcliff Mansion on the site.

Willie Radcliff's first brush with the law came during the spring of 1930. He was hunting jackrabbits a quarter mile south of Radcliff Mansion when he spotted a yearling doe browsing on freshly sprouted oak leaves near the river's edge. Taking careful aim with the same rifle he'd used to shoot Abe Kinsel's goat, Willie put a bullet behind the deer's right ear. The local game warden, Jed Sutton, heard the shot and spotted Willie dragging the deer down over the riverbank. Sutton left his patrol car behind, marched across the field, and intercepted the junior scofflaw as he was hotfooting it home.

"Young man, I'd like to talk to you," shouted Sutton.

Willie pretended he didn't hear and kept on walking.

"Young man, I'm ordering you to stop!"

Willie stopped, turned around, and looked back at the approaching officer. Skinny as a rail and bowlegged, Sutton wore khaki trousers, a khaki shirt, gold-rimmed glasses, and a star-shaped badge that was pinned above his left shirt pocket. What really captured Willie's attention was the long-barreled Colt revolver hanging from Warden Sutton's right hip.

"Point that rifle in the other direction and place it on the ground!" said Sutton.

"Why are you bothering me?" said Willie, leaning the rifle against the trunk of a nearby valley oak.

"What's your name, son?"

"Willie Radcliff."

"How old are you?"

"Thirteen."

"Are you pulling my leg?" Young Radcliff was already six feet tall and outweighed Sutton by forty pounds.

"No. I'll be fourteen in July."

"Do you have a hunting license or some kind of identification?"

"No. This is my parents' property, and that's our house over there."

"You and I are going to take a walk."

"Where we goin'?"

"Back to where you left that deer."

Two weeks later, Willie Radcliff appeared in Butte County Juvenile Court to answer for the deer he'd killed. His wealthy and influential father appeared with him. "My son is sorry for his mistake," said Preston to the hearing officer. "His mother and I can assure you it won't happen again." The case was dismissed, and Willie's rifle was ordered returned.

The following February, after waterfowl season had closed, Warden Sutton caught Willie with a pile of mallards he'd killed while hunting on one of his father's farm ponds. Again, the young man was ordered to appear in Butte County Juvenile Court, and, again, his father accompanied him. "Our son is a good boy," said Preston. "His mother and I believe he was a little confused about when the season closed."

"Your Honor," said Sutton, "I've received a half-dozen reports of this young man committing other wildlife violations. Unless there's a consequence to his actions, he'll keep right on violating the law and progress to more serious crimes."

The hearing officer gently chastised Willie and instructed him to write a two-hundred-word essay explaining why it was wrong to kill ducks out of season. Case closed. Willie's shotgun was ordered returned.

JULY 18, 1932, FOUND WILLIE RADCLIFF headed for Chico in the 1927 Model T Ford pickup his father had given him for his sixteenth birthday. Willie's plan was to pick up his high-school friend Ray Smithers and watch the double-feature matinee, *Frankenstein* and *Dracula*, at the National Theater.

OOGA-OOGA! trumpeted the Model T's horn, as Willie raced up Third Street and skidded to a stop in front of the Smithers residence. "Ray!" Willie shouted. "The show starts in a half hour, and there's already a long line." *OOGA-OOGA!*

Ray's father, wearing a sleeveless white undershirt, suspenders, and brown slacks pulled up to his chest, opened the screen door. "He'll be out in a minute. Stop honking that horn!"

"Tell him to hurry." *OOGA-OOGA!*

"Raymond, that smart-aleck friend of yours is outside waiting for you."

"I can't find my other sneaker, Dad. Tell him I'll be right there."

"You tell him yourself. Hurry up, so he'll stop honking that horn."

"Be sure to be home by 6:00," said Ray's mother. "Uncle Fred and Aunt Louella are coming for dinner."

Ray ignored his mother, threw open the screen door, and raced out to the curb.

The ambient temperature was ninety-five degrees when Willie Radcliff and Ray Smithers walked out of the National Theater into the blazing, early-evening sunlight. "It's hotter out here than it was inside," said Smithers.

"How would you like to drive up to Bear Hole and go for a swim?" said Willie, leading Smithers down the street to the city library, where his pickup was parked.

"That sounds great, but my mom told me I had to be home by 6:00."

"I didn't know you were such a mama's boy, Ray. Are we going, or aren't we?"

"Okay, I'll go, but I have to be home before dark."

Willie's Model T bounced and sputtered up the rocky road to upper Bidwell Park before pulling up beside a basalt cliff overlooking Big Chico Creek.

"Look at this," said Smithers, peering at the swirling, cerulean-blue water below. "There's a school of salmon swimming upstream through that shallow riffle."

"Let's have some fun," said Willie. "Follow me."

Smithers followed Radcliff down a path to the water's edge, where Willie picked up a rock and chucked it at a passing fish. "Damn! I missed."

One salmon after another swam the shallow gauntlet to deeper water, tempting Radcliff and Smithers to pelt them with the myriad river rocks that lay on the bank. A half hour had passed when a familiar voice rang out from the cliff above. "Unless you boys want to spend the next two weeks in juvenile hall, I suggest you stop what you're doing and put down those rocks!"

A flat-brimmed ranger hat shaded the uniformed officer's face, but for Willie Radcliff, there was no mistaking the gruff voice, the skinny bowlegs, and that long-barreled Colt revolver hanging from the officer's right hip.

"We were just throwing rocks in the water," said Smithers.

"I know what you're doing. Stay right where you are until I get down there."

"Keep your mouth shut," mumbled Willie. "I know how to handle this guy."

"How many times are we going to meet like this?" said Sutton, sweat dripping down his cheek.

"I don't know," said Willie, a detectable smirk on his face. "I guess that's up to you."

"You think this is funny, do you?"

"Yeah-kinda. We haven't hurt nothin', so you can't do nothin'."

"Who told you that?"

"I think it was a little bird."

"If you keep listening to that little bird, you're going to end up back in juvenile court. Not a month goes by that I don't receive a report of someone ground-sluicing quail from the seat of that little Model T pickup up there."

"I haven't killed a quail since the season closed," said Willie.

"Of course you haven't. Do you mind if I give you some advice?"

"You're the one wearing the badge."

"I've run into a lot of cocky young fellas like you during my years as a game warden. Some of them finally learn to respect the law, and some of them don't. The ones who don't go on to commit more serious crimes and sometimes end up in prison. Your father isn't always going to be around to save you, Willie."

"What did you say?" said Radcliff, looking over at his friend and grinning. "I wasn't paying attention."

WILLIE RADCLIFF GRADUATED FROM CHICO HIGH School on Friday evening, June 15, 1934. Preston and Molly Radcliff were there to meet him as he walked off the stage, diploma in hand. "We're proud of you," said Molly, giving her son a hug.

"Thanks, Mom," said Willie, glancing over his shoulder.

"Congratulations, son," said Preston, shaking Willie's hand. "Would you mind coming straight home tonight? We have something important we'd like to talk to you about."

"I'm not coming home," said Willie, turning to his left and walking away. "My friends are waiting, and we're gonna celebrate."

"This is more important than celebrating with your friends, dear," said Molly. "We can talk tomorrow."

"I'm leaving on a two-week business trip early tomorrow morning," said Preston.

"Then we'll talk when you get back. Hey, Ray! Wait up!"

Preston asked Molly to wait for him at the end of the bleachers. When she'd gone, he turned to his son. "If you leave now, you can expect the gate to be locked when you get home."

"Go ahead and lock it. Mom will let me in."

"Not this time, she won't. And I won't be supporting your lazy, good-for-nothing lifestyle any longer. You can get yourself a job and find another place to live."

"Is he coming?" said Molly, walking to the parking lot with her husband.

"He is if he knows what's good for him," said Preston, climbing in the driver's seat of their jet-black, 1934 Buick sedan.

"Don't you think you were a little hard on him? All the other kids are going out to celebrate."

"Celebrate?" said Preston, rolling up the window so others in the parking lot wouldn't hear. "That kid has been pampered and mollycoddled since the day he was born. All he does is hunt and fish. Do you know how many times I've stepped in and gotten him out of trouble? I've given him a dozen summer jobs, and he hasn't completed a single one. I bought him a truck, and what thanks do I get? He disrespects me in front of his friends. I mean it, Molly—if Willie blows off this opportunity, he can find another place to live, he can find a job, and he can forget about receiving a nickel of inheritance."

Preston must have made an impression on his son. Willie's pickup was parked in front of the mansion when his parents drove into the garage.

"What did you want to talk to me about?" said Willie, following his parents up the porch steps and into the house.

"Actually, there are a number of things," said Preston. "Go wait in the parlor with your mother. I'll be there in a minute."

"What's this all about?" said Willie, sitting on the couch next to his mother. "If he starts yelling at me, I'm gonna leave and find my friends."

"Willie, you've made some pretty bad mistakes in your life. Leaving right now would probably be the worst. For once, just sit here and listen to what your father has to say. It also wouldn't hurt to show him some appreciation and respect."

Preston sat down in his easy chair and began. "It would ease my mind considerably to know that my son is willing and able to take over the family business when I'm gone."

"That's a long way off, dear," said Molly. "Why are you bringing it up now?"

"It may not be such a long way off. I'm forty-four. My father passed away at age fifty-nine, and his father at age fifty-three. Right now, Willie isn't qualified to operate a wheelbarrow, let alone take over the family business."

"I'm only seventeen, Dad. What do you expect?"

"Now you sound like your mother. Just hear me out before you get excited."

"I'm listening."

"My father left me the nest egg I used to create what some people call an agricultural empire. Radcliff Farms is now the largest private land-owner in Glenn and Butte counties. Your mother and I, with the help of Mel Pendergast, started the business by leasing grazing rights and running cattle in the foothills west of Orland and Willows. A few years later, we expanded by purchasing choice farmland and growing crops like milo, corn, alfalfa, almonds, apples, oranges, walnuts, prunes, and apricots."

"I've heard you tell that same story a hundred times, Dad. I'm impressed by all your accomplishments. Where do I fit in?"

"I've recently purchased three sections of rice-growing property. One is near Princeton, one is near Williams, and one is in the Butte Sink, east of Colusa."

"I don't know anything about growing rice."

"Of course you don't. That's where my proposition comes in."

"What kind of proposition?"

"For the last two summers, I've hired a soil consultant named Dale Stewart to help us increase efficiency."

"Why don't you explain that to Willie, dear."

"It means improving the soil so we can reap the greatest possible yield from every acre of cropland. Professor Stewart teaches at the University of California's agricultural campus in Davis. To make a long story short, I told him how much I would love to get my son into an institution like that."

"What did he say?" said Molly, leaning forward and staring into her husband's eyes.

"He asked about Willie's grades."

"So much for that idea, huh, Dad?"

"Not necessarily. I told him you were a C student but that wasn't a good indicator of your potential. With the right amount of motivation, you could become an A or B student."

"What did Professor Stewart say, dear?"

"He said with his recommendation, we might be able to get Willie admitted on a probationary basis."

"What does that mean?" said Willie.

"It means if you end your first semester with a grade-point average of B or better, you get to stay in school for another semester . . . and so on and so on, until you establish yourself as a qualified student."

"What makes you think I can do that?"

"That's where motivation comes in. On the day you graduate with a degree in agriculture, I'll put you in charge of the company's new Rice Production Division. How many students have a job like that waiting for them when they graduate from college?"

"What do you have to say to your father, Willie?"

"How do you know I'll be accepted?"

"You already have been. I filed an enrollment application for you six months ago. It also didn't hurt that I donated a hundred acres of prime agricultural land to the school."

"What if I refuse to go?"

"If you refuse to go, you can begin looking for a job and another place to live tomorrow morning."

"What if I go and can't hack it?"

"Your mother and I will support you as long as you stay in school and maintain the necessary grade-point average. If you drop out or get kicked out, you're on your own."

"Preston, you don't really mean that."

"I mean every word of it," said Preston, rising to his feet. "Party's over, son. I'm taking a train to Chicago at 5:00 tomorrow morning. Let me know what you decide before I leave."

WITH HIS BACK AGAINST THE WALL, Willie accepted his father's proposition and agreed to enter the University of California's Northern Branch of the College of Agriculture, in Davis. Taking a full load of classes and maintaining a passable grade-point average wasn't going to be easy for a young man who had never been pressured to work hard, never had to apply himself, never learned to organize his time, and never followed through on a commitment. Now it was up to him to succeed or forfeit any chance of one day inheriting the Radcliff Farms fortune.

Classes began the third week of September 1934. Willie drove down the week before to check into his dormitory and attend orientation. "Room 211," mumbled Willie, as he approached the half-open door and gave it a light shove.

"Hello. You must be Willie Radcliff," came a husky male voice from across the room.

"Who are you, and how do you know my name?"

"I'm Lincoln Hirsch. Come in and make yourself at home." Barechested and clad in checkered boxers, Hirsch was lying on his back, reading a textbook.

Willie couldn't help noticing that Hirsch's legs hung six inches off the end of the bed. "How long have you been here?" he said.

"Almost a week. I work in the student bookstore part time, so I came down from Doris a week early to help with inventory."

"Doris? You mean way up north, on the way to Tule Lake?"

"That's the place. My parents own a small hay farm up there."

"I've been through there a few times."

"You must be a duck hunter."

"And you must be smarter than you look. Are you a freshman?"

"No. I'm a junior."

"A junior! Why are you still living in the dorm?"

"I'm on a limited budget and was offered a proposition I couldn't afford to pass up."

"What kind of proposition?"

"It's a private matter I'd rather not discuss."

An honor student, Hirsch had been recommended to Preston Radcliff by Professor Dale Stewart. As Willie suspected, Hirsch was hired by his father to make sure his unmotivated son succeeded. In return for his services, Hirsch's room, board, and tuition would be covered through the 1935-1936 school year. After graduation, Hirsch would assume the role of assistant supervisor in one of Radcliff Farms' six divisions.

"You still haven't told me how you know my name," said Willie.

"It's on the plaque next to the door," said Hirsch, growing weary of Radcliff's cocky attitude. "Any more questions?"

"Yeah. How 'bout trading me bunks? I like sleeping next to an open window."

Hirsch chuckled. "You've got quite a sense of humor, Radcliff."

"Nothing funny about it. I want that bunk."

Hirsch sat up, put his book down, and walked across the room in his bare feet. "I guess you could fight me for it," he said.

Willie picked up his suitcase and dropped it on the bunk nearest the door.

"Smart boy," said Hirsch. "Freshman orientation begins tomorrow morning at 7:00, McDonald Hall. That's the big red building that looks like a barn."

At 5:00 a.m. on Monday, September 10, 1934, Willie awoke to the sound of his roommate playing reveille on a trumpet. For the next two years, Lincoln Hirsch made sure Willie never missed a class, studied regularly, and turned his work in on time.

"MY JOB IS DONE," HIRSCH SAID to Radcliff on June 11, 1936. "Tomorrow, I graduate and move on to my new job. You're going to have to find somebody else to help you study and write your term papers for you."

As disappointed as Willie was, it didn't take him long to find someone else willing and able to tutor him fulltime and guide him through the next two years. This time, it was an unassuming junior transfer from Sacramento Junior College named Rebecca Walsh. Whatever Rebecca lacked in self-confidence, she made up for in intelligence, study habits, test-taking ability, and report-writing skills. Rebecca and Willie graduated together on June 10, 1938—Willie with an overall grade-point average of 2.95 and Rebecca with a grade-point average of 4.00. Blessed with just enough common sense to know he had a good thing going, Willie proposed to Rebecca that same evening.

FOUR

EARLY MONDAY MORNING, MAY 22, 1972, Warden Glance hopped into his VW Beetle and drove for three and a half hours to Fallon, Nevada. Turning north on Highway 95, he crossed the Carson River, passed the Municipal Airport turnoff, and was just outside the city limits when he spotted a hundred-yard-long corrugated metal fence with concertina wire strung across the top.

Parking outside the open gate, Glance moseyed toward a metal building with a sign above the door reading LUKE'S AUTO DISMANTLING. On his right, a large, mixed-breed dog paced back and forth at the end of a chain attached to a wire clothesline.

"Whatcha lookin' for?" said an elderly gentleman wearing grease-stained overalls.

"I need a hubcap for a 1957 VW Beetle," said Glance, turning to his left and noticing three parked vehicles over the old man's shoulder. None of the vehicles matched the description of the Jeep Wagoneer Glance was looking for.

"We ain't got but three VW Beetles on the lot. You're probably not gonna find what you're lookin' for, but you can check with the boys inside."

Glance entered the metal building to find a phone ringing off the hook and a swamp cooler blowing so loudly, he failed to hear the clerk addressing him from behind the counter.

"Whatcha need?" repeated a surly beanpole in his early thirties with long, red hair tied in a ponytail.

"Alvis, it's your girlfriend on the phone," shouted a second employee standing next to the cash register.

"Tell her I'm busy," said Alvis, turning to his left and exposing a three-inch gash on the right side of his neck. "Hey, buddy, I ain't got all day."

"Sorry," said Glance. "I need a hubcap for a 1957 VW Beetle."

"Don't have it. Anything else?"

"What time do you close?"

"Five o'clock. Who's next?"

Glance walked back to his car convinced that the employee identified as Alvis had been the driver of the Jeep Wagoneer and one of the men who'd robbed the peregrine-falcon nest two days earlier. Contemplating his next move, he drove south on Highway 95 and stopped to gather his thoughts at a viewpoint overlooking the Carson River. *Do I start for home, satisfied that I've located one of the suspects, or do I wait around here for six hours and find out where Alvis lives?*

Choosing the latter, Glance polished off a deli sandwich and an iced tea at the market in Fallon. He then telephoned Anne from a pay phone in front of the store.

"Manzanita Elementary School. Rosemary speaking."

"Hi, Rosemary. This is Hank Glance. May I leave a message for Anne?"

"Hi, Hank. Anne just returned from her field trip, and she's right here."

"Henry, where are you?"

"Hi, Sweetheart. I'm still in Fallon, and it looks like I won't be home until 10:00 or 11:00 tonight."

"What's wrong?"

"Nothing's wrong. I found one of my suspects. I'm waiting for him to get off work so I can follow him home."

"Henry, I'm worried about you."

"Don't worry. I just want to see where this guy lives, then I'll head west."

"You be careful. I love you."

"I love you too. I'm looking forward to seeing you when I get home."

Glance drove back out Highway 95 past the airport turnoff and found a cottonwood tree on the west side of the road within binocular range of the auto-wrecking yard. The time was 1:05 p.m. At 2:15, a Nevada highway patrolman drove by, headed north. At 3:30, the same highway patrolman passed Glance, headed south. Watching in his rearview mirror, Glance saw the dark-blue patrol car stop on the side of the highway, make a U-turn, and pull into the shade of the cottonwood tree, twenty feet behind him.

"Is everything all right?" said the officer, standing at Glance's open window.

"So far, so good," said Glance, smiling and handing him his law-enforcement identification.

The officer appeared to be about Glance's age.

"What are you doing in Nevada, Warden Glance?"

Glance stepped out, shook the officer's hand, and explained his purpose for being there.

"I'm Ted Mellow," said the officer. "Good to meet you, Hank. You aren't gonna believe this, but my next-door neighbor is a Nevada game warden. His name is Ron Weise. Do you know him?"

"No, but I could sure use his help right about now."

"He's off on sick leave, after falling off a ladder and injuring his back."

"I hope he's all right."

"I talked to him yesterday. He was up and moving around."

"Ted, one of the suspects I'm investigating works at that auto-wrecking yard up the road."

"Do you have a name?"

"I heard a fellow employee call him Alvis."

"That would be Alvis Treat. You wanna be careful dealing with him."

"What makes you say that?"

"He's unstable and dangerous. A couple years ago, Alvis took a shot at the game warden who was stationed here at the time."

"Did they arrest him?"

"Oh yeah! There was a jury trial and everything. Alvis came up with some cock-and-bull story about shooting at a deer with his .30-30 rifle and not knowing the game warden was there. One of the jurors either believed him or was a shirttail relative of some kind. Treat got off scot-free."

"What does Alvis drive?"

"Every time I've stopped him, he's been driving a black Chevy pickup. When Alvis isn't at work, he's usually rock climbing. I think that's why he stays so skinny. There's some cliffs about twenty miles north of here. People sometimes stop along the highway to watch him climb."

"Have you ever been to his home?"

"Once or twice, looking for stolen property. Did you say Alvis and another man had robbed a falcon nest in California?"

"Alvis is a prime suspect. Just in case I lose him, would you mind telling me how to get to his home?"

"Sure. About three miles past the wrecking yard, you'll see a road on the left called Jackrabbit Trail. It isn't paved, and there may be a few rough spots for that bug you're driving. Follow it for about three miles until you come to a fork. Take the right fork onto Cottontail Path. It meanders up a hill and drops down into a canyon. Treat's place is at the end of the road. You'll have a pretty good view of it from the top of the hill. As I remember, it's a mobile home next to a large metal building that houses his beat-up Winnebago and all the junk he collects."

"Ted, you've been a big help. I can't thank you enough."

"No problem, Hank. Next time I see Ron, I'll tell him I ran into you."

A black Chevy pickup left the auto-wrecking yard at 5:05 p.m., heading north on Highway 95. Glance waited until it was out of sight, then slowly pulled out from under the cottonwood tree and followed. He was a mile from the Jackrabbit Trail turnoff when a white limo blew by and quickly disappeared into the distance.

Jackrabbit Trail turned out to be even rougher than Officer Mellow had described. Reaching Cottontail Path, Glance shifted his VW Beetle into second, sputtered up the hillside, and came to a stop thirty yards from the crest. "This is close enough," he said, grabbing his binoculars.

The crest of the hill proved to be the perfect vantage point. It provided a bird's-eye view of the dry streambed at the bottom of the canyon, the last two hundred yards of Cottontail Path, and Alvis Treat's residence. Scanning the scene with binoculars, Glance spotted the faded blue Jeep Wagoneer he'd been searching for. It was parked in the shade of a cottonwood tree behind Treat's mobile home. A large metal building, with an early-model Winnebago backed halfway inside, sat to the left of the mobile home.

While Glance continued to check out the scene below, a white limousine came rolling in from the east and stopped in front of the mobile home. "I wondered where you were going in such a hurry," said Glance. He watched the driver, dressed in a chauffeur's uniform, walk around to the other side of the limo and open the right-rear passenger door.

"Who's this dude?" mumbled Glance, as a slender man looking to be in his early thirties stepped from the car. He sported shoulder-length, perfectly coiffed, bleached-blond hair and wore a sand-colored leisure suit. The visitor walked toward the mobile home and stopped at the wooden picnic table out front.

Alvis Treat emerged from his mobile home, carrying what Glance recognized as a cardboard, live-bird shipping box. He set the box down on the picnic table. Treat then pulled a fledgling falcon from the box and held it up for the visitor's inspection.

When the visitor was finished inspecting the first falcon, Treat put it back in the box and pulled out a second. The fledglings were identical to the Bangor-aerie peregrines Glance had seen the day before. With both birds back in the box, the visitor pulled a number of bills from the inside pocket of his coat and, one by one, placed ten of them on the table. Treat folded the bills and tucked them inside his pants pocket. The visitor, who Glance now identified as the falcon buyer, picked up the box and carried it back to the limo, where his driver was waiting next to an open door.

As the limo rolled eastward along the canyon floor, Glance suddenly realized that his VW Beetle was parked next to the road on which the limo was traveling. He raced down the hill, jumped in the Beetle, and made a mad dash back to the Cottontail Path-Jackrabbit Trail intersection. Back on Jackrabbit Trail, Glance slowed to a snail's pace, placed a baseball cap on his head backwards, and acted as if he were one of the local yokels headed into town for beer and cigarettes.

Glance was a mile from Highway 95 when the white limousine came bombing up behind him, horn honking and headlights blinking. Failing to yield, Glance kept the limo driver honking his horn and shouting expletives to within two hundred yards of the highway intersection. Seeing a wide spot at the left side of the road, the limo driver gunned his engine, roared past Glance, and was fishtailing back onto Jackrabbit Trail, when a dark-blue Nevada Highway Patrol sedan turned left from Highway 95 and met the car head on; the officer switched on his red spotlight and brought the oncoming limo to a skidding stop. Seconds later, a Nevada Department of Wildlife patrol car, with two uniformed officers inside, made a left turn onto Jackrabbit Trail and stopped behind the highway-patrol unit.

Glance climbed out of his VW Beetle and walked over to meet officer Ted Mellow and the two Nevada wildlife officers. By the time he got there, they had pulled the two limo occupants out of the car, frisked them, and instructed them to stand at the front of the highway-patrol unit.

"Hey, my client is in a hurry to get to the airport," shouted the limo driver. "That asshole wouldn't let us pass."

"You two just stand there and keep quiet," said Mellow. "We'll get back to you in a minute."

"I just watched the man on the right buy two fledgling peregrine falcons from Alvis Treat," said Glance, pointing to the man in the leisure suit. "Treat stole the falcons from a nest near Bangor, California, the day before yesterday."

"Treat is the reason we're here," said the younger wildlife officer, slightly bent over at the waist and moving gingerly. "I'm Ron Weise and this is my supervisor, Larry Jacobs. When Ted told me you were up here by yourself spying on Alvis Treat, I became concerned. Treat is crazy as hell. He took a shot at the warden whose position I filled two years ago."

"Officer Mellow told me about that," said Glance. "You must be the warden who fell off the ladder. I called your department, but they told me you were unavailable."

"That's him," said Jacobs, gray haired and twenty-five pounds overweight. "I told him to stay home and rest, but he insisted on coming."

"Where are the falcons now?" said Weise.

"They're inside a cardboard box on the back seat of the limo," said Glance, walking over and peeking inside. "It looks like the guy over there in the leisure suit covered them with his coat."

"Where do we go from here?" said Mellow. "I should have gone off duty an hour ago."

"May I make a suggestion?" said Glance.

"Absolutely," said Jacobs.

"Book these two. As soon as possible, take a team of officers into the canyon and arrest Alvis Treat. I watched the man over there on the right pay Treat ten bills for the birds. Based on what I know about the black market for peregrine falcons, each of those bills was a thousand dollars."

"Sounds like Alvis has finally stepped in it big time," said Weise.

"Yes," said Glance. "In addition to whatever state charges you come up with, I suggest you get U.S. Fish and Wildlife involved and consider charging all three of them, as well as a fourth man I'll tell you about in my report, with violations of the U.S. Endangered Species Conservation Act and the federal Lacey Act; the Lacey Act came into play when the illegally taken falcons were transported across the state line into Nevada. I'll fax you my report by tomorrow morning."

"What about the falcons?" said Weise.

"After you photograph the fledgling peregrines, I'd like to take them to UC Davis. They have a wonderful raptor program, and one of the professors in charge is a friend of mine. There may be a chance of returning these birds to the nest."

FIVE

Times were hard for everyone during the 1930s, but people still had to eat, so Radcliff Farms had come through the Great Depression in reasonably good shape. True to his word—almost—Preston Radcliff appointed his son assistant business manager of the newly formed Radcliff Farms Rice Production Division. Until such time as Willie proved himself capable of handling the actual business manager's position, he would serve the company by driving from work site to work site, checking on progress and fooling the laborers into thinking he knew what he was doing. The real workhorse—the man who got the job done—was Robert Giles Masterson, one of six field supervisors employed by Radcliff Farms to run the day-to-day operation. By the time Willie was hired, Masterson had placed 1,920 acres of the company's newly acquired property into rice production—six hundred and forty acres near Princeton, six hundred and forty acres near Willows, and six hundred and forty acres in a marshy, low-lying slice of Butte County called Butte Sink.

Rebecca Radcliff, Preston's new daughter-in-law, was a diamond in the rough. So impressed was Preston with her knowledge and accounting skills, he hired her to replace Melvin Pendergast as Radcliff Farms' chief financial officer. Reaching the age of sixty-five, Pendergast had retired, sold his interest in the company back to the Radcliffs, and moved to his dream home on a hillside overlooking Santa Barbara.

Radcliff Farms Duck Club was established in late December 1939, and Willie Radcliff was chosen by his father to be its first manager. For decades, waterfowl hunters had ogled the flooded wetlands now under the ownership of Radcliff Farms. Like flies to honey, waterfowl hunters were drawn to the seemingly endless flocks of ducks and geese that flew in and out of the three privately owned properties. When duck blinds were advertised at top-dollar prices in newspapers as far away as Sacramento, San Francisco, and Los Angeles, they were quickly snatched up by wealthy industrialists, business executives, and movie stars.

Cash came pouring in, and the first duck season for Radcliff Farms Duck Club was a huge success. Preston was so pleased with the job Willie had done, he built his son and Rebecca a ranch-style home on ten acres south of Willows.

Willie and Rebecca moved into their new home on June 6, 1940. A few weeks later, while Rebecca was at work and Willie was puttering in the front yard, a 1934 Ford pickup stopped in front of the house.

"What the hell do *they* want?" mumbled Radcliff, as two scruffy-looking, twenty-plus-year-old men climbed out of the pickup and walked up the driveway. "See that little sign next to the front door?" barked Radcliff. "It says NO PEDDLERS OR AGENTS ALLOWED."

"Ain't you Willie Radcliff, the guy who runs the duck club?" said the tall, lanky one.

"That's right. We're not hiring right now."

"My name's Eli. Most people around here call me Gooseneck. This here's Mitch. We got a business proposition for ya."

"Oh yeah? What kind of business proposition?"

"Ducks."

"What about ducks?"

"Next duck season, we can supply you with as many ducks as you need."

"Why would I need ducks? I run the most successful duck club in Northern California."

"We can keep it that way by supplyin' your club members with ducks when the huntin' ain't so good," said Mitch, a gnomish character with greasy black hair and a crooked nose that looked like it had been punched too many times and incorrectly pushed back into place.

"And how do you propose to do that?"

"It ain't none a your concern how we do it. All you gotta do is pay us for 'em."

Eli "Gooseneck" Strode and Mitch Leatherwood were market hunters, engaged in the illegal practice of duck dragging—sneaking up on flocks of feeding waterfowl during the hours of darkness and slaughtering large numbers of the hapless birds at the same time. They generally sold their ill-gotten bounty to restaurants in San Francisco and other large cities, but these two would-be entrepreneurs were looking to branch out and expand their clientele.

"And what would this cost me?" said Radcliff.

"Seventy-five cents for mallards and pintails, and four bits for everything else," said Strode.

"Let me think about it. Is there a way I can get in touch with you guys?"

Strode handed Radcliff a matchbook with the phone number of a Maxwell auto shop emblazoned across the front. "Call this number and ask for Gooseneck or Mitch," he said. "If we ain't there, one of us will get back to ya."

"Who shall I say is calling? I don't want to leave my real name."

"Hell if I know," said Strode. "How 'bout Hopalong Cassidy?"

DURING THE OFF-SEASON BETWEEN FEBRUARY AND October 1940, Willie Radcliff, with financial assistance from his father, built a state-of-the-art clubhouse at Radcliff Farms' Butte Sink duck club. Butte Sink was the largest and most exclusive of the three Radcliff Farms duck-club sites, with hunting blinds that only the wealthiest clients could afford. The two-story clubhouse contained an office, private sleeping quarters, a community kitchen, a well-stocked bar, a card room, and a walk-in cooler for temporary storage of ducks and geese. Ten acres were set aside at each of the Radcliff Farms duck-club properties for members who chose to bring their own travel trailers.

When duck season opened in October 1940, the weather was still hot and dry, with most of the Pacific Flyway's duck and goose populations remaining up north at Tule Lake, Lower Klamath, and beyond.

"Jack and I hunted all day, and all we killed were a hen wigeon and a drake spoony," complained a famous 1940s movie star.

"It's the warm, dry weather," said Radcliff. "Wait until the rain comes. We'll have more ducks and geese than you can shake a stick at."

"That may be true, but until then, it's not worth our time to drive all the way up here from Los Angeles."

That afternoon, Willie made a phone call.

"Bud's Garage," said the man answering the phone.

"Is Gooseneck there?"

"He ain't here today."

"What about Mitch?"

"Mitch is busy and don't have time to come to the phone."

Willie heard another man in the background: "Pop, don't hang up. I'll be right there."

"Don't be spendin' all day on that phone," said Bud, handing the receiver to his son. "You've still got three more lube jobs and a flat tire to take care of before you go anywhere."

"I know, I know," said Mitch, grabbing the receiver. "Hello. Who's this?"

"It's Hoppy."

"Who?"

"Hopalong Cassidy. You and a guy who called himself Gooseneck came to see me at my home last summer. The two of you were gonna supply me with ducks when I needed 'em."

"Oh yeah! You're that big sonofabitch from the duck club."

"That's me. I need ducks, and lots of 'em."

"It's been pretty slow, weather bein' the way it is, but I know where I can get ya a few birds."

"How fresh are they?"

"We killed 'em last night. It was the first flock of any size this season. They were all bull sprig, if you can believe that. Not a hen in the bunch."

"You mean drake pintails?"

"Yeah, drake pintails. Gooseneck took most of 'em to the Bay Area early this morning. We kept a few in case somebody like you called."

"How much are you guys asking?"

"A buck apiece."

"You said seventy-five cents apiece before."

"That was then, and this is now. How soon do ya need 'em?"

"I need 'em today."

"What's your number? I'll call you back."

That afternoon, Mitch Leatherwood delivered forty-six freshly killed drake pintails to the Butte Sink clubhouse. Radcliff hung them in a separate compartment at the back of the walk-in cooler. The ducks he'd purchased sent the movie star and a handful of other club members home happy, but those who were left out continued to complain.

Willie Radcliff bought forty or fifty ducks at a time from Gooseneck Strode and Mitch Leatherwood throughout the remainder of October and into November. The third week in November brought a cold snap, followed by ten days of pouring rain. With a change in the weather came a substantial influx of ducks and geese from up north. Market hunters like Strode and Leatherwood were running drags two nights a week and killing over a hundred ducks on each occasion. From mid-November through the end of January, Radcliff purchased over three hundred ducks, most of them mallards and pintails.

On the last Wednesday of the 1940-1941 duck season, a wealthy restauranteur named Louis Griffin walked out of the field after a day of hunting and back to the Butte Sink clubhouse.

"Well, Griff, how'd ya do?" said Radcliff, handing him a cold beer.

"Thanks," said Griffin. "I can sure use this after the day I've had. Lots of ducks to shoot at, but I couldn't hit the broad side of a barn."

"I'm sorry to hear that. Are you stickin' around for the party? Some of the boys are already in the clubhouse celebrating."

"I know. I heard 'em from way out in my duck blind. I'd love to stay, but I have to drive back to Los Angeles tonight. I've got a meeting with my Santa Monica restaurant manager late tomorrow afternoon. When I'm finished there, I'm makin' tracks for Palm Springs."

"What's happening in Palm Springs?"

"The Hollywood crowd is coming into town for the weekend, and everyone is meeting at my restaurant for dinner and a Friday-night party. I had planned to add a few roast ducks to the menu, but I've only got a couple wigeons to show for my entire day of hunting."

"I can take care of that. Pull your car up to the clubhouse before you leave."

After finishing off two more beers and taking a shower, Griffin pulled up to the clubhouse in his 1940 Cadillac coupe.

"Pop the trunk and open the lid on your cooler," said Radcliff. "I'll be right back." He returned carrying six bull sprig and four greenhead mallards, all of them picked and field dressed.

"Boy, that's sure nice of you!" said Griffin. "Now I can have my Palm Springs chef cook up a feast."

"There's plenty more where these came from."

"Doesn't the season close this Sunday?"

Willie hesitated. "The season is closing, but I may be able to help you out for three or four more weeks."

"Willie, please correct me if I'm misinterpreting your offer. Are you saying you're willing to supply me with wild ducks for my restaurants?"

One of Radcliff's employees walked by carrying a case of liquor bottles for the party inside.

"Is the war in Europe having any effect on your business?" said Radcliff.

"Customer numbers have fallen off a little," said Griffin, watching Radcliff's employee carry the liquor bottles into the clubhouse. "Is it safe to talk about ducks again?"

"It's safe," said Radcliff, chuckling.

Willie Radcliff had become well-acquainted with the market-hunting practices of his business associates, Gooseneck Strode and Mitch Leatherwood. Motivated by greed, Strode, Leatherwood, and two unknown members of their duck-poaching ring would continue killing and selling wild ducks until the birds migrated north in late February.

"How much would this cost me?" said Griffin.

"Two bucks a bird and the cost of transportation. I'll have my driver bootleg them as far as Fresno if you can have someone meet him there. That will save you a few bucks."

"I believe I can arrange that. What's the chance of getting caught with all those ducks? It wouldn't be good for business if my name were plastered all over the newspapers."

"Slim to none," said Radcliff, snickering. "I haven't heard a peep about any feds sneaking around since that bust they made a couple years ago. The state wardens are so few and far between, I haven't seen one of them in three months."

"Maybe they all got drafted," said Griffin. "A couple of my waiters at the Santa Monica restaurant received their notices to report last week. With Hitler running roughshod over Europe, it's only a matter of time before we get in the war."

During February 1941, Willie arranged three deliveries, totaling 135 ducks, to Griff's Seafood restaurants in Santa Monica and Palm Springs. By doing so, he promoted himself from a duck buyer to what state and federal wildlife officers called a ringleader or middleman.

SIX

W ARDEN HENRY GLANCE HAD ACCUMULATED A mountain of over-time during his investigation into Warden Norman Bettis's disap-pearance and the resulting murder trial that concluded in May of 1972. This prompted Captain Odom, who had dropped by the Glance farm-house, to say, "Hank, I want you to park your truck in the barn, spend June with that beautiful bride of yours, and be ready to go back to work in July. If the state phone rings, ignore it. I'll call if I need to get in touch with you."

"What if someone reports a spotlighter in the middle of the night?"

"I've already asked the dispatcher to call me if anything important comes up in your district. I'll either handle it myself or farm it out to the new guy."

"The new guy?"

"Yeah, a young fella named Thaddeus Calloway transferred into the Willows position while you were involved with the trial. He starts June first."

"I know him!" said Glance. "Tad Calloway was the Blythe warden who provided backup during the bighorn-sheep investigation two years ago."

"That was some case," said Odom. "I remember you and the feds tak-ing down that crooked taxidermist who had the secret shop way out in the desert. Do you ever hear from that Oklahoma oil tycoon who worked undercover with you on the sting?"

"He sent me a Christmas card last December. There was a photograph of him and his new bride on the cover. She's apparently the host of a popular Oklahoma City TV show."

Odom chuckled. "Back to Warden Calloway. His captain said he's a damn good warden but he doesn't know when to quit. Does that sound like someone you know?"

"I'm not sure I know what you're getting at," said Glance, a sheepish grin on his face.

"Like hell you don't," said Odom, slapping Henry on the back and opening the door of his patrol car. "That reminds me. How did your falcon caper turn out?"

"The falcon caper?" said Glance. "Oh, the falcon caper! Everything turned out well, thank you."

"Something tells me there's a lot more to that story than you're telling me," said Odom, "but I've got a meeting in Sacramento to get to, so it'll have to wait."

"Thanks for coming by, Chuck."

Climbing into the driver's seat, Odom looked back. "I'm dead serious about your overtime, Hank. When you come back to work in July, I want it down to zero."

ANNE GLANCE HAD JUST BUTTONED DOWN her classroom for the summer when Henry walked in and told her he'd been ordered to take the entire month of June off. "That's wonderful!" she said, removing the last stack of textbooks from a cart and placing them on the shelf. Anne reached up, wrapped her arms around Henry's neck, and kissed him on the lips. "Let's go to Hawai'i!"

"Hawai'i?" said Henry. "I had my heart set on finally planting a garden."

"You can do that when we get back. Janet Wilks, in the classroom next door, has a condo in Maui. She and her husband rent it out to other teachers when they're not staying there themselves. This summer, they're taking a cruise to Alaska."

"Are you serious about Hawai'i?"

"I am. We never did go on a honeymoon. You were always involved in one of your investigations."

"Do you think we can afford it?"

"As hard as you and I work, I think we deserve it," said Anne, locking her desk at the back of the classroom and preparing to leave. "Janet said Maui is the best place to see lots of fish, so that should please you. She drew me a map to an isolated bay at the southern tip of the island called La Perouse."

"Sounds intriguing."

"I thought that would get your attention. Wait till you hear the rest."

"I'm all ears."

"We have to swim across this bay to reach the cove Janet told me about and the open ocean. She said the cove is so full of marine life, it's like swimming in an aquarium."

"Maui is known for that," mumbled Henry, thumbing through a science textbook that one of Anne's students had left behind.

"You mean you've been there before?"

"I've never been to La Perouse, but I have been to Maui."

"Why haven't you mentioned it?"

"We didn't have sexy young teachers like you when I was in seventh grade."

"No changing the subject, young man. Sit yourself down at one of those desks and tell me about Maui."

"Yes, Mrs. Glance. When Larry Jansen and I turned eighteen, we took a scuba-diving course at the Riverside YMCA. Our instructor was a dive-shop owner who said he'd been hooked on scuba diving since the first time he watched Lloyd Bridges on TV."

"*Sea Hunt!*" blurted Anne. "My dad and I used to watch that show together."

"After each lesson, the instructor would tell us a story about one of his dive adventures," said Henry, lifting the lid on the desk he'd chosen and finding a pile of gum wrappers inside. "When I asked him to describe his all-time favorite dive spot, he said, 'No contest—the back wall of Molokini.'"

"Is Molokini in Maui?"

"It's actually a tiny island off the coast of Maui. Most beginning divers and snorkelers go to the Molokini Crater, inside the wall."

"Is that where you and Larry went?"

"Not a chance. After hearing stories about sharks, whales, and manta rays off the back wall, Larry and I decided to skip the beginner stuff and go where the adventure was."

"Somehow, that doesn't surprise me. Weren't you a little concerned about diving with sharks?"

"Not really. All we saw during our back-wall dive were harmless whitetip reef sharks. We did spot one gray reef shark out in the blue."

"Out in the blue?"

"Yeah. When you're diving near a reef, it's customary to occasionally glance out into the open ocean. You never know what you might see at the outer limits of your visibility."

"Were you frightened when you spotted the gray reef shark?"

"I was excited, but the idea of being attacked never crossed my mind. Gray reef sharks are potentially dangerous, but if you don't provoke them, they'll generally keep their distance. It's tiger sharks that divers have to be concerned about. They're fairly common throughout the Hawaiian Islands and have a reputation for taking a bite out of just about anything . . . even an occasional swimmer."

"Did you have your own dive equipment, Henry?"

"We rented our tanks but brought the rest with us. I used to have a regulator, BC, wetsuit . . . everything. After I broke my wrist and lost my Stanford baseball scholarship, I had to sell my dive gear to help pay for my living expenses and first-semester tuition fees at Chico State. All I have left are my mask, fins, and a well-used snorkel."

"How did you manage to pay for the trip to Maui? It must have been expensive."

"My uncle Roscoe paid for our trip as a high-school graduation present."

"Wow! That's quite a gift."

"Uncle Roscoe never had kids of his own. He always thought of me as his son. Roscoe never missed one of my baseball games, from Little League all the way through my freshman year in college. Early in my sophomore year, the engineering company Roscoe worked for opened an office in Portland and sent him there to run it. Soon after that, Uncle Roscoe passed away."

"That's so sad, Henry. What happened?"

"My mom said he was born with a weak heart. Uncle Roscoe was frail but incredibly intelligent. One of his inventions sold for over a million dollars. Now that you've heard my story, when do we leave for Hawai'i?"

"I'll call the travel agent Janet told me about. We can fly directly from San Francisco to Maui, rent a car at the airport, and drive to the condo in Kihei."

MONDAY MORNING, JUNE 7, 1972, FOUND Henry and Anne Glance rumbling to the end of the lava-rock road leading to La Perouse Bay. "I guess this is as far as we go," said Henry.

"Where's the beach?" said Anne. "All I see are black lava rocks."

"I see a few patches of sand between the rocks," said Henry, stepping from the compact rental car. He reached into the back seat for a mesh bag containing two towels and his and Anne's snorkeling equipment. "I can't wait to get in the water."

"The ocean is gorgeous," said Anne, "but if you don't mind, I'd like to take our time getting in."

"We'll take as much time as you need," said Henry, looking back to find that Anne had removed her tank top, revealing a peach-colored, two-piece swimsuit he'd never seen before.

"What's the matter, Henry? Is it my new bathing suit? I bought it at Osers before we left."

"Uh . . ."

"Henry, we've been married over a year now," said Anne, chuckling. "Why are you acting so shy? You've seen me in a swimsuit before."

"Not like that one! I hope I can keep my mind on where we're going."

Henry led Anne across an expanse of flat lava rocks to what he described as the perfect entry point.

"Remember, you promised to help me adjust my facemask and attach my snorkel," said Anne.

Henry rinsed Anne's facemask with water, spit in it, and rubbed the inside glass with his fingertips. Then he rinsed the mask again before adjusting the strap and attaching the snorkel. "Tell me how this feels," he said.

"Perfect," said Anne, peering back at her smiling husband through the glass.

"Good. Let's walk out until we're waist-deep before putting our fins on. As calm as this water is, it should be easy."

"Easy for you, you mean. Henry, is there anything you're not good at?"

"Lots of things."

"Like what?"

"Well, I never learned to dance."

"Are you serious?"

"I'm as serious as that sea urchin next to your left foot. Be careful not to poke yourself. They sting."

"You mean you didn't go to dances in high school?"

"Not a single one," said Henry, ducking beneath the water's surface and clearing his facemask. "I was kind of a geek in high school. All I did was play baseball and basketball during the school year. In the summertime, I worked at the grocery store and played baseball. About once a month, Larry and I would drive over to Oceanside and go surfing."

"Henry, I'm a little apprehensive about this," said Anne, leaning back in the water and straining to put her fins on. "Please don't swim off and leave me."

"I'm gonna be right beside you the entire time. Let's swim across the bay and work our way along that rock wall until we reach the cove Janet told you about."

"How deep do you think this bay is? The water doesn't look very clear."

"You're a good swimmer, Anne. Just keep swimming until you get to the other side."

"What about sharks? I've read that sharks are most likely to attack when the water's murky."

"That's true, but sharks aren't likely to be in this little bay."

"That's reassuring," said Anne, a worried look on her face. "Just in case, I'm going to swim to the other side as fast as I can."

"Okay. Let's go!"

Facedown and breathing through their snorkels, Henry and Anne raced across the bay. It wasn't until they approached the steep lava-rock wall on the other side that they could see anything but opaque, pale-blue water.

Anne pushed her snorkel aside. "I'm glad that's over with. I kept thinking something was going to come up from the deep and grab me."

Henry laughed. "It was a little spooky, wasn't it? Visibility should improve the closer we get to the open ocean."

Henry and Anne snorkeled westward along the naturally formed lava-rock wall. The water became clearer with every kick of their fins, until visibility was nearly limitless. Two-foot waves rolled in from the ocean, breaking against the wall and creating a surge zone where schools of brightly colored yellow tang, orange-spine unicornfish, whitebar surgeonfish, and Achilles tang darted in and out. Immediately beyond the surge zone lay a deep, crystal-clear cove inhabited by cauliflower coral, lobe coral, parrotfish, wrasse, Moorish idols, and a half-dozen species of multicolored butterflyfish.

Anne lifted her head from the water and removed the snorkel from her mouth. "Henry, I've never seen anything so beautiful in my life. It really *is* like swimming in an aquarium!"

Henry had purchased a book titled *Hawaiian Reef Fish* at the Kahului Airport and had read it from cover to cover the night before. He and Anne spent the next hour mesmerized by the spectacular display of marine life swimming, crawling, and growing in the cove. Each time they surfaced, Henry would identify the species of fish they'd seen.

The ocean was as flat as a mountain lake that day, beckoning the young couple to continue around the outside edge of the lava-rock barrier and explore the open ocean beyond.

"Maybe we'll come across a sea turtle or a pod of dolphins," said Anne.

"Wouldn't that be great?" said Henry. "We could see just about anything out here. Let's keep this rocky ledge on your right. I'll be on your left. Any time you want to turn around and head back, just reach over and tap me on the shoulder."

Henry and Anne snorkeled farther and farther from the opening to La Perouse Bay. As they swam, Henry noticed that the coral outcroppings they'd seen in the cove were absent. Instead, massive lava rocks—some of them as large as a city bus—peppered the ocean floor. Something else captured his attention: scores of tiny damselfish and chromis darted in and out of rock crevices, but the larger parrotfish, peacock groupers, and jacks were nowhere to be seen.

Henry and Anne were about to turn around and begin the long swim back to La Perouse Bay when they came upon a large, oval-shaped object floating just under the surface, ten yards ahead. Engulfed in a milky-white soup, the subject of their curiosity was being tossed back and forth in the surge. Every time the object collided with the lava-rock cliff, particles of flesh spewed forth and the sound of someone smacking a wooden ball with a croquet mallet echoed across the water.

"Let's head back, Anne."

"What's wrong, Henry? I've never seen that look on your face before."

"There's no way we can climb this cliff, so we're going to have to swim back the same way we came. Stay as close as you can to the rocks and try not to splash. I'll be right beside you."

"Henry, you're scaring me. What's wrong?"

"No time to talk now."

With Anne swimming parallel to the rock cliff and Henry on her right—parallel with the open ocean—they snorkeled their way back toward La Perouse Bay. Henry kept a watchful eye out in the blue, turning on his backside every fifty yards or so, in case something approached from behind. Halfway to the bay's entrance, Henry's greatest fear was realized: he and Anne were being shadowed by a dark-gray figure with vertical stripes, a boomerang-shaped tail, and the classic dorsal fin that had titillated moviegoers for decades. Rather than alert his wife to the possible danger, he remained steadfast at her starboard side and motioned for her to keep on swimming.

SEVEN

WILLIE RADCLIFF WAS DRAFTED INTO THE U.S. Army on January 12, 1942, at the age of twenty-five. With a little help from his father, he was assigned to the newly formed 7th Infantry Division at Fort Ord. Willie never left California during the war and was discharged on September 5, 1945, having risen to the rank of Class I supply sergeant. Monday morning, September 10, 1945, found Willie waiting in his father's office at Radcliff Farms headquarters in Chico.

"It's about time you got here," said Preston, storming into the room, a stack of papers in his hand. "I told Rebecca I wanted to see you at 8:00."

"She told me," said Willie. "I had to pick up my work truck and gas it up after she dropped me off at the equipment yard."

"Close the door and sit down."

Willie was about to push his father's office door closed, when he peered through the doorway and saw Rebecca sitting at her desk, a worried look on her face. As Radcliff Farms' chief financial officer, Rebecca Radcliff already had a good idea what her father-in-law was going to talk about.

"Before you get started, there's something I want to say," said Willie, taking a seat in front of his father's desk.

"What's that?" said Preston. Willie hesitated, searching for the right words. "Spit it out, son. I haven't got all day."

"I don't like taking orders from Bob Masterson. If he's still gonna be my boss, I'm not sure I want to manage the duck club anymore."

Stone-faced, Preston leaned back in his chair.

"Dad, are you gonna say something?"

"We're hiring apple pickers up in Paradise," said Preston. "I tell you what—if you'll work your tail off for an entire week, I'll put you in charge of one of the picking crews."

Speechless, Willie leaned forward in his chair.

"Keep in mind that the work week for fruit pickers is Monday through Saturday," said Preston.

Willie's poorly timed complaint had backfired badly, and he knew it.

"I'm offering you a new job, son. Forty cents a box. Whaddaya think?"

Willie stood up from his chair and headed for the door.

"Sit down, Willie. I think the duck club may not have been such a good idea after all."

"What makes you say that?"

"The money came pouring in for a while, but during the three years you were passing out uniforms at Fort Ord, half of those rich clients of yours dropped their memberships. If this continues, I'll never recoup the truckload of money I've invested."

"What investments are you talking about?"

"Are you kidding? Who do you think paid for that palatial clubhouse at the Butte Sink site?"

"It's gonna take time, Dad. You'll eventually get your money back."

"I've just scratched the surface," said Preston. "There's also the booze. Do you realize what a bottle of whiskey costs these days? As if that weren't enough, you've taken thirty acres of prime agricultural land out of production and turned them into parking lots. I thought duck hunters were supposed to rough it, not be mollycoddled and pampered like a bunch of spoiled movie stars."

"Is that all?" said Willie, again coming to his feet.

"No. There's one more thing. What were all those petty-cash requisitions Rebecca kept handing me? I asked what they were for, and she had no idea. I counted a dozen or more, all of them for three hundred dollars."

"You don't forget anything, do you?"

"No, I don't. That's what makes me a good businessman. I'm waiting for an answer."

"They were the cost of doing business," said Willie, thinking about all the ducks he'd purchased with the money. "So why did you call me in here—to fire me?"

"Not just yet, but we need to straighten out a few things before you go back to work."

"I'm listening."

"First, Bob Masterson is manager of the Rice Production Division. He is your immediate supervisor, and you'll do what he tells you to do whether you like it or not. Second, I'm going to give you one year to get your duck club back in order and turn it into a profitable enterprise. If you don't, I'll close you down and turn that fancy clubhouse into storage space. Any questions?"

"No."

"Good. You've got work to do. Get to it!"

STILL FUMING FROM THE MEETING WITH his father, Willie drove from Radcliff Farms headquarters directly to the Butte Sink clubhouse. "I'll show him," he said, storming through the kitchen, kicking a chair out of his way, and unlocking the door to his office. Neatly stacked on Willie's desk were three years of records and field notes left by Division Manager Bob Masterson. Willie ignored them and directed his attention to the current roster of duck-club members that lay beneath. Twelve duck-blind leases had expired—five of them at the Willows club, six at the Princeton club, and one at the Butte Sink club.

It was the unleased Butte Sink duck blind that bothered Willie the most. The last lessee had been millionaire restauranteur Lou Griffin, the man he'd illegally sold 135 ducks to in February 1941. Willie picked up the phone and called him.

"There's a name I haven't heard in a while," said Griffin. "How the hell are you, Willie?"

"Right now, I'm trying to put my duck club back together, Lou. I see that you've dropped your membership."

"The hunting wasn't that good the season you went into the army, so I decided not to renew my lease until you came back. I hated to do it, but driving all the way up there for a couple wigeons didn't make much sense."

"I understand. Does that mean I can count on you for this season?"

"What the hell. Send me a contract, and I'll sign it and send it back with a check."

"That's great, Lou. How is the restaurant business going?"

"It was slow for a while after the war ended, but lately it's picked up considerably. I'm opening my third restaurant in a few weeks."

"Where's this one gonna be?"

"San Francisco. We're right on Fisherman's Wharf and twenty minutes from Kezar Stadium, where a brand-new professional football team will be playing in the fall of 1946."

"Wow! That new football team should draw a lot of potential customers."

"You bet it will. Speaking of bringing in customers, if you're able to accommodate some of my regulars like you did three years ago, I'd be interested in continuing our previous arrangement."

"I'll see what I can do, but I can't guarantee the same price."

"Understood. I'll buy as many of those items as I can get."

Willie hung up the phone after a long and productive conversation with Lou Griffin. Excited about Griffin's return to the fold, Willie drove straight to Maxwell. As was usually the case between noon and 1:00 p.m., Gooseneck Strode was sitting on the shaded side of Bud's Garage with a lunchbox in his lap and a peanut-butter sandwich in his hand.

"I heard you was back from the army," said Strode, looking leaner and rougher around the edges than Radcliff remembered.

"Why didn't you call me?"

"I figured you needed time to get settled."

"Where's your partner Mitch?"

"Haven't you heard? Mitch is in Kansas."

"Kansas! What's he doing in Kansas?"

"He got caught sellin' army property and they sent him to Leavenworth."

"How long is he supposed to be there?"

"Two years, with the possibility of cutting it to one for good behavior."

"Where does that leave our business?"

"Right now, we ain't got no business. Mitch is in prison, and Vince Hawkins is somewhere in France. Me and Clyde Tweedy are the only ones still here."

"Can you do it with three?"

"Why? Are you volunteerin'?"

"The thought did cross my mind."

"No offense, but I don't think somebody as big as you could keep up. We cover a lot of ground in a short amount of time. How are you at belly crawlin' through the mud?"

"What if I became the driver?"

Strode held back a chuckle. "Here's how it works," he said. "Clyde doesn't just drop us off and pick us up. He also acts as a lookout and warns us if there's any game wardens in the area. Clyde knows all the roads and levees like the back of his hand, which is pretty damned important when you're drivin' around in the dark with the headlights off. If he makes a mistake, we end up in jail, stuck in the mud, or upside down at the bottom of a ditch."

"How 'bout giving me a try as a shooter? I walk through these rice fields every day. You'd be surprised how fast a big man like me can move."

EIGHT

"IT WAS AT LEAST TWELVE FEET long," said Henry Glance.

"Tiger shark?" said fisheries biologist Ron Jennings.

"Stripes and all."

"Were you frightened, Anne?" said Ron Jennings's wife, Mildred.

"I didn't even see it!"

"Why not?"

"Because Henry waited until we were back in the safety of the bay before he told me the shark had been following us."

"Hank, why did you do that?"

"You need to know the whole story, Millie. The shark had been feeding on a sea turtle when we unknowingly ventured into its territory. I felt our best chance of avoiding an attack was remaining calm and leaving the area without doing anything further to attract its attention."

"I would have been swimming away as fast as I could," said Rose Calloway, Warden Tad Calloway's wife.

"It's not like in the movies," said Henry. "Even if Anne and I had been Olympic swimmers, that shark could have been on us with one flick of its tail."

The doorbell rang at the Paradise home of Captain Chuck Odom and his wife, Barbara.

"Jack and Maggie, welcome to our home," said Chuck, a highball in his hand. "We're so glad you could make it."

Chuck and Barbara led the middle-aged couple through the living room and out to the backyard patio where the rest of the guests were seated. Warden Jack Mayberry sported a neatly trimmed flattop over his Hawaiian shirt and checkered Bermuda shorts. His most remarkable features, other than his snow-white legs, were his protruding chin and his unusually large forearms.

"May I have your attention?" said Chuck, clinking his highball glass with a spoon. "Barbara and I would like to introduce Jack 'Popeye' Mayberry and his better half, Maggie. Jack transferred into the Chico warden's position that's been unoccupied since Tom Austin retired last June."

"Jack and I know each other from down in Southern California," said Tad Calloway, the new Willows warden.

"Then you know what a hard charger he is," said Chuck. "Jack's only been here two weeks, and he's already shaking things up."

When everyone had greeted the new couple, the Mayberrys found empty chairs next to Henry and Anne Glance.

"Jack, why did Chuck refer to you as Popeye?" said Anne.

"That's a long story," said Mayberry. "The Popeye moniker was bestowed upon me by an abalone poacher years ago."

"Let me tell it," said Chuck, taking a seat in the circle. "I was there when it happened."

"Go ahead, Chuck," said Jack. "I'm sure you can tell it better than I."

"Jack was our new boarding officer on the patrol boat *Yellowtail*, out of San Pedro. I had recently been hired as the *Yellowtail*'s deckhand. Les Milton was our engineer, and Gary Plant was captain."

"I remember Les being a great cook," said Jack. "He could make a mackerel taste good."

"Are you going to tell the story, or shall I?"

"Sorry, Chuck. You go right ahead."

"We were patrolling the backside of San Clemente Island when we spotted this commercial abalone boat."

"How'd ya know it was a commercial abalone boat?" said Ron.

"It was about twenty-six feet long and had a davit crane attached to the stern. There was a dripping-wet burlap bag filled with abalone hanging from the crane. I remember one of the divers removing his wetsuit as we approached."

"How many people were on board?" said Henry.

"Three. Is that right, Jack?"

"You're telling the story," said Mayberry, smiling and sipping on a high-ball Chuck had made for him.

"The boat owner was a big, loudmouthed character named Salvatore Balducci. I can still hear his buddies saying, 'Sal, calm down. Sal, calm down.' Balducci and the man in the wetsuit were the divers. The third man operated the hose and the air pump. When Jack climbed on board and said he wanted to inspect their abalone, Balducci came running across the deck and got in his face. Jack was young, inexperienced, and had the face of a sixteen-year-old in those days. Balducci probably figured he could intimidate him."

"I've been trying for years," said Maggie, "and it hasn't worked yet."

Everyone laughed.

"Did anyone try to help Jack?" said Anne.

"I started to jump on board, when Captain Plant grabbed me by the arm and yanked me back," said Chuck.

"Why would he do that?" said Rose.

"He told me he wanted to see how the rookie handled himself, but I later learned he had an ulterior motive."

"How *did* Jack handle himself?" said Tad.

"He remained as cool as a cucumber and went about his business, inspecting and measuring every abalone on board."

"How many abalone were there?" said Henry.

"It's been twenty years, but I think they had well over a hundred. When Jack told Balducci half of them were short and all three men on board were going to be charged with possession of undersized abalone, Balducci blew a cork."

"Wha'd he do?" said Ron.

"First, he started stomping around the deck, whining about losing his commercial fishing license. When that didn't work, he climbed back in Jack's face and started calling him Popeye. 'Look here, Popeye!' he shouted. 'If you weren't wearing that badge, I'd throw your ass overboard.'"

"Jack, you never told me about this," said Maggie.

"There's probably a lot he hasn't told you," said Barbara.

"Anyway, Jack just stood there and took it until Balducci made the mistake of poking him in the chest with his finger."

"He shouldn't oughta done that," said Tad.

"You got that right," said Chuck. "In the blink of an eye, Jack grabbed Balducci's wrist and twisted it upside down."

"Did Balducci cooperate then?" said Ron.

"Not until Jack talked him to his knees, sprawled him face down on the deck, and cuffed his hands behind his back. We hauled Balducci and his crew before Judge Andrews in Avalon that same afternoon."

"What was the outcome?" said Tad.

"At first, all three abalone poachers pled not guilty and demanded jury trials. When Judge Andrews learned that Balducci had threatened and assaulted Warden Mayberry, he told him he could await his trial in the L.A. County Jail. I'll never forget the look on Balducci's face when his crew members raised their hands and said they wanted to change their pleas to guilty."

"Did Balducci get his jury trial?" said Henry.

"The last time I saw him, he was cussing a blue streak as the bailiff led him out the back door of the courtroom," said Chuck.

"He did get his trial three months later," said Jack. "The jury found him guilty."

"What kind of sentence did he get?" said Tad.

"He got six months in the can. A couple months later, I testified before the Fish and Game Commission and Balducci lost his commercial fishing license for life."

"Served him right!" said Rose. "Chuck, are you going to tell us why Captain Plant grabbed your arm and wouldn't let you help Jack?"

"Thanks for reminding me, Rose. Gary Plant and Sal Balducci both lived in Avalon. Every time Plant ran into Balducci in the grocery store or anywhere else on Catalina Island, Balducci would make a crass remark and try to goad him into a fight. Plant knew if he punched that big sonofabitch in the nose, he could lose his job, so he never took the bait."

"I get it!" said Ron, laughing. "Plant knew that Balducci was finally going to get the ass kicking he deserved."

"That's right," said Chuck. "Jack wasn't just an expert in defensive tactics. He was also a black belt in karate."

"Great story!" said Anne.

"There's an addendum," said Chuck. "Twenty-four hours after the incident, everyone in the Long Beach Fish and Game office was calling Jack Mayberry Popeye. That's been his nickname ever since."

After a dinner of barbequed chicken, tossed salad, and corn on the cob, everyone sat around the patio, telling stories and getting acquainted.

"Jack, Chuck said you've been shaking things up since you got here," said Henry. "Would you mind telling us what he meant?"

"Not at all. I spent all day last Saturday checking fishermen on Deer Creek. I'd see a car parked along the road up ahead, leave my patrol car fifty yards back, and quietly work my way down the canyon. In this case, I heard a waterfall and men hollering."

"Would anyone like another drink?" said Chuck.

"I'll take another one of these," said Tad, holding up an empty beer can.

"Coming right up."

"Where was I?" said Jack.

"You heard men hollering."

"Thank you, Anne. When I heard the commotion, I ducked down and crept up on what turned out to be three men in their early twenties. They were casting weighted treble hooks into this deep pool at the base of a waterfall. Pretty soon, one of 'em hooked a fish in the back and horsed it up on the bank. At that point, I knew they were violators."

"Was it a trout or a salmon?" said Ron.

"It was almost three feet long and weighed seven or eight pounds."

"That had to have been a spring-run salmon," said Ron, judging from his knowledge and experience as a fisheries biologist. "They run up Deer Creek in the springtime and stack up in the deeper pools during the summer months. I know right where that waterfall is."

"These guys had already killed three salmon. The one they'd just foul-hooked seemed unharmed, except for the gash in its tail, so I made them release it."

"What did you do next?" said Henry.

"I marched them up to my patrol car and made them sit on the side of the road while I researched the regulations. They all had good IDs, so I seized their fishing gear and their fish, and told them I'd be filing formal complaints with the Butte County District Attorney's Office. Since Deer Creek is closed to the take of salmon, I let them slide for the snagging violations and charged them with unlawful take and possession of four salmon in Deer Creek."

"It sounds like you handled it perfectly," said Henry. "If you ever need help, let me know. I became pretty familiar with that neck of the woods after Tom Austin retired and his position was left open for almost a year."

"There is something you can help me with, Hank. I was patrolling near Butte Meadows the other day when this guy ran out of his cabin and flagged me down. He said two old codgers have been parking their truck up the road in the morning and again in the evening. He thinks they're sneaking into this little trout stream that runs through the back of his property. The stream is supposed to be chock-full of gorgeous little brown trout."

"What's the name of this stream?" said Henry.

"He called it Secret Creek, but I'm not sure it really has a name."

"It sounds like they're milk running," said Henry.

"What does that mean?" said Anne.

"It usually means they catch a limit of trout, take them home or back to camp, then come back later that same day and catch another limit," said Henry. "Jack, do you mind if I run an idea by you?"

"Sure, Hank. Go ahead."

"Saturday is the first day of Fourth of July weekend. Those two geriatric desperadoes will probably be camping near Butte Meadows somewhere. What would you think about dropping me off by the stream before they arrive? I'll hide in the bushes and see what they're up to. When you come back to pick me up, we'll pay them a visit."

NINE

WILLIE RADCLIFF SPENT THE FIRST HALF of October 1945 on the phone, trying to talk his former customers into renewing their leases. "I just got back from a scouting trip to Lower Klamath," he told them. "It's swarming with ducks, and as soon as the weather changes, they'll head south into the valley." By the first of November, Willie had convinced all but one of his former duck-club members to renew their leases.

Luck was on Radcliff's side. South winds and heavy rains did come to the Sacramento Valley, bringing waterfowl down from up north in numbers that hadn't been seen in years.

On Sunday morning, November 11, 1945, Willie received the phone call he'd been waiting for.

"Ducks are all over the valley!" said Gooseneck Strode.

"Tell me about it," said Radcliff. "My club members have been in the field for two hours, and some of them have already returned with limits."

"Did you mean what you said about joinin' us?"

"Damn right I meant it."

"There's an old, abandoned barn at the intersection of Knudson Road and County Road 38. A rusted-out tractor is stuck in the mud out front. We'll meet you there at 10:00 tomorrow night. The barn door is always open, so you can hide your truck inside."

"What should I bring?"

"You're gonna get wet and muddy, so dress light and wear shoes you can run in. Bring your shotgun and ten high-base, number 4 shotgun shells."

"Why only ten?"

"Remember what I said about movin' fast? No sense luggin' around excess weight. We fire one volley and don't make another sound. There's a reason why me and the boys have been doin' this since high school and never been caught."

"Okay," said Willie, his throat suddenly dry. "I'll see you tomorrow night."

The weekend storm had passed, and the night air was crisp and clear, with a first-quarter moon overhead. Radcliff drove into the broken-down old barn Gooseneck had described and cut his headlights. With just enough natural light to find his way, he climbed from his silver-gray, 1943 Chevy pickup and walked back toward the barn's entrance.

Fifteen minutes passed and no one came. Radcliff walked out to the road where a rusted-out tractor sat in the mud. "This has to be the right place," he mumbled.

Radcliff had begun a slow walk back to the barn when he heard the roar of rubber on pavement and saw headlights approaching. He dashed back to the tractor and hid behind one of the giant rear tires. The car stopped at the intersection of County Road 38 and Knudson Road.

"It's gotta be them," mumbled Radcliff. "Who else would be way out here in the middle of the night?"

The car made a right turn on Knudson Road and sped away.

Disappointed and confused, Radcliff ambled back to the barn. It was pitch dark inside, but a gaping hole in the roof allowed moonlight to stream through and illuminate the outline of his pickup. He shuffled toward the driver's-side door and was about to reach for the handle when he tripped over something and almost fell.

"Game warden!" came a shout from the other side of the barn. A flashlight came on and lit up a pile of ducks at Radcliff's feet. "Put your hands in the air and don't move."

"Oh shit!" blurted Radcliff, his heart pounding. "Those aren't mine!"

"A likely story," came a second voice. "You're under arrest!"

"Wait a minute," said Radcliff. "I recognize *that* voice."

Gooseneck Strode and another man emerged from the darkness, both bent over, laughing. "You've just been initiated into the gang," said Strode. "This here's Vince. He got home yesterday, a couple hours after me and you talked on the phone."

"How did you get here?"

"Clyde dropped us off a few minutes before you showed up. That was him who stopped at the intersection while you were out by the tractor. I think he realized he'd come back too early and took off."

"Here he comes now," said Vince Hawkins, short, husky, and still sporting a butch haircut from his stint in the army.

"Let's go to work," said Strode. "Willie, grab your shotgun and whatever else you're bringin'. Hop in back with Vince."

Gooseneck Strode, Clyde Tweedy, and Vince Hawkins had already located a large congregation of feeding ducks on a section of rice ten miles southwest of Willows. On the way back to the planned drag site, Willie peppered them with questions about the operation.

"Do you guys have any competition?"

"What do ya mean?" said Strode.

"You know—other duck draggers who might beat you to the same ducks."

"It's understood that we operate in the area west of the river, from Willows to Williams. Dud Bogar and his gang work east of the river, includin' Biggs, Gridley, and the Butte Sink. Russ Louderback's crew stays down around Yuba City and the Sutter Buttes. That way we don't come to blows like some a the old-timers did back in the thirties."

"You mean there were actual fights?"

"Things get pretty serious when money's involved," said Tweedy, slender, about Radcliff's height, with bushy blond hair. "Dud Bogar has made it clear he'll shoot anyone who poaches his territory."

"Have you run into him yet?" said Strode. "He's usually cruisin' around the Butte Sink area."

"Is he that big hillbilly who drives the ugly green Studebaker?"

"That's Dud. He talks like he just climbed off the bus from Oklahoma, but he's dumb like a fox."

"Who does this Dud character sell his ducks to?"

"I heard a rumor that he sells to some turkey rancher down around Lincoln," said Strode, "but nobody knows for sure."

"We're comin' up on the drop-off site," said Tweedy. "You guys get ready. I'll open the trunk so you can grab your shotguns."

GOOSENECK STRODE AND HIS GETAWAY DRIVER, Clyde Tweedy, were whooping it up in the Silver Dollar Bar the night after Willie Radcliff's first duck drag. "I wish you'd a been there," said Strode, chugging down his third beer.

"What happened?" said Tweedy, laughing.

"The shootin' started and ducks were droppin' like flies when that big sonofabitch started hollerin' like he was crazy or somethin'. I've never seen anyone so out-of-his-mind excited."

Pulling his first duck drag was like taking a massive dose of testosterone for Willie Radcliff. He would later tell his new friends that blasting away at all those ducks was the most fun he'd ever had in his life. Three hundred and twenty-nine ducks were harvested that memorable night, not counting all the wounded ones that limped into the weeds, suffered a gangrenous death, or were dragged away and eaten by rats, skunks, and other scavengers.

Radcliff saved twenty-five percent of his share for the less-skillful shooters at his Butte Sink duck club. He sold the rest to restauranteur Lou Griffin for two dollars and fifty cents apiece. Willie pulled seven drags with Strode's gang during the bountiful 1945-46 duck season and two more in late February, after the season had closed. If Strode's calculations were correct, his gang sold over nineteen hundred ducks that year and most of them were pintails.

Willie Radcliff's good fortune didn't end with the money he made illegally selling wild ducks. Radcliff Farms Duck Club ended the year financially in the black, with every blind leased and a lengthy list of hunters waiting to get in.

"I couldn't be more pleased," said Preston. "To show my appreciation for the fine job you've done, I have a surprise for you."

"Are you finally gonna give Bob Masterson the boot?"

"No, Willie. Bob Masterson is going to remain your boss as long as I'm president of Radcliff Farms. Bob has been working for me a long time, and I trust him almost as much as I trust your mother. You'd be wise to stop your sniveling and make the most of it."

"So, what's the surprise?"

"The surprise is I'm negotiating the purchase of another six hundred and forty acres of rice-growing land near Williams. How would you like to turn it into another Radcliff Farms duck club?"

NOTHING BROUGHT WILLIE RADCLIFF MORE JOY and excitement than the thrill of duck-dragging with Gooseneck Strode and the gang, but that ended when Mitch Leatherwood returned from prison in October 1946. Leatherwood was welcomed back with open arms, lending credence to the phrase, "There's no honor among thieves."

In spite of Rebecca's becoming pregnant in 1946, and the birth of William Junior in 1947, Willie's black-market duck-selling business never missed a beat. He continued to buy ducks from Gooseneck Strode and sell them to Lou Griffin until Bob Masterson caught wind of what was going on in January 1948.

Forty-year-old Bob Masterson was an average-sized man, with muscular arms and exceptionally strong hands from his career wrestling with irrigation pipes and heavy equipment. He'd also been a champion middle-weight boxer during his earlier years in the U.S. Navy.

Masterson received word that shipments of wild ducks were leaving the Butte Sink clubhouse just after daylight on Tuesday mornings. According to Masterson's anonymous informant, the transport vehicle was a green-and-white Chevrolet panel truck belonging to Radcliff Farms.

On the second Tuesday in January 1948, Masterson hid his work truck near the entrance to the Butte Sink clubhouse and waited patiently, a cup of hot coffee warming his hands. Just before daylight, a panel truck meeting his informant's description drove past the open gate and down the dirt road to the clubhouse. Masterson closed the gate behind it. Ten minutes later, the truck returned and stopped at the gate. When the driver got out, Masterson was waiting for him.

"What's your name, son?"

"Seth Deason," said the young man, visibly shaken.

"Haven't I seen you somewhere before?"

"Yes, Mr. Masterson. I run the check station at the Radcliff Farms Princeton duck club."

"I take it you know who I am?"

"Everybody who works for Radcliff Farms knows who Bob Masterson is."

"I'm going to ask you a few questions. Your future as a Radcliff Farms employee will depend on how truthful your answers are. Do I make myself clear?"

"Yes, Mr. Masterson."

"What did you just pick up at the clubhouse?"

"A load of ducks."

"Open the back of the truck so I can see them." Deason opened the back of the truck, removed a tarp, and showed Masterson fifty field-dressed mallards and pintails. "Who gave you these ducks?"

"Willie Radcliff."

"Where were you taking them?"

"To San Francisco."

"Where in San Francisco?"

"To Griff's Seafood Restaurant, on Fisherman's Wharf."

"How often do you do this?"

"Every other week."

"Where else do you deliver ducks for Willie Radcliff?"

"I meet a man in Fresno on alternate Thursdays. He takes them to Griff's Seafood restaurants in Santa Monica and Palm Springs."

"How do you know that?"

"Mr. Griffin's driver and I have become pretty good friends over the past two years, and he told me."

"Are you telling me that you've been doing this for the past two years?"

"Yes, between mid-November and the end of February."

"Who pays you?"

"Willie Radcliff."

"Who pays the man you meet in Fresno?"

"Mr. Griffin, I suppose."

"Who authorized you to use a Radcliff Farms delivery truck to haul the ducks?"

"Willie Radcliff."

"I want you to sit here by the gate until I return," said Masterson, as he climbed into the panel truck and drove to the clubhouse.

"What's wrong?" said Willie, walking out to the panel truck. "Did you forget something?"

"Game's over," said Masterson, cutting the motor and stepping out.

"What are *you* doing here?"

Masterson doubled his fist and punched Radcliff in the mouth. "I've put up with your arrogant attitude and your insubordination long enough," he said. "Now I'm going to give you the beating your father should have given you a long time ago."

"When he hears about this, he'll fire you for sure," blubbered Radcliff.

"You're what my old man used to call a bad actor," said Masterson, punching Radcliff again—this time with so much force, Willie's feet flew out from under him, and he hit the ground like a two-hundred-and-sixty-pound sack of potatoes. "You don't care about anyone but yourself, and there's not a decent bone in your body. If you mention one word about this to your father, I'll tell Mike Prescott, the Willows game warden, about the black-market duck-selling business you've been running for the last two years."

"It's your word against mine," said Radcliff, struggling to his feet and taking a wild swing at Masterson.

Masterson ducked the swing and battered Willie's face until his lower lip swelled up like a tomato. "I can't wait to tell Warden Prescott about that crooked seafood restaurant on Fisherman's Wharf."

Willie figured he could lie his way out of just about anything with his parents, but the thought of Lou Griffin and his shady business partners thinking he'd squealed on them sent shivers down his spine. "You win!" he whimpered. "What do you want from me?"

"You're going to put an end to your outlaw activities, clean up your act, and show me some respect."

"And what if I don't?"

"I was hoping you'd say that," said Masterson, administering the coup de grace with a haymaker to Radcliff's jaw—knocking him out cold. While Willie lay on the wet ground, Masterson reached into the back of the delivery truck, gathered up all the dead ducks, and dumped them on his long-time antagonist's head. Masterson then drove back to the entrance gate to deal with Deason.

"Here's what you're going to do," said Masterson. "Return this truck to the equipment yard, wash it, gas it up, and make sure there's not a feather or a spot of blood left anywhere."

"Yes, Mr. Masterson."

"I'll allow you to return to your regular job, but if you do anything like this again, I'll not only fire you, I'll turn you in to the game warden."

"I understand," said Deason. "What if Willie tries to fire me for telling you everything?"

"You just leave Willie Radcliff to me."

TEN

J ACK "POPEYE" MAYBERRY AND HIS WIFE, Margaret, had rented a small house east of Mangrove Avenue until they were able to find a suitable home in or near Chico to purchase. An hour before daylight on Saturday, July 1, 1972—three days after the barbeque at Captain Odom's house—Jack watched Warden Glance's patrol truck pull up to the curb in front. He walked out and invited Henry in for a cup of coffee.

"Thanks for the offer, Jack, but I've never developed a taste for the stuff."

"Hank, you're the first game warden I've ever met who didn't drink coffee."

"Your predecessor, Tom Austin, said the same thing the first time I rode with him."

"I'll run back in the house and grab my keys while you gather whatever gear you're taking."

Dressed in full camos, Glance reached into the cab of his truck and pulled out a pair of binoculars. "Can't conduct a stakeout without these," he said, locking the door and walking up the driveway to a dark-green, 1968 Ford sedan—the same patrol car Warden Tom Austin had driven for the previous three years.

"How many miles did Tom put on this car before you inherited it?" said Glance, as Mayberry backed it down the driveway and headed southeast toward Highway 32.

"Ninety-nine thousand, seven hundred and twenty-five. I've added another seven thousand since I've been here."

"Are you going to request a four-wheel-drive pickup when they finally put this clunker out to pasture?"

"Absolutely! All the Fish and Game vehicles I've ever been issued were sedans. I never needed four-wheel drive to commute from my house in Seal Beach to the harbor where our patrol boat was moored."

"Do you miss working marine patrol?"

"Let's just say I miss the ocean and leave it at that," said Mayberry, looking over at his passenger with a hint of rancor in his voice.

"I understand," said Glance, believing he'd struck a nerve. "No need to explain."

"Dealing with commercial fishermen every day of my career was no picnic, let me tell you. Have you ever boarded a trawler after it's just dragged the bottom of the ocean for three miles?"

"No, I haven't."

"What I've seen in those nets would make your skin crawl, Hank. You wouldn't believe the damage they do to the ocean floor."

"I've read about the non-target species that are scooped up and killed by trawlers."

"They call that bycatch. I call it blatant destruction of the ocean and every critter in it. I did my best to protect the resource for twenty-two years, but the stress was killing me." Mayberry removed his Stetson. "I used to have hair like yours. Now look at me!"

"Do you feel better now that you've gotten that off your chest?"

"Sorry about that, Hank. Maggie's tired of hearing it, so I guess I used you as my sounding board this morning."

"You're welcome to sound off to me any time you want, Jack. I feel the same way you do. I think that destructive practice should have been outlawed years ago. On the lighter side, how far from Butte Meadows is the little stream you were talking about at the barbeque?"

"It actually meanders through Butte Meadows. The stream is so small and overgrown with willows, most people don't even know it's there."

"I bet after working the Channel Islands for twenty years, you've seen some pretty big fish."

"I've seen just about every large fish that swims off the California coast,

Hank—marlin, swordfish, giant seabass, bluefin tuna, yellowfin tuna, great white sharks, basking sharks, thresher sharks—you name it. The biggest fish I've ever seen was a forty-foot whale shark off La Jolla."

"Wow! Do you know how fortunate you are to have had those experiences?"

"Those experiences were what I loved about the job. Dealing with commercial fishermen—that's another story."

"Where did you see the great white sharks?"

"I've seen lots of them out around the Farallon Islands. The only one I've ever seen while diving was in the kelp forest fifty yards from the Avalon Casino on Catalina Island. It came out of nowhere, cruised right by me, and disappeared."

"How big was it?"

"You know how everything looks twice as big underwater?"

"I do."

"That shark could have passed for a submarine. It was the most frightening thing that's ever happened to me, but I wouldn't trade the experience for anything in the world. Ya know what I mean?"

"I know exactly what you mean, Jack. Anne and I had a similar experience in Maui, just last week. I was telling everyone about it when you and Maggie arrived at the barbeque."

"If you were in Maui, I bet it was a tiger shark."

"As a matter of fact, it was."

"Are you a scuba diver, Hank?"

"I am, but Anne and I were snorkeling when this happened."

"The department may be putting together a dive team. Are you interested?"

"What are the requirements?"

"Ya gotta be a certified scuba diver. That's about it for now. The chief of patrol asked me to put together a plan before the end of the year. I'm supposed to provide him with a set of qualifications and requirements."

"What would it involve?"

"We could be dealing with just about anything related to water—abalone, lobsters, commercial fishing, evidence recovery, surveillance, pollution, rescue—the whole nine yards."

"Would I have to change districts?"

"Not if I have anything to say about it. The way I see it, team members would remain in their own patrol districts and be called in as needed. It makes sense that most of them will occupy districts on or near the ocean, but resource-related investigations occur in lakes and streams too."

"It all sounds exciting, but I should probably talk to Anne about it before I commit. Please keep me in mind when you begin recruiting."

When they reached Butte Meadows, Mayberry turned up a well-traveled dirt road that snaked its way through a mile of tall timber and skirted two mountain cabins. "My informant lives in the one with the blue pickup parked in front," he said.

"I guessed that when I saw someone watching us from the window," said Glance. "And the little stream you told us about flows behind the cabin we just passed?"

"It does, but it meanders through a grassy meadow first. According to my informant, these two old-timers park their pickup at the meadow, walk out to the creek, and fish downstream from there."

The grassy meadow Mayberry had described was drenched in early-morning dew when Mayberry pulled his patrol car up beside it. "See that jungle of stunted willows out there?" he said, pointing. "That's where the stream is."

"It's almost 6:00 now," said Glance. "How 'bout picking me up about 10:00?"

"Sounds good," said Mayberry. "I'll find a place to hide and catch up on my daily activity reports."

Glance quietly closed the passenger door and waded out through the wet grass toward a distant patch of wild blackberries. He lay prone behind the thorny bushes for thirty minutes before a brown Ford pickup crested the hill, stopped at the side of the road, and two gray-haired gentlemen climbed out. The passenger wasted no time dropping the tailgate and rigging his line; he was dressed in khaki slacks, a long-sleeved shirt, and a canvas visor that shielded his eyes from the brilliant morning sunlight. The driver, who bore a striking resemblance to the passenger, wore a navy-blue, zip-up sweatshirt and a tan fishing vest.

"George, aren't you gonna wait for me?" said the driver, as the passenger donned a forest-green fishing vest, picked up his rod, and began walking toward the stream.

"I didn't know you were gonna take all day, Fred. Put on that little gold hook I gave you, and let's get going. As slow as you are, it'll be noon before we catch our first fish."

"Are you using one split shot or two?"

"For crying out loud! Do I have to do everything for you?" George leaned his rod against a tree and walked back to the truck. Reaching the tailgate, he suddenly let out with a holler. "Ow!"

"Wha'd ya do?"

"I banged my shin on that damned trailer hitch of yours. Didn't I tell you to remove it after we unhooked the trailer?"

"I'm sorry to be such a pain in the ass, George. I thought we came up here to relax and enjoy ourselves."

"Here, give me that!" said George. "You take one BB-sized split shot with the needle-nose pliers and pinch it onto your line. If you add too much weight, it'll just sit there in one place and won't drift under the ledge where the fish are."

Finally ready, Fred followed George across the meadow and down the hill to the stream.

Glance pulled a notepad from his shirt pocket as he watched George creep up to the streambank, dangle his rod over the water, and drop his baited hook into the current. Within seconds, he lifted a wriggling eight-inch trout from the water and dropped it into his wicker creel. Henry couldn't tell if George removed earthworms or mealworms from the Bobbet bait box that hung from his belt. Whatever they were, they proved to be deadly effective. Within twenty minutes, the determined fisherman had caught and kept seven trout. Each time George deposited a trout in his creel, Henry placed a hash mark next to his name.

While George busied himself catching fish, Fred spent most of his time snagged on willow roots and tree branches. In the time it took George to catch seven fish, Fred had caught and kept one. Henry noticed that George's behavior changed once he'd caught and kept nine trout. Instead of depositing the fish in his own wicker creel, he walked over and placed them in Fred's green canvas creel. When Fred and George drove away at 9:55 a.m., Henry's tally showed that George had caught and kept seventeen trout. Fred had caught and kept three.

"How'd it go?" said Mayberry, as Glance walked out from behind the blackberry patch and climbed inside Mayberry's patrol car.

"I watched one fisherman catch seventeen trout and put seven of them in his fishing buddy's creel. I have a hunch they were brothers."

"What makes you say that?"

"They looked alike, and the passenger ridiculed the driver from the time he stepped out of the pickup until the time they left. Like your informant said, all the fish they caught were about eight inches long."

Glance handed Mayberry a detailed written account of what he'd witnessed. "I see you wrote down their license number," said Mayberry. "Let's run a radio check and find out where these guys live."

"That may not be necessary. I suspect we'll find their trailer at the Butte Meadows Campground."

"What makes you think that?"

"Their pickup had a trailer hitch, and I heard them talking about being in camp last night."

As Mayberry and Glance drove by the Butte Meadows Campground, Glance spotted the brown Ford pickup he'd seen earlier.

"That looks like one of those little Shasta camp trailers parked next to it," said Mayberry. "Do you see anyone around?"

"No, but the door is open, so they must be close by."

"How 'bout we patrol on up to Jonesville and check them out on our way back?"

"Sounds good," said Glance.

It was pushing 6:30 in the evening when Mayberry and Glance drove back by the Butte Meadows Campground. The camp trailer was still there, but the brown Ford pickup was gone. "I have a hunch where they might be," said Glance.

"Great minds think alike," said Mayberry, turning north on the same dirt road he and Glance had taken that morning.

The wardens had driven a half mile when Glance recognized the suspects' pickup approaching. "Here they come," he said.

Mayberry stepped from the patrol car and waved for the oncoming pickup to stop. "Hello. Have you gentlemen been fishing?"

The driver looked over at the passenger, then turned his attention to Warden Mayberry. "We have," he said.

"We'd like to see your fishing licenses and your fish."

Each fisherman handed Mayberry a valid California Fishing License through the driver's-side window. "Thank you," said Mayberry, handing the licenses back. "Now, if you'd show us your fish."

"Sure," said the driver, his hands trembling. "They're in back."

While the passenger stood by at the rear of the pickup, the driver dropped the tailgate and showed Mayberry each of their creels. Glance, still wearing camos, was observing from the right-front fender of the patrol car. Seeing the two fishermen up close for the first time, he pegged them as twins. Both men were short and plump, with flawless pink skin. The driver wore gold-rimmed glasses.

"Which creel is yours?" said Mayberry, looking at the driver.

"The canvas creel is mine, and the basket creel belongs to my brother."

The passenger's basket creel contained ten eight-inch brown trout. The driver's canvas creel contained four.

"Did you catch all four fish in this one?" said Mayberry, holding up the canvas creel.

"Yes," said the driver.

"Did you catch any trout earlier in the day?"

"I caught three this morning."

Looking at the passenger, Mayberry said, "How many trout did you catch this morning?"

"I didn't catch any this morning. If you've finished your business, we're hungry and would like to get going."

"Let me ask you again," said Mayberry. "Did you catch and keep any fish today, other than the ten here in your creel?"

"How many times do I have to tell you? What you have in your hand is all the fish I've caught today. You saw my fishing license. What more do you need?"

"For starters, I'd like to see identification from each of you."

The driver was identified as eighty-one-year-old Frederick Michael Carlisle of Chico, California. The passenger, eighty-one-year-old George Robert Carlisle, lived seven miles south of Chico, in Durham.

"I'm going to keep your driver's licenses and your creels until we see what's back at your camp," said Mayberry.

"Our camp!" spouted George Carlisle. "How do you know about our camp?"

"You gentlemen are in the blue-and-white Shasta trailer, aren't you?"

Fred Carlisle's chin dropped and an expression of pending doom spread across his face.

"I guess that answers my question," said Mayberry. "You gentlemen go ahead. We'll be right behind you."

"Looks like George is getting an earful," said Glance, watching the Carlisle brothers through the rear window of their pickup.

"He sure is," said Mayberry, chuckling.

"What's this all about?" said George Carlisle, meeting the two wardens as they pulled up to the campsite and climbed out of Mayberry's patrol car.

"Since you asked, I'll tell you," said Mayberry. "The daily bag limit is ten trout per person. That doesn't mean you can catch ten for yourself and another seven for your brother. This morning, you were observed doing just that. Before we go any further, I'd like to see any fish you have in camp. Let me remind you that failure to show your fish when I ask to see them is another violation."

"We have two ice chests," said George, before his brother could say anything. "One is right there on the table. The other one is inside the trailer."

George opened the trailer door and carried the second ice chest outside so Warden Mayberry could inspect it. While Mayberry searched the two ice chests, Glance watched George slide over and close the trailer door.

Finding no fish inside either of the ice chests, Mayberry turned to the Carlisle brothers. "I'm going to ask you gentlemen one more time if you have any other coolers, refrigerators, or ice chests that might contain fish."

Neither brother responded.

"Which one of you is the owner of this nice little Shasta trailer?"

"I am," said Fred.

"How long have you owned it?"

"I bought it new in 1955, right after I retired."

"Unless my memory fails me, these Shasta trailers have built-in iceboxes below the sink."

Seeing no way out of their predicament, Fred threw open the trailer door. "I told him we were gonna get caught, but that stubborn brother of mine wouldn't listen. Go ahead and look in the icebox. You obviously know where it is."

Mayberry opened the built-in icebox and found the twenty small brown trout that Warden Glance had seen the Carlisle brothers take that morning. Mixed with the smaller trout were four twelve-inch brown trout.

Glance watched as Mayberry explained to the Carlisle brothers what was going to happen.

"Without getting into who caught what, if there's anything either of you gentlemen would like to tell me, now's the time to do it."

Fred looked at George, expecting him to respond. "George, you stubborn old fool. If you stick me with this, you're going to have to hitchhike home. I told you this was going to happen if you kept putting your fish in my creel. You were a stingy little miser when we were kids, and you haven't changed a bit."

"Why don't you tell us what really happened," said Glance.

"Who's this guy?" said George. "If he's not a game warden, I don't have to tell him anything."

"I am a game warden," said Glance, displaying his identification. "I'm also the person who watched the two of you fishing in that small stream this morning."

"Then you know I only caught seven trout all day," said Fred. "My brother can tell you the rest."

"Yeah, I caught the rest of 'em," said George.

"What about the four larger brown trout?" said Glance.

"I caught those here in Butte Creek this afternoon, while Fred was taking a nap."

TWO MONTHS LATER, JACK MAYBERRY WAS patrolling through the Butte Meadows Campground.

"Warden Mayberry!" shouted Fred Carlisle, seated in a lawn chair next to his blue-and-white Shasta trailer. Another elderly gentleman sat next to him.

"Hello, Mr. Carlisle," said Mayberry through his open window. "How ya been?"

"Life is good now that I have a new fishing partner."

"I see that," said Mayberry. "Where's your brother?"

"That tightwad was so angry about paying his two-hundred-and-fifty-dollar fine, he moved to a senior community in Surprise, Arizona. Now he spends his days cheating at shuffleboard and his nights playing bingo."

ELEVEN

WILLIE RADCLIFF HAD HIS HANDS FULL between 1948 and 1957, opening two new duck-club properties, leasing sixty additional duck blinds, and helping Rebecca raise their young son. During all that time, he never severed his relationship with Gooseneck Strode. Every time the two men met, Willie would remind his former business partner of how much he'd enjoyed blasting away at all those ducks.

Early one evening during the summer of 1957, Radcliff walked out of Willows Market and was approaching his spanking-new, Chevy Bel Air convertible, when he heard a familiar voice coming from a rusted-out old tow truck in the next parking space. "Hey, Willie, how ya doin'?"

"If it isn't my old pal Gooseneck Strode!" said Radcliff, leaning over and dropping his shopping bag on the front passenger seat of his convertible. "How long's it been—five years?"

"At least," said Strode. "I don't go by Gooseneck no more."

"Why not?"

"It's a long story." Strode reached into a metal cooler, pulled out a cold, dripping-wet beer, and offered it to his friend.

"Don't mind if I do," said Radcliff, hopping up on the flatbed beside Strode. "You look like you've had a rough day."

"Yeah. I had to run clear up to Plaskett Meadows and pull a couple flatlanders outta the mud."

"I'm curious why you no longer go by Gooseneck."

"Haven't you heard about the game warden over in Gridley who disappeared last December?"

"I did hear something about that. What does it have to do with you?"

"Nothin', but ever since it happened, I've been harassed by every game warden, deputy sheriff, and detective in Northern California."

"Why are they harassing you?"

"Because Gooseneck Strode has a reputation for bein' an outlaw duck poacher who hates game wardens. One night, I was leavin' the Silver Dollar bar over in Gridley, when everything suddenly went dark."

"What happened?"

"Someone threw a blanket over my head, wrapped a rope around my waist, and kicked the livin' shit outta me. I was in the hospital for three days with cracked ribs and a broken nose."

"Did you ever find out who did it?"

"I heard it was four game wardens from Southern California, but that was just a rumor and nothin' ever came of it."

"Did you hear any of their voices?"

"I heard a few grunts when they picked me up and dropped me on the parking lot, but no one said a word. The next mornin', I woke up in the hospital."

"I was going to ask if the old gang was still together. Maybe I shouldn't, after what you just told me."

"Three of us were still pullin' a few drags until I got beat up. Since then, we ain't fired a shot."

"Did I ever tell you about the game warden who followed me around when I was a kid?"

"No. What was his name?"

"I don't remember his name."

"Wha'd he look like?"

"Skinny little guy with bowlegs. He wore gold-rimmed glasses, a Smokey the Bear hat, and he toted a big hogleg on his right hip."

"That sounds like Jed Sutton. Ornery old cuss. Did he ever catch you doin' anything?"

"He caught me a couple times, but for every time he did, there were twenty other times he didn't. I musta plinked five or six deer and a dozen or more hawks and owls with that sweet little Model 56 .22 rifle of mine."

Strode chuckled.

"I gave that rifle to my son, Butch, for his tenth birthday," said Radcliff. "You aren't gonna believe what he did with it."

"Wha'd he do?"

"He shot our neighbor's goat."

"I bet he caught hell for that."

"No. I couldn't very well punish my son for something I did when I was his age."

"Where did you shoot a goat?" said Strode, laughing.

"In Newville, where my parents and I lived until I was thirteen."

"You mean that old ghost town out west of Orland?" said Strode, handing Radcliff another beer.

"That's the place, only it wasn't a ghost town then. Just one more, then I gotta go. My wife will be on my ass if I don't show up with those groceries. By the way, did you or Mitch ever get married?"

"Mitch did. He's got a couple boys who look and act just like him."

"What about you?"

"I'm forty-one and still livin' by myself in the trailer my old man left me."

"Thanks for the beers," said Radcliff, chugging the last one. "It's been good talking to you."

"Hey, Willie. Do ya like fishin'?"

"I love to fish, but I've been so busy with the duck clubs these last few years, I haven't had time to go."

"I know where we can catch catfish as long as your leg. Are ya interested?"

"You bet!"

"How 'bout tomorrow night?"

"What time?"

"I'll pick you up about 8:00."

"I don't have a fishing license."

"A fishing license? What's that?"

WILLIE WAITED UNTIL JUST BEFORE STRODE arrived to tell Rebecca he was going fishing. "I might not be home until after daylight," he said.

Being passive by nature, and willing to overlook just about anything to avoid a confrontation, Rebecca shrugged her shoulders and went back to her knitting.

"What do they call this place where we're going?" said Radcliff, climbing into Strode's 1947 Chevy pickup and placing a cooler between them on the bench seat.

"My grandpa called it Sam's Slough."

"Who's Sam?" said Radcliff, handing Strode a beer.

"Hell if I know."

From Radcliff's home south of Willows, the two fishermen headed toward Colusa on Highway 99 for a half hour, traveled east for five miles, then headed south again on a washboard dirt road that ended at a barbed-wire Hampshire gate. The sign on the gate read NO HUNTING, FISHING, OR TRESPASSING. VIOLATORS WILL BE PROSECUTED.

"Don't pay attention to that sign," said Strode. "I been fishin' here since I was a kid and ain't been kicked out yet."

Radcliff opened the gate and dragged it across the road.

"Leave it open," said Strode, tossing his empty beer can out the window into a patch of star thistle. "We'll close it when we come out."

Strode's headlights lit up two forked tree branches stuck in the mud at the water's edge. He wheeled around, backed up to the makeshift rod stands, and cut the motor. Climbing from the truck, Strode reached into a wooden box behind the cab and pulled out a lantern.

"What do you want me to do?" said Radcliff.

"Just sit on the tailgate and drink your beer. I'll get everything ready."

Both rods and reels were already set up with sinkers and number-two treble hooks. While Radcliff downed his fourth beer, Strode reached inside the bait bucket and pulled out a baseball-sized gob of chicken entrails. Like a surgeon, he attached the gooey mess to Radcliff's hook and deftly secured it with yarn.

"Cast it out there by that snag," said Strode. "Be careful not to cast so hard you yank your bait off."

"Are you ready for another beer?" said Radcliff.

"Sure," said Strode, wiping his bloody hands on a filthy green rag and taking a long slug.

With their fishing rods leaning against the makeshift rod stands, Strode and Radcliff sat patiently on the tailgate, drinking beer and swapping hunting and fishing stories for the next four hours.

"The biggest buck I ever killed was a four-pointer up near a place called Surprise Valley," said Strode.

"How big was it?"

"The antlers measured forty-one inches, and it weighed three hundred and five pounds field dressed."

"I'd pay big money to bag a deer like that. How did you happen to kill it?"

"My Uncle Roy owns a little ranch just outside of Cedarville. It's about ten miles from where I killed the buck. Roy knows where all the big bucks hang out 'cause he's kind of a guide."

"What do you mean he's *kind of* a guide?"

"He ain't licensed or nothin' like that, but if somebody's got the money, Uncle Roy can guarantee him a trophy buck or a trophy bear."

"Tell me more."

"Two years ago, the night before the 1955 deer season opened, Uncle Roy drove me to this alfalfa field. He was shinin' his spotlight around when he lit up the monster buck he'd been tellin' me about. I stepped outta the truck, rested my .30-30 Winchester on the hood, and dropped that big boy right where he stood."

"Then what happened?"

"Uncle Roy handed me a flashlight and told me to run out and field dress it. He said he'd be back in an hour. When he got back, he parked out on the highway and left the motor runnin'."

"Why'd he do that?"

"That way he wouldn't leave any tire tracks in the soft sand next to the road."

"Weren't you worried about another car coming along?"

Strode laughed. "It was 2:00 in the mornin'. Everybody in Cedarville was asleep, and the only other outpost of any kind was Old Yella Dog, forty miles away, in Nevada."

"Hey, I think I just had a bite!" said Radcliff.

"Better grab your rod. If he hits it again, give it a hard yank."

Radcliff hopped down from the tailgate, picked up his rod, and hopped back up. "It sounds like your Uncle Roy's done this before," he said.

"Yup. The followin' Monday, me and Uncle Roy drove the head and hide to Quincy and left it with Rudd Hostetter to be mounted. I ain't got a pot to pee in, but that big buck is hangin' in my trailer alongside the biggest bear I ever killed."

"Did your Uncle Roy help you kill the bear too?"

"He sure did. Uncle Roy's Walker coonhounds are the best bear dogs in Modoc County. They ain't bad at treein' lions neither."

"Now that's something I've always wanted to do—kill a mountain lion."

"Just say the word, and I'll set you up with Uncle Roy."

"How much do you think he'd charge me?"

"If a client wants a kitty—that's what Uncle Roy calls a mountain lion—he charges five-fifty. He might give ya a deal if I was to refer you."

Strode turned to find Radcliff fast asleep and his fishing rod bouncing up and down on the bed of the truck. "Willie, wake up!" he shouted as the rod and reel flew off the tailgate, bounced on the ground, and were about to disappear into the gray-green water.

Radcliff awoke to find Strode standing waist-deep in the slough with the butt end of the rod clutched in his right hand and the rod tip bent in half.

"Get out here and take this rod, or I'll land this fish myself."

Radcliff took the rod from Strode and was surprised by the awesome strength of the fish on the other end of his line.

"Ride 'em, cowboy!" hollered Strode. "I told ya these fish were big."

Radcliff walked up and down the shoreline, fighting the fish, while Strode shouted instructions. "Let him run with it and don't try to horse him in, or he'll snap your line."

"What do you think it is?"

"It's a damn big channel cat. They always head straight for the bottom."

The sun was coming up as Strode and Radcliff drove north on Highway 99 into Maxwell. "Where we goin'?" said Radcliff.

"The feed store opens at 6:00, and I want to find out how much that fish of yours weighs."

The weighmaster at the feed store said Radcliff's channel catfish weighed just over forty-two pounds, which would have been a state record had Radcliff possessed a current fishing license and certified his catch. As it was, Willie would settle for having his fish mounted by a professional taxidermist.

Early Monday morning, while Rebecca and Butch were still in bed, Willie removed his prize from their garage freezer and drove 108 miles up the Feather River Canyon to the lumber town of Quincy. Down at the east end of Main Street was a defunct furniture store with a mounted grizzly bear in the window. "This has to be the place Eli told me about," said Radcliff. The bell above the door tinkled as he stepped inside.

"What can I do for ya?" said a heavyset, gray-haired man who was putting the finishing touches on an elk head.

"Are you Rudd Hostetter?"

"That's what my mother used to call me."

"I have a catfish I'd like you to mount."

"I don't do fish much anymore. Put it on top of that freezer over there and I'll be with you in a minute."

Radcliff flopped his fish on the top of the freezer and rolled back the tarp in which it was wrapped.

"That's a damn big catfish," said Hostetter. "Where'd ya catch it?"

"In a slough near Colusa. My friend Eli Strode took me there a couple nights ago."

"How's my buddy Gooseneck doin'?"

"He's doin' great, except he doesn't go by Gooseneck anymore."

"Why not?"

"Haven't you heard about the game warden who disappeared?"

"I heard," mumbled Hostetter. "One less pain-in-the-ass game warden comin' into my shop and hassling me."

"What was that?"

"Never mind. I was just thinkin' out loud. I hope Gooseneck didn't have anything to do with that game warden's disappearance. I know he likes them about as much as I do."

Radcliff scanned the taxidermy studio. His attention was drawn to a mountain lion perched on an artificial rock, poised to pounce. He imagined how great a mount like that would look in the trophy room he planned for Radcliff Mansion when his ship came in.

"I did that for Gooseneck's uncle Roy and one of Roy's clients," said Hostetter, leaving the elk head to dry. "What's your name?"

"Willie Radcliff. I manage all the Radcliff Farms duck clubs down in the valley."

"Some of my regular customers are members of that club. I mounted a pair of green-winged teal for one of them just the other day. How much do you charge to lease a blind for the season?"

"That depends on the blind and which unit it's in. I tell ya what," said Radcliff, handing Hostetter his business card. "Give me a call next week and we'll set up a day for you to come down and look around. If you like what you see, maybe we can work out an arrangement that benefits both of us. I plan on doing some serious big-game hunting this fall."

"I'll do that," said Hostetter. "Meanwhile, let's have a look at that fish."

TWELVE

Every year during the third week of July, Inspector Bill Matson scheduled two days of training at the Region 2 Department of Fish and Game headquarters, in Sacramento. Some of the training was required by the state so each officer could continue to carry a badge and a gun. Some of the training was designed to help each officer perform his/her duties more effectively. The rest was mostly time-consuming filler, learned one day and forgotten the next.

"We'll go ahead and take our break now," said the afternoon instructor. "Everyone please be back by 2:15."

Wardens Glance and Calloway walked out the back door of the Region 2 office into the sweltering summer heat.

"I have something I want to show you," said Glance. "It's parked in the back lot where they keep all the retired state vehicles."

"Do you think they'd miss us if we didn't come back after the break?" said Calloway.

Glance laughed. "What are you driving at?"

"If I hear one more word about visions and mission statements, my head is going to explode."

"There it is," said Glance, pointing to a scratched-up, dark-blue 1965 Ford Econoline van.

"Isn't that the radio tech's old van?" said Calloway. "Too bad they're gonna auction it off. That would make a great undercover rig."

"That's exactly what I was thinking," said Glance. "Let's drop in on the inspector before we leave today. Maybe we can talk him into letting us have it."

Later that afternoon, when the training session was finally over, Glance and Calloway caught Inspector Bill Matson walking out of his office. "Here comes trouble," said Matson. "If only I'd left five minutes earlier."

"Bill, may we have a few minutes of your time?" said Glance.

"Sure. Come on in and have a seat."

"Tad and I need an undercover rig to work spotlighters and duck poachers this winter. We think the radio tech's decommissioned van would work perfectly."

"What's wrong with the Bronco your captain's squad already has?"

"That rig has been around so long, every hunter and fisherman in three counties knows it belongs to Fish and Game," said Glance.

"Yeah," said Calloway. "I was working undercover in it just the other day, when a fisherman walked up and asked me what the limit was on steelhead."

"I'd like to help you fellas out, but I don't have any money in my budget to get that van back in working order. Last I looked, it had a hundred and forty thousand miles on it."

"I have a proposition for you," said Glance.

"Hank, the last time I accepted one of your propositions, you disappeared for almost a year and ended up solving a thirteen-year-old murder. I hope this isn't anything like that. My heart couldn't take it."

"This one's pretty simple, Bill. If you'll arrange to have Pat Sturgess's old van turned over to Tad and me, I'll guarantee it won't cost the department a penny."

"How are you gonna do that?" said Matson.

"Don't worry—it's all legal and aboveboard."

"That scares the hell out of me, Hank, but I'll run it by the business officer and see if I can have it turned over to you guys on a temporary basis. How soon do you need it?"

"Today is Friday. How 'bout Monday?"

"Damn, Hank! You know the state doesn't work that fast. Give me a week to talk to the business officer and another day or two to get that rattletrap started. It's been sitting out in the back lot all summer. I'm sure the battery's dead."

"Thanks so much, Bill. You won't regret it."

"I'd better not. The department has open warden's positions in Barstow and Brawley. I could easily arrange a couple transfers."

After meeting with Inspector Matson, Glance and Calloway hopped in Glance's patrol truck and drove north out of Sacramento toward Calloway's home in Willows.

"All right, go ahead and ask," said Glance, looking over at Calloway seated in the passenger seat.

"How are you gonna get that van running smoothly without it costing the department an arm and a leg?"

"I have an old baseball buddy named Don Hartline. Don went to work for Corrections about the same time I was hired by Fish and Game. He's now the head instructor in charge of the auto shop at the California Correctional Center in Susanville. Don and his wife, Barbara, spent the night with us last week. We got to talking, and I mentioned my idea of turning an old van into an undercover surveillance vehicle."

"What did your friend say?"

"He said to draw up a plan and tell them exactly what we want. His inmates enjoy a challenge and do great work. As long as it's a state vehicle, it won't cost us anything—except for the cost of the paint—to have it completely overhauled and painted."

"You told the inspector it wouldn't cost anything."

"I'll pay for the paint myself, Tadpole. My vision is—"

"Your *vision*? How long have you been thinking about this?"

"I started thinking about it the first afternoon of that training session we just attended. That's what kept me awake."

Calloway laughed.

"My vision is to have that van purring like a kitten by this fall," said Glance. "We paint three-quarters of it primer gray and leave the dented right-front fender just the way it is."

"I get it," said Calloway. "Make the van look like you started to paint it, then got distracted and ended up blowing your paycheck on beer and cigarettes."

"Exactly, Tadpole. And I'm just getting started."

"Hank, does your mind ever rest?"

"Anne asks me that three times a week."

"Where are we going to house this secret weapon of ours?"

"I'll find room for it in the old hay barn behind our house."

SIX WEEKS AFTER THE JULY TRAINING session and meeting with Inspector Matson, Glance telephoned Calloway and asked him to come to his farmhouse near Gridley. "When you get here, drive back to the barn," said Glance. "I'll be out there working on something."

When Calloway arrived at the Glance farmhouse, Henry was outside the barn loading what he described as essentials into his new project.

"How did you get it here?" said Calloway, seeing the refurbished undercover van for the first time.

"Don Hartline drove it down from Susanville last week. He and his wife were on their way to visit relatives in Riverside, so Barbara followed Don in their family car. Give it a good once-over and tell me what you think."

Calloway walked around the van, checking out the paint job. Three-fourths of the vehicle had been painted primer gray, leaving the dented right-front fender faded blue. "It looks like shit," he said. "Just the way we wanted it!"

"Look under the passenger seat. The mic is in that little box next to the console. Just lift the lid."

"Who did this?"

"Pat Sturgess. He reinstalled the original radio, and it works like a charm. Pat also hooked up the tape deck you see under the dash. While he was at it, I had him hide a sneak light beneath the front bumper and attach the toggle switch to the left side of the tape deck."

"When and where did he do this?"

"I talked him into doing everything ten days ago, while he was up in Susanville working at the state wildlife area. Don Hartline drove the van over from the prison after they had finished with it."

Calloway shook his head in disbelief. "What else is in here?"

"An ice box, a built-in closet, two reclinable seats in back, and two chests. The closet contains an assortment of old coats and well-worn army fatigue jackets. The chest on the left is full of props and disguises."

Calloway lifted the lid of the chest on the left. "Where in the world did you get all this?"

"Dale Bagley, another one of my old baseball buddies, works for a company in Los Angeles that provides props for movie and TV productions. He's what they call a prop master. I called and asked Dale if he knew where I could get my hands on some used cowboy hats, a few wigs, and maybe a fake beard or two. He sent me a cardboard box filled with this stuff. There must be a dozen wigs and five or six ratty old cowboy hats in there."

"That white cowboy hat looks like the one Gene Autrey used to wear," said Calloway.

"Maybe it is!"

"Hank, you never cease to amaze me. What's in the other chest?"

"The other chest contains a sawed-off shotgun, a couple batons, two sets of binoculars, two sets of regular cuffs, a package of flex cuffs, a stack of notepads, and a first-aid kit. All the back windows are tinted so we can see out but no one can see in."

ONE OF THE LESSONS HENRY GLANCE had learned during his first three years on the job was about walking into a crowded deer camp on opening weekend of deer season—things weren't always as they seemed and a significant amount of gamesmanship could be going on. Glance looked for clues to what he called a dirty camp: A normally raucous crowd suddenly becomes quiet. People stop what they're doing and train their eyes on the uniformed intruder. People drop out of sight or try to leave camp. And, most importantly, tricks are played with deer tags—indications of unlawfully taken deer.

"What do you think?" said Glance from the passenger seat, as he and Calloway set out on a Friday afternoon in late September to work the 1972 deer-season opener.

"She runs smooth as silk," said Calloway, excited about their first overnight detail in the undercover van. "I told Rose I wouldn't be home until tomorrow evening, so you point the way."

"Steer us north, toward Chico. We'll run up Highway 32 to Butte Meadows. From there, take Humboldt Road to Jonesville."

"What's in Jonesville?"

"Not much of anything, but it's the gateway to our next adventure, Tadpole."

"You know how I like adventures, Hank. Tell me about this one."

"Well, there's a deer camp east of Jonesville where this rowdy bunch out of Quincy always spends opening weekend. I learned about them last year when I was covering three patrol districts."

"What is it about this deer camp?"

"I think they've been getting the jump on deer season for the last couple years by going out spotlighting the night before it opens."

"What makes you think that?"

"Last year, at 8:15 on opening morning, everyone was fast asleep. Doesn't that seem a little odd to you?"

"It sure does. You'd think they'd all be out hunting. How many hunters were there?"

"I counted six rifles locked up in the cabs of three pickups. One of the pickups was still attached to a horse trailer. The other two were detached and parked behind two camp trailers. A man was sleeping in the bed of each of the detached pickups. Based on all the snoring that was going on, I figured the other four were sleeping in the trailers."

"How long do you think they'd been there?"

"I felt the hoods of all three pickups. The one attached to the horse trailer was ice cold. The other two were still warm to the touch. The temperature that morning was just above freezing. I was about to look around for any signs of deer being taken, when I received a radio call from dispatch."

"Don't tell me. They needed you to respond to something way over in Glenn County, seventy-five miles away."

"You guessed it. A hunter trespass altercation near Elk Creek."

"Did you go?"

"I had to—I was the only warden available in three warden's districts. Late that afternoon, I returned to the deer camp."

"You mean you drove all the way back up there on a hunch that something was hinky?"

"You know me. When I arrived, I found everyone sitting around drinking beer and telling stories. Four of the hunters looked like they were in their early forties. The two younger ones were probably nineteen or twenty. As I climbed out of my truck and walked into camp, someone shouted, 'The game warden's here. Hide all the deer.'"

"Was he being a smart-ass, or did they really have deer in camp?"

"Both. One of the younger guys was pretty mouthy, and they did have four deer hanging in camp. All of the deer were tagged and in game bags. The times of kill written on the tags were obviously bogus, but I figured rather than provoking an argument I couldn't win, I'd play dumb and file it away for the following year."

"What do you think happened?"

"I wasn't sure at the time, but it bothered me so much, I decided to drive back up late that Sunday afternoon."

"Did you find anything?"

"Everyone in camp had gone home. I looked everywhere and didn't find a thing. On my way out of the area, I stopped at a half-dozen other camps and asked if they'd had any luck."

"What did they say?"

"Everyone said pretty much the same thing: 'Where's all the deer?' A man from Corning said he had hunted all day Saturday and half of Sunday and didn't even see a doe."

"So what you're telling me is the people in your hinky deer camp slept in on opening morning and still managed to bag four bucks by that afternoon? Something was rotten in Denmark, huh, Hank?"

"Exactly. There's no doubt in my mind that they spotlighted those four bucks the night before deer season opened. I'd bet my next paycheck that they did it on the private ranch about six miles north of their camp."

Glance and Calloway had driven through Butte Meadows and were five miles from Jonesville when Glance said, "Before we go any farther, let's assume the roles of two wild and woolly young deer hunters out to pop a couple bucks on opening weekend of deer season."

"Sounds like fun," said Calloway, turning off at the next logging spur and cutting the engine.

"You get first pick," said Glance.

Calloway opened the disguise chest, reached for a brown, shoulder-length wig, and placed it on his head. He topped the wig with a gray cowboy hat. "What do ya think?" he said.

"It's you, Tadpole."

"What are you gonna wear, Hank?"

"I thought I'd wear this blond, surfer-dude wig. I wore it to gas up the van this morning before you arrived. No one even gave me a second look. It also reminds me of summer days at the beach in Oceanside."

"Aren't you gonna wear a hat?"

"I don't think so," said Glance, chuckling. "It might mess up my hair."

THIRTEEN

Two weeks after Rudd Hostetter and Willie Radcliff met in Hostetter's Quincy taxidermy studio, Hostetter spent the day riding around with Radcliff, looking at available duck blinds to lease. By the end of the day, Hostetter had signed a contract stipulating that he would mount Willie Radcliff's catfish and one big-game trophy in return for the exclusive use of blind number 12 at Radcliff Farms' Williams duck club for the 1957-58 waterfowl season.

During the ten years that followed, Roy Strode, Eli Strode's uncle, would guide Willie Radcliff in the taking of six big-game trophies, all of which would be professionally mounted by Rudd Hostetter. In return for his services, Hostetter would retain exclusive use of blind number 12.

On a cold morning in late November 1958, while Willie Radcliff slept in the cab of Roy Strode's pickup, Strode's hounds treed a mountain lion in a canyon north of Shasta Lake. "Willie, wake up," said Ed Cooley, the twenty-seven-year-old helper Strode paid to skin and pack his clients' trophies. "Bring your rifle and follow me."

Cooley and Radcliff passed through an abandoned apple orchard, skidded down a leaf-strewn ravine, and pushed their way through a half mile of tick-infested brush before finding Strode and his longtime dog handler, Leon Pancake, standing at the trunk of a three-hundred-year-old California black oak.

"It's a big Tom," shouted Strode, over the deafening bawl of baying hounds.

Radcliff walked back and forth beneath the massive oak until he came to the perfect spot from which to bag his trophy.

"Better take him before he comes down and kills one of my dogs," shouted Strode.

"He's not going anywhere," mumbled Radcliff, peering up through a tangle of gnarled tree limbs at a pair of piercing yellow eyes.

The frightened cat stared back at his pursuer and was about to attempt an escape when a sharp crack from Radcliff's .30-06 rifle echoed down the canyon.

"Nice shot," said Strode, as the hounds raced toward the lion's limp carcass and began to gnaw on it. "That's the biggest cat I've ever seen in this part of the country. I bet he weighs close to two hundred pounds."

Radcliff beamed. "My first kitty!" he said.

PRESTON EARL RADCLIFF DIED OF A massive heart attack on June 9, 1959. Molly Radcliff arranged for her husband to be buried in what was to become the Radcliff family plot, a hundred yards north of Radcliff Mansion. Molly became sole owner of Radcliff Farms, its properties, and all of its assets. In accordance with Preston's wishes, Molly promoted Bob Masterson to president of the company and Rebecca Radcliff to vice president. When Willie heard the news, he drove straight to Radcliff Mansion.

"Hello, dear," said Molly, dressed in her bathrobe. "I haven't seen you since the funeral."

"How could you make Bob Masterson president of the company and completely ignore your own son?"

"When I saw you drive up, I thought you were here to console me," said Molly, wiping tears from her eyes. "Can't you at least give me time to grieve your father's passing?"

"How do you think I feel, having to take orders from a man I've despised for the last twenty years, not to mention from my own wife?"

"Your father and I both felt that Bob was the best person to take over the company and keep it running smoothly. There are a lot of people to think about besides yourself, son. You may not want to hear this, but you're not qualified or responsible enough to handle a difficult job like president of Radcliff Farms."

"What do you expect me to do—go on back to my duck club and pretend everything's all right? Maybe Rebecca can give me my orders every morning before we send your grandson off to school."

While Willie continued his rant, Molly shuffled across the hardwood floor to the living-room couch. "I couldn't be more disappointed in your behavior," she said. "I must have talked your father out of firing you a dozen times. Do you think we didn't know about your running an illicit duck-selling business and using company cars to make your deliveries?"

Realizing he'd made a mistake confronting his mother in her present emotional state, Willie turned and walked out the door.

IN LATE SEPTEMBER 1960, ROY STRODE telephoned Willie Radcliff with a proposition. "Remember that mountain lion we killed north of Shasta Lake?"

"Of course I do. It's mounted, crated, and sitting in my warehouse right now."

"How would you like to kill a trophy black bear?"

"What do you consider a trophy?"

"The big cinnamon-colored boar I saw this mornin' should go well over four hundred pounds."

"What was he doing when you saw him?"

"He was gobbling up that crate full of two-day-old donuts I threw on the bait pile yesterday afternoon. I picked up the donuts, ten loaves of stale bread, and a garbage can full of rotten produce from a grocery store in Central Valley. The manager usually gives the stuff to one of the local pig farmers, but when I offered him ten bucks, he gave it to me."

"How much will this well-fed bear set me back?" said Radcliff, chuckling.

"Since my current client just backed out on me, I'll only charge you four hundred. Rudd owes you for this year's duck blind, so mounting this bear won't cost you anything."

"Make it three-fifty, and we have a deal. I didn't get that promotion I was counting on, so I'm a little short on cash right now."

The following Sunday, after returning from his successful bear hunt, Willie received an unexpected telephone call from his mother. "If it's not too much of an inconvenience, I'd like to see you right away," she said.

Willie arrived at the mansion just after 3:00 in the afternoon. Molly was sitting in her rocking chair, staring out the living-room window.

"What is it you wanted to talk to me about?"

"Get right to it, huh, son? No Hi, Mom, how ya feeling?"

"Sorry. I've been kinda busy."

"Busy doing what—bear hunting?"

"Who told you that?"

"Rebecca talks to me, even if you don't."

"Are you gonna tell me what's on your mind, or should I leave?"

"Please do your poor mother a favor and sit down."

Willie sat on the couch, across from his mother.

"Had your father outlived me, everything we owned would have been sold and the money placed in some kind of nonprofit, charitable organization."

"I knew he was disappointed with me, but I had no idea he hated me that much."

"Your father didn't hate you, Willie. He just believed that everything a person receives should be based on what he's earned. When Bob told Preston what you'd been up to, he had our attorney erase you from his will."

"What are *you* gonna do, Mom?"

"Preston would roll over in his grave if he knew what I'm about to tell you."

Willie leaned forward and stared into his mother's teary eyes.

"As much as I wanted to honor your father's wishes, I just couldn't do that to my son. I met with our attorney last Thursday and told him I wanted to leave my entire estate to you."

"What did he say to that?"

"What *could* he say? The company and the family fortune belong to me. I'm free to do with them whatever I please. As long as I'm alive, the company will be run in accordance with your father's wishes. When I pass on, it will all be yours—the company, the land, the money . . . everything. I'm counting on you to do the right thing and consider all those Radcliff Farms employees who depend upon us for their livelihoods."

"I will," said Willie, giving his mother a hug. "I will!"

Molly Radcliff's love for her son was strong but so was her fondness for her daughter-in-law. Unbeknownst to Willie, she had her attorney set aside ten million dollars in Rebecca Walsh Radcliff's name.

ON THE MORNING OF OCTOBER 11, 1961, Willie Radcliff told his wife, Rebecca, he was leaving for a two-day business meeting in Eureka. What he didn't tell her was the trunk of his Chevy Bel Air was loaded with his .30-06 rifle, a box of .30-06 cartridges, rain gear, binoculars, and a pair of hiking boots.

Radcliff arrived in Eureka at 4:00 p.m., ate dinner at a popular seafood restaurant, and checked into a motor inn at the north end of town. At 7:00 p.m., he telephoned Roy Strode, using a number Strode had given him. At 8:00 p.m., Radcliff went to bed and slept until midnight, when he was awakened by the sound of the phone ringing in his room.

"I'll be by to pick you up in a half hour," said Strode. "Dress warm and don't forget your rifle."

Roy Strode and Willie Radcliff headed north on Highway 101 and didn't encounter another car until they passed through the tiny coastal community of Orick.

"That asshole is right on our tail," said Radcliff, noticing the headlights in his right rearview mirror.

"That asshole is my brother, Mel," said Strode. "He and his son Jake live here in Orick. Jake is the butcher at Orick Store. Jake's brother, Eli, is with them."

"I'll be damned," said Radcliff. "It's been a while since I've seen Eli."

Radcliff's watch read 2:15 a.m. when Roy Strode's and Mel Strode's pickups passed through Berry Glenn and Roy Strode pulled to the right side of the highway. Mel Strode pulled in behind him. Hearing a thump in back, Radcliff turned in his seat to find Jake and Eli hopping into the bed of Roy Strode's pickup. Jake tapped on the cab, signaling his uncle to take off.

Roy Strode and his three passengers continued north on Highway 101 for another mile or so before turning left onto a winding paved road leading west. When they reached a large lagoon, Roy slowed his pickup to a stop and instructed Radcliff to retrieve his rifle and a spotlight from behind the seat.

"Are we gettin' close?" said Radcliff, handing Strode the end of the spotlight cord.

"Can't ya hear the waves?" said Strode, rolling his window down and plugging the spotlight cord into his cigarette lighter.

"Yeah!" said Radcliff. "I didn't realize we'd be this close to the ocean."

"That's where this herd likes to hang out. Sometimes they're right down on the beach. That seven-by-seven Mel and I saw yesterday could be anywhere, so be ready."

Strode steered his pickup off the pavement, onto a gravel path that veered north and paralleled the ocean. He stopped at intervals and lit up the immediate area. The hunting party had traveled a quarter mile off the pavement when Strode's spotlight settled on three majestic bull elk lying next to each other on a grassy knoll.

"The biggest one just stood up," said Strode, shining the spotlight in its eyes.

Radcliff quietly slipped out the passenger door and rested his left shoulder on the hood of Strode's pickup.

"That's the seven-by-seven," said Strode. "Take him!"

BOOM! came a blast from Radcliff's rifle. The mighty bull's legs buckled under his eleven-hundred-pound torso, and he flopped to the ground.

"Nice shot," said Jake Strode, jumping down from the pickup bed and running toward the fallen animal. Strapped to Jake's back was a mainframe and a backpack filled with butchering tools.

"Congratulations," said Eli Strode, right behind his older brother. "You guys better skedaddle. We'll take it from here."

Roy Strode wheeled his pickup around, flipped on his headlights, and stomped on the gas. Minutes later, he and his client were back on Highway 101, headed south.

Two hundred yards south of Berry Glenn, on the side of a hill, sat an abandoned shack partially covered by blackberry vines. Roy Strode slowed his pickup to a crawl and blinked his headlights as they rolled by. Headlights appeared from behind the shack, blinked back twice, and went off.

"Is that your brother?" said Radcliff.

"Yup. He'll sit up there in the dark for another hour then drive in and pick up the boys. Jake will have your trophy caped out and ready to go by the time Mel gets there."

"You guys have this down to a science, don't you?"

"Years of practice, Willie. I'll have you back at your motel in an hour. You can get a little shuteye before daylight."

MOLLY RADCLIFF PASSED AWAY ON APRIL 2, 1962. Rebecca Radcliff arranged a small service for her mother-in-law and made plans to have her buried next to her husband, Preston, in the Radcliff family plot. In Willie Radcliff's mind, any promises he'd made to his mother paled in comparison to the humiliation he'd felt being passed over as president of the company. To make matters worse, the man his parents had chosen to be president was the same man who'd beaten Willie half to death and left him lying in the mud under a pile of dead ducks. Within days of receiving his inheritance, Willie fired Bob Masterson and put the company and all its land holdings up for sale. The only properties he didn't put up for sale were Radcliff Mansion and 2,000 acres of adjacent riparian forest.

"What are you planning to do with all that money?" said Rebecca, dead set against the idea of selling Radcliff Farms and putting its employees out of work.

"I have big plans for a business of my own," said Willie, puffing on a big cigar.

"What kind of business?"

"I'm going to build a retirement resort."

"Where?"

"On our riverfront property downstream from Radcliff Mansion. I'm meeting with a Sacramento contractor tomorrow."

"What else is floating around in that demented mind of yours?"

"Soon we'll be moving to Radcliff Mansion."

"What makes you think I want to live in that old firetrap?"

"It won't be a firetrap when I get through with it. I've already found a contractor to do the renovation. After that, we hire an interior decorator to completely refurnish the place. If you play your cards right, I might let you help pick out the furniture."

FOURTEEN

Still entertained by the collection of disguises Glance had come up with, Calloway and Glance laughed all the way to Jonesville.

"About five miles up the road, we'll take a left and head north across a big meadow," said Glance. "Just inside the tree line, on the other side of the meadow, is the campsite I told you about."

"Do you think that bunch from Quincy will be there?" said Calloway.

"They have been the last two deer openers."

"Is all of this U.S. Forest Service land?"

"I think everything up here is national forest until we come to the private ranch and a locked gate."

"And that's where you think they're doing the spotlighting?"

"I'd bet on it. See that sign up ahead?"

"I do."

"Turn left there and head across the meadow. When we reach the stream crossing, stop."

Reaching the stream crossing, Glance rested his rifle stock on the passenger-side window frame and focused his spotting scope on a circular congregation of trucks and camp trailers three hundred yards away. "Welcome back, boys," he said, chuckling. "I see you still have that jacked-up, black Dodge pickup."

"How do you wanna work this?" said Calloway.

"Let's drive right past their camp. We'll act as if we're a couple of country boys on our way to find a campsite."

"Do you want them to get a good look at us?"

"That's the general idea," said Glance, reaching behind the passenger seat. "I might even pop in one of these tapes."

With the windows rolled down and Buck Owens and his Buckaroos belting out "I've Got a Tiger by the Tail," Calloway steered the van within thirty yards of the suspected deer poachers' camp.

"Interesting," said Glance, when the van had passed the camp and was out of earshot.

"What's interesting?"

"They brought that same horse trailer."

"What's so interesting about the horse trailer?"

"Just like last year, there's not a horse in sight."

A quarter mile farther down the road, the wardens pulled into a camp-site next to a gurgling little brook. "It's only 6:30, and it won't be dark for another two hours," said Calloway. "Now what do we do?"

"Now we wait," said Glance, removing his disguise.

"What if they don't go out hunting tonight?"

"Then I apologize for getting you involved in this boondoggle and offer to buy you dinner the next time we work together."

"I have to admit that most of your boondoggles have paid off. I'll reserve judgement on this one until it's over."

"That's awfully benevolent of you, Tadpole. If you look in the ice chest behind your seat, you'll find a couple of sandwiches and some drinks Anne prepared for us. Next to the chest, there's a shopping bag filled with corn chips, cookies, and a bag of peanuts in the shell."

"Hank, what did you do to deserve a dream wife like Anne? Tell me the truth: Did you find her in a bottle on some deserted island?"

Glance laughed. "I often ask myself that question, especially when we're working one of these all-night details and Anne's at home by herself in that drafty old farmhouse."

"No offense, Hank, but I think you're crazy."

By 10:00 that evening, Glance and Calloway were sitting quietly in the dark and had run out of subjects to talk about. Glance was behind the wheel shelling peanuts, and Calloway was in the passenger seat draining the last drop of coffee from his thermos. Glance was hanging ten on the biggest wave of his life when the telltale *knock-knock-knock-knock-knock* of a diesel engine stirred him awake.

"Tad, wake up!"

"What time is it?" said Calloway, rubbing his eyes.

"It's after midnight," whispered Glance, slipping out the driver's-side door and scampering from tree to tree until he reached the road. He arrived just in time to see the black Dodge pickup roll by with a man standing in back. The man in back was leaning over the cab, cradling a rifle.

"What did you see?" said Calloway, when Glance returned to the van.

"It was our boys from the deer camp. I think they're headed for the private property I told you about. They should be out most of the night, so let's put our uniforms on and work our way down to their camp."

Before leaving the van, Glance radioed the dispatcher and asked her to telephone Warden Jack Mayberry and ask him to come up on the air.

"Two-five-three, two-five-one," said Mayberry, ten minutes after receiving the dispatcher's call.

"Two-five-one, proceed with the plan."

"Ten-four. Two-five-one."

"Jack's gonna drive to Jonesville and wait for our call," said Glance. "It'll take him a couple hours to get up here from Chico."

With flashlights turned off and a portable radio pack in hand, Glance and Calloway followed the dirt road south to the suspects' deer camp. The camp was dark when the wardens arrived. Two of the three pickups were gone, not so much as a peep was heard coming from the two trailers, and the campfire was completely out. Being careful not to trip over any of the aluminum chairs spaced around the fire pit, Glance and Calloway tiptoed down a well-worn footpath leading to the horse trailer.

Glance couldn't help noticing that the horse trailer's doors were open and the ramp was down. He flashed his light inside and quickly turned it off. The trailer was empty. Lying beside it was a short stack of firewood with a folded canvas tarp on top.

The sleepy wardens dozed on and off against a couple of old-growth pine trees until 4:15 a.m., when the clank of a dropping tailgate announced the suspects' return.

"This big sonofabitch is probably gonna give me a hernia," came a booming voice from one of the arriving pickups.

Glance and Calloway watched two men carry a large buck through camp and out to the horse trailer. The barrel-chested man with the booming voice was later identified as forty-two-year-old Hugh Blocker. The smaller man, wearing a gray sweatshirt and Levis, was later identified as forty-three-year-old Rod Laurel. Winded, they swung the deer up on the ramp and dropped it with a thud.

"Rod, shine your flashlight over here while I fill out my tag," said Blocker.

"That's sure a nice buck," said Laurel, holding the light.

"It's the biggest damn buck I've ever killed."

"Are you gonna have it mounted?"

"Hell yes, I'm gonna have it mounted! Monday morning, I'm taking the head and cape to Rudd Hostetter's shop at the east end of town."

Two more hunters arrived at the back of the horse trailer as Blocker and Laurel were sliding Blocker's buck inside.

"Flop it down on the ramp and fill out your deer tag," said Rod Laurel to his son, later identified as twenty-year-old Webb Laurel.

"Hugh's four-pointer makes my forky look dinky," said Webb Laurel.

"That's all right, son. Yours will be a lot better eatin'."

"What's keeping Hardy and Scott?" said Blocker.

"Scott had to get rid of all that beer he's been drinkin'," said the fourth hunter, later identified as forty-two-year-old Arthur Turner. "It's a damn shame about that spike we had to leave out there to rot. Hardy was still checking it out with his binoculars when Scott went ahead and shot it."

"Hugh, what did you put down for location and time of kill?" said Webb Laurel.

"I wrote Butt Mountain for my location and 7:30 a.m. for time of kill. You'd be wise to make your time of kill a little later."

"How 'bout 8:15?"

"That'll work."

"Here comes Scott and Hardy with Scott's three-pointer," said Turner. "Oh, no! Scott just tripped over one of the lawn chairs and dropped the rear end of his deer in the fire pit."

When all three bucks had been tagged and placed inside the horse trailer, Hugh Blocker and Hardy Jessup picked up the tarp that was lying on the woodpile and used it to cover them.

"Scott," said Hardy Jessup, "you and Webb stack them logs on top of the tarp and pull up the ramp in case a game warden comes snoopin' around."

"What about the two spotlights?" said Blocker. "Maybe we should hide them too."

"Good idea," said Jessup. "Scott, grab them spotlights outta the two pickups and hide 'em under the tarp before you pile the wood on top."

"Why do I have to do everything?"

"Because I told ya to! You've already caused enough trouble tonight. Let's see if you can do somethin' right for a change. The rest of us are gonna hit the sack."

Glance and Calloway remained still for a half hour after everyone had gone to bed. Making sure no one was milling around, Glance walked down to the streambank and unzipped the canvas bag containing the battery-powered, portable radio. "Two-five-one, two-five-three, car-to-car."

"Two-five-one. Go ahead."

"Let's eleven-ninety-eight this morning at 7:30. We'll have plenty of light by then."

"Will you be at the camp you described to me on Thursday?"

"Affirmative."

"How'd everything go?"

"Everything went as planned."

"Good. Be advised, two-five-five is with me."

"Ten-four."

Chico warden Jack Mayberry and Orland warden Roy Harrelson drove into the deer camp at 7:30 a.m. Mayberry was driving his shiny new Dodge Power Wagon patrol truck. Glance and Calloway met them as they stepped from the warm pickup into the biting, early-morning air.

While the hunters slept, Glance and Calloway led Mayberry and Harrelson through camp to the horse trailer in back. Harrelson took photographs before and after Glance and Calloway uncovered the deer.

"Let's leave the deer where they lay and roust these guys out of their bunks," whispered Glance.

As each hunter was rousted from his warm sleeping bag, he and the immediate area around him were searched for weapons. Rodney Laurel, Hardy Jessup, and Art Turner still had unused deer tags in their possession. Scott Jessup was the only hunter who possessed a bear tag. Bear season opened on the same day in September as the general deer season.

"Warden Calloway and I were in camp when the six of you arrived with three illegally taken deer," said Glance to the assembled group. "By illegally taken, I mean they were killed during closed season, during closed hours, and with the use of artificial lights."

"I thought deer season opened today," said Blocker, his boot laces untied and his muscular, uncovered arms folded in front of his chest.

"Deer season didn't open until legal shoot time," said Calloway. "Legal shoot time was 6:30 a.m. Warden Glance and I watched you gentlemen hide three deer inside that horse trailer at 4:15."

"We also watched three of you falsify your deer tags," said Glance. "A few minutes after that, Hardy Jessup ordered his son, Scott, to remove two spotlights from the pickups and hide them under the tarp."

"I guess we're screwed," said Rodney Laurel, barefooted, with a blanket wrapped around his body.

"Shut up, Rod," said Hardy Jessup, spitting tobacco onto the ground and wiping the dribble from his chin with the back of his hand.

"We're not through yet," said Glance, "but before we continue, I'm going to advise you of your Miranda rights." Glance recited the Miranda warning from memory. When he'd finished and each of the hunters in camp had acknowledged that he understood, Glance continued: "Warden Calloway and I heard you men talking about a spike buck that Scott Jessup shot and left to rot last night."

"I never shot no spike buck!" barked Scott Jessup, standing in his stocking feet and wearing the clothes he'd slept in.

"It would be a crying shame to let that deer go to waste," said Glance. "If you or some of your companions were willing to show us where you left it, we won't have to charge you with waste of game along with everything else."

"I didn't shoot no spike buck, and I ain't gonna help you game wardens find anything!"

"If my son said he didn't shoot a spike buck, he didn't shoot a spike buck," said Hardy Jessup.

"Is it you who has the key to the posted property?" said Warden Mayberry.

"No," said Hardy Jessup. "That would be Hugh."

"Thanks a whole hell of a lot," said Blocker. "This'll be the last time I hunt with you or that drunken kid of yours. It was your idea to hunt at night in the first place."

"Do you have written permission to hunt on the Jamison Ranch?" said Mayberry.

"Not on me," said Blocker.

"Where is it?" said Mayberry.

"I must have left it at home."

Glance handed Blocker's identification to Mayberry.

"So if I go to your home on Bucks Lake Road in Quincy, you will be able to provide me with written permission from the landowner?"

"Not exactly," said Blocker.

"What does that mean?"

"One of my business associates loans the key to me every year, in return for letting him and his wife use our timeshare in Las Vegas."

Mayberry held out his hand. Blocker pulled the key from his pocket and handed it to him.

"So what's gonna happen to us?" said Rodney Laurel. "Are you gonna write us tickets, or are we gonna be arrested?"

"Since we're in Butte County, formal criminal complaints will be filed with the Butte County District Attorney's Office," said Glance. "In a few weeks, each of you will receive a notice to appear in court. All of the deer and your rifles will be seized into evidence."

"Will we get our rifles back?" said Hardy Jessup. "That lever-action .30-30 of mine has been in the family for over sixty years."

"That will be up to the court," said Glance. "You'll be given receipts before we leave."

Final photographs were taken of the three illegally taken deer and the seized and tagged rifles before wardens Mayberry and Harrelson transported them to Chico. The deer would be donated to charitable organizations in the Chico area, and the rifles would be stored in the Department of Fish and Game Region 2 evidence locker, in Sacramento.

Glance and Calloway slipped out of camp and followed a trail upstream to the undercover van. "I feel badly about that spike buck going to waste," said Glance, removing his uniform and changing back into civilian clothing. "What would you think about taking a ride out on that ranch to see if we can find it?"

"Do you have the key to the gate?" said Calloway.

"Yes. Jack gave it to me before he and Ron left."

"Then let's give it a try."

Glance and Calloway were following the black Dodge pickup's tire tracks down a dead-end logging spur on the Jamison Ranch when Glance spotted a brown, furry object on the hillside, forty yards away. "I think it's a bear," he said, focusing his binoculars.

"Are you sure?" said Calloway.

"I don't know what else it could be. It's definitely not a deer. I'll be right back."

Glance slid down an embankment and dropped into a shallow ravine overgrown with bracken ferns. Reaching a clearing on the other side, he discovered a blood trail that led up the hillside to the dead animal.

"What is it?" shouted Calloway from the van.

"It's a cub bear."

"Was it shot?"

"There's a bullet hole in the upper left ham," said Glance, rolling the bear over. "I don't see an exit wound."

"Is the body warm?"

"Barely."

"I'll bring the camera."

"Let's carry him back to the van," said Glance, after Calloway took photos of the bear and the blood trail. "It looks to me like this little guy was wounded and hid in the fern thicket until the hunters were gone. He was probably trying to make it up this hill when his heart gave out."

"It had to be that bunch from the deer camp," said Calloway.

"I agree. That black Dodge pickup is registered to Hardy Jessup. His son, Scott, was the only one in camp with a bear tag. Let's walk this stretch of road and see if we can find a shell casing."

Unable to find a shell casing, Glance and Calloway stopped at the stream and carried the bear to the water's edge. Glance used his knowledge from biology lab and a razor-sharp knife to probe for the bullet. It had passed through the upper portion of the cub's left hip, followed a slightly downward trajectory, and lodged itself inside the left lung. After photographing the slug in place, Glance removed it, placed it in an evidence envelope, and washed his hands in the stream.

Glance and Calloway spent another two hours searching for the abandoned spike buck, to no avail. They drove out to the gate, locked it behind them, and began their journey back to the valley. Donning their previous disguises, the wardens drove past the poachers' deer camp and waved as they went by.

"Say, weren't those the same longhaired hippies who drove past us yesterday evening?" said Hugh Blocker, from his lawn chair.

"Yup," said Rod Laurel. "I recognize that ugly, half-painted van."

"I wonder how they did," said Art Turner.

"They couldn't have done any worse than us," said Blocker.

MONDAY MORNING AFTER THE DEER-SEASON OPENER, Warden Glance picked up Scott Jessup's Winchester .30-30 rifle at the Region 2 evidence locker and drove across Sacramento to the California Department of Justice evidence laboratory. It took the technician less than an hour to confirm that the slug Glance had dug out of the small California black bear had been fired from Scott Jessup's rifle. Three days later, Glance delivered a ten-page arrest report to the Butte County District Attorney's Office. Formal criminal charges were brought against Scott Jessup, Hugh Blocker, Webb Laurel, Hardy Jessup, Rodney Laurel, and Arthur Turner.

Rodney Laurel, Hardy Jessup, and Arthur Turner eventually pled guilty to possession of deer during closed season and spotlighting. They were each fined $650 and placed on three-years' summary probation. Conditions of probation prohibited them from hunting or being in the field with anyone who was hunting. All their rifles, including Hardy Jessup's family heirloom, were ordered forfeited by the court.

Webb Laurel pled guilty to possession of deer during closed season, spotlighting, and falsifying a deer tag. He was fined $850 and placed on three-years' summary probation. His rifle was ordered forfeited by the court.

Hugh Blocker was represented by an attorney and originally pled not guilty. After three months of delays, postponements, and attempted plea bargains, he pled guilty to take and possession of deer during closed season and spotlighting. The charge of falsifying a deer tag was dismissed. Blocker was fined $1,150 and placed on three-years' summary probation. His rifle was ordered forfeited by the court.

Scott Jessup was represented by a public defender, pled not guilty, and requested a jury trial. The jury found Jessup guilty on all counts: possession of deer during closed season, take of bear during closed season, spotlighting, and falsifying a deer tag. Jessup was sentenced to serve six months in the Butte County Jail and ordered to pay a fine of $1,750. His rifle was ordered forfeited by the court.

FIFTEEN

R ADCLIFF FARMS AND ALL ITS LAND holdings sold to a consortium of San Joaquin Valley agribusinesses on January 2, 1963, for $89 million. Willie Radcliff sealed the deal with his Sacramento contractor the next day, setting in motion the first phase of a fifteen-year excavation and building project on 2,000 acres of riparian forest downstream from Radcliff Mansion. The first phase included vegetation removal and the leveling of 150 acres and ended with the building of 100 mobile-home sites, a swimming pool, a boat dock, and a restaurant.

Work on Radcliff Mansion began March 2, 1963. The renovation included ripping out two walls and turning Preston Radcliff's four-hundred-square-foot study into a six-hundred-square-foot trophy and card room. When the renovation, redecorating, and refurnishing were completed on September 2, 1963, Willie Radcliff, Rebecca Radcliff, and sixteen-year-old William Radcliff Junior—also known as Butch—moved in.

Willie Radcliff's long-awaited ship had come in. He wasted no time satisfying his manic obsession with killing everything that walked, crawled, or swam. During the first nine years after receiving his inheritance, Radcliff traveled to Alaska, Africa, Florida, Southeast Arizona, and Hawai'i, searching for big game and monster fish to line the walls of his new trophy room.

While on a marlin-fishing trip to the big island of Hawai'i in late June 1972, Radcliff met a wealthy San Francisco real-estate broker named Bill

Kellogg. The two men were sitting in a motel bar, comparing stories about the largest trout each of them had ever landed, when Kellogg told Radcliff about having caught a five-foot-long trout weighing over a hundred pounds. "It's called a taimen," he said.

"No wonder," said Radcliff. "You're talking about an alligator, not a fish."

"Have another highball," said Kellogg, laughing. "I said taimen, not caiman."

Soon after returning from his Hawaiian fishing trip, Radcliff sat down at the antique oak desk in his remodeled Victorian mansion, looked up at the moose staring down at him from the wall, and began to type on a sheet of Willie's Sacramento River Resort letterhead:

> Nicolas Cantor Enterprises
> 196 Ocean View Terrace
> Sausalito, California
>
> July 10, 1972
>
> Dear Mr. Cantor:
> I recently learned from a fisherman friend named Bill Kellogg that you arranged a fishing trip to Far Eastern Russia, inside the Soviet Union. Bill told me that on that trip he caught a five-foot-long trout that weighed over a hundred pounds. He called the fish a taimen. If Mr. Kellogg's story is true, I would spare no expense to arrange such a trip for myself.
> Sincerely,
> William L. Radcliff

Ten days after sending his letter, Radcliff received the following reply:

> Willie's Sacramento River Resort
> 160 River Road
> Chico, California
>
> July 14, 1972

> Dear Mr. Radcliff:
> Regarding your recent inquiry, I am not acquainted with anyone named Bill Kellogg, have no knowledge of the fish you described, and have no business dealings in the Soviet Union.
> N. Cantor

Radcliff was about to toss Cantor's letter in the wastebasket when his telephone rang. "Yeah," he said, thinking it was one of his employees down at the resort.

"Is this my friend Willie Radcliff?"

"Who's this?"

"It's Bill Kellogg, and judging from the tone of your voice, you've received a letter from Nic Cantor."

"I was just about to throw it in the trash."

"Nic sends a letter like that to everyone who asks about his business in the Soviet Union. Then he has his attorney do a little investigating to make sure the inquiry he received didn't come from a government agent of some kind. I just got off the phone with Nic and gave you a glowing recommendation. You're in, my friend, you're in! Nic will be calling you shortly."

Fifty-nine-year-old Nicolas Cantor had emigrated from the Soviet Union to the United States at the end of World War II, when his name was still Alexey Nikolaev. Being a shrewd businessman with the ability to speak fluent English, it didn't take Cantor long to poke his fingers into a number of lucrative investment opportunities, including shipping, real estate, banking, and outfitting.

Cantor had maintained and monetarily nurtured government and business contacts in Russia for decades. These connections enabled him to establish an outfitting business for wealthy Americans willing to pay whatever it took to kill the trophy big-game mammal or catch the trophy fish they'd always dreamed of. In the case of Willie Radcliff, it was a five-foot-long trout that weighed over a hundred pounds. On the afternoon of July 20, 1972, an hour after Radcliff had spoken with Bill Kellogg, Cantor dialed Radcliff's number.

"Hello."

"Mr. Radcliff, this is Nic Cantor. How are you on this gorgeous day?"

"It may be gorgeous where you are, but it's a hundred and four here in Chico."

"I can't do anything about the weather, but I can offer you the trip of a lifetime, where the air is cool, the scenery is spectacular, and the streams are teeming with monster trout. Be assured that my fee covers virtually everything: transportation, food, equipment, lodging, guide service, tips, taxidermy work if you so desire, and shipping of the finished product right to your door."

"It all sounds good to me," said Radcliff. "How soon can we set up a trip?"

"How does September first sound?"

"Perfect!"

"Wonderful! I'm going to turn you over to my assistant, who will answer any additional questions you have and get things rolling. It was great talking to you, Willie. May I call you Willie?"

"Sure. Everybody else does."

"I'll look forward to your spending the night at my home in Sausalito on August thirty-first, the day before you leave on your adventure. You may leave your car here and ride to the airport with Adrian early the next morning."

"Who's Adrian?"

"Adrian Petrov will be your guide and constant companion from the time you leave here September first until you return on September tenth."

NEIL DIAMOND WAS SINGING HIS LATEST hit, "Cracklin' Rosie," as Willie Radcliff drove across the Golden Gate Bridge in his gold, 1972 Cadillac Coupe de Ville. He'd never been to Sausalito and marveled at all the stately homes perched on the forested hillside above the bay. Following directions given to him by Nic Cantor's assistant, Radcliff located Ocean View Terrace and wound his way up the steep hill until he came to a red brick wall framing an electric gate. The address on the call box next to the gate read 196.

"Hello. Is anybody home?" said Radcliff, releasing the button.

"Who, may I ask, is calling?" came a female voice.

"Willie Radcliff."

The gate opened. Radcliff followed a terra-cotta-colored cement drive-way through a grove of trees to a quarter-acre parking lot and a four-car garage. The garage housed a black Mercedes, a red Corvette convertible, and a silver Aston Martin. The fourth door was closed and locked. A beige Mercedes, a blue Ford station wagon, a green Oldsmobile Cutlass, and a white Dodge van were parked in the spaces to the right of the garage.

"Welcome, Mr. Radcliff," came a voice from the nearby stairway. Radcliff turned to find a tall young man with light-brown hair walking in his direction. He was wearing sandals and a gray tank top with the words SAN FRANCISCO STATE BASKETBALL emblazoned across the front. "I'm Adrian Petrov," he said. "It's so good to meet you."

"Petrov?" said Radcliff. "Are you the guy who's supposed to be my guide for the trip?"

"I am."

"Kinda young, aren't you?"

"I'm twenty-six."

"What kind of qualifications do you have?"

"I grew up in Khabarovsk, Russia. I studied language and international relations at the university there, and I speak fluent English as well as Russian. I'm also a graduate student at UC Berkeley, and I teach courses at San Francisco State."

Petrov handed Radcliff his crisp new California State University, San Francisco, business card, then led him down a cement stairway to the back entrance of Nicolas Cantor's three-story home. Each of the three stories had its own wraparound-view terrace looking out on the bay. The master suite and Cantor's home office were on the top floor. Guest rooms were on the second floor. Common living quarters—complete with a living room, den, bar, home gym, gourmet kitchen, lap pool, spa, three baths, and a changing room—were housed on the bottom level.

When Radcliff was settled into one of the guest rooms, he walked downstairs to the main terrace where Nic Cantor, Adrian Petrov, and a well-tanned, middle-aged man smoking a nine-inch Gran Corona cigar were seated.

"Willie, it's so good to meet you in person," said Cantor, a fit-looking, middle-aged man dressed in casual slacks, a silk Hawaiian shirt, and sandals. "What can we get you to drink?"

"A cold beer would hit the spot," said Radcliff.

"Adrian, please get Mr. Radcliff whatever brand of beer he desires and make Dick another Scotch on the rocks."

"Coming right up," said Petrov.

"You've got a pretty nice place here," said Radcliff. "Where do you keep your yacht?"

"I keep my sailing boat at the harbor north of here, but I'm not sure you'd classify it as a yacht. Why don't we all relax here on the deck and discuss tomorrow's adventure? Willie Radcliff, I'd like you to meet Dick Bridger. Dick will be joining you and Adrian on your fishing trip to the wilds of Far Eastern Russia."

Bridger stood up from his chair and extended his right hand.

"You're dressed like you just stepped off the golf course," said Radcliff, noticing Bridger's expensive golf trousers, collared polo shirt, and white golf cap.

"I did," said Bridger. "Nic and I always play a round when I'm in the Bay Area on business. I drove up this morning in the Mercedes."

"Oh yeah?" said Radcliff. "What kind of business are you in?"

"Property management."

"Whose property do you manage?"

"My own. What do you do, Willie?"

"I own a resort up in Butte County, but mostly I hunt and fish."

"That must be nice. I enjoy hunting and fishing but seldom find the time. Every year, I let Nic talk me into one of his boondoggles."

"He's kidding, Willie," said Cantor. "You'll find that Dick is quite a jokester."

"Say, Dick," said Radcliff, "you wouldn't happen to have another one of those fancy cigars, would you? I smoked my last one on the way down here."

"I do," said Bridger, "but I'd have to run up to my room to get it."

"That's okay. I'll bum one off you during the trip."

Petrov rolled his eyes.

"Nic, was that your wife I saw in the kitchen?" said Radcliff.

"No. I'm not married. The woman you saw in the kitchen is Maria, my cook."

After spending the next fifteen minutes making small talk, Cantor steered the conversation to the business at hand.

"You three will fly on a commercial airline from San Francisco to Seoul.

The flight takes over twelve hours, so you'll have plenty of time to talk and get to know each other. You'll arrive at 6:00 p.m. San Francisco time, but it will be 10:00 a.m. the next day in South Korea."

"I ran into that on a few of my hunting trips," said Radcliff. "Kinda messes with your head."

"A young gentleman named Chang-ho will be waiting when you enter the terminal. He and Adrian have become pretty good friends. Chang-ho will help collect your bags and drive you to the cargo section of the airport. From there, you'll fly on a cargo plane to the Russian city of Khabarovsk."

"How long will that take?" said Radcliff.

"About four hours. Khabarovsk is a beautiful city on the Amur River. I was born and raised there. Unfortunately, you will not be able to spend any time sightseeing."

"Why is that?" said Radcliff. "I was hoping to take a few pictures."

"Adrian, have you explained to Mr. Radcliff that he will be inside the Soviet Union and must remain with you at all times?"

"I haven't had the opportunity."

"Then I'll fill him in. Dick has been on two hunting trips behind the Iron Curtain, so he already knows the drill."

"Now you're scaring me!" said Radcliff.

"Nothing to be afraid of, as long as you follow instructions. After you leave San Francisco, the only document you'll need is your passport. Adrian will carry all of the other necessary papers and answer any questions you might be asked. Adrian speaks Russian and is familiar with most of the government officials you'll encounter. I suggest you leave your camera out of sight until you reach base camp. Under no circumstances should you take photographs of power installations, dams, or government buildings of any kind. Have I been absolutely clear about that?"

"Yeah. I get the picture."

"A Russian gentleman named Oleg will be waiting as you exit the cargo plane in Khabarovsk. He will drive you to my sister, Sasha's, house, where you will spend the night. The three of you will leave early the next morning and drive north on the Amur River Highway to Komsomolsk."

"Why is he snickering?" said Radcliff, pointing at Petrov.

"Because the Amur River Highway is unlike any highway you've driven on in America."

"How long will it take?"

"All day. I own a cabin on the northern outskirts of Komsomolsk. You'll sleep there and leave early the next morning to meet the helicopter."

"You mean we get to ride in a helicopter?"

"There are no roads where you're going. The only way a person can get there is by helicopter. You'll experience wilderness that you didn't know still existed and fish some of the most spectacular streams in the world."

"I'm looking forward to that! How 'bout you, Dick?"

Bridger didn't answer.

"Adrian, please give Dick a nudge," said Cantor.

"Huh?" said Bridger.

"Dick," said Cantor, "Willie asked if you were looking forward to fishing all of those spectacular streams in Far Eastern Russia."

"Can't wait."

"Grischa and Dimitri will be waiting with lunch and two boats when you step off the helicopter," said Cantor. "After you've eaten your fill of barbequed salmon steaks, they'll transport the three of you upriver into a labyrinth of smaller side channels until you reach base camp. I hope you've brought some good, strong rods. These taimen trout are quite large and extremely powerful."

"I've caught seven-foot tarpons on the rods I brought," said Radcliff. "How 'bout you, Dick?"

"I believe I came prepared."

"What type of flies do they use to catch these monster trout?" said Radcliff.

"I've seen a few smaller ones caught on dry flies, but taimen are piscivorous," said Petrov.

"I'm glad you said something," said Radcliff, chugging his third beer. "Which way to the nearest head?"

"There's a washroom on the other side of the pool," said Cantor, pointing.

"It means they feed on other fish," persisted Petrov, as Radcliff walked away.

"What was that?" said Radcliff, turning around.

"Piscivorous means they feed on other fish. To answer your question, your best bet for catching taimen is a large streamer that resembles a school of bream."

Radcliff mumbled an inaudible response then turned back around and continued toward the restroom.

"What did he say?" said Bridger, laughing.

"I think he said thank you," said Cantor.

"Like hell, he did!"

"He's coming back," whispered Cantor, wiping the smile from his face. "Don't worry, Willie. Grischa and Dimitri will help you find the right lure. Boxes of everything you'll need are included in the package."

"I can't wait to get a line in the water," said Radcliff.

"Then I suggest the three of you hit the sheets early. Your flight to Seoul leaves at 6:00 a.m. You'll need to leave here by 4:00 to be at the airport in plenty of time to check in and take care of your baggage. Do either of you have any questions?"

"I have one," said Radcliff. "Suppose I catch one of those giant trout and decide to have it mounted. How are you gonna deliver it to my door, like you said on the phone?"

"I'm part owner of two shipping companies," said Cantor, "one head-quartered in Anchorage, Alaska, and one headquartered in Oakland. The one headquartered in Oakland makes regular trips between the Bay Area and Seattle. Your trophy will be delivered right to your door three months from the day you return from Far Eastern Russia. The taxidermist I use does outstanding work."

"Oh yeah? What's his name? I might know him."

"I'm sure you'll be quite satisfied. Here is my business card, if you have any questions about delivery of your mounted trophy. Now let's get ready for dinner. Maria has prepared something extra special for us."

"It sure smells good," said Radcliff. "What is it?"

"Barbequed moose backstrap. You'll find it much like eating a choice cut of beefsteak, without the fat."

"Sounds great!" said Radcliff. "Right now, I could eat a moose."

SIXTEEN

"WHO WOULD BE CALLING AT 2:15 on a Sunday morning?" said Anne, as Henry climbed out of bed and made his way down the dark hallway to the kitchen.

"Hello."

"Is this Warden Glance?"

"Yes."

"My name is Ira Benson. I apologize for calling at this hour, but I had to wait until the bar closed and everyone left."

"Henry, who is it?" said Anne, standing in the doorway wearing the new nightgown she'd purchased on sale the previous day.

"Everything's okay," Henry whispered. "Go back to bed."

Anne poured herself a glass of water and stood at the kitchen table while she drank it.

"No need for an apology, Mr. Benson. I'm happy to listen to whatever you have to say."

"Please call me Ira."

"Okay, Ira. Please call me Hank."

"Psst."

Henry returned his attention to Anne, who winked at him with her left eye and smiled playfully.

"Would you please excuse me for one minute, Ira?"

"Sure, go ahead."

Henry walked over to Anne, gave her a long kiss on the lips, and nudged her down the hall to the bedroom. "I'll be there in a few minutes," he whispered.

"I'm back, Ira. Sorry for the interruption."

"No problem," said Benson, chuckling. "I wish I still experienced those kinds of interruptions. In case you're wondering, I'm the bald, heavyset guy in the brown sports coat who sat in the back row of the courtroom every day during the murder trial."

"I remember you! You were always the first spectator to arrive and the last one to leave at the end of the day."

"You're a very observant young man. That's probably one of the reasons you're such a good investigator. By the way, I thought you did a remarkable job."

"I appreciate your saying that."

"Norm Bettis was a good friend of mine. It must have been about thirty-five years ago when he started dropping in the bar for what he called a horn of corn. It was always on a Tuesday afternoon, when the bar was empty except for Norm and me."

"What did you guys talk about?"

"He would tell me what was on his mind, and I'd listen. As I got to know him better, I began giving Norm tips on who was doin' the serious poaching around here. You wouldn't believe what I hear from behind this bar. That's why I'm calling."

"What bar are we talking about?"

"The Silver Dollar, at the north end of Gridley. Believe it or not, I was a deputy sheriff until I was twenty-seven. When my old man passed away and left me this business, I decided it was safer and more lucrative to pour drinks and listen to people's troubles than it was to carry a badge and a gun. I'm sixty-four now, so you do the math."

"Thirty-seven years," said Glance, stifling a yawn.

"What?"

"Thirty-seven years. That's how long you've been tending bar."

"Thanks for reminding me. Anyway, I think every good case Norm Bettis ever made around here was because of information I'd given him. I told him about Gastineau's duck-poaching gang long before he heard it from that gas-station attendant."

"No kidding?"

"No kidding. But everything I told him went in one ear and out the other. By the time Norm turned sixty, he was so burned out and bitter, all he wanted to do was sit in Pearl's Diner and drink coffee."

"Why was he so bitter?"

"Norm was a hard charger, like you, until he hit fifty and decided it was time to promote. He passed the captain's exam and interviewed for the Chico captain's position, which he wanted badly. They passed him over and gave the job to some desk jockey out of Sacramento who didn't know the difference between a mallard and a mud hen. Norm never forgave them for it."

Glance looked at the clock and saw that almost an hour had gone by. "Ira, it's been a pleasure."

"I appreciate your listening to me ramble on, Hank. I don't have anyone at home anymore, so sometimes I get carried away and forget what time it is. Here's what I wanted to tell you."

"Go right ahead," said Glance.

"Winter is coming on, and I've been hearing two of my regulars talking about running duck drags again this year. Based on bits and pieces of information I've gleaned from their conversations, it's a gang of four."

"You've piqued my interest. Please tell me more."

"The ringleader is a big, tough-looking guy named Randy Farnham. Randy's got an ugly scar on his left cheek that you can't miss. He claims his brother accidently shot him when they were kids fooling around with their old man's revolver."

"I think I've run into Farnham a time or two. Does he drive a Chevy crew-cab pickup with a homemade camper shell? If I remember correctly, the truck is grayish-green."

"That's him. Would you like his license number?"

"I think I have it, but, sure, go ahead."

"It's L603725. Before I forget, Randy works swing shift at the cannery in Oroville. His nights off are Sunday and Monday."

"That's valuable information, Ira. It could save us a lot of time."

"Farnham lives in his parents' old place out in East Biggs. I don't know the name of the road, but the property backs up to Johnson Ditch. You can't miss it. There's an old hay barn out behind the house, and every car and tractor his old man ever owned is sitting out in the weeds, right where it was when it quit running."

"Are his parents still living?"

"No. Bud Farnham kicked the bucket two years ago. He was a piece a work, just like his kid."

"Who else is involved?"

"Randy's partner is a loudmouthed punk named Chuck Carney. Carney works the same hours at the cannery. I think Randy got him the job. It's because of Carney's big mouth and lack of common sense that I know so much. He and Farnham were pretty well plastered this evening when Carney asked Farnham how much Charlie was gonna pay them for their ducks this year."

"Charlie?" said Glance.

"Yeah. Based on what I'm hearing, Charlie owns a restaurant in Chinatown and drives a powder-blue Mercedes."

"By Chinatown, are we talking about San Francisco?"

"I believe so. I heard Farnham say he has to drive 290 miles round trip every time he makes a delivery."

"What does Chuck Carney look like?"

"He must be twenty-nine or thirty, maybe five-nine, short dark hair. He has this grubby-looking Mitch Miller goatee."

"Do you know what he drives?"

"He drives an old Plymouth with the long tail fins. Randy calls it the Batmobile."

"You said there were four in the gang. What about the other two?"

"That would be the Leatherwood brothers, Mitch and Sonny. Mitch just turned twenty. I know because I checked his ID just the other night and asked him to leave. I think Sonny is about two years younger. Both cocky little squirts, just like their old man. Mitch Senior spent half his life in this bar until he got married and stopped running around with Gooseneck Strode."

"Please tell me about Gooseneck Strode. I keep hearing his name mentioned."

"Next to Dud Bogar, Gooseneck Strode was the most notorious duck poacher this part of the country has ever known."

"You said *was*. What happened to him?"

"It was about the time Norm Bettis disappeared and the big investigation began. Everyone was sure Gooseneck had something to do with Norm's disappearance. The investigators were relentless and wouldn't leave him alone. Late one night, Gooseneck staggered out of this bar and was about to climb into that rusted-out old pickup of his, when someone threw a blanket over his head and beat him half to death. He was in the hospital for several days with a broken nose, cracked ribs, and bruises all over his body. After that, Strode kinda dropped out of sight. Last I heard, he was still drivin' the tow truck at Bud's Garage, in Maxwell."

"What nights are Farnham and Carney most likely to be at the Silver Dollar?"

"Just about any night except Sunday. That's when we're closed. Once the weather changes and the ducks come down from up north, it's a crap shoot."

"Ira, you've given me a lot of good information. Rest assured, no one will ever find out where it came from. If you hear anything else, feel free to call me any time. Answering the phone at 2:00 in the morning is what I get paid for."

Hanging up the phone, Henry took a drink from the glass of water Anne had left for him, crept into the bedroom, and pulled back the covers.

"I thought you'd never get off that phone."

"I didn't know you were—"

"Who's more important—me or Ira Benson?"

"Who's Ira Benson?"

MONDAY MORNING, HENRY AWOKE TO THE sound of Anne running her hair dryer. "Sorry I woke you," she said.

"I was awake."

"Sure you were," said Anne, kissing her husband goodbye. "I'll see you this evening. We have a teachers' meeting before classes begin, so I have to go."

"Have a good day. I love you."

"I love you too."

Henry faded back to sleep and was awakened at 8:00 by the ringing of the phone in the kitchen. "I'm coming," he said, climbing out of bed and stumbling down the hallway in his bare feet. "Hello."

"Good morning, Sherlock. Did I wake you?"

"You know Monday and Tuesday are my days off."

"Since when does that make any difference? Hey, what do ya think about working duck opener in the undercover van this Saturday?"

"Normally, I'd like that idea, but we may have to wait until November before any birds come down from up north. The only ducks I've seen lately have been a couple resident mallards on the pond at the end of our road."

"You're probably right, Hank. I haven't seen many birds on the west side of the valley either."

"I'm actually glad you called, Tadpole."

"Oh yeah? What do ya have in mind?"

"I had an informant telephone me yesterday morning at 2:15."

"Musta been important to call at that hour. What did this informant have to say?"

"Way too much to talk about over the phone. If you're out and about this afternoon, why don't you come by?"

"Sounds good. How 'bout 3:00?"

"Perfect. I'll see you then." Glance hung up and dialed the phone.

"Sheriff's office. Records."

"Hi, Lois. This is Hank Glance."

"Hank Glance! How does it feel to be a celebrity?"

"Fame is fleeting, Lois. Besides, I couldn't have done it without you."

"You should go into politics."

Henry laughed. "I don't think I have the stomach for it."

"Why haven't you come by to see me?"

"The captain made me take a month off to burn all the overtime I built up during the murder investigation and the trial that followed. I've been trying to catch up ever since."

"A likely story. What can I do for you, Hank?"

"I'm working on another investigation."

"Uh-oh! Who's the unlucky person this time?"

"It's too early to say. Could I talk you into running a registration check on California plate L603725? If this guy has a criminal history, would you please put a copy of his rap sheet in my box?"

"How soon do you need it?"

"Sometime today, if possible."

Glance was finishing his breakfast when the phone rang.

"Are you ready?"

"Go ahead, Lois."

"Your license number comes back to a 1967 Chevrolet crew-cab pickup. The registered owner is Randal John Farnham, 100 Johnson Ditch Road, East Biggs. I put a copy of his criminal history in your box."

"What does it look like?"

"A couple local DUIs. That's about it."

"Thanks so much, Lois."

"Any time, Hank. Stay out of trouble."

"I'll try, but I can't promise anything."

WHEN TAD CALLOWAY DROVE UP GLANCE'S driveway at 3:15, Glance was dressed in shorts, a pair of low-top Converse All Stars, and a gray T-shirt with the Chico State Wildcat logo splashed across the front. The undercover van was parked outside, its side door open.

"Why don't you park your work truck in the barn, next to mine?" said Glance.

"Do I detect another adventure, Hank?"

"That's a good possibility, Tadpole."

Calloway walked out of the barn, closed and locked the barn doors, and climbed into the undercover van through the side door.

"You know the drill," said Glance. "There's a clean T-shirt hanging in the closet. I washed everything after the Jonesville deer-camp caper."

"You'd make somebody a good wife," said Calloway, opening the door to the van's built-in closet. He hung his Sam Browne duty belt on a hook, placed his uniform shirt on a hanger, and donned a green-and-black-striped T-shirt. "Why do I suddenly feel like Dennis the Menace?"

Glance laughed. "Let's take a drive out to East Biggs. One of the duck poachers my informant told me about lives on property that backs up to Johnson Ditch. I'd like to check it out."

"Will this duck poacher be there?"

"He works swing shift at the cannery in Oroville, so I'm hoping he'll be on his way to work."

"What's this guy's name?"

"Randy Farnham. According to my informant, he and three other outlaws have been duck dragging for the last couple years and selling their ducks to a man in San Francisco named Charlie."

"He shouldn't be difficult to find," said Calloway. "There can't be more than a thousand Charlies in San Francisco!"

Traveling north on Highway 99 toward East Biggs, Glance turned right onto a county road, drove two miles, and took another right into a mature peach orchard. When they'd followed the gravel pathway to the last row of trees, Glance stopped and turned off the engine. "Grab a pair of binoculars and follow me," he said.

Calloway followed Glance through the orchard for a hundred yards before Henry hunched down, turned to his right, and crept up to a four-foot-high barbed-wire fence. Forty yards beyond the fence was a man-made watercourse overgrown with tules, known to the locals as Johnson Ditch.

"That's where Farnham lives," said Glance, pointing across the ditch to a rundown farmhouse and a dilapidated hay barn. "I'm gonna sneak over there and take a peek inside that barn."

"How are you gonna get across that ditch without sinking up to your ass in mud?"

"Watch me."

Glance straddled the fence and stepped over. "Whistle if you see anyone coming," he said, before sprinting toward the ditch and clearing it by four feet.

While Calloway kept an eye out, Glance quietly circled the barn. He found a few boards missing on the west side, allowing him to peek in. The first items of interest were a water faucet, a large tub, and a circular contraption with an electric motor attached. "That has to be some kind of duck-plucking setup," Glance mumbled. "And those fifty-five-gallon drums must serve as receptacles for the feathers, guts, and other duck parts."

Ten feet from the fifty-five-gallon drums was a workbench covered by a canvas tarp. Eight stainless-steel ice chests sat on top. Convinced that Farnham was running a commercial duck-selling operation, Glance continued walking around the outside of the barn to the back, where he found a tractor and four more fifty-five-gallon drums—three of them containing bits and pieces of dried duck down. He had begun searching the

three-foot-high weeds for bare spots where feathers might have been buried, when Calloway whistled.

Glance dove for cover as a Chevy crew-cab pickup raced up the gravel
driveway, wheeled around to the back of the house, and skidded to a stop.
Leaving the motor running, a man Glance recognized as Randy Farnham
ran up the back steps and went inside.

It was well-known to anyone who worked with Henry Glance that the
young game warden possessed a photographic memory and a keen eye
for detail. On this occasion, the warden's attention was drawn to a faded,
sixteen-inch yellow-and-red bumper sticker with black lettering attached
to the rear of Farnham's truck. While Farnham was still inside the house,
Glance sprinted to the back of the barn for a closer look. With binoculars focused on the sticker, he read EAT AT HONG KONG CHARLIE'S,
CHINATOWN, SAN FRANCISCO.

Suddenly, the back door of Farnham's house flew open and Farnham
reappeared with an envelope in his hand. He ran to his pickup, backed up,
and sped away.

"Wha'd ya see?" said Calloway, as he and Glance trekked back through
the orchard to the undercover van.

"I saw enough to confirm that Farnham is running a commercial duck-
selling operation. He has a plucking machine in the barn and a tractor out
back that he uses to bury the entrails and feathers."

"What's our next move, Hank?"

"As long as this warm weather continues, they're not going to be killing
any ducks. I'd like to take a ride to San Francisco and check out a restaurant called Hong Kong Charlie's."

"Where'd that come from?"

"From the bumper sticker on the back of Farnham's truck."

"Are you kidding?"

"No, Tadpole. That bumper sticker could be the key to our next adventure. How would you like to have lunch in Chinatown tomorrow?"

"What will the captain say about that?"

"Nothing, because we're not going to tell him. We'll take my bug and go
on our own time. Do you have a suit or a sports coat?"

"I have a blue suit that I wore to my warden's oral three years ago. It's
been hanging in my closet ever since."

"I have a gray sports coat. What would you think about posing as a couple junior business executives enjoying a lunch out after a stressful morning at the office? We'll order a couple beers with our chicken chow mein, get to know the waiter, and find out as much as we can about Hong Kong Charlie."

EARLY AFTERNOON, OCTOBER 17, 1972, FOUND wardens Glance and Calloway driving across the San Francisco-Oakland Bay Bridge in Glance's Volkswagen Beetle. Taking the Embarcadero toward Fisherman's Wharf, they turned left on Washington Street and took another left on Stockton before entering a world of neon signs, brightly colored lanterns, and Chinese markets.

"I see it!" said Calloway, pointing to a vertical neon sign that dwarfed all the others. "It's down at the end of this block."

As luck would have it, a red MG pulled away from Hong Kong Charlie's as Glance and Calloway approached. "That space has barely enough room for a bicycle, let alone a car," said Calloway.

"Piece of cake," said Glance, backing in. "Be sure to bring your brief-case. We want to look like businessmen."

"I will," said Calloway, concentrating on the car parked in front of them. "You missed the fender of that Cadillac by less than an inch."

"What's in the briefcase?" said Glance.

"My son's coloring books. He carries the case around, pretending to be Perry Mason."

Glance and Calloway stepped from the bright afternoon sunlight into a dimly lit room filled with immaculate ivory-black tables—each one set with fine linen and polished silverware.

"Two for lunch?" said an alluring Asian hostess dressed in a white satin miniskirt. Glance nodded. "Right this way. Have you gentlemen been here before?"

"No," said Calloway. "My associate and I are here in San Francisco on business."

"Oh? What kind of business?"

"Finance," said Glance.

"Your waitress will be with you in a minute," said the hostess, placing two menus on the table.

"Hank, did you mean what you said about buying my lunch? I was going to let you off the hook, but all I could find in Rose's purse this morning were a ten and two ones."

"Don't worry. I've got it," said Glance, turning to the second page of his menu and pointing to the item he was looking for: roast duck.

"Do you think they're selling wild ducks this time of year?" said Calloway, lowering his voice so the party at the next table wouldn't hear.

"No. I suspect they're selling domestic white Pekins this time of year. Any time this restaurant is selling wild ducks, they're probably doing it on the sly, to special customers they know and trust."

"Hello. My name is Suyin," said the twenty-something waitress with long, black hair. She was dressed in dark slacks and a white linen blouse that accentuated her hourglass figure. "May I offer you gentlemen something to drink before you order?"

"Do you have draft beer?" said Glance.

"Yes, we do."

"Please bring me a glass."

"I'll have one, also," said Calloway. "This is a nice place. How long have you worked here?"

"Two years. I only work the lunch shift. I'm a student at San Francisco State."

"Really?" said Glance. "What are you majoring in?"

"Biology. I plan to attend medical school when I graduate."

"Tell me, Suyin," said Glance, "is the owner of this fine establishment really named Hong Kong Charlie?"

"That's the owner over there talking to the bartender," said the waitress, motioning with her hand.

Glance and Calloway directed their attention to a handsome, forty-plus-year-old Asian man wearing beige slacks and a collared golf shirt.

"His name is Zhao Peng, but he goes by Charlie to make it easier for his customers and his American business partners. Mr. Zhao has investments all over the Bay Area."

"How long has he owned this restaurant?" said Calloway.

"I will answer your questions when I return with your drinks. It will give you time to decide what you'd like for lunch."

Glance stood from his chair and followed Suyin past a row of tables, through two swinging doors, and into a bustling, brightly lit kitchen.

"You not come in here!" shouted one of the cooks.

"I'm looking for the restroom," said Glance, making a mental note of two walk-in coolers, a spacious private office, and a back entrance leading to the alleyway.

"I'll show you," said Suyin, leading Glance back into the seating area and pointing to a hallway at the other end of the bar.

During the time it took Glance and Calloway to eat their lunch and drink two draft beers, they learned a wealth of information from their new friend, Suyin: Charlie Zhao was divorced; he and Suyin had dated once; he golfed every Wednesday morning; Hong Kong Charlie's business hours were Tuesday through Sunday, from 11:00 a.m. to 9:00 p.m.; business was especially good during November, December, January, and February; and Charlie Zhao had owned the restaurant for at least three years.

"Where we goin' now?" said Calloway, as he and Glance walked out of the restaurant.

"Hop in and I'll show you."

Glance made a sharp right immediately south of Hong Kong Charlie's front entrance. Following the east-west alleyway, he turned right at the first north-south alleyway intersection and stopped at the rear entrance to Hong Kong Charlie's. "Did you bring anything to write with?" he said.

"Where's your pen?" said Calloway.

"I must have left it on the table after writing down what our waitress told us."

"I'm not sure I have anything," said Calloway, rummaging through his briefcase. "Will this work?"

"I guess it'll have to," said Glance, looking at the green crayon in his partner's hand.

Using Glance's notepad, Calloway wrote down the license number of a powder-blue, 1971 Mercedes-Benz 350SL parked in the reserved space between the back door of the restaurant and two dumpsters.

"That's the car my informant told me about," said Glance. "I think we've confirmed that Zhao is our duck buyer."

"Are we heading home now?" said Calloway. "We don't want to get caught in rush-hour traffic."

"Let's take one more spin around the block."

"What for?"

"You'll see," said Glance, steering his VW Beetle around the block and back to Hong Kong Charlie's front entrance. Again, he turned right into the east-west alleyway, but this time he turned left at the first north-south alleyway.

"*Now* where are we goin'?" said Calloway.

"See that row of dumpsters near the end of the block?"

"Yeah."

"Keep watching."

Glance passed the row of dumpsters, then backed in behind them. "Perfect!" he said.

"What's perfect?" said Calloway.

"Next time, we'll be driving the undercover van, which will allow us to see over the top of these dumpsters, through our tinted back window, to Charlie Zhao's back door."

SEVENTEEN

"**T**HAT BARBEQUED MOOSE WE HAD FOR dinner last night was sure tasty," said Radcliff.

"Yes, it was," said Petrov, sitting in the first-class passenger seat next to him. "One of Mr. Cantor's longtime clients was so thrilled about killing a trophy bull moose in Kamchatka last fall, he sent him the backstrap packed in dry ice."

"I bet that's not all he sent him," said Radcliff. "That moose must have cost plenty."

"I make it a point not to discuss money with clients. Mr. Cantor handles all the financial matters. Have you ever heard the phrase 'Money is no object'?"

"I have, but even us rich folks don't wanna be bamboozled. Ain't that right, Dick?" Dick Bridger was sleeping soundly in the seat across the aisle.

"When your business is based entirely on word of mouth, no one gets bamboozled," said Petrov. "Most of Mr. Cantor's clients come back year after year. Where else can they arrange a world-class hunting or fishing trip behind the Iron Curtain?"

"Since you mentioned it, how is it that Cantor is able to do that when other outfitters can't?"

"Mr. Cantor lived half of his life in Far Eastern Russia before coming to America. He maintains what he calls dual citizenship in America and the Soviet Union. Nic still has business associates in the Primorsky Krai, Khabarovsk Krai, Komsomolsk, Magadan, and Kamchatka. There's an agency in the Soviet Union that authorizes hunting and fishing trips for wealthy foreigners; Nic has established a mutually beneficial working relationship with the heads of that agency."

"You scratch my back, and I'll scratch yours. Is that it?"

"Let's just say money talks, even behind the Iron Curtain."

"Don't you mean money talks, *especially* behind the Iron Curtain?"

Petrov didn't take the bait. Ten silent minutes had gone by when Radcliff reached over with his fist and lightly punched him on the right shoulder. "If I asked your boss to arrange a hunt for me in Far Eastern Russia, would he do it?"

"He might—under the right circumstances."

"You mean for the right price, don't you?"

Petrov leaned toward Radcliff and whispered, "If Nic Cantor likes you and thinks you're worthy of his trust, he can arrange for you to kill any wild animal that walks, flies, or swims in the Soviet Union."

"Can you be more specific?" Radcliff whispered back.

"Moose, bear, deer, sheep, elk, wolf . . . even lynx."

"Lynx? I've never killed a lynx. Aren't they like a bobcat, only bigger?"

"Yes. The ones in Russia are much bigger."

"You don't say! I wouldn't mind adding one of those to my kitty collection."

"Your kitty collection?" said Petrov.

"Yeah. I've killed big cats all over the world. They're on display, full figure, in my private trophy museum. I killed two lions and a leopard in Africa. It cost me a bundle to have 'em mounted and shipped home, but it was worth it."

"What other big cats have you killed?"

"I killed a jaguar in Southeast Arizona and a two-hundred-pound mountain lion in Northern California."

"Sounds like you're quite the hunter, Willie. We'll talk more about Nic's outfitting business on the flight from Seoul to Khabarovsk. Right now, I'd like to get some sleep."

Having drunk two cups of coffee at the San Francisco Airport and three more after the jet had taken off, Radcliff kept right on talking. "There's something about putting the crosshairs on a big cat that really gets my juices flowing. Ya know what I mean?"

Petrov didn't respond. He had finally drifted off and remained asleep until the plane began its descent into Seoul.

A smiling young Korean gentleman wearing camo pants, work boots, and a gray jacket was waiting as Petrov, Bridger, and Radcliff entered the terminal.

"Hello, Chang-ho," said Petrov. "This is Mr. Bridger and Mr. Radcliff."

"It is a pleasure to meet you both," said Chang-ho, extending his right hand.

Bridger shook Chang-ho's hand and said hello.

"Which way to the head?" said Radcliff, walking on by.

Chang-ho helped the fishing party gather their baggage and drove them to the other side of the airport, where a World War II-era cargo plane was ready for takeoff. "Our seats are in the rear of the plane," shouted Petrov, over the roar of the engines. "Be careful not to trip over those crates."

When everyone was seated, Chang-ho jumped to the ground and signaled the pilot to take off. Five hours later, the plane landed in Khabarovsk, where another Korean gentleman slid open the hatch door and allowed the early-evening light to pour in.

"Oleg is parked over by that warehouse," said Petrov. "As soon as they hand us our baggage, we'll load up and get out of here."

Fifty-two-year-old Oleg Kozlov waited patiently behind the wheel of an army-green, four-wheel-drive Russian carryall.

"What about that guy over there?" said Radcliff, pointing to a uniformed official with a rifle slung over his shoulder.

"Don't point!" whispered Petrov. "He won't bother us as long as we act naturally and go about our business."

As Petrov, Bridger, and Radcliff lugged their gear to the van, the man in uniform waved to Petrov and shouted something in Russian. Petrov laughed and shouted back.

"What did he say?" said Radcliff.

"He said to bring him back a bottle of vodka at the end of our fishing trip. I told him I would."

"How'd he know we were going fishing?"

"He probably saw your fishing-rod case."

"Do they still have those terrible work camps in the Soviet Union?"

"You mean the gulags?"

"Yeah, the gulags."

"They officially did away with them ten or twelve years ago, but I'd watch my step if I were you."

"Why do you say that?"

"Word is, there's still a few of them around."

"Is he serious, or is that supposed to be funny?" said Radcliff, looking over at Bridger.

Bridger shrugged his shoulders and kept walking toward the carryall.

"This is Oleg Kozlov, our driver," said Petrov. "He understands most of what we say, as long as we speak slowly and enounce our words. Oleg is going to take us to a house here in Khabarovsk where we'll spend the night. The house belongs to Mr. Cantor, but his sister, Sasha, lives there and accommodates Nic's clients. Willie, since you haven't been here before, why don't you ride up front and take in the sights."

Kozlov drove the van to a two-story house overlooking the Amur River. He parked on a cement driveway next to a sparse garden of scattered green cabbage. The rest of the front yard was bare.

After a dinner of beef stroganoff and cabbage rolls, with marlenka honey cake for dessert, Petrov and Bridger went up to bed. Radcliff and Kozlov stayed up drinking vodka and fraternizing with Sasha, who spoke passable English. At 9:00, Kozlov went up to bed, leaving Sasha, who was still quite shapely at age forty-nine, to fend for herself.

Petrov awoke at 3:30 a.m. to the sound of Kozlov and Sasha carrying on a lively conversation downstairs. He knocked on Radcliff's and Bridger's bedroom doors on his way to the bathroom. When Petrov came out of the bathroom, Bridger was on his way in. Radcliff was still snoring, so Petrov knocked again. "Willie, it's time to get up."

"I'm up," grumbled Radcliff. "I'll be down in a couple minutes. Where the hell did I leave my boots?"

Petrov found Kozlov sitting at the kitchen table, a cigarette in one hand and a cup of coffee in the other. Sasha, dressed in a bathrobe and slippers, was busy removing a pan of sharlotka from the oven. "Where is that pig who drank all my vodka and chased me around the living room last night?" she said, in Russian. "I finally had to slap him."

Kozlov laughed.

"Mr. Radcliff will be down in a minute," said Petrov, in Russian. "It's important that we show him respect, even if he is an ill-mannered pig."

Sasha and Kozlov burst into laughter.

"What's everybody laughing about?" said Radcliff, finding his boots at the bottom of the stairway.

"Oleg just told a funny joke," said Petrov.

"Oh yeah? I'd like to hear it."

"It loses its humor in translation. We'd better hurry up and eat so we can get going. It's a long way to Komsomolsk."

Kozlov took his seat behind the wheel, Radcliff rode shotgun, and Petrov and Bridger sat in back. The fishing party headed southeast for the first hour before turning north on an unpaved road that Petrov jokingly called the Amur Highway. They had traveled ten miles along the north-west base of a low-lying mountain range—passing through a forest of oak, spruce, and scattered junipers—when an enormous animal flashed in front of the headlights.

"What was that?" shouted Radcliff, suddenly wide awake.

"Probably a deer," said Petrov, awakened by Radcliff's outburst. "We see them quite often on this road."

"Deer don't have long tails," said Radcliff. "And the animal I saw was much bigger than any deer I've ever seen."

"What color was it?" said Petrov.

"I only saw it for a split second, but what I saw was light brown on top and white on its underside."

"Did it have stripes?"

"It was a blur, so I couldn't tell."

"Did you see it, Oleg?" said Petrov.

"Tiger," said Kozlov. "I live here all my life and only see three."

"Where did you see them?" said Radcliff.

"Two times at night in these mountains. Once during the day while camping in the Primorsky Krai."

"Do you think we'll see any tigers where we're going to be fishing?" said Radcliff.

"We have a better chance of seeing a flying saucer," said Petrov. "But you never know."

"Boy, would I like to add one of those to my kitty collection! I'd pay any amount of money to make that happen."

Known as Siberian tigers until 1984, Amur tigers were on the brink of extinction in the 1940s. They were granted full protection by the Soviet government in 1947. At the time of the fishing party's sighting, numbers of this tiger subspecies (*Panthera tigris altaica*) were estimated to be between 130 and 150 animals—most of them living in Russian geographic areas known as the Primorsky and Khabarovsk krais.

"Look, the sun is coming up," said Petrov, hoping to distract Radcliff and wipe the crazy idea of killing a fully protected Siberian tiger from his mind.

As the fishing party continued deeper into the Khabarovsk Krai, Kozlov began rambling in Russian about a Siberian tigress and her cub that had been killed by an old school chum of his.

Petrov leaned forward and rested his arms on the back of Radcliff's seat so he could hear the driver's story.

"My friend Igor Popov and I were in a Khabarovsk bar last week, buying each other drinks," said Kozlov. "I asked what Igor had been doing since leaving school. He said he works in Nakhodka, loading and unloading ships, and had come back to Khabarovsk to visit his mother. I asked what he did in his spare time. He said during the winter months, he and his cousin, Yegor, are trappers. I remember Yegor from school. He was a big, husky brute, boorish and ill-mannered."

"Like Willie?" said Petrov, in Russian.

"Yes," said Kozlov, laughing out loud. "Very much so."

"Did I hear my name mentioned?" said Radcliff, opening his eyes.

"No," said Petrov. "Oleg, please continue."

"Igor said he and Yegor had inherited a tract of land from their grandfather, who'd been a high-ranking member of the Soviet Union's Communist Party. According to Igor, the land has a shack and a barn on it. Igor and Yegor hunt and trap from the shack during the winter months and make enough money selling hides to buy vodka and essentials at the Lazo store."

"I wish I could understand what he's saying," said Radcliff.

"Go back to sleep," said Petrov. "I'll tell you the whole story tonight when we get to Komsomolsk."

"We were into our second bottle of vodka when Igor pulled a photo-graph out of his handbag," said Kozlov. "It showed him standing over a large tiger and what looked like a half-grown cub. Igor held an AK-47 rifle in his hand."

"Are you saying that Igor killed a mother Siberian tiger and her cub?" said Petrov.

"Yes."

"Igor must trust you to show you a photograph like that. Tigers are protected in the Soviet Union."

"I think Igor would have told me where all of his money was buried if I had asked him. He was pretty drunk. According to Igor, he and Yegor were wading through the snow, checking their trap line, when they came upon a trail of large cat tracks."

"Too large to be anything but tiger tracks?" said Petrov.

"Yes, way too large. Igor said they ran back to their cabin and returned with three large steel-jawed leghold traps, each one connected to a length of chain. They set the traps in a half circle, anchored them to a tree, and covered them with snow."

"This is unbelievable!" said Petrov.

"I thought so too," said Kozlov. "They hung a chunk of deer meat directly over the traps. Igor said this setup was similar to the ones they used to trap lynx. They had apparently killed a deer the day before to use as lynx bait."

"So, they poached a deer, as well as the two tigers?"

"Yes," said Kozlov. "Early the next morning, Igor and Yegor walked through the snow to where they'd set the traps. Igor said the forest was unusually quiet, causing him to believe a tiger might be nearby. They crept up to the tree where the traps were buried and saw the adult tiger lying in the snow, panting heavily. Her front paw was caught in one of the traps and the anchor chain was tangled around both of her front legs."

"Where was the cub?"

"Igor said the cub was lying in the snow next to its mother. When it saw Igor and Yegor approaching, it folded its ears back and snarled. That's when Igor raised his rifle, fired twice, and killed them both."

"Did Igor tell you what he and his cousin did with the tigers they'd killed?" said Petrov, disgusted by what he'd heard.

"According to Igor, they used their sled to haul the tigers back to their shack. Then they loaded the carcasses into the back of Yegor's truck and covered them with firewood. That afternoon, they drove all the way to Pogranichny, near the Chinese border. When it was good and dark, they slipped across the border into China and met with a Chinese businessman from Mudanjiang."

"How'd they happen to meet with the Chinese businessman?" said Petrov.

"I asked that," said Kozlov. "Igor said it was common knowledge among Russian trappers that they could make good money selling tigers and tiger parts to certain Chinese businessmen. Apparently, this Chinese business-man wanted the hide, the bones, the heart . . . everything. I asked Igor how much he was paid for the tigers. That's when he got up from the table, staggered over to the window, and pointed to his new four-wheel-drive vehicle. 'Enough to buy that,' he said."

EIGHTEEN

A MONTH HAD PASSED SINCE WARDENS GLANCE and Calloway had visited Hong Kong Charlie's San Francisco restaurant. Three weeks of Indian summer in October and early November had given way to one Pineapple Express after another. Prompted by strong winds and heavy rains out of the south, tens of thousands of migrating ducks and geese poured into the Sacramento Valley from the north. The national wildlife refuges and state wildlife areas were full to the brim with waterfowl. When the sun went down, great numbers of these ravenous birds ventured out from their sanctuaries to feed in the surrounding rice fields.

At 2:15 on Sunday morning, November 19, 1972, the kitchen phone rang at the Glance farmhouse. "I'm sure it's for you," said Anne, pulling the pillow over her head.

Henry felt his way down the dark hallway, bouncing off the walls and fumbling for the light switch that was never where it should be. "Hello."

"Hank, this is Ira Benson. You said to call when I heard something."

"Absolutely! Just give me a second to orient myself and turn on the light. Okay, Ira. I'm ready."

"Farnham and Carney left the bar about two hours ago. All they talked about this evening was how many ducks there are in the valley. Carney said he knows of a field about five miles northwest of Gray Lodge Wildlife Area where the birds have been feeding the last two nights."

"Did they happen to say when they were going to meet?"

"Tonight at 7:00, at Randy's place."

"Did they mention Charlie?"

"Randy did say he'd gotten a call from Charlie, asking when they were gonna bring him some ducks."

"Ira, thanks so much for the call. If you think of anything else, please feel free to call me any time."

"I will, Hank. I hope it helped."

GLANCE WAITED UNTIL 8:00 A.M. TO telephone his friend Mark Wilcox, a veteran California Fish and Game warden who'd worked the San Francisco patrol district for twenty-five years.

"How ya doin', Hank?" said Wilcox. "The last time I saw you, you had just graduated from POST training at the Riverside Sheriff's Academy and we were serving warrants together in Oakland."

"I learned a lot that week, Mark. You're one of the best instructors I've ever had, and everything you taught me has made me a better game warden and a better law-enforcement officer."

"I appreciate your saying that, Hank. What can I do for you?"

"I called to tell you about a restaurant in San Francisco's Chinatown that is buying and selling wild ducks."

"What's the name of the restaurant?"

"Hong Kong Charlie's. The owner is a forty-one-year-old Asian man named Zhao Peng. To avoid any confusion, Zhao is his last name and he goes by Charlie Zhao. Please don't ask me to explain that. Zhao drives a powder-blue, 1971 Mercedes 350SL, California plate 406RYL. We believe a buy will take place tomorrow."

"Any idea what time?" said Wilcox.

"I'll contact you as soon as I know. The restaurant will be closed. A pair of Butte County outlaws named Randy Farnham and Chuck Carney will most likely enter through the alleyway and meet Zhao at the back door. My partner, Tad Calloway, and I will be staked out down the alley from Hong Kong Charlie's and radio you when it's time for the takedown."

"Sounds good," said Wilcox. "Meanwhile, I'll see what I can find out about Zhao. If he's buying and selling wild ducks, that's probably not all he's into."

Hanging up the phone, Glance called Tad Calloway. "They're meeting at Farnham's tonight at 7:00."

"Does that mean they're planning to pull a drag?"

"Yes. According to my informant, Carney knows of a field where the ducks have been feeding in large concentrations for the last two nights. It's about five miles northwest of Gray Lodge. I bet it's that section of rice that butts up against Howard Slough. The ducks were swarming in and out of there yesterday evening when I drove by in the van."

"So what's the plan, Hank?"

"If we try to follow these guys around, we're liable to spook 'em and nix the whole operation. I'm thinking we let them do their thing and wait for them to come back to Farnham's barn."

GLANCE AND CALLOWAY RETURNED TO THE same East Biggs peach orchard they'd used to check out Randy Farnham's place back in October. At that time it was a sunny afternoon. This time it was pitch dark, so before leaving the paved county road and entering the gravel path that led through the orchard, Glance cut the undercover van's headlights and flipped a switch beneath the dashboard. With the aid of the tiny sneak light mounted under the van's front bumper, the wardens slowly drove to the second-to-last row of trees and stopped. "We'd better go the rest of the way on foot," said Glance, stepping from the van and quietly pushing his door closed.

Dressed in full camos and each carrying a turned-off flashlight, Glance and Calloway trekked through the orchard for a hundred yards before hunching down, turning to the right, and creeping up to the same four-foot-high barbed-wire fence Glance had negotiated in October. "Let's watch from here until they leave," whispered Glance.

With the aid of Farnham's overhead barnyard light, Glance and Calloway watched Randy Farnham, Chuck Carney, and two men believed to be the Leatherwood brothers climb into Farnham's Chevy crew-cab pickup and drive away at 7:30 p.m. When the suspected outlaws were out of sight, Glance and Calloway used a splintered two-by-six to cross Johnson Ditch. Safely on the other side, they made their way to Farnham's barn.

"What do we do now?" said Calloway.

Glance motioned for Calloway to follow and led him to a patch of three-foot-high weeds on the west side of the building where Glance had previously discovered the missing boards. "It's going to be a long night," he said. "We might as well make ourselves comfortable."

It was 3:45 the next morning when Glance and Calloway were awakened by the sounds of slamming doors and people talking. The lights came on in Farnham's barn, after which the man Glance recognized as Randy Farnham began barking orders: "You guys start bringin' the ducks in while I fill the tub and get the plucker goin'. The knives are on the work bench. Mitch, you and Nic start guttin' 'em as soon as we get the wings and feathers off. Throw the guts, heads, and legs in those barrels. I'll bury 'em when me and Chuck get back from San Francisco."

"Do you want us to stack the finished ones in the coolers?" said Mitch Leatherwood.

"Yeah. Gut fifteen or twenty at a time, rinse 'em off with the hose, and stack 'em in the coolers. Don't leave the hose runnin' while you're guttin' the birds. Last time we had a muddy mess in here."

Glance and Calloway were sickened by the carnage. Load after load of dead ducks had been hauled in by the Leatherwood brothers and unceremoniously dumped on the barn floor. Most of them were pintails, with a few mallards and wigeons mixed in. It took every ounce of self-control the wardens could muster not to crash the party and arrest everyone on the spot.

When the picking and cleaning were finished at 6:15 a.m., Farnham and his crew carried four large ice chests to Farnham's pickup, lowered the tailgate, and slid them inside. Farnham closed and locked the camper shell. "You boys go home and get some sleep," he said. "As soon as I make a pot of coffee, me and Chuck are gonna head for San Francisco."

Glance and Calloway watched from the weeds at the north side of the barn as Farnham and Carney walked inside the house and the Leatherwood brothers drove out from under the barnyard light in a green, early-model Chevy pickup. "Fifty-six or fifty-seven?" whispered Glance, watching them drive away.

"Fifty-six," said Calloway. "My older brother had one just like it, only his was fire-engine red."

"Are you ready?"

"You lead the way."

Glance and Calloway slipped back across the ditch, hustled their way to the undercover van, and made a beeline for Glance's farmhouse near

Gridley. "Keep the motor running," he said. "I'll be right back." Glance ran up the steps into the kitchen and telephoned Warden Mark Wilcox.

"What's the latest?" said Wilcox.

"The delivery should take place sometime between 11:00 this morning and 2:00 this afternoon. I'll radio you when the ducks have been taken inside the restaurant."

"Thanks, Hank. We'll stay out of the area until I receive your radio call."

Glance and Calloway headed for San Francisco's Chinatown at 7:45 and arrived at 10:30. At 10:50, they were in position. As Glance had predicted, the undercover van's tinted rear window was just high enough for the wardens to see over the top of the dumpsters and enjoy a clear view of Hong Kong Charlie's rear entrance.

The wardens took turns standing and watching until 12:15 p.m., when a Ford sedan turned right at the alleyway intersection, parked behind Hong Kong Charlie's, and a heavyset Asian man climbed out and went inside.

"That's not Zhao," said Glance. "He may be the manager. I remember seeing him the day we were in the restaurant for lunch."

Twenty minutes after the suspected manager arrived and went inside, a powder-blue Mercedes rolled into Zhao's reserved-parking space. "That's definitely Zhao," said Calloway, training his binoculars on a thin Asian man dressed in golfing attire. Zhao pulled the screen door open and walked inside.

"The stage is set," said Glance. "All we need now is for Farnham and Carney to show up with the ducks."

"All we *don't* need now is the San Francisco Police Department," said Calloway. "There's a patrol car headed up the alley in our direction."

The San Francisco PD unit stopped at the rear of the undercover van and a uniformed officer climbed out. With his right hand resting on his holstered duty weapon, the officer cautiously approached the van's driver's-side window and peeked inside. He found Glance sitting in the driver's seat with his identification in one hand and his badge in the other. Glance slowly rolled down the window and whispered, "My partner and I are conducting a stakeout. We expect the perps to arrive any minute."

"Fish cops?" the officer whispered back.

"Yes. It would help us greatly if you would act as if there's no one in this vehicle and drive away."

"No problem," said the officer. "Let us know if we can help."

"Thanks so much," said Glance. "We will."

The SFPD officer hadn't been gone five minutes, when Randy Farnham's pickup turned right at the alleyway intersection and parked in front of Hong Kong Charlie's rear entrance. Farnham and Carney climbed from the truck, tapped on the screen door, and were invited inside. Seconds later, Farnham and Carney, followed by the restaurant manager and Zhao, walked out to Farnham's pickup.

Farnham unlocked the camper shell, dropped the tailgate, and reached for the first ice chest; he and Carney carried it inside the restaurant. Zhao and the restaurant manager pulled a second chest out onto the tailgate and carried it inside. Farnham and Carney were carrying the third chest into the restaurant when Zhao and the restaurant manager reached inside the bed of the pickup for the fourth; they had just lifted it from the tailgate when Farnham came out of the restaurant, shook his head, and motioned for them to stop and put it back. Farnham then locked the camper shell with the fourth chest still inside and followed Zhao and his manager back into the restaurant.

Glance and Calloway waited patiently for Farnham and Carney to leave. "They must have another delivery to make," said Glance. "Otherwise, Farnham would have let Zhao take the fourth chest."

"What do you think is taking them so long?"

"Zhao is probably counting the ducks before paying Farnham."

"Here they come."

Farnham and Carney emerged from the restaurant carrying three ice chests. Judging from the ease with which they carried them, the ice chests were empty. After stowing the chests in back, Farnham and Carney hopped in the pickup and drove north down the alley. Glance and Calloway followed from a distance, with Calloway driving and Glance reaching for the radio mic. "Three-two-one, two-five-three," he said.

"Three-two-one. Go ahead," said Wilcox.

"Three large chests were delivered to the location we discussed earlier. We're following the delivery boys. You guys take over from here. Please let me know when you've made contact."

"Ten-four. ETA five."

Farnham turned right onto an alleyway that led to Stockton Street, followed Stockton north to Jackson Street, drove west on Jackson to Taylor, and proceeded north on Taylor all the way to Beach Street. He turned east on Beach, north again on Mason, and took a sharp left into a one-way alley leading to the rear entrance of Bomba's Fish House, located a few blocks from Fisherman's Wharf.

NINETEEN

B Y THE TIME THE FISHING PARTY arrived at Nicolas Cantor's log cabin on a grass-covered hillside north of Komsomolsk, Willie Radcliff needed help climbing out of the carryall.

"Sorry about your back," said Petrov.

"Nothing a good stiff drink won't cure," said Radcliff.

"Our housekeeper keeps the bar well stocked. It's on the right as you come in the door."

"Adrian, are we supposed to carry our own bags inside, or does Oleg do that for us?" said Dick Bridger.

"Oleg will bring everything in after he makes a fire."

"I see that the shed in back is stacked to the ceiling with firewood," said Bridger.

"Winter comes early here in Far Eastern Russia," said Petrov. "Having a good supply of firewood can be a matter of life and death."

"Yeah, but I'd rather live out here than in one of those ten-story concrete buildings we passed driving through Komsomolsk," said Bridger.

"I grew up in Soviet public housing," said Petrov, opening the cabin door and inviting everyone inside. "Our apartment was on the ninth floor."

"Hey, Bridger," said Radcliff, moving his bulky frame out of the doorway so Kozlov could get by, "speaking of apartment buildings, I heard you talking to Cantor about some run-down dump you bought in East L.A."

"I own seven apartment buildings," said Bridger, beating a path to the bar. "I buy them cheap, make a few improvements, raise everybody's rent, and rake in a handsome profit. It's the American way, Radcliff. Stick with me and you might learn something. What can I fix you to drink?"

"Scotch on the rocks."

"A man after my own heart. Here's to a successful week of fishing."

"Down the hatch," said Radcliff. "Where does a man in your income bracket live?"

"I own a house in Corona del Mar, where I spend most of my time. I also own houses in Palm Springs and Poipu, Kaua'i. What about you? I'm interested in that resort I heard you talking about."

"I live in a Victorian mansion I inherited from my mother. I had it completely renovated before we moved in."

"Where *is* this mansion of yours?"

"It's on the east bank of the Sacramento River, nine miles west of Chico."

"I've heard of Chico. The daughter of one of my business associates goes to college there and loves it."

"I hear that from a lot of people. I'm building a world-class retirement resort down the road from the mansion. It's a work in progress, but I already have a hundred-space mobile-home park, a swimming pool, a restaurant, and a boat dock."

"Interesting. Have you had any problems?"

"I've had to deal with a few bumps in the road."

"There you go again," said Petrov, "complaining about the bumps in the road."

"My first problem was zoning," said Radcliff. "Every acre my father owned was zoned agriculture. He operated a multimillion-dollar agricultural empire for almost forty years."

"And you weren't interested in taking over the family business?"

"Not in the slightest! When I was a kid, my old man made me knock almonds, pick apricots, dig irrigation ditches, and endlessly sweep out those giant packing sheds you see along the highway. He said it would toughen me up and make me appreciate the value of hard work."

"Did it?"

"Hell no. I hated hard work and still do. All I ever wanted to do was hunt and fish."

"So, what did you end up doing about the zoning problem?"

"I was told if I wanted to build a resort on my 2,000 acres, I'd have to get a zoning variance. It just so happened that Dell Kickbusch, my county supervisor at the time, was planning on running for the state legislature. I offered to contribute to his campaign if he would pull a few strings and arrange to have my zoning designation changed. He was hesitant at first, but when I sweetened the pot, he changed his mind."

"That usually works for me too," said Bridger, holding a half-full bottle of Scotch whiskey in his hand. "Here, give me your glass."

"Throw in a couple more ice cubes while you're at it," said Radcliff. "I have a hundred occupied spaces in the mobile-home park, and the restaurant is packed almost every night since I opened it up to the general public. You should see the crowd on Fish Taco Fridays. The college kids drive clear over from Chico."

"Sounds like you've got a winner."

"That's not all. The next stage of my development is the golf course. We start pushing over trees and leveling the land in 1974."

"Attaboy! We know what we want and won't stop at anything to get it. Right, Willie?"

"Right, Dick," shouted Radcliff, tromping down the hallway to the bathroom. "And woe to anyone who gets in our way!"

"Is there anything special you gentlemen would like for dinner?" said Petrov.

"Anything but cabbage rolls," said Radcliff, throwing open the bathroom door. "Dick, you asked if I'd had any other problems. I did have one."

"Lay it on me, buddy."

"This past summer, I was arrested."

"That *is* a problem," said Bridger, laughing. "How did an upstanding pillar of the community like Willie Radcliff get arrested?"

Petrov rolled his eyes.

"We were having a Fourth of July celebration on the deck behind the restaurant. It was after 10:00, and the band was really cookin'. They were so loud, one of my tenants called the sheriff and complained. Can you believe that? Most of those old geezers go to bed before the sun goes down so they can get up at five and take Fido out for his morning constitutional. If I ever find out who complained, I'll drown his ass in the river."

"And it'll serve him right," said Bridger, laughing so hard he rolled off the couch onto a brown-bear rug. "You still haven't told me how you got arrested."

"Oh," said Radcliff, wrapping his right arm around Petrov's neck to keep from stumbling over Bridger. "I got into a scuffle with one of the sheriff's deputies and knocked his tooth out."

"I can see how that might be a problem."

"They charged me with battery on a peace officer, but my attorney convinced the DA it was an accident."

"Off course it was!" said Bridger. "Your fist just happened to hit the deputy in the mouth. What was the final outcome?"

"They reduced the charge to disturbing the peace, and I had to pay for the deputy's dental work. Hey, what does a man have to do to get a little service around here?"

"Coming right up," said Bridger. "Hand me your glass."

IT TOOK EVERY OUNCE OF STRENGTH Petrov and Kozlov had to drag Radcliff and Bridger out of bed and into the van the next morning. "When do we eat?" said Radcliff, awakened by the sound of swishing propeller blades.

"You two will have to wait until we reach our destination," said Petrov. "Oleg and I ate breakfast an hour ago."

"Wha'd ya have," said Radcliff, "some of that salty porridge slop we ate yesterday morning at your boss's sister's house? What was her problem, anyway? All I wanted was a little kiss."

The morning sun had climbed over the mountains to the east, illuminating rolling green hills in one direction and an endless landscape of grasslands and flooded river basins in the other. The higher the helicopter rose, the more spectacular the scenery became. Soon, grasslands, wetlands, and the occasional lake gave way to forests of oak, spruce, ash, birch, elm, pine, and maple. The pilot followed a course up the main river, which was replete with oxbows and side channels, before setting his craft down on a sandbar. Two twelve-foot, rugged-hull inflatables, each equipped with a forty-horse outboard motor, rested on the shore.

Busy preparing a lunch of barbequed salmon steaks were Grischa Alexeyev and Dimitri Garin, twenty-three-year-old bilingual graduate students from Komsomolsk. Alexeyev was tall and slender, with shoulder-length dark hair. Gregarious and outspoken, he was a big fan of Lennon—not Vladimir (spelled differently)—but John. Alexeyev made no secret of his affinity for Western ways.

Garin was of average height and weight, with short brown hair. The soft-spoken son of a former high-ranking Soviet army officer, he was skeptical of Soviet propaganda but kept his doubts to himself.

While the others helped prepare lunch, Radcliff grabbed a rod and reel from one of the inflatable rafts and cast a gold, number-2 Mepps spinner into the slow-moving current. "Watch this," he said, flicking his second offering all the way to a patch of dark water near the opposite shore. The split second his lure hit the water, a fish smacked it so hard, it almost pulled the rod from Radcliff's hand. "Fish on!" bellowed Radcliff, so loudly it startled Garin, causing him to drop a freshly cooked salmon steak onto the ground.

"That one's Radcliff's," said Bridger, holding a metal plate in one hand and a bottle of Russian pale lager in the other.

"I thought these taimen were supposed to be hard to catch," scoffed Radcliff.

"It's not a taimen," said Alexeyev, in a low voice so Radcliff wouldn't hear.

"What do you think it is?" said Bridger.

"A pike or a lenok. A taimen would snap that ultralight rod like a twig."

"Damn!" blurted Radcliff. "My first taimen, and it got away."

After lunch, Kozlov and the helicopter pilot flew back to the helipad near Komsomolsk. The fishing party loaded into the inflatables and began their journey upstream through a snarl of swift currents, side channels, and natural obstacles. Along the way, Garin's boat caromed off a submerged log and nearly capsized. Radcliff, who refused to wear a life jacket, was jettisoned overboard. He was about to be sucked under a tangle of tree limbs when Petrov grabbed him by the shirt collar and hung on until Garin was able to steer the boat into slower water. When Petrov asked if he'd learned his lesson about not wearing a life jacket, Radcliff replied, "I didn't need help from you or anybody else."

Base camp consisted of a canopy-covered table and chairs, three large tents, and a three-sided lean-to made of tarps and wooden posts. Alexeyev and Garin would sleep in one tent, Petrov and Bridger would sleep in another, and Radcliff, whose snoring had shaken the walls of Sasha's house, would sleep in a tent by himself.

Willie Radcliff and Dick Bridger fished four different tributary streams over the next five days, using flies, streamers, imitation mice, and every lure in the camp tacklebox. Bridger hooked and landed one eighteen-inch pike on the second day. Radcliff felt a couple of hard strikes but never caught a fish. He complained mercilessly from the time he got up in the morning until he climbed into his sleeping bag at night. "I could have stayed home and fished off the dock behind my restaurant," he said. "This is the worst fishing trip I've ever been on. Petrov, you tell your boss I want my money back!"

The two discouraged clients had given up on catching much of anything, let alone a hundred-pound taimen. On the last afternoon before heading home, they decided to stick around camp and drink whatever alcoholic beverages were left in the coolers. Radcliff downed four bottles of Russian beer, staggered into his tent, and slept the afternoon away. Bridger sipped Crimean wine with Petrov and Alexeyev. Garin, a non-drinker, started packing for the trip back to civilization.

Everything was quiet and peaceful until a family of Russian wild hogs trotted into camp.

"Don't move!" said Garin.

"What are you going to do?" said Bridger, as Garin leaned over the bow of his inflatable and pulled out the Mosin-Nagant Model 1891, World War II rifle he'd been given by his father.

"I'm going to make sure we have pork chops for dinner."

Two adult females, six half-grown piglets, and a massive, three-hundred-pound boar grunted and snorted their way around camp while Dimitri Garin took careful aim and squeezed the trigger. The ear-shattering crack from Garin's rifle scattered the squealing swine back into the forest. All except one.

"What happened?" said Radcliff, poking his head outside the tent.

"Dimitri shot a pig," said Bridger. "I thought he was gonna shoot that big, ugly boar, but he shot Porky instead."

Radcliff returned to his cot and drifted back to sleep.

"Those big tuskers taste like shoe leather," said Garin, walking over to examine his kill. "This young one will barbeque up nice and tender, with meat as sweet as honey."

As Bridger, Petrov, and Alexeyev watched, Garin pulled a knife from the sheath he wore on his belt and began to gut and skin his prize. "What are you going to do with the entrails?" said Alexeyev. "Don't forget what happened two years ago."

"What happened two years ago?" said Bridger, watching Garin climb into one of the inflatables and return with a long-handled dip net.

"A certain someone had cleaned the day's catch and left a pile of fish guts lying right over there," said Alexeyev, pointing to a shady spot next to the water's edge. "An hour later, we received a visit from a Russian brown bear and her two cubs. Adult Russian brown bears are the size of that tent you're sleeping in. We had to jump in the boats and leave for fear of being ripped apart. When we returned, our bear-proof icebox was in six pieces. Mama bear couldn't get it open, so she jumped on it and batted it around until it fell apart. We still had two days to go before the helicopter returned and nothing to eat. Fortunately, the fishing was good on that trip, so we ate fish for breakfast, lunch, and dinner."

"Hold this net just above the ground," said Garin.

"Don't get any of those pig guts on me," said Petrov, with outstretched arms.

Garin placed a rock in the net and dropped the entrails—including heart, intestines, and liver—in on top. After washing the blood from his hands, he clipped the net from its frame and tied it off with twine. "Now I want you to take that spinning reel on the table and attach it to one of those stout rods," Garin said to Dick Bridger. "Then pick out an assortment of taimen lures and follow me."

Garin removed a thirty-foot length of five-eighths-inch nylon line from the boat, picked up the netting containing the pig entrails, and began walking upstream. Bridger and Petrov followed.

"I'll stay here and keep an eye on the camp," said Alexeyev.

Garin stopped when he reached the first deep pool.

"Now what are you going to do?" said Petrov.

"Watch and learn," said Garin. He tied the nylon line to the entrail-laden netting and tossed it as far as he could into the deepest part of the stream. "I know there's a large taimen in this hole. I saw it break the water's surface a couple days ago, chasing a school of bream."

"If they're not biting, you can throw everything in your tacklebox at them, and they won't come near it," said Petrov. "What makes you think those pig guts will do the trick?"

"The object is to attract small fish, not the taimen. The congregation of fish around the pig guts will trigger the taimen's predatory instinct and lead to what I hope will be a feeding frenzy."

"You have it all figured out, do you?"

"It's worth a try," said Garin. "During a feeding frenzy, a taimen will attack any moving object. I've seen them come clear out of the water after birds scratching for seeds along the shore."

TWENTY

GLANCE AND CALLOWAY WATCHED FROM A distant parking lot as a younger man wearing a blood-stained white apron walked out of Bomba's Fish House and met Farnham and Carney at the back of Farnham's pickup. The restaurant employee pointed to the rear entrance of the restaurant, after which Farnham and Carney carried the fourth ice chest inside.

"Two-five-three, three-two-one, car to car," said Warden Wilcox.

"Two-five-three. Go ahead," said Glance.

"The owner of the business we just contacted and his manager are in custody. We found three chests full of ducks and a lot more. I'll fill you in by landline tonight."

"Ten-four. We have another one for you, if you're available."

"We are! Ten-twenty?"

"We're near Fisherman's Wharf, in a parking lot at the intersection of Beach and Mason streets. Primer-gray van with a blue right-front fender."

"ETA fifteen."

Ten minutes had passed when two dark-green, California Department of Fish and Game Ford sedans entered the parking lot, circled the van, and drove up. "Whatcha got?" said Wilcox, window to window with Calloway.

"Mark, this is Tad Calloway," said Glance, from the passenger seat.

"Good to meet you, Tad."

"The pleasure is mine," said Calloway.

"The young whippersnapper next to me is Phil Simpson," said Wilcox. "This is his first week on the job and, thanks to you guys, he's havin' a ball."

"Glad we could help," said Glance. "Farnham and Carney started out with four ice chests full of ducks this morning and only carried three into Hong Kong Charlie's. We decided to follow them and see where the fourth ice chest was going. Down at the end of that alley over there is the back entrance to a restaurant called Bomba's Fish House."

"We know it well," said Wilcox. "One of the wardens in the car behind us busted Bomba with a cooler full of short abs six months ago. Some people never learn."

"Farnham and Carney are in there with an ice chest full of ducks, mostly pintails," said Glance. "You guys have at 'em. If you're going the formal complaint route, I'll coordinate with you tonight and send you a narrative tomorrow."

"Sounds good," said Wilcox. "Are you sure you guys don't want in on the fun?"

"We have two more customers to deal with up in Glenn County," said Glance. "Besides, we'd rather not burn this rig if we don't have to."

"Thanks a million, Hank. You too, Tad. Good to meet you."

"Where did you meet Mark Wilcox?" said Calloway, as he and Glance watched the two Fish and Game sedans head for Bomba's back door.

"When I first came on the job, I spent a week in the Bay Area serving arrest warrants with big Mark. You wouldn't believe how good he was at tracking down flakes who failed to pay their fines."

"Sounds like fun," said Calloway.

"It was. Mark is the nicest guy in the world, but he's all business when there's an arrest to be made. I almost feel sorry for Farnham and Carney."

"How long has Mark been here in the Bay Area?"

"He's spent his entire career working these docks and butting heads with cantankerous commercial fishermen. I don't think Mark would have it any other way. I'm eager to hear what they found at Hong Kong Charlie's besides ducks. I meant to ask, but I wanted them to hit Bomba's before Farnham and Carney had a chance to leave. Knowing Mark, he'll book them both and have Farnham's truck towed to the impound yard."

"That would serve them right, after slaughtering all those ducks."

"You can say that again! It's 2:30 now. Let's pay the Leatherwood brothers a visit before they hear from Farnham and split."

"Do you know where they live?"

"Yes. I called Brad Foster at the Glenn County Sheriff's Office last week. He did some digging for me and came up with a mobile home on Lausten Road, east of Maxwell. Mitch Leatherwood Junior lives there and Brad thinks Sonny does too."

"Are you sure we want to show up in the undercover van?"

"Good point, Tadpole. Let's go to Willows first, change into our uniforms, and leave the van at your house. We'll pay a visit to the Leatherwood boys in your patrol truck."

It was after 7:00, and the stars were out when Glance and Calloway drove up the gravel driveway to a single-wide mobile home with a green, older-model Chevy pickup parked in front.

"There's that fifty-six Chevy pickup we saw at Farnham's place," said Calloway. A quick license-plate check over the radio confirmed the pickup belonged to Mitchel Ray Leatherwood Junior. The gun rack behind the seat contained two shotguns—a 12-gauge pump and a 12-gauge semi-automatic. An empty box of 12-gauge, number 4 shotgun shells lay on its side in the bed.

While Glance and Calloway inspected the Chevy pickup, an overhead light came on in the yard and two short, wiry young men with greasy, reddish-colored hair walked out of the trailer and approached. They were wearing the same clothes they'd worn that morning at Farnham's barn.

"What do you want to do first?" mumbled Calloway.

"Let's ID 'em and seize those shotguns. It's your district, so you do the talking."

"Whatcha doin'?" said Mitch Leatherwood Junior.

"I'm Warden Calloway. This is Warden Glance. You two, along with Randy Farnham and Chuck Carney, were involved in a serious wildlife violation late last night and early this morning. We'll explain the rest after we see your identification and inspect your weapons."

Each brother produced a hunting license and current state and federal duck stamps. When asked for their driver's licenses, Sonny Leatherwood produced one and Mitch said his had been suspended. Mitch Leatherwood unlocked his pickup and stepped back. Glance kept an eye on the

Leatherwoods while Calloway removed the two shotguns, made sure they were unloaded, and placed them on the hood of his patrol truck.

With the Leatherwood brothers properly identified and their shotguns seized into evidence, Calloway advised them of their violations and that criminal charges would be filed with the Butte County District Attorney's Office. "You'll receive notices from the court as to when and where to appear," said Calloway, as he and Glance climbed into Calloway's patrol truck and drove away.

HENRY DRAGGED HIMSELF UP THE BACK steps of the Glance farmhouse and into the kitchen. "Here he is now," said Anne, handing her husband the phone. "It's Mark Wilcox."

"Hi, Mark."

"When was the last time you slept, young man?"

"I slept for a couple hours in the weeds behind Farnham's barn early this morning. Does that count?"

"We have a ton of things to talk about, so how 'bout I call you again tomorrow morning, after you've had a good night's sleep?"

"Sounds great, Mark."

"Thanks again for everything, Hank. I've been on the job for twenty-five years and never had a day like this one."

"I'm glad everything worked out. I'll talk to you tomorrow."

"Hello, stranger," said Anne, wrapping her arms around her husband and kissing him on the lips. "Would you like something to eat now or after you shower?"

THE MORNING AFTER THE BIG DUCK-SELLING bust, Henry was sitting at the kitchen table typing arrest reports when the phone rang. "That's probably Mark Wilcox," said Anne. "Unlike some of your other game-warden buddies, he waited until after 8:00."

Henry smiled back at his wife, then reached up and answered the phone. "Hi, Mark."

"How'd ya know it was me?"

"A wild guess."

"Do you feel better after a good night's sleep?"

"I sure do, and I'm eagerly waiting to hear what happened at the restaurants yesterday. Why don't you start with Hong Kong Charlie's."

"You're gonna love this. Zhao had just walked out of the restaurant and was climbing into his Mercedes when we drove up. I told him we had reason to believe an illegal wild-duck sale had taken place in his restaurant and we were there to make an inspection. Right away, he goes into a tirade and says we can't come in without a search warrant. I explained that his business wasn't a dwelling and we had a legal right to inspect all boxes, packages, and receptacles that might contain birds, mammals—"

"Fish, reptiles, or amphibians?" said Glance. "That's one of the best sections in the *Fish and Game Code.*"

"One of my favorites," said Wilcox. "Zhao knew he was screwed, so he led us through the back door into the kitchen. The first place we searched was the walk-in cooler on the right. I opened the door and there was Zhao's manager, standing next to ninety freshly picked and cleaned ducks. He had 'em all spread out on a tarp, separated according to size. Like you said, most of 'em were pintails."

"Did you find anything else?"

"We found two boxes of undersized abalone and one box filled to the brim with short lobsters. I thought Zhao was gonna have a stroke. He and his manager started shouting at each other in Chinese. When they finally settled down, I sat Zhao down and read him his Miranda rights. With no prompting from me, he offered to tell us everything we wanted to know."

"What did he tell you?"

"I asked how much he'd paid for the ducks. He said five bucks apiece, for a total of four hundred and fifty dollars."

"I bet he paid Farnham in cash."

"Yup. Nine fifty-dollar bills. Remind me to tell you a funny story about that when we get to the other restaurant."

"How many times had he bought ducks from Farnham?"

"Twice last year and twice the year before. Zhao gave me this hangdog look and said he had customers willing to pay any price for a wild-duck dinner. 'I would have been a poor businessman, had I not provided them with what they wanted,' he said."

"Did he tell you where he got the abs and the lobsters?"

"He said he bought them all from the same man, a wholesaler named Ivan Jelic."

"What happened at Bomba's Fish House?"

"Boris Bomba moved up here from Long Beach a couple years ago. He's a pathological liar and wouldn't tell the truth if his life depended on it. We walked in the back door as Bomba was handing Farnham a wad of cash. 'I'll take that,' I said. Bomba claimed he was paying Farnham back for some money he owed him. That's when I noticed a bulge in Farnham's shirt pocket. I pointed to it and said, 'I bet you have nine fifty-dollar bills in there, don't you?'"

"How did Farnham respond?"

"He just stood there, looking like the cat that ate the canary. I waited a few seconds then told him if he didn't hand me the money, I was gonna cuff him first, then take it from him."

"Did he give it to you?"

"Damn right he did. Then I cuffed him and his partner."

"Did you find the ducks?"

"I turned to Bomba and asked him if he'd ever heard me say anything I didn't mean. When he said no, I told him he had three minutes to produce the chest full of ducks. If he didn't, we were gonna search the entire restaurant."

"Did that convince him to cooperate?"

"Not at first. Then I said, 'Who knows what else we might find—short abs, short lobsters, illegal fish, drugs . . . the possibilities are endless.' Bomba ordered one of his dishwashers to go get the chest and bring it out to us. It contained thirty ducks."

"Did you end up booking Farnham and Carney?"

"You bet your life we booked 'em. If word ever got out around the docks that I let two duck-poaching sonsabitches come into my patrol district, sell a hundred and twenty ducks, and drive away, I'd lose all the respect I've earned over the last twenty-five years. We not only booked 'em, we also had Farnham's pickup towed. It cost him two hundred dollars to get it out of the impoundment yard and another five hundred to the bail bondsman to cover ten percent of his bail."

"You mean the bail was five thousand?"

"Five thousand each. Farnham had to sign a deed of trust, deeding his house to the bail company. I don't know what kind of collateral Carney came up with."

"You guys did a fantastic job, Mark."

"You and your sidekick did all the work. We enjoyed the spoils. How do you want to handle this, Hank?"

Glance thought for a minute before answering. "The way I see it, you charge Farnham and Carney in San Francisco. There were two other men involved with killing, picking, and cleaning all those ducks. We'll charge them here in Butte County."

"What about the rest of 'em?" said Wilcox.

"Why don't you decide what to charge Zhao, Jelic, and Bomba with. I wouldn't cut them any slack. It might be a long time before anyone catches them again."

"Sounds good, Hank. Needless to say, you and Tad will receive subpoenas if any of this goes to trial. I can't tell you how much we appreciate all the incredible work you've done."

"I'm glad everything paid off. I'll send you the reports I promised. If you need anything else, let me know."

After hanging up the phone, Glance telephoned Ira Benson to thank him for the information he'd provided and tell him how the investigation turned out. Benson answered on the second ring.

"Hello."

"Hi, Ira. This is Hank Glance."

"Hank! I'm so glad you called. I've been cleaning out my old files and found some information I wanted to give you before I toss it in the burn barrel. This happened twenty-seven years ago. I gave this same information to Norm Bettis at the time, but I don't know if he ever followed up on it."

"I'm all ears, Ira."

"Gooseneck Strode and a guy named Clyde Tweedy got liquored up in here and started talking about a duck drag they had pulled the previous night with a man named Willie Radcliff. Strode went on and on about this Radcliff character laughing his ass off every time he pulled the trigger and watched all those ducks fall from the sky. I have it written down that they killed 329 ducks that night. Radcliff apparently ran a big duck club down in the Butte Sink area. From what I gathered, Gooseneck and his crew of outlaws were regularly selling ducks to Radcliff so he could turn around and sell them to some restaurant in San Francisco."

"Would you happen to know the exact date this happened?"

"November 13, 1945. I know it's old stuff and you can't do anything about it now, but I thought I'd give it to you in case Willie Radcliff is still around. He was about the same age as Strode, so he'd be in his late fifties now."

"Thanks so much, Ira. I'll do some snooping around and see what I can come up with on Mr. Radcliff."

"You know what they say about leopards," said Benson, chuckling.

"They don't change their spots?"

"Exactly!"

TWENTY-ONE

A N HOUR HAD PASSED SINCE DIMITRI Garin chummed the stream bottom with pig entrails. He and Adrian Petrov were standing on the shore, and Dick Bridger was wading waist-deep in the current, when a school of silver bream raced along the water's surface in front of Bridger.

"I've never seen them do that before," said Petrov.

"They were being chased," said Garin.

"Whatever was doing the chasing swam right by me," said Bridger.

"What did it look like?" said Garin.

"From what I could see, it was about four feet long, kinda snaky, and had a reddish-colored tail."

"That had to be a taimen. Cast your plug near the spot where I tossed those pig entrails."

Seconds after Bridger's lure hit the water, it was engulfed in the taimen's cavernous maw, and the fight was on. "I've caught lots of steelhead," shouted Bridger, grimacing, "but none of them fought like this. It feels like I have a marlin on the end of my line."

"If he heads downstream, you'll have to go with him," said Garin. "If you don't, he'll snap your line."

"There he goes!" shouted Petrov, reaching for a long-handled dip net and following Bridger downstream.

"You won't need that for another hour," said Garin.

Bridger fought his taimen for almost an hour before Petrov was able to slip behind it, capture the lower half of its body in the net, and slosh the leviathan trout to shore.

"Congratulations!" said Petrov. "Now you can say you've landed a Russian taimen."

"A damn big one at that," said Bridger, cradling the fish and smiling for photographs. "This thing must weigh a ton."

Garin pulled a measuring tape from his pocket, and Petrov helped him stretch it across the full length of the fish. "Fifty-four inches," said Garin. "My guess is about sixty-five pounds. We can officially weigh it when we get back to camp, or we can release it and let it live to fight another day. Your choice."

Bridger thought for a minute or two. "I think I'd like to have it hanging in camp when Radcliff wakes up from his nap. I can't wait to see the look on his face."

"Is that why you don't want to release it?" said Garin. "So you can prove to Mr. Radcliff that you're a better fisherman than he is?"

"I'm not sure I like your tone," said Bridger. "It's my fish, I paid for it, and I'll do whatever the hell I choose with it."

"He didn't mean anything by it," said Petrov, stepping between the two men. "If you don't intend to have your fish mounted, it's customary to release it so someone else can experience the same thrill you did."

"It's not his place to question my motives," said Bridger. "He's supposed to take me where the fish are and keep his mouth shut."

Not wanting to provoke Bridger any further, Garin retrieved the baiting device he'd rigged up and started back to camp.

"Dimitri is concerned about the survival of this species here in Far Eastern Russia," said Petrov. "We've seen fewer of them over the last several years. Taxidermists have developed a way to create lifelike fiberglass reproductions. That way, fishermen like you can have their well-earned trophies without killing the fish."

"I like that idea," said Bridger. "Let's get him back in the water."

"A wise decision," said Petrov. "What would you think about us sending an eight-by-ten glossy of you and your taimen to Mr. Radcliff's Chico, California, address?"

"I love it!"

IT WAS APPROACHING MIDNIGHT ON SEPTEMBER 10, 1972, when Petrov, Bridger, and Radcliff passed through the electric gate and entered Nic Cantor's Sausalito estate. "Just drop me off at my car," said Radcliff.

"There's a shower and a warm bed waiting for you in the house," said Petrov. "Don't you want to sleep here tonight and drive to Chico in the morning?"

"Nope."

"You're staying, aren't you, Dick?"

"You bet. I can't wait to take a shower and hit the sheets. It was a great trip, Adrian. Thanks for everything."

"Speak for yourself," mumbled Radcliff, still fuming about his lack of success. Climbing from the van, he unloaded his gear and tossed it in the trunk of his Cadillac. "Petrov," he said, "tell your boss I'll be in touch."

NIC CANTOR RECEIVED A PHONE CALL on Tuesday morning, September 17, 1972. "Nic, this is Willie Radcliff."

"Willie! I was hoping to hear from you. Adrian tells me you weren't too happy about your trip."

"That's an understatement. I'd like to talk to you about a way you can redeem yourself."

"Redeem myself? Didn't I provide you with everything written in your contract?"

"You promised me a taimen, and I didn't catch a damn thing. I could have done better fishing off the dock behind my restaurant."

"I'm sorry, Willie, but there's no way I can control how many fish you catch. Dick Bridger caught a beautiful taimen. Maybe you should have watched to see how he did it."

"When can we meet?" said Radcliff, unamused by Cantor's remark.

"I'm a busy man, Willie. Do you mind if I check my schedule and get back to you?"

"I'll be waiting for your call."

Willie Radcliff was not used to being ignored. When Cantor hadn't called him back after two weeks' time, Radcliff picked up the phone and dialed his number again. This time, Cantor relented and agreed to meet the following afternoon, September 30, 1972, at the Sausalito harbor where he kept his boat. Radcliff was waiting at the gate when Cantor walked up with a key in his hand.

"Hello, Willie," said Cantor, a contemplative look on his face Radcliff hadn't seen before. "Let's talk on the boat."

"Sounds good."

Cantor's watercraft turned out to be more than a modest sailboat. It was a fifty-seven-foot, custom-built sloop designed to accommodate six people on voyages to California's Channel Islands, Mexico, and beyond.

"Nice boat," said Radcliff.

"It gets me where I want to go. Step aboard and have a seat."

Radcliff took a seat in one of the deck chairs.

"I have a tennis date in an hour," said Cantor. "What is it you were so eager to talk to me about?"

"Like I said on the phone, I'm not satisfied with the way my fishing trip turned out."

"Get to the point, Willie. What is it, exactly, that you want?"

"I want you to arrange a hunting trip for me."

"What makes you think I can do that?"

"Didn't you arrange for someone to kill that moose you barbequed a few weeks ago? Petrov told me you have connections all over Far Eastern Russia and you can arrange for me to hunt moose, brown bear, elk, sheep, even lynx."

"Oh he did, did he?"

"Yes, he did. That's when I told him about my big-game trophy room and my kitty collection."

"Your kitty collection?"

"Yeah. I have two African lions, a mountain lion, a leopard, and a jaguar in my kitty collection. What I don't have is the biggest kitty of them all—a Siberian tiger."

Cantor laughed out loud. "You can't be serious!"

"I'm dead serious. I think you owe it to me, anyway, but I'm willing to forget about that and pay you a hundred thousand dollars to get me the Siberian tiger I want for my collection."

"Siberian tigers are quite rare, Willie. They're also protected by the Soviet government. You must be out of your mind if you think I'm going to help you kill one."

"If they're so rare, why did I see one on the drive from Khabarovsk to Komsomolsk?"

"Now you're making things up."

"Ask your flunky Petrov if you don't believe me. A tiger ran across the road in front of us."

"Regardless of what you think you saw, locating one of those elusive kitties, as you call them, would be like finding a needle in a haystack."

"Is that what's stopping you, or is it the amount of money I'm willing to pay?"

"It's out of the question, Willie. Unless there's something else you'd like to talk to me about, I'm going to get ready for my tennis date."

"How does a hundred and fifty thousand grab you?"

"You're wasting your breath," said Cantor, coming to his feet and beginning to lock up.

"I'm willing to pay you a quarter million dollars, under these conditions . . ." said Radcliff.

Cantor stopped what he was doing and sat back down.

"First, the tiger must be wild, fully grown, and in good condition. I don't want a broken-down old cat you bought from some circus."

"I'm an honest businessman, Willie. I wouldn't do that to you."

"Like hell you wouldn't. Second, I want a museum-quality full mount delivered to my door within three months of the day of the kill. In case you've forgotten, that's what you promised had I caught a taimen."

"Give me a couple minutes to think about this," said Cantor, coming to his feet and walking toward the stern of the boat. Kamchatka brown-bear hunts had been the most lucrative part of Nic Cantor's and Leonid Grekov's outfitting business for two decades. Wealthy hunters from all over the United States had paid exorbitant prices to travel to Far Eastern Russia and bag the massive bruins for their trophy rooms. On rare occasions, when bears were scarce, it was necessary to employ a baited culvert trap—a length of metal culvert closed at one end, with a trapdoor at the other.

"I'm waiting," said Radcliff.

"Here's the only way we'd have any chance of providing you with what you want," said Cantor, turning around and walking into the shade. "We'd have to employ a culvert trap."

"A culvert trap?"

"I know what you're thinking, but without one, you have a better chance of catching Bigfoot than a Siberian tiger."

"You don't expect me to shoot a tiger while it's in a trap, do you?"

"It's up to you, Willie, but I'd prefer to release it and allow you the thrill of the hunt. Listen closely, because this is my first and only offer."

"I'm listening."

"It could take months to fill an order like this, maybe never. If we do get lucky and find you a tiger, I'll expect half payment up front and the other half on delivery of the mounted trophy. There will be no written contract, and if I hear one word from anyone about today's conversation, the deal's off."

"If that's the only way I can get my tiger, I guess that'll have to do," said Radcliff.

"Keep in mind, this could take months. If we catch a tiger, you'll have to be ready to leave for the Primorsky Krai at the drop of a hat. I'll arrange to get you there and back, like I did before, and Adrian Petrov will go along to keep you out of trouble."

"I like this boat," said Radcliff, feeling better since he'd once again gotten his way. "Have you ever thought of selling it?"

"No, I haven't. Don't get too pleased with yourself, Willie. We haven't found you a tiger yet."

"No, but for the amount of money I'm offering, I have a hunch you will."

"Before you leave, there's one more thing," said Cantor.

"What's that?"

"I'll need a fifty-thousand-dollar deposit."

"What for?"

"Insurance. If you happen to lose your nerve or change your mind once I've begun making phone calls and putting this agreement in motion, the fifty thousand will be forfeited."

"I guess I can go along with that. I'll send you a check when I get back to my office."

Cantor snickered and shook his head.

"What's the problem?"

"Willie, you wanted to play in the big leagues, and you got your wish. I expect to be paid in cash. The wheels won't begin to turn until I receive the fifty thousand."

"How am I supposed to get it to you?"

"That's your problem, not mine. If we're through, I have a tennis date with a beautiful woman."

"What's her name?" said Radcliff, chuckling. "I might know her."

"Her name is Joy. I doubt very much that you know her."

PART TWO

Crossing Paths

1973 - 1975

TWENTY-TWO

SEPTEMBER 1973 IN BUTTE COUNTY WAS hot and dry, with the exception of one thunderstorm that rumbled for an hour, spit out a few raindrops, and moved eastward toward Bangor. Warden Henry Glance left the house at 5:00, an hour after the storm had passed. His plan was to fly the colors—let himself and his patrol truck be seen—during the early evening hours and stake out one of the Feather River's more popular salmon-snagging riffles in the light of a full moon.

Glance had developed positive working relationships with most of the landowners in his patrol district. They, in turn, provided him with keys and combinations for any locked gates he might encounter. On this evening, Glance entered the Mapes Orchard property by way of a locked gate, parked his patrol truck between two rows of nectarine trees, and hiked a quarter mile to his well-hidden vantage point overlooking Hawkins Riffle.

The county road came to an "L" turn a half mile north of Glance's position. Over the years, salmon poachers, most of them drop-offs, had straddled the Mapes Orchard barbed-wire fence at the turn. They followed a well-worn path through a jungle of Himalayan blackberry bushes out to the rock-strewn riverbed. From there, it was a short hike downstream to the shallow riffle where, over the years, untold numbers of spawning salmon had been illegally hooked by the back or tail and dragged unceremoniously from the water.

A few minutes after sunset, Glance spotted two men walking across the rubble and climbing over washed-up tree limbs at the water's edge on his side of the river. The husky man in front was shirtless and dressed in gray overalls. Trailing ten feet behind was a much thinner man wearing a dark-colored T-shirt and cutoff jeans. Both suspected salmon snaggers sloshed across a narrow, waist-deep river channel to the sandbar in the middle of the river.

Glance heard the sand crunching under the men's feet and the squeaking of their water-soaked tennis shoes as they trudged their way across the sandbar to Hawkins Riffle. Reaching their destination, they dropped their gear and began casting their lines toward the opposite riverbank, engaging in a series of slashing motions during the retrieval process.

Just as I suspected, thought Glance, focusing his binoculars on the violators and sickened by what he saw. *Starting out as four-inch smolts, these incredible fish have dodged predators for a hundred and fifty miles all the way downstream to San Francisco Bay, survived in the ocean for three or four years, then navigated manmade obstacles all the way back up here— only to be foul-hooked and dragged out of the river before they've had the chance to spawn.*

The weighted, three-pronged hook directed by the man in overalls hit home on his second cast, puncturing the dorsal region of a ten-pound Chinook and holding fast. Rather than waste time playing the fish, the experienced salmon snagger tightened the drag on his reel, backed across the sandbar, and dragged his flopping quarry up on the bank. He then placed his first salmon inside a burlap bag, secured the bag to an exposed willow root, and tossed it in the water.

The same series of events played out eight more times, each one documented in the notepad Glance pulled from his uniform-shirt pocket. At 11:15, the outlaws packed up their gear, pulled their gunny sacks from the water, and headed back upstream. Glance kept meticulous records. According to his notes, the man wearing overalls had illegally taken five salmon and the man in the T-shirt had illegally taken four. When the violators were out of sight, Glance climbed from his hiding place and sprinted back to his patrol truck.

"Two-five-three, two-five-four, car-to-car," came Warden Tad Calloway's voice over the radio.

"Two-five-three. Go ahead," said Glance, having just climbed into his patrol truck and still struggling to catch his breath.

"Are you working the river?"

"Affirmative," said Glance, breathing heavily. "I'm south of the L turn . . . near Hawkins Riffle."

"I'm in the area if you need assistance."

"Stand by. I'll get back to you in five, when I've returned to the county road."

"Ten-four."

Glance had made it back to the county road using only the moon to light his way. With his patrol truck hidden behind a pump shed, he radioed Calloway. "Two-five-four, two-five-three."

"Two-five-four. Go ahead."

"The two salmon snaggers I've been watching all evening just walked out to the county road and are waiting to be picked up."

"Ten-nine. I didn't catch the first part of your transmission."

"Stand by," said Glance. "I see a car coming."

As Glance watched, the driver of the apparent getaway car pulled up against the Mapes Orchard fence, cut his engine, and turned off his headlights. His dome light came on as he stepped from the car, walked to the rear, and popped open the trunk.

"Where the hell ya been?" came a voice from the darkness. "I told you to pick us up at 11:30. It's after midnight."

"Sorry, Butch. I had to unplug a sink for one of the trailer-park residents and got a late start."

Glance heard the trunk slam shut, followed by the repeated opening and closing of car doors. "Two-five-four," he said into the radio mic, "start heading this way."

"I'm almost there!" Calloway shouted.

When the 1965 Ford Galaxy's backup lights came on, Glance engaged his headlights and his red spotlight, stomped on the gas, and roared to within three feet of the getaway car's rear bumper. "Department of Fish and Game!" he shouted as he stepped from the patrol truck. "Driver, turn off your engine and hand me the keys."

"Of course, officer," said the driver, in a British accent. "I'm only too happy to comply."

"Everyone remain in the car and keep your hands where I can see them," said Glance, securing the car keys in his pocket.

Glance walked to the rear of the Ford sedan and shined his five-cell flashlight on the license plate. He then returned to his patrol truck, reached for the mic, and advised Sacramento dispatch of his location, the suspect vehicle's license number, and the number of adult males inside.

Warden Calloway roared up to the scene and jumped out of his patrol truck as Glance was about to demand identification from the three poaching suspects. Glance turned his attention to Calloway just long enough for the man sitting in the front passenger seat to throw open his door, scurry under the barbed-wire fence, and run off into the darkness.

"Tad, would you watch these two?" said Glance, hurdling the fence and dashing after the fleeing suspect.

"He'll never catch him," said the man in the back seat.

"I wouldn't bet on that," said Calloway.

"Stop!" shouted Glance, drawing closer with every stride.

Glance's command fell on deaf ears, and the suspect quickened his pace.

The farther the suspect ran from Warden Calloway's headlight beams, the darker his chosen path became. Realizing that his flashlight was the only thing still lighting the suspect's way, Glance shouted, "Last chance. Stop, or I'll—"

The next sound Glance heard was a barrage of expletives spewing from a blackberry thicket ten yards ahead.

"I warned you," said Glance, turning his flashlight back on and finding the suspect lying face down in a tangle of thorny branches. "I'm not in the mood for any more of your nonsense, so place your hands behind your back and don't move another muscle until I tell you to."

"That was a dirty trick!" said the suspect, as Glance helped him to his feet. "You never would have caught me if I hadn't tripped and fallen into those blackberries."

"Uh-huh. Start walking. I'll be right behind you."

"My arms are all scratched up, and my overalls are torn," complained the suspect as he walked toward the road.

"What's your name?"

"Butch."

"What's your real name?"

"I don't have to tell you anything."

"Suit yourself. The booking officer in Oroville is going to ask you the same question."

"It's William Radcliff Junior. You're not planning on taking me to jail, are you?"

Glance was deep in thought and didn't answer.

"Hey, warden—I asked if you were planning on taking me to jail."

"Are you related to Willie Radcliff?" said Glance, recalling the name of the 1940s-era outlaw Ira Benson had given him ten months earlier.

"That's my old man. He's gonna be madder than hell when he finds out about this. If you're smart, you'll take these cuffs off and let me go."

"I'll take my chances. Do you have any identification?"

"No. I left it at home."

"You just struck out, Mr. Radcliff."

"What's that supposed to mean?"

"Strike one was when you decided to snag salmon. Strike two was when you ran off and put my partner and me in danger. Strike three was your failure to carry identification. If you're going to break the law, it's always a good idea to carry valid identification. Now turn back around and keep walking. We're almost there."

Warden Calloway had collected driver's-license information from the getaway-car driver, fifty-six-year-old Martin Fletcher. Fletcher was sitting on the ground next to Calloway's patrol truck, uncuffed. The second salmon snagger, twenty-five-year-old Travis Blunt, was cuffed and sitting on the ground next to Fletcher. Like Radcliff, Blunt wasn't carrying identification.

"Thanks for showing up when you did," said Glance to Calloway. "Did these guys give you any trouble?"

"Not a bit. The driver even apologized for the man who ran."

Glance instructed Butch Radcliff to sit on the ground next to Blunt and Fletcher. Removing Fletcher's car keys from his pocket, Glance popped open the Ford Galaxy's trunk. Inside, he found a pair of broken-down rod and reel setups, a canvas backpack filled with snagging equipment, and two wet gunny sacks containing a total of nine salmon.

While Calloway kept an eye on the three suspects, Glance unlocked his camper shell, spread a canvas tarp across the bed, and loaded the salmon and all the suspects' snagging equipment inside. When he'd finished, he took a notepad from his shirt pocket and rejoined the group.

"Mr. Radcliff, do you have any identification at all?" said Glance.

"I told ya, it's at home on my dresser."

"What's your date of birth?"

"June 10, 1947."

"Where's home?"

"Willie's Sacramento River Resort."

"What's your address?"

"One hundred and five River Road, Space 11, Chico, California."

"Does Willie Radcliff also live at that address?"

"No. He lives in the mansion up the road. Why do you keep asking about my father? He doesn't have anything to do with this."

Glance examined Fletcher's driver's license and ignored Radcliff's question. "Mr. Fletcher . . ."

"Yes, officer?"

"Do you go by Martin or Marty?"

"Either is perfectly all right. I'm so sorry for the trouble my young associate has caused you."

"Martin, I'd like to speak with you in private," said Glance, motioning for Fletcher to stand up and follow. "Tad, we'll be back in a few minutes."

"Take as much time as you need," said Calloway. "These two aren't going anywhere. I think I'll have myself a cup of coffee while we're waiting."

TWENTY-THREE

GLANCE LED MARTIN FLETCHER UP THE road into the darkness and out of Butch Radcliff's and Travis Blunt's earshot.

"Am I going to be arrested?" said Fletcher.

"You're carrying valid identification, so I don't think that will be necessary," said Glance.

"May I ask why you've separated me from the others?"

"Because something tells me you don't belong with them."

"Is it my British accent?"

"That's part of it. Do you mind telling me how a seemingly intelligent gentleman like you got mixed up with those two outlaws?"

"Would you like to hear the long answer or the shorter version?"

"Let's start with the shorter version."

"Very well. When my employer's son tells me to do something, I feel compelled to do it. By the way, I was quite impressed with the way you handled young Master Radcliff. He used to be a reasonably pleasant young man, but lately he's become a bully, like his father."

"And his father is?"

"Willie Radcliff."

With the two cuffed prisoners back at the vehicles, Glance knew he had a brief window of opportunity to find out as much as he could about Willie Radcliff, the outlaw Ira Benson had told him about.

"Martin, I'd like to ask you a few questions, but before I do, I want to make sure you understand your rights." Glance recited the Miranda warning from memory.

"What is it you wish to know?"

"Does that mean you're willing to answer my questions without an attorney present?"

"You seem like an honorable chap. I suppose that would be all right."

"How long have you known Willie Radcliff?"

"It all started in 1964. At the time, I was a journeyman plumber, an accomplished musician, and the lead singer of a folk group called the Martin Fletcher Trio."

"Here in the United States?"

"No. In Sheffield, England. We were regularly playing pubs in Sheffield, Manchester, and Liverpool, when someone suggested we go to America and try to hit it big."

"You mean like the Beetles?" said Glance, chuckling.

"Not quite that big, but we were pretty pleased with how popular we'd become. I was hesitant to make the move at first, but the more I thought about it, the better it sounded. My wife had left me five years earlier, we didn't have any kids, and I was tired of unplugging backed-up sewer lines."

"So you took the leap?"

"Right off the proverbial cliff. We played one gig in a seedy Brooklyn bar, and the other two members of my group flew back to England."

"Where did that leave you?"

"People are always looking for a good plumber, so I spent the next five years working my way across America. One afternoon in 1969, I walked into the restaurant at Willie's Sacramento River Resort. It was Fish Taco Friday, and the place was hopping with raucous college students."

"I know that place," said Glance. "Some friends and I dropped in a couple years ago when I was a student at Chico State."

"I walked up to the cashier and told him I was in need of employment," said Fletcher. "'Hey, boss,' he shouted to a large, middle-aged man ogling a table full of attractive coeds, 'this guy says he wants a job.'"

"Did his boss happen to be Willie Radcliff?"

"In the flesh."

"What did he say?"

"'Tell him to take a hike. We don't want any bums hangin' around here.'"

Glance shook his head.

"I had started for the door, when one of the cooks walked out of the kitchen and shouted to Radcliff, 'The dishwashing machine has broken down, we've run out of clean glasses, and the sink is backed up again.' Seizing the opportunity, I walked up to Radcliff and said, 'I'm a journeyman plumber. Whatever your problem is, I can fix it.'"

"Did he take the bait?"

"Like a hungry salmon. He pointed to the kitchen and told me to get my ass in there. I had everything running smoothly in less than an hour. Instead of officially hiring me, he offered me two meals a day in the restaurant's kitchen, free utilities, and an old trailer at the back of the park to sleep in."

"No salary?"

"He pays for my services out of his pocket. You must understand that in spite of Willie Radcliff's great wealth, he's tighter than the paper on the wall."

"How did he become so wealthy?"

"Willie's parents once owned the largest farming operation in Northern California. When they passed away, Willie inherited the business, all the land, Radcliff Mansion, and a substantial amount of cash. He sold the business and most of the land, keeping the mansion and 2,000 acres of adjoining property for himself."

"How do you know all this?" said Glance, looking back toward the vehicles to make sure everything was all right.

"Suffice it to say I have it on good authority," said Fletcher. "Radcliff took some of the millions he received from the land sales to create what is now Willie's Sacramento River Resort."

"Please tell me more about Butch Radcliff," said Glance, thinking about what Ira Benson had told him and searching for a foot in the door to Willie Radcliff's history of wildlife crimes.

"Butch's behavior tonight was reprehensible," said Fletcher, "but he's not inherently bad, like his father. You'll be surprised to learn that Butch is a talented guitar player."

"No kidding!" said Glance. "I play guitar myself."

"I play banjo and guitar," said Fletcher. "Maybe the three of us can get together and jam sometime."

"I'd like that, but right now I'd better get down to business. How many times have you been the getaway driver for Butch and his salmon-snagging buddies?"

"Perhaps a dozen or more since the salmon have been running. Sometimes it's Travis with Butch, and sometimes it's one of his other friends."

"When you pick them up, do they usually have fish?"

"Yes. They're always dragging those heavy burlap bags behind them when they come running back to the car. Butch sells the fish to his father and splits the proceeds with his friends. I've heard him say he gets seven bucks for the fresh-looking salmon and five for those that have begun to break down and turn black."

"So, in spite of having all that money, Willie Radcliff is involved in this nickel-and-dime salmon-poaching enterprise?"

"I know this is hard to believe," said Fletcher, "but he's involved in it up to his nineteen-inch neck. I think it gives him some kind of maniacal thrill to break the law and beat what he frequently calls 'the system.'"

"You're right," said Glance, shaking his head. "It is hard to believe."

"Just yesterday, Willie caught me looking at a pile of fresh salmon in the walk-in cooler. I had one of Butch's cottage-cheese containers in my hand. 'What the hell are you doing in here?' he said. I tried to explain that I was looking for a mop, but he grabbed me by the back of the neck and said, 'If I catch you in here again, I'll drown your skinny ass in the river.'"

"What does Radcliff do with the salmon Butch sells him? Please tell me he's not feeding those spawned-out, decomposing fish to his customers."

"The restaurant has twenty tables inside and ten more on the deck overlooking the river. It draws a reliable lunch and dinner crowd, but it's standing room only on Fish Taco Fridays. Sometimes, the cars are parked a mile down River Road. Most of them belong to college students. Being the tightwad that he is, Willie mixes the river salmon Butch provides with fresh ocean salmon he purchases from one of the fish dealers over on the coast."

"You said you had one of Butch's cottage-cheese containers in your hand when Willie caught you in the cooler. What was that about?"

"There was a cardboard box on the floor of the cooler. It was packed with cottage-cheese containers. The cottage-cheese containers were stuffed with salmon skeins. Butch and his friends have been ripping these skeins out of the female salmon they kill. They sell them to bait dealers up and down the river when the steelhead are running."

"Where is this walk-in cooler?"

"It's in the utility building connected to the restaurant."

"Hank," came a shout from Warden Calloway. "Are you about ready to wrap this up?"

"Just a couple more minutes," Glance shouted back. "Martin, what does Willie Radcliff drive?"

"When he's trying to impress people, he drives his gold Coupe de Ville. The rest of the time, he bangs about in a beat-up, forty-seven Chevy pickup. Whenever Willie shifts from first to second, he grinds the gears so badly, you can hear him coming from a mile away."

"Do you have any idea where he keeps his records?"

"Willie Radcliff is quite secretive about his business dealings. He has a fancy office on the first floor of the mansion. I caught a glimpse of it earlier this year when his wife, Rebecca, asked me to fix a leaky bathroom faucet."

"Really!"

"Yes. Willie was away on one of his hunting trips at the time. He hunts and fishes all over the world and has quite a trophy collection."

"By trophies, are you talking about mounted animals?"

"Yes, mostly big game, but also some very large fish."

"Have you seen this collection?" said Glance, again reflecting on what Ira Benson had told him.

Fletcher hesitated.

"Martin, is there something you're afraid to tell me?"

"It's not me I'm concerned about."

"Who are you concerned about?"

"My friend."

"Hank," shouted Calloway. "How much longer are you going to be?"

"We're almost finished," shouted Glance, gesturing for Fletcher to continue.

"I peeked into Willie's office on the way down the hall to the bathroom with the leaky faucet," said Fletcher. "Rebecca caught me staring at a moose head hanging on the wall."

"Did she say anything?"

"She said the moose in Willie's office was just a sample of what her no-good husband had locked away in his trophy room."

"She actually said that?"

"She didn't just say it, she offered to show me. It was about 5:00 in the evening, and Rebecca had a highball in her hand."

"Did you take her up on her offer?"

"Not at first, but she insisted. I was also concerned about her swollen left eye."

"Her swollen left eye? How well did you know Rebecca Radcliff?"

"I had talked to her a few times when she'd come into the restaurant. That's how she learned about my plumbing skills."

Knowing he was running out of time, Glance fired questions at Fletcher in rapid succession.

"What did you see in the trophy room?"

"The door was locked at first. Rebecca said not to worry—she knew where her husband kept the key. The trophy room reeked of cigar smoke. It was the size of a small dance hall and furnished with expensive Persian rugs. In the center was an antique poker table with six wooden chairs."

"What about the mounted animals?"

"Everything is labeled, like in public museums," said Fletcher. "I remember seeing a huge bear standing on his hind legs, a couple African lions, a leopard, and an enormous Siberian tiger."

"Are you sure it was a Siberian tiger?" said Glance.

"That's what the label said."

"Do you remember the approximate date you saw these things?"

"It was the first week in August."

"You mean this year?"

"Yes, 1973."

"Are Willie and Rebecca still married?"

"Why do you ask that?"

"Her swollen eye and the comment she made about her no-good husband."

"Willie and Rebecca are still married on paper. Rebecca still does book-keeping for the business, but they no longer live together."

"Where were you planning on sleeping tonight?"

"After what's happened, I'll probably sleep on my friend's couch in Chico."

"I hope you're not offended when I ask this, but would your friend be Rebecca Radcliff?"

"Hank!" shouted Calloway. "We need to get these guys into Oroville now!"

"We're on our way," shouted Glance.

"Call me in the morning," said Fletcher, handing Glance a Willie's Sacramento River Resort business card with a Chico address and phone number handwritten on the back.

TWENTY-FOUR

Glance handed Martin Fletcher the keys to his car and watched him drive away. "Take these cuffs off and we'll see how tough you are," said Butch Radcliff, still sitting on the ground next to Calloway's patrol truck.

"I've been listening to that for the last half hour," said Calloway. "Blunt is strapped in the passenger seat of my truck and ready to go. Let's run these two into Oroville and get them out of our hair."

"Good idea," said Glance, helping Butch Radcliff to his feet and leading him to the passenger side of his patrol truck.

"You're gonna be sorry you did this," said Radcliff.

"Climb in and try not to bump your head," said Glance.

When Radcliff was safely buckled in, Glance and Calloway walked out of the prisoners' earshot to discuss plans for the remainder of the night and early morning.

"What did you find out from Fletcher?" said Calloway.

"Plenty! If half of what Fletcher told me is true, Butch's father is far worse than any outlaw you or I have ever dealt with."

"Have you considered the possibility that Fletcher might have been feeding you a load of bullshit?"

"I have, but my gut tells me this is well worth following up on. I'm not just talking about salmon. The man has a trophy room filled with big game from all over the world. Fletcher said everything is labeled, like in a public museum. He's seen African lions, a leopard, and a huge Siberian tiger."

"What makes you think this stuff is illegal?"

"I'd bet my life on it—especially the Siberian tiger. I've read that there are fewer than a hundred wild ones left on Earth. Most of those are in Far Eastern Russia."

"I'm still not convinced that this isn't a wild-goose chase," said Calloway.

"Remember the informant who tipped us off about Randy Farnham and his gang?"

"Of course."

"Had we not followed up on the information that informant gave me, Randy Farnham would still be slaughtering ducks and selling them to restaurants in San Francisco. That same informant told me about Willie Radcliff."

"What'd he say?"

"He said Willie Radcliff was poaching ducks and selling them back in the 1940s. Based on what Martin Fletcher just told me, he's far worse than that now. After we book these two, I think we should stake out Willie's Sacramento River Resort."

"Where is this resort located?" said Calloway, yawning.

"It's about nine miles northwest of Chico."

"And we're going to drive there after we book Blunt and Radcliff in Oroville?"

"That's the idea. We have to get there before Butch calls his father and his father gets rid of the evidence."

"What evidence are we talking about?"

"To start with, the illegal salmon and salmon eggs that are stacked inside the resort's walk-in cooler."

"What about the lions and tigers?"

"In due time, Tadpole, in due time."

"I should know better than to ask a question like that," said Calloway. "You're always three steps ahead of me."

"Are you ready to go?"

"You lead the way, Sherlock."

Glance hopped into the driver's seat of his Dodge Power Wagon and started the engine. "How 'bout some music?" he said. "I found this great station out of Los Angeles that only comes in during the wee hours of the morning. Do you like folk music, Butch?"

"I'd like to kick your ass."

"That's no way to talk," said Glance, turning the dial on his music radio. "Hey, we're in luck! It's Gordon Lightfoot, and he's singing one of my favorite songs. I've been practicing this on my guitar. Speaking of guitars, I understand you play."

"A hell of a lot better than you."

"You may be right about that."

"ALAN, HOW SOON WILL THOSE TWO be allowed to make phone calls?" said Glance, after booking Blunt and Radcliff.

"It'll be at least two hours," said Sergeant Ragsdale, the officer in charge of the Butte County Jail's graveyard shift. "We're pretty busy tonight."

"That's perfect," said Glance. He and Calloway would need that much time to drive to Willie's Sacramento River Resort and set up a stakeout before Butch could telephone his father.

"We're always happy to help you fish cops," said Ragsdale. "What were these two doing—fishing without a license?"

Glance laughed at Ragsdale's well-worn joke and asked if he and Calloway could use the office typewriter to knock out a couple of arrest reports.

"Sure, go ahead," said Ragsdale.

Glance's list of charges against Butch Radcliff included resisting a peace officer in the discharge of his duties, snagging salmon, take and possession of an overlimit of salmon, and taking salmon during closed hours. The charges against Travis Blunt were identical but did not include the resisting-arrest violation. Glance asked Ragsdale if he could arrange to have the two arrest reports delivered to the deputy DA handling arraignments later that morning, since he and Calloway would be involved in a stakeout.

"No problem," said Ragsdale. "We'll take your reports over to the courthouse with the prisoners."

"Thanks so much, Alan. Do you mind if we use your phone to call our wives?"

"It's on the desk," said Ragsdale, dashing off to help one of his deputies control an uncooperative prisoner. "Dial nine first to call out."

"Henry, I've been worried about you," said Anne, rubbing her eyes.

"I'm fine, Sweetheart. Tad and I just booked two salmon snaggers, and now we're on our way to set up a stakeout."

"I bet Rose Calloway was happy to hear that."

"Such is the life of a game warden's wife."

"Henry, you need to come up with another line. That one doesn't wear well at 3:00 in the morning."

"I'm sorry, Sweetheart. I didn't know what else to say."

"Say you're coming home to get some sleep. You get so wrapped up in these investigations, it's going to affect your health."

"I agree with what you're saying, but I'm too far into this one to take a break now. Time is critical, so I have to go."

"Please be careful. I love you."

"I love you too. Bye."

Seconds after ending his phone call with Anne, Henry threw caution to the wind and telephoned U.S. Fish and Wildlife Special Agent Kurt Remington. "Hello," said Remington, on the fourth ring.

"Hello, Kurt. This is Hank Glance. I apologize for calling at this hour."

Silence.

"Kurt, are you there?"

"I'm here, Hank. I was just taking a minute to wake up and gather my senses."

"Tad Calloway and I are involved in an investigation that could lead to some serious federal Lacey Act violations. Are you available?"

"You mean now?"

"Sometime after 7:00 this morning, depending on what happens in the next couple hours."

"Just tell me when and where, Hank. I'll be there."

"Do you have a pencil?"

"I'm ready. Go ahead."

It was 3:10 a.m. when Glance ended his conversation with Agent Remington and left the Butte County Jail, in Oroville, with Tad Calloway.

Calloway followed Glance in his own patrol truck as the sleepy wardens plodded north to Chico. Once in Chico, they headed west on Highway 32 and continued north on River Road to a stand of mature valley oaks fifty yards downstream from Willie's Sacramento River Resort.

"We walk from here," whispered Glance, looking at his watch. "If my calculations are correct, Butch should be calling his father right about now."

"It looks like all the lights are off in the trailer park," whispered Calloway, glassing the property with binoculars. "I see a streetlight at the entrance and another one next to what looks like a cinder-block building. Where did you say Willie Radcliff lives?"

"According to Fletcher, he lives in a mansion upriver."

North of the wardens' location and west of the trailer-park entrance sat the restaurant and the utility building Fletcher had described. The restaurant was an Old West-style structure with a wraparound porch and a deck that jutted out onto the grass-covered riverbank. A ten-by-twenty-foot sign reading WILLIE'S SACRAMENTO RIVER RESORT was perched on the restaurant's rooftop.

"I see another light down by the boat dock," whispered Calloway, as he and Glance approached. "By the way, what does Willie Radcliff look like?"

"Fletcher said he's a large man, in his mid-fifties, with an explosive temper."

"I wouldn't have it any other way. What does he drive?"

"He drives around in an old Chevy pickup when he's at the resort. Every time he shifts from first to second, he grinds the gears so badly, you can hear him coming from a mile away."

"That must be him now," said Calloway, following Glance to a row of Leyland cypress trees and hunkering down behind them. Seconds later, a pickup matching Fletcher's description entered the complex, turned left at the restaurant, and cruised down a chip-sealed road to the mobile-home park.

"Where do you think he's going?" said Calloway.

"I have no idea. Did you get a look at the driver?"

"It was too dark to see his face, but I saw a little red flame about eight inches from his nose."

"That has to be Willie Radcliff. Fletcher said he's usually sucking on a big stogie."

"His brake lights just came on at the cinder-block building," said Calloway. "Now he's dropping the tailgate and propping a wooden plank against the pickup bed."

"I don't see him," said Glance. "Where'd he go?"

"He walked behind the building. Here he comes, pushing a wheelbarrow."

While Radcliff loaded the wheelbarrow into the pickup bed, Glance and Calloway sprinted across the restaurant parking lot, dashed around the southeast corner of the restaurant, and ducked under the elevated deck that looked out on the river.

"Here he comes!" said Glance, watching the Chevy pickup cross the restaurant parking lot and swing around to the rear of the attached utility building.

Glance and Calloway scampered to the back of the utility building and peeked around the corner as Radcliff lowered his wheelbarrow to the ground. He then unlocked the utility building, propped a rock in front of the door, and pushed the wheelbarrow inside. The next sound Glance and Calloway heard was the clank of a metal latch on the walk-in-cooler door.

Five minutes had gone by, when the cooler door clanked shut and out came the wheelbarrow, overloaded with salmon carcasses and cottage-cheese containers. Instead of unloading the contraband into his pickup bed, as Glance and Calloway expected him to do, Radcliff turned and hustled down a gravel path to the boat dock.

"I don't believe it," said Calloway. "He's gonna dump it all in the river."

"Not if I can help it," said Glance, jumping to his feet and bounding down the hill after Radcliff. "Department of Fish and Game. Stop right where you are!"

"Try to stop me!" Radcliff shouted back, pushing the wheelbarrow as fast as his draft-horse legs could carry him.

"I'm ordering you not to dump that evidence in the river!"

Radcliff kept running. He was ten feet from the end of the boat dock when Glance grabbed him by the shirt collar and jerked him back, causing the wheelbarrow handles to slip from Radcliff's sweaty hands and sending the wheelbarrow skidding to a stop six inches from the dock's edge.

"You're under arrest!" said Glance, maintaining his grip on Radcliff's collar and reaching for his handcuffs.

"Like hell I am!" shouted Radcliff, thrusting his right elbow to the rear, striking Glance just above the cheekbone and rocking him backwards.

Radcliff had started for the wheelbarrow, when former Downey High School linebacker Tad Calloway came flying through the air and made the tackle of his life. Radcliff's two-hundred-sixty-pound frame slammed against the dock so hard, it caused the wooden planks to buckle and sent waves of river water washing up on shore. Glance and Calloway wrestled Radcliff's arms behind his back and applied the cuffs before he could catch his breath.

TWENTY-FIVE

"Hello, Willie," said Butte County Deputy Sheriff Boyd Hightower. "We meet again."

Radcliff grunted an expletive.

"Thanks for coming," said Glance, helping Hightower and Calloway walk Radcliff over to the caged sheriff's unit and secure him in the back seat.

"Did he do that to you?" said Hightower, closing the car door and walking far enough away so Radcliff couldn't hear.

"I'm afraid so," said Glance.

"Wha'd he do, coldcock you?"

"He caught me with his elbow out there on the dock."

"Radcliff was about to dump a wheelbarrow full of evidence into the river," said Calloway.

"I suggest you have one of your warden buddies take a photograph while it's still swollen like that," said Hightower, pointing at Glance's face. "I had to do the same thing the night I came here to break up a party and that ornery SOB knocked my tooth out."

"I will," said Glance. "Thanks for the advice."

"What would you like me to put on the booking sheet?"

"PC 148 should work for now," said Glance, referring to the *California Penal Code* section for resisting arrest. "I'll have a formal arrest report at the DA's office by 9:00 this morning."

"Sounds good. What are you guys up to, anyway?"

"Kurt Remington and I are going to Sacramento to request a federal search-and-seizure warrant," said Glance. "Tad and Jack Mayberry will secure Radcliff Mansion until we return."

"Radcliff Mansion?" said Hightower. "I responded to a domestic disturbance there a couple months ago."

"Do you mind if I ask what prompted the call?" said Glance.

"Willie doesn't just hit cops and game wardens."

"Who else did he hit?"

"His wife."

Glance shook his head in disgust. "I have to run up to the mansion and write down a description of the place for the search warrant. How far north on River Road is it?"

"About a half mile. You can't miss the gaudy iron archway."

"Thanks again for responding, Boyd. And I really appreciate your advice about documenting what Radcliff did to my face. It must be getting close to the end of your shift."

"No problem, Hank. I'll see if I can talk the day-shift duty sergeant into sending a deputy out to the mansion this afternoon. No telling what Willie will do if he bails out of jail and finds you fish cops searching his house."

The sun was peeking over the horizon when Deputy Hightower pulled away from Willie's Sacramento River Resort. As Hightower turned right and headed toward Highway 32, he passed a dark-green Dodge Power Wagon headed in the opposite direction. Glance had requested that Warden Jack Mayberry meet him and Calloway in the restaurant parking lot.

"Jack, thanks for coming," said Glance, climbing into his patrol truck. "It may be late afternoon before Kurt Remington and I return from Sacramento with a federal search warrant. Tad will fill you in on the situation."

"Jack and I will photograph and secure the evidence out on the dock before we head up to the mansion," said Calloway.

"Thanks, Tad," said Glance, starting to drive away. He drove to the east end of the parking lot then stopped and walked back.

"Wha'd ya forget?" said Calloway.

Glance removed a ring of keys from his pocket and tossed it to him.

"Where'd ya get these?"

"They fell out of Radcliff's pocket when you tackled him. I picked them up so they wouldn't fall through the cracks and into the river."

ANNE WAS LOADING SCHOOL SUPPLIES AND a folder full of corrected papers into her 1966 Chevy Chevelle when her face lit up at the sight of Henry's patrol truck rolling up the long, gravel driveway.

"Henry, what happened to your face?" she said as Henry greeted her with a kiss and a hug.

"I got elbowed by the man we just arrested."

"You poor dear," said Anne, lightly touching her husband's right cheekbone.

Henry flinched.

"I'm sorry. Does it hurt badly?"

"I'll be all right."

"All right, my foot! You need to see a doctor."

"That will have to wait. Kurt and I are going to Sacramento to get a search warrant."

"Who's Kurt?"

"He's coming up the driveway right now."

Muscularly built, with sandy-brown hair just over his ears, thirty-two-year-old Kurt Remington stepped from his beige-colored undercover van and walked up to greet the Glances.

"Anne, this is U.S. Fish and Wildlife Special Agent Kurt Remington. He transferred into the Chico agent's position after Bob Northrup retired."

"Nice to meet you, Kurt. I'd love to stay and talk, but our principal has scheduled a staff meeting for 7:30 and I have to go. Henry, will I see you when I get home this evening?"

"That depends on how long it takes us to get the search warrant in Sacramento and search a mansion nine miles west of Chico."

"When were you planning on getting some sleep? Never mind—I already know the answer to that question." Anne kissed Henry goodbye and drove off to work.

Glance led Remington up the back steps of the rented farmhouse and into the kitchen. "I hope this works," he said, grabbing the phone and dialing the number Martin Fletcher had given him. "Our success today may depend on it."

"Hello," came a woman's voice.

"Hello. This is Warden Hank Glance with the Department of Fish and Game. I was given this number by Martin Fletcher."

"Yes, Warden Glance. Martin told me you may be calling. I'm going to let you speak with him."

"Thank you."

"Hello, Warden Glance. I hope everything went well after I left last night."

"It went as well as possible, Martin. Is your friend willing to meet with us this morning?"

"We just had a long talk about that, and Rebecca has agreed to meet with you. What time will you be here?"

"How does 10:00 sound?"

"Just a minute, I'll ask." Fletcher returned to the phone. "Rebecca says that will be fine. Her Chico address is on the card I gave you."

"We're in business!" said Glance, hanging up the kitchen phone and handing the receiver to Remington. "Now you'd better make your calls."

Agent Remington telephoned his supervisor at the U.S. Fish and Wildlife office in Sacramento. After a short conversation with the agent in charge, he telephoned the U.S. Attorney's Office, also in Sacramento, and made arrangements to meet with one of the federal prosecutors that afternoon at 2:00.

With all three of the important phone calls made, Glance led Remington into the farmhouse's vintage-1930s dining room.

"My wife would love these wainscoted walls," said Remington.

"This is my favorite room in the house," said Glance. "It's situated so the morning sun comes in through those east-facing windows. Anne likes to snuggle up in the window seat and read on Sunday mornings during the wintertime."

While Remington explored the old farmhouse, Glance typed Willie Radcliff's preliminary arrest report—charging him with battery on a peace officer, resisting arrest, obstructing a peace officer in the performance of his duties, and possession of unlawfully taken salmon.

Glance and Remington left the farmhouse at 8:15 a.m. and raced to the Butte County District Attorney's Office, in Oroville. Henry handed his arrest report to Deputy DA Will Freeman as Freeman was leaving for the 9:00 arraignments.

"When was the last time you slept?" said Freeman, noticing the dark circles under Glance's eyes. "And what happened to the side of your face?"

"Can't talk now," said Glance, racing back to the parking lot. "You'll read all about it in the report."

"WOW! MY WIFE WOULD LOVE TO see the inside of this house," said Remington, as he and Glance pulled up in front of a vintage Craftsman bungalow near Chico's Bidwell Park. "She has her heart set on finding a home like this that we can afford."

"Many of the houses in this neighborhood are like this. Anne's parents and her two sisters live in a Dutch Colonial a few blocks from here."

Martin Fletcher greeted Glance and Remington at the curb and led them up the wooden steps to a covered, wraparound front porch where Rebecca Radcliff sat waiting.

"Rebecca, this is Warden Hank Glance and U.S. Fish and Wildlife Agent Kurt Remington," said Fletcher.

"It's very nice to meet you both," said Rebecca. "Please sit down and make yourselves comfortable."

Glance sat in an antique, mission-style rocking chair while Remington chose an oak-framed loveseat.

"We really appreciate your agreeing to meet with us," said Glance.

"Yes, we do," said Remington. "I can't get over how beautiful your house is."

"Thank you," said Rebecca, her hands noticeably shaking as she checked through her notes.

"Anything you're willing to tell us about Mr. Radcliff's trophy collection would be helpful," said Glance. "We're also interested in any records he might have kept."

"William keeps his trophy room under lock and key," said Rebecca. "I've been inside three times—twice by myself and once when I showed it to Martin."

"How did you get inside?" said Remington.

"The key to the trophy room is inside a little metal box. The magnetized box is attached to the inside wall of the safe, and the safe is inside my husband's office."

"I take it you know the combination to the safe?" said Glance.

"Yes. When the Radcliff Farms office building was sold, the safe was removed and brought to Radcliff Mansion. I already knew the combination from all my years as Radcliff Farms' chief financial officer. I've written it on this piece of paper for you."

Glance walked over to accept the paper. In doing so, he noticed Rebecca's hands had stopped trembling.

"You'll find a diagram of the house on the other side," said Rebecca. "It shows where to find the safe and my husband's trophy room."

"This is so helpful," said Glance.

"Glad I could help. If you gentlemen are looking for records of William's hunting transgressions, you'll find them in the safe. His journal contains information about every animal in the mansion: when he killed it, where he killed it, whom he paid for the privilege of killing it, and how much he paid to kill it. Also inside the safe are two small file cabinets filled with photographs."

"What do you remember seeing in Mr. Radcliff's trophy room?" said Remington.

"The first thing you'll see when you walk through the doorway is a nine-foot Alaskan brown bear standing on his hind legs. William describes in his journal how he killed it on what was supposed to be a legal moose hunt."

"You seem to know your wildlife," said Glance.

Rebecca smiled. "I started out as a zoology major, switched to agriculture, and ended up serving as Radcliff Farms' chief financial officer for twenty-four years."

"You'll find that Rebecca is quite an accomplished woman," said Fletcher.

"We're beginning to realize that," said Remington. "What other wildlife do you remember seeing in Mr. Radcliff's trophy room?"

"I remember several big cats, deer, elk, a black bear, a bighorn sheep, and a pronghorn. Mementos from William's fishing trips also cover the walls."

"Were the mammals full-body mounts, like the Alaskan brown bear, or were they shoulder mounts?" said Glance.

"All of the big cats are full-body mounts. The other mammals are what you refer to as shoulder mounts."

"They're hanging on the walls?" said Remington.

"Yes," said Rebecca, "along with the fish."

"Do you remember anything else about the items in your husband's trophy room?" said Glance, taking notes.

"Yes. I've saved this item for last because it upset me so much."

"Agent Remington and I are eager to hear about it."

"I was upstairs in the mansion on June 16 of this year, when a delivery truck pulled up in the driveway. I watched the driver and my husband unload a large wooden crate and roll it into the house. William locked whatever it was in his trophy room. The next morning, while William was down at the resort, I removed the key from his safe and investigated. The crate had been opened, and there it was—a magnificent Siberian tiger staring back at me from inside a glass case."

"Are you sure it was June 16 when the crate arrived, and are you sure it was a Siberian tiger?" said Glance.

"Yes, and yes. I wrote about it in my diary, and I read about the tiger in William's journal. He killed it March 12, 1973, on a trip to Far Eastern Russia. Two weeks after the tiger was delivered, I opened William's safe and found a letter stapled inside his journal. The letter was postmarked Sausalito, California. I copied what it said on this piece of paper."

Rebecca handed the sheet of paper to Glance. It read:

> Our records show that the finished product was delivered
> to 160 River Road, Chico, California, on June 16, 1973.
> Payment is due upon receipt.

"Do you know how much your husband paid to kill the tiger?" said Glance.

"It's in the journal, along with the letter I just told you about and an earlier letter from the same person. William made three payments: one for $50,000, one for $125,000, and the last one for $75,000."

"A quarter million dollars?" said Glance.

"Yes, my husband paid a quarter million dollars to satisfy his enormous ego. I know those figures are correct because I found the corresponding withdrawals in one of our bank accounts. William and I no longer live together, but I still keep the books."

"Interesting," said Remington.

"William is meticulous about his hunting journal, but he has no clue how to keep accurate books for multimillion-dollar accounts. I managed

Radcliff Farms' books for twenty-four years, so I have plenty of experience."

"Who keeps the resort's books?" said Glance.

"I do. If I didn't, William would already be bankrupt."

"Are there photographs of this tiger you told us about?" said Glance.

"Six of them," said Rebecca. "Each one shows William standing over the tiger, like the great white hunter, with a rifle in his hand."

"Are there any other people in those six photographs?" said Remington.

"One photograph shows a tall, thin man in the background. I don't think he wanted to be in the picture, because his hand is raised and partially covers his face."

"Is his face identifiable at all?" said Remington.

"It may be, if you have a way to blow up the image."

"And these photographs are all in the safe?" said Glance.

"Yes. They're filed chronologically."

"How do you think your husband will react when he finds out you're cooperating with us?" said Glance. "I understand that he's been physically abusive in the past."

"During the early years, William's abuse was strictly verbal. I think his mother would have disinherited him had he hit me. After Molly died and William inherited the Radcliff Farms fortune, things got worse."

"In what way?" said Remington.

"Being a CPA and Radcliff Farms' chief financial officer, I made the mistake of questioning William's decision to sell the company and squander millions of dollars on that glorified trailer park down the road from the mansion. He was determined to prove he could be just as successful in business as his father."

"And Mr. Radcliff didn't appreciate your questioning him?" said Remington.

"He showed his appreciation by slapping me across the face."

"Did he hit you on any other occasions?" said Glance.

"Two others," said Rebecca. "The last time, he also threatened to throw me out of the second-story window. William spent that night in jail, and I moved out the next morning. That was two months ago, when Deputy Hightower came."

"Are you okay financially?" said Glance.

"Yes. Thanks to Molly Radcliff, I'm secure in that category."

TWENTY-SIX

G LANCE AND REMINGTON THANKED REBECCA RADCLIFF and Martin Fletcher for their help and drove directly to the U.S. Fish and Wildlife office in Sacramento, where U.S. Fish and Wildlife Special Agent in Charge Roy Campbell maintained the necessary search-and-seizure warrant templates. Since the officers were requesting a federal search-and-seizure warrant, U.S. Fish and Wildlife Special Agent Kurt Remington would act as the affiant. Remington prepared the necessary documents—an affidavit in support of a federal search warrant and a federal search-and-seizure warrant—using probable-cause information collected and put together by Glance and Remington.

While the documents were being prepared, Glance telephoned the California Department of Fish and Game Records Division, asking if William Lawson Radcliff had ever submitted a Declaration of Importation, required of anyone importing a legally taken and legally possessed bird, mammal, fish, reptile, or amphibian into California from another state or country. Only one Declaration of Importation had ever been submitted by William Lawson Radcliff; it was submitted in September 1970 for an Alaskan moose.

Agent Campbell contacted U.S. Fish and Wildlife Service headquarters, in Washington D.C., and asked if William Lawson Radcliff had ever legally imported trophy big game of any kind into the United States. Records showed that Radcliff had legally killed a male African lion, a female African lion, and a male leopard in 1967. He had imported mounted trophies of these mammals from South Africa into the United States by means of a common carrier. No other federal permits had ever been issued to Radcliff.

"Based on everything I've learned about Willie Radcliff, including all the big-game mammals my informants have seen in Radcliff's trophy room, it surprises me that he's killed or imported anything in accordance with the law," said Glance.

"He must have made a mistake and hired a legitimate outfitter for the South Africa trip," scoffed Campbell.

"You sound like you've had some experience with South African hunting guides," said Glance.

"I tagged along on a two-week safari with a friend of mine a couple years ago."

"Was your friend successful?"

"He killed a cape buffalo. The outfitter caped it out, prepared the hide so it wouldn't spoil, and recommended a reputable African taxidermist. When it was time to ship my friend's shoulder-mounted trophy to the United States, the outfitter made sure all the required permits were shipped with it."

"We're all set," said Remington, walking into Campbell's office with a set of prepared documents in hand. "Our appointment with the federal prosecutor is in a half hour, so Hank and I should get going."

"Have you gentlemen thought about what you're going to do with all those mounted trophies?" said Campbell. "They take up a lot of room, they don't do well under extreme temperatures, and they hate the bright sunlight."

"I've reserved a seventeen-foot U-Haul truck in Chico," said Glance.

"That's fine and good, but where are you planning on storing the trophies?"

"In the storeroom behind this office," said Remington. "Once they're forfeited by the court, we'll probably donate them to Chico State and some of the other educational institutions."

"What did our business manager have to say about your keeping them in the storeroom?"

"He said he'd give me a year to get them out."

"Good," said Campbell. "I'm glad you two have thought this out and aren't going off half-cocked."

"Mr. Marsden, Agent Remington and Warden Glance are here for their 2:00 appointment," said Marsden's secretary through the open doorway.

"Send them in," came a young-sounding male voice.

The walls of Marsden's office were covered with framed awards and certificates, each one issued to Heathcliff R. Marsden. As Marsden pushed aside a pile of case folders, Glance and Remington perused a series of framed photographs: Marsden shaking hands with Governor Ronald Reagan, Marsden receiving an award from the dean of the UC Davis School of Law, and Marsden standing next to former U.S. Attorney General John Mitchell.

"Come in and sit down," said the young prosecutor with a firm hand-shake and a welcoming smile. An inch or two shorter than Glance and Remington with neatly trimmed blond hair, Assistant U.S. Attorney Heath Marsden appeared to be in his late twenties.

"We have an affidavit and a search-and-seizure warrant for you to review," said Remington, placing the papers on Marsden's desk.

Marsden was preoccupied with Glance's uniform. "I once thought about becoming a game warden," he said.

"What changed your mind?" said Glance.

"After graduating from Chico State, I wasn't sure what I wanted to do. My dad wanted me to get a law degree and come to work for his firm. I wasn't excited about being a defense attorney, but I went ahead and entered law school anyway."

"You must have done pretty well," said Remington.

Marsden laughed. "I did so well the school gave me my own office. After acing the bar exam, a job was waiting for me here."

"I graduated from Chico State, also," said Glance.

"I thought you looked familiar."

"You probably saw him on the front page of *The Bee*," said Remington. "Remember the story of the game warden up in Gridley who disappeared back in 1956? It was a cold case for thirteen years until Hank came along. He's the officer who solved the mystery."

"That's where I've seen you before! Everyone in this office was talking about it the day that article came out. Hey, Susan, we have a celebrity in here."

"I'm on the phone," said Marsden's secretary.

Uncomfortable with the attention he was receiving, Glance smiled and pointed to the documents on Marsden's desk. "We have two wardens securing the house we're going to search," he said. "I'm concerned that the person you're going to read about in the affidavit will bail out of jail and cause them serious trouble."

"Then let's get down to business," said Marsden. The more he read, the more engrossed he became. Each time Marsden finished reading a page and proceeded to the next, he looked over at the two wildlife officers and shook his head.

Marsden's secretary appeared in the doorway. "Did you want something?" she said.

"Yes, Susan," said Marsden, signing off on the documents and handing them to her. "When you've finished making copies, I'm going to walk these gentlemen over to Judge Sanford's office."

The Honorable Matthew B. Sanford was the only district-court judge available that day. He was involved in a painfully boring trial at the time. When the judge's secretary handed him a note saying Heath Marsden and two wildlife officers were waiting to have a search-and-seizure warrant signed, Sanford tapped the bench with his gavel and said, "Court is adjourned until tomorrow morning at 9:00." Judge Sanford reviewed and signed the warrant, reminded Marsden about the following Saturday's golf date at Ancil Hoffman Park, and wished the officers good luck.

"My calendar is clear tomorrow," said Marsden. "Is there any chance of my accompanying you officers on the search this evening?"

"Absolutely!" said Glance. "We'd consider it an honor to have you along."

"What would you think about my dropping my car off at my parents' house in Chico and riding out to the search site with one of you?"

"That will work," said Remington.

Glance and Remington left the U.S. Attorney's Office at 3:45 on the afternoon of September 10, 1973. Glance dropped Remington off at the Chico U-Haul facility, picked up Marsden at his parents' house near East First Avenue, and headed west on Highway 32. Glance and Marsden

approached Radcliff Mansion at 5:05. A heated conversation was in progress at the top of the front-porch steps.

"This is what I was afraid of," said Glance, reaching for the truck-door
handle. "That big thug doing all the shouting is Willie Radcliff."

Warden Calloway broke away from the squabble between Radcliff and
Mayberry and ran down the porch steps to meet Glance. "Boy, am I glad
to see you!"

"How long has Radcliff been here?"

"About fifteen minutes. He ordered Jack and me off his property and
demanded that I turn over the keys to his house. I told him a search warrant was on the way and if he went inside, we'd have to go with him."

"Whad he say to that?"

"His exact words were—"

"Never mind—I can guess. Warden Tad Calloway, this is Assistant U.S.
Attorney Heath Marsden."

"Nice to meet you," said Calloway, shaking Marsden's hand. "Hank, I'm
afraid if Radcliff pokes Jack with his finger one more time, all hell is going
to break loose."

Glance walked up the steps to Radcliff, handed him a copy of the federal search-and-seizure warrant, and said, "Mr. Radcliff, this is a lawful
warrant to search your house and seize any items we have probable cause
to believe are illegally possessed."

As Radcliff read the warrant, Agent Remington roared up the driveway
in a U-Haul truck.

"What's that truck doing here?" shouted Radcliff. He threw his copy
of the warrant down on the porch, rumbled down the steps, and almost
knocked Marsden over as he stormed down the driveway. "Get the hell off
my property!" shouted Radcliff, waving his fist in the air.

"I see why you were so concerned," said Marsden, as Glance ran down
the steps in pursuit of Radcliff.

Radcliff was about to accost Agent Remington, when Glance caught up
with him. "Mr. Radcliff, the document I gave you should have explained
why we're here."

"I'll kill the first one of you who tries to remove anything from my
house!" shouted Radcliff, clenching his right fist and telegraphing a
punch to Glance's face. Glance ducked the blow, wrapped his arm around

Radcliff's bull-like neck, and heaved him over his hip. Radcliff landed on the pavement with a thud, then Glance, Calloway, and Mayberry rolled him over, wrestled his arms behind his back, and applied the cuffs for the second time that day.

"I'll get you for this!" Radcliff shouted at Glance.

"Should I radio the sheriff's office and ask them to send out a caged unit?" said Calloway.

"That won't be necessary," said Mayberry. "There's one coming up the driveway now."

Radcliff's nonstop tirade ended abruptly when he saw Butte County Deputy Sheriff Ron Hilliard climb out of the sheriff's unit. Soft-spoken and as big as a house, Hilliard was a dead ringer for Western TV star Clint Walker—so much so, his fellow law-enforcement officers had christened him with the moniker Cheyenne.

"Boyd Hightower asked me to come by and check on you fish cops," said Hilliard, smiling. "Is that my buddy Willie on the ground over there?"

"Your buddy likes the county jail so much, he can't wait to go back," said Mayberry. "Hank, why don't you guys get started. I'll help Ron with Mr. Radcliff."

"Thanks, Jack."

"Are these your cuffs?" said Hilliard to Mayberry.

"No. They belong to Hank."

"I'll take them off and replace them with mine. That way Hank can have his back."

"Are you sure you want to do that?" said Mayberry. "It took three of us to put those cuffs on. His wrists are so large, we were down to the last click."

"Willie's not going to give me any trouble, are you, Willie?"

Radcliff didn't respond.

While Glance, Calloway, Remington, and Marsden climbed the steps to Radcliff Mansion, Warden Mayberry helped Deputy Hilliard load Radcliff into the caged sheriff's unit.

"What's all this about?" said Hilliard, after Radcliff had been secured and the officers were out of earshot.

"We're serving a federal search-and-seizure warrant," said Mayberry.

"Let me guess. Does this have something to do with Willie's big-game collection?"

"How did you know about that?"

"A few of the businessmen in Chico come here once a month to play cards. I arrested one of them for DUI the other night. He told me all about the stuffed animals during his ride to the county jail."

"Whad he say?"

"He blabbered somethin' about Willie paying a quarter million dollars to kill a tiger in the Soviet Union. I asked if he'd actually seen the tiger. He said he had and that Willie has a trophy room filled with animals from all over the world."

TWENTY-SEVEN

A GENT REMINGTON REACHED INTO HIS FOLDER and pulled out Rebecca Radcliff's hand-drawn diagram as the search team climbed the steps to Radcliff Mansion and walked across the wraparound covered porch to the front door.

"Tad, I hope you still have that key ring I gave you this morning," said Glance.

"It's right here," said Calloway, removing it from his pocket and handing it to Glance. "If you hadn't shown up when you did, I might have had to wrestle Radcliff to keep it."

Everyone laughed.

Glance unlocked the door and stepped back. "Kurt, since you're the affiant, why don't you do the honors."

It had been decided beforehand that Glance and Remington would supervise the search, Calloway would carry the clipboard and manage the evidence log, Mayberry would take necessary photographs, and Assistant U.S. Attorney Heath Marsden would simply observe.

Having waited until Deputy Hilliard transported Willie Radcliff off the premises, Mayberry ran up the steps and entered the forty-four-year-old mansion. He caught up with the rest of the search team as they were navigating the long hallway on the south side of the house and about to enter Willie Radcliff's office.

"Thanks so much for taking care of that," said Glance.

"No problem," said Mayberry. "I'm glad Hilliard showed up when he did. He saved us a lot of time and trouble."

"He sure did," said Glance. "Before the rest of us go inside, I think you should photograph the office in its existing condition."

"Good idea," said Mayberry. "I'll photograph it again as we leave."

In the corner of Willie Radcliff's carpeted office sat a coal-black safe, sixty inches high and forty-two inches wide. Using the combination Rebecca Radcliff had provided, Remington turned the dial and swung open the heavy metal door to a lifetime of wildlife crimes. Radcliff's journal, two metal file cabinets filled with photographs, and a magnetic metal box containing the key to Radcliff's trophy room would reveal his well-kept secrets.

Rebecca Radcliff had forgotten to tell Glance and Remington that her husband's ten-by-thirteen-inch, leatherbound journal was secured by leather straps attached to a metal locking device.

"I thought things were going a little too smoothly," said Calloway. "Now what do we do?"

"I have a pocketknife," said Mayberry.

Glance pulled Radcliff's key ring from his pocket and searched it for the appropriately sized key. "Let's try this," he said, turning the key in the miniature lock.

Radcliff's journal opened to a treasure trove of incriminating evidence: handwritten notes and descriptions, letters, business cards, and receipts. The journal and two metal file cabinets containing photographs were seized and Calloway made the appropriate notations in the evidence log.

Before closing and relocking the safe, Remington reached inside and pulled out the small magnetic box containing the key to Willie Radcliff's trophy room.

"Let me see that key," said Glance, comparing it with one of the keys on Radcliff's key ring. "This one is identical, so you might as well put that one back in the safe."

"That key ring has sure come in handy," said Marsden.

"Yes, it has," said Glance. "We can thank Tad and his tackling skills for that."

"What about the moose head?" said Mayberry.

"Go ahead and photograph it," said Glance, "but the moose stays here. According to our records, Radcliff killed it and imported it into California legally."

"That's hard to believe," mumbled Calloway.

"I thought so too," said Remington.

No other items of interest were found in Radcliff's office, so Mayberry photographed it one last time and the search team proceeded back up the hallway, through the parlor, and into the north side of the mansion. When they came to an elaborately crafted set of teakwood double doors, Glance said, "Let's enter cautiously, being extra careful around anything that might be breakable or harmful to our health."

Glance unlocked and opened the doors. A nine-foot Alaskan brown bear guarded the entryway.

"Wow!" said Mayberry, snapping photographs. "How would you like to have this guy poke his head into your tent some night?"

"They're a lot larger than they appear on TV," said Marsden. "His head probably weighs more than I do."

"It's going to be a chore getting him into the U-Haul," said Glance. "I hope the four of us can manage it."

"I'd be happy to help," said Marsden, "but because I might end up prosecuting this case, it's better that I just observe and not participate in the seizing of evidence."

"I haven't seen anything like this since I was eight years old, visiting the San Diego Natural History Museum in Balboa Park," said Glance.

The stench of cigar smoke wafted from the card table at the center of the room as the search team entered. Rhythmically spaced throughout the 600-square-foot trophy room were a full-body mounted male African lion, a full-body mounted female African lion, a full-body mounted jaguar, a full-body mounted leopard, a full-body mounted mountain lion, and a full-body mounted Siberian tiger.

All four walls were adorned with shoulder-mounted big-game mammals, including a California black bear, a seven-point Roosevelt elk, a full-curl Sierra Nevada bighorn, and what Calloway proclaimed was a Boon and Crocket-sized pronghorn. Interspersed with the mammals on the walls were skin mounts and fiberglass replicas of trophy fish Radcliff had caught and probably boasted about at one time or another.

"Look at this," said Calloway, "a gold engraved plaque claiming this catfish is a California state record."

"I bet he didn't have a fishing license when he caught it," said Remington. "He probably had the plaque made himself."

"Nobody's gonna take that bet," said Glance. "Look at this thresher shark. Its tail stretches all the way to the ceiling."

Other fish on display were a fifteen-foot black marlin, a sailfish, a tarpon, a South American peacock bass, a giant sea bass, and a bluefin tuna.

Rebecca Radcliff's descriptions had been spot-on. Over the next four hours, the search team carefully examined every mounted specimen in the room. In each case, they considered when it was taken, where it was taken, who—besides Willie Radcliff—had been involved, payments Radcliff had made, who had done the taxidermy work, and whether or not the specimen was currently illegal to possess. All of the seizures were based on the wildlife officers' knowledge of state and federal wildlife regulations and information and photographs found in Willie Radcliff's safe. The seized mounts were tagged, photographed, and loaded into the U-Haul.

When the search team had completed their task, final photographs were taken and the trophy room was locked. Remington placed a copy of the evidence log on a shelf by the front door. After locking the front door, the search team assembled on the circular driveway at the bottom of the porch steps.

"I was impressed by the professional way you gentlemen conducted the search," said Marsden.

"How did you like the way we handled Radcliff?" said Calloway.

"I thought we were off to the races when he took a swing at Hank, but before I knew it, that big lug was face down on the pavement with his arms cuffed behind his back."

"We owe that to Jack Mayberry," said Calloway. "He's our expert at hand-to-hand combat, self-defense, and cuffing techniques."

"No kidding?" said Marsden.

"No kidding. Jack drums it into us every other month during our all-day training sessions. I thought it was a waste of time at first, but dealing with brutes like Radcliff has made a believer out of me."

"I've also taught you not to use any more force than is necessary to subdue the recalcitrant," said Mayberry. "I know cops who would have kicked Radcliff in the slats after what he did to Hank. Not Golden Boy—he reached for his handcuffs."

"Speaking of Hank," said Marsden, "where did he go?"

"He's sawing logs over in the seat of his pickup," said Calloway. "Hank and I have been working this case for thirty straight hours without sleep. The only reason I'm still awake is the thermos of coffee in my truck."

"And Hank doesn't drink coffee?" said Marsden.

"Tell him, Jack," said Calloway.

"Golden Boy subsists on a diet of milk and cookies."

Everyone laughed.

"What's all the commotion about?" said Glance, appearing suddenly.

"I'm afraid we've been having fun at your expense," said Marsden. "Where were you and Kurt planning on parking that U-Haul full of animals tonight?"

"It's probably not a good idea to park it on the street in front of my house," said Remington.

"I'll park it in our barn," said Glance. "Kurt, why don't you take my pickup and bring it back tomorrow afternoon. I was thinking we could all meet at my place about 1:00. We can talk about the evidence we just seized and how we're going to proceed with the investigation."

"Great idea!" said Remington. "I'll drop our esteemed assistant U.S. attorney off at his parents' house on my way home."

"One o'clock works for me," said Calloway.

"Me too," said Mayberry. "If you'd like, I can run Radcliff's keys out to the jail on my way to your place."

"I'm afraid I won't be able to make it," said Marsden. "I have to be in court tomorrow."

"Understood," said Glance. "Heath, it's been a pleasure having you as part of the team."

"The pleasure was all mine, Hank. I'd appreciate either you or Kurt calling me once a week and letting me know how the investigation is progressing."

"You can count on it," said Glance.

BOTH HANDS ON HENRY'S WATCH WERE straight up when he locked the barn door and trudged up the back steps to the kitchen.

"My God!" said Anne, dressed in her bathrobe and slippers. "The side of your face looks even worse than it did this morning. What is going on?"

"I'm not sure where to start," said Henry, removing his gun belt and hanging it on a hook in the kitchen.

"Start by kissing your wife and giving me one of those bear hugs I love so much. I'm worried about you!"

"Nothing to worry about."

"Have you looked in the mirror lately? You're going to see the doctor tomorrow!"

"Uh . . . maybe Friday, if it doesn't look any better. Tomorrow is going to be a busy day."

"Henry, what am I going to do with you? You get so wrapped up in these investigations, you refuse to take care of yourself."

"I appreciate your concern, Sweetheart, but what I need most right now is a good night's sleep."

"Have you had anything to eat?"

"Kurt and I grabbed a sandwich about 1:00 this afternoon, on our way to Sacramento."

"That's what I thought. Why don't I make you a fried-egg sandwich while you take a shower?"

"That sounds great," said Henry, staggering into the bedroom, kicking off his boots, and lying back on the bed.

"What would you like on your sandwich besides ketchup and mustard?" shouted Anne from the kitchen.

Henry was already back in Oceanside, this time riding that monster wave all the way to the beach.

TWENTY-EIGHT

HENRY HAD SLEPT LIKE A BABY after working thirty hours straight and executing the search-and-seizure warrant at Radcliff Mansion. When Anne climbed out of bed at 6:00 a.m., her husband popped up right behind her.

"Henry, why don't you stay in bed and get some more rest?"

"I want to go through all that stuff on the dining-room table before everyone gets here."

"What time are they coming? I hope it's not before I leave for work."

"Not to worry. We're meeting at 1:00 to go through the evidence and talk about the Radcliff case."

Anne just shook her head.

After breakfast, Henry brushed his teeth, kissed Anne goodbye at 7:30, and spent the next five and a half hours probing Willie Radcliff's records.

"Hank, I'm worried about you," said Remington, the first to arrive. "I hope you weren't up doing this all night."

"No. I got a good night's sleep," said Glance, watching out the dining-room window as Calloway and Mayberry arrived in Mayberry's new Dodge Power Wagon.

"What have you learned?" said Remington.

"A lot," said Glance, leaving to meet Calloway and Mayberry at the back door.

"Why don't you all have a seat around the table," said Glance, leading Calloway and Mayberry into the dining room. "I'd offer you coffee, but I don't know how to make it."

Mayberry and Calloway looked at each other and nodded.

"In early September 1970, Willie Radcliff went on a moose-hunting trip to Alaska with two men, named Roy Strode and Rudd Hostetter," said Glance. "As near as I can figure, Strode and Hostetter introduced him to a local guide named Clint Neevee. Neevee took the three of them on a guided hunt, which resulted in Radcliff killing a trophy bull moose."

"And that's the one hanging in his office?" said Mayberry.

"Yes. I'll read a passage about it from Radcliff's journal. It's dated September 9, 1970."

> This morning, Clint Neevee drove Roy Strode, Rudd Hostetter, and me to a secluded pond where a trophy bull moose had been coming to feed. Roy and Rudd waited in the Jeep while Clint and I crept up to the pond for a peek. There he was, the biggest moose I'd ever seen, standing neck-deep in the water, feeding on pond weeds. I was preparing to fire when Clint tapped me on the shoulder and asked how I felt about swimming in forty-degree water and dragging a three-quarter-ton moose with five-foot antlers back to shore. We waited two more hours before the moose finished his breakfast, waded to shore, and I finally got my shot.

"He even filed a Declaration of Importation with the California Department of Fish and Game before bringing it into the state," said Glance, holding up Radcliff's copies of permits from Alaska and California.

"Is Neevee a licensed guide?" said Remington.

"Based on Radcliff's records, Neevee was a licensed guide at the time the moose was killed. Neevee is now in prison for knifing a man in an Anchorage bar fight."

"These are nice people Radcliff hangs out with," said Calloway. "How did you find out about the knifing?"

"One of the wardens I attended the Riverside Sheriff's Academy with ended up quitting our department and going to work for Alaska Department of Fish and Game. He took a warden's position in Kodiak, Alaska, and has been a wealth of information ever since."

"What's his name?" said Calloway.

"Paul Comstock."

"I remember him. He was the warden in Baker when I first came on the job. Let me think: Would I rather be stationed in one of the hottest places on Earth or a wildlife paradise like Kodiak, Alaska?"

"There's another reason Bob wanted to go to Kodiak," said Glance. "His brother, Neil, is a Coast Guard helicopter pilot at the air station up there."

"We'd better pick up the pace," said Remington. "We have a lot to do today."

"I agree," said Glance. "This next passage from Radcliff's journal is dated September 13, 1970—four days after he killed the moose."

> This morning before daylight, Clint drove the three of us
> north for fifty miles before shifting into four-wheel drive
> and following a jeep trail to an open meadow with a stream
> running through it. Roy asked Clint if this was where he'd
> dumped the bait. Clint said it was and he and Rudd would
> be wise to stay in the jeep until they heard a shot or we
> returned. Clint and I hiked along the edge of the meadow
> for a hundred yards or so before smelling the stench of rot-
> ting flesh and hearing a lot of grunting and groaning going
> on. Clint said the road-kill moose calf he'd dumped was
> right around the next bend and I should be ready to fire
> at a moment's notice. He was also carrying a rifle, in case I
> missed. We crept around the bend to find a huge Alaskan
> brown bear feeding on the carcass. I put a bullet behind his
> left shoulder before he even knew we were there.

"Radcliff goes on to say that Neevee drove Strode and Hostetter to the kill site, where the two of them gutted and skinned the bear."

Glance passed around two photographs showing Radcliff standing next to the bear with a rifle in his hands. Flanking Radcliff were two mid-dle-aged men believed to be Roy Strode and Rudd Hostetter. "I checked with the Alaska Department of Fish and Game," said Glance. "There is no record of William Lawson Radcliff ever being issued a permit to kill a bear of any kind in Alaska."

"Are you sure the other two men in the photographs are Roy Strode and Rudd Hostetter?" said Remington.

"I'm ninety-nine percent sure," said Glance. "I ordered photographs of Strode and Hostetter from DMV this morning. They should arrive in a few days. Unless I'm mistaken, Roy Strode is a relative of Gooseneck Strode, a legendary duck poacher here in the valley. Hostetter is a well-known taxidermist with a studio in Quincy; I suspect he processed the bear hide and smuggled it back to his studio, along with the legally taken moose. According to Radcliff's journal, he paid Hostetter $9,450 for the moose shoulder mount and the full-body bear mount. There's no mention of what he paid Strode for his services."

"This is clearly a federal Lacey Act violation," said Agent Remington. "The bear was illegally taken in Alaska, therefore, it was illegally imported into California."

"Then you should handle it, with able assistance from Golden Boy here," said Mayberry.

"Jack, would you mind dropping the Golden Boy stuff?" said Glance. "It makes me uncomfortable."

"Sorry, Hank. You're a hard act to follow. Sometimes it makes us mortals feel a little inadequate."

"Lighten up, Hank," said Calloway. "If Jack didn't respect you, he wouldn't be kidding around."

"If you state game wardens have settled your little spat, can we move on?" said Remington. "We still have a truck full of animal mounts to drop off at the Fish and Wildlife office in Sacramento, a search warrant to return to the district court in Sacramento, and a rented truck to return to the U-Haul facility in Chico."

"That's up to Hank," said Calloway.

"All right," said Glance. "I'm sorry I said anything."

"You should be," mumbled Calloway.

"Would you guys stop!" said Remington.

Everyone burst into laughter and didn't stop until they were interrupted by the phone ringing in Glance's kitchen.

"Five bucks it's the captain," said Calloway.

"Why would Chuck be calling now?" said Mayberry.

"The inspector probably got a call from Radcliff's attorney."

Glance strolled into the farmhouse kitchen and reached for the phone receiver on the wall. "Hello."

"Hank, this is Chuck."

"Good morning, Chuck," said Glance, looking back to find three wild-life officers listening from the doorway between the kitchen and the dining room.

"The last time I looked, it was 1:00 in the afternoon," said Odom.

"Sorry, Chuck. I must have lost track of the time."

"I just received a call from the inspector. An attorney who represents multimillionaire William Radcliff just spent a half hour on the phone with him. According to the attorney, Radcliff is livid and wants everything you took from his house last night returned."

"How long has this guy been an attorney?"

"What difference does that make?"

"Everything taken from Radcliff's home last night was seized under a federal search-and-seizure warrant. A federal prosecutor out of Sacramento accompanied us while we conducted the search."

"Who was with you besides this federal prosecutor?"

"Kurt Remington, Tad Calloway, and Jack Mayberry. They're here now, going through the evidence with me. One of the items we seized was an endangered Siberian tiger that Radcliff illegally killed in the Soviet Union on March 12 of this year."

"Soviet Union! What the hell are you into now—espionage?"

"I'm just doing my job, Chuck. It leads where it leads."

"What am I supposed to tell this attorney?"

"Tell him to pound sand down a rathole."

Glance heard muffled laughter coming from the dining room.

"What!" shouted Odom.

"Tell him if his client gets anything back, it won't be until this investigation is completed and the adjudication process has played out. There's also the matter of assault and battery on a peace officer."

"Assault and battery! What peace officer?"

"Me. Yesterday morning, Radcliff elbowed me in the face and may have fractured my cheekbone. Last evening, he took a swing at me with his fist."

"Barbara, bring me my blood pressure medicine and a glass of water."

"I didn't catch that," said Glance.

"Never mind. Have you written an incident report?"

"Not yet."

"How do you do it, Hank?"

"How do I do what?"

"Get yourself involved in all these entanglements."

"Isn't that what we're paid to do?"

"Thanks, Honey."

"You're welcome."

"Not you! I'm talking to my wife. Make sure I receive that incident report by Monday."

"Will do. Thanks, Chuck. Goodbye."

TWENTY-NINE

G LANCE COULD HAVE HEARD A PIN drop when he reentered the dining room after talking to Captain Odom on the phone. "Why is it so quiet in here?" he said.

Remington, Calloway, and Mayberry rose from their chairs and gave Glance a standing ovation.

"That was a work of art," said Remington, laughing.

"Masterful," said Calloway.

"Hank," said Mayberry, slapping Glance on the back, "you're our golden boy, so you'd better get used to it."

When everyone had settled down and stopped laughing, Remington said, "It may be too late for felony conspiracy charges, but we should be able to prove that Strode and Hostetter were accomplices in the Lacey Act violation involving the Alaskan brown bear."

"That's great," said Glance. "Let's move on to the jaguar. According to Radcliff's journal, he killed it October 17, 1971, on a private ranch east of Douglas, Arizona."

"I didn't know we had jaguars in the United States," said Mayberry.

"Not very many," said Glance. "They used to come across the Mexican border into Arizona, New Mexico, and even Texas, but now only a handful have been seen in New Mexico and Southeastern Arizona. The private property where Radcliff killed this one butts up against the Mexican border."

"How do you know that?" said Mayberry.

"This morning, I called Arizona Game and Fish. They connected me with the warden who covers the southeastern corner of the state. He told me the property I mentioned is in the San Bernardino Valley and takes in a wetland that's loaded with wildlife."

"I don't think jaguars were placed on the U.S. Endangered Species List until 1972," said Remington.

"That's true," said Glance, "but the Arizona Game and Fish Commission outlawed jaguar hunting in 1969. This violation appears to be well within the statute of limitations for the Lacey Act."

"What else can you tell us about the case?" said Remington.

"Radcliff employed a guide named Raul Espinoza. Espinoza was introduced to Radcliff by Roy Strode. The hide preparation was done by a taxidermist named Phillip Rose, who lives in Douglas. The actual mount was completed by Rudd Hostetter, in Quincy." Glance reached across the table and picked up a small stack of photos. "I found these in one of Radcliff's file cabinets."

"It was sure nice of Radcliff to provide us with all these photographs," said Remington. "It makes our job so much easier."

"It *was* thoughtful of him," said Glance. "If the side of my face didn't hurt so much, I might feel more benevolent toward the sonofabitch."

"Attaboy, Hank!" said Calloway, laughing. "Don't you feel better now that you've gotten that off your chest?"

"Yeah!" said Mayberry. "Maybe Hank is human after all."

"How does it feel, Hank?" said Remington.

"You mean to be human?"

"No. I'm talking about your face. It looks worse than it did yesterday."

"Anne thinks I have a fractured cheekbone. She wants me to see a doctor."

"What's it feel like?"

"It feels kinda numb."

"You'd better listen to your wife and have it checked out."

"We were talking about the jaguar," said Glance, anguished by the poaching of such a rare, iconic species inside the United States. He passed the photos around. "One of these photos shows Radcliff standing over the cat in what appears to be a marshy area. Another one shows Radcliff and a dark-skinned man, possibly Espinoza, standing over the dead jaguar, with hounds milling around in the background."

"I'd like to have our agent in Tucson contact the taxidermist in Douglas before we contact Hostetter up here," said Remington. "I'll call him tonight and explain the situation."

"I think that's a great idea," said Glance.

"What about the other mounted animals we seized?" said Calloway.

"That's where you and Jack come in," said Glance. "According to Radcliff's journal, the black bear was killed off a bait pile north of Shasta Lake in October 1959. Radcliff drew a little sketch next to this entry. It shows a bear eating a box of donuts."

"Don't tell me Radcliff has a sense of humor," said Mayberry.

"I don't know about that," said Glance, "but he and his buddy Strode are sure brazen."

"What makes you say that?" said Remington.

"Remember the seven-point Roosevelt elk we had trouble taking down from the wall last night?"

"I do," said Mayberry. "I think I strained my back."

"Guess where they killed it?"

"In the Eureka Zoo?" said Remington, chuckling.

"No, but you're close. On November 12, 1964, Willie Radcliff and Roy Strode spotlighted the elk on a beach inside Prairie Creek Redwoods State Park. Roy Strode's nephews, Jake and Eli, helped them pull this caper off."

"Didn't you tell me Eli Strode and Gooseneck Strode were one and the same?" said Calloway.

"I did," said Glance.

"Tell us about the bighorn," said Remington, trying to speed things along.

"The bighorn ram was killed in a place called Sawmill Canyon, west of Independence, California, on September 14, 1965. Radcliff didn't provide dates of kill for the other two big-game mammals we seized last night. He did provide the locations, however: the pronghorn was grazing in an irrigated pasture near Goose Lake, and the mule-deer buck was spotlighted in an alfalfa field east of Cedarville."

"So we're going to pursue the black-bear, elk, bighorn, pronghorn, and mule-deer cases as California violations?" said Calloway.

"That's the way I see it," said Glance. "You don't have to worry about the statute of limitations because all of those illegally taken mammals were in Radcliff's possession."

"Let's talk about the tiger," said Remington.

"I've been waiting for you to say that," said Glance. "Only about a hundred and fifty wild Siberian tigers are left on Earth. Most of those live in the Primorsky Krai region of Far Eastern Russia. According to Radcliff's journal, that's where this one came from."

"Did he happen to say when it was killed?" said Remington.

"March 12, 1973."

"How do you know so much about Siberian tigers?" said Mayberry.

"Have you seen Hank's library?" said Calloway.

"No."

"Show him, Hank."

"I'd like to see it, too," said Remington.

Glance led everyone through the spacious country kitchen to a two-hundred-square-foot adjoining room with a single window and multiple rows of barnwood shelves on all four walls.

"This is where the original owner and his wife stored their Mason jars full of canned fruit and vegetables back in the 1930s," said Glance. "It turned out to be a perfect home for every book Anne and I own."

"How many of these books have you read?" said Mayberry.

"All of them at least once and some of them several times," said Glance, leading the group back into the dining room.

"Where would you suggest we start the tiger investigation?" said Remington.

Glance showed Remington, Calloway, and Mayberry the first of two typed letters he'd found in Radcliff's journal. "This one is dated July 14, 1972, and the return address is Nicolas Cantor Enterprises, 196 Ocean View Terrace, Sausalito, California. I found one of Cantor's business cards stapled to it."

"And you think this Cantor fella is involved?" said Remington.

"Up to his neck," said Glance. "Reading between the lines, Radcliff had sent Cantor a letter asking about a taimen-fishing trip to the Soviet Union. Unsure about Radcliff, Cantor wrote back that he had no business dealings in the Soviet Union."

"What does that have to do with the tiger?" said Remington.

"This second letter from Cantor to Radcliff arrived in June 1973," said Glance, handing the letter to Remington. "It tells Radcliff that the final product was delivered on June 16, 1973, and payment was due upon delivery."

"That confirms what Rebecca Radcliff told us yesterday," said Remington. "I remember her saying that her husband made three payments: $50,000, $125,000, and $75,000. Should we pay Mr. Cantor a visit?"

"Yes, but not just yet," said Glance, pointing to a second business card stapled to Cantor's first letter. "This card belonged to a man named Adrian Petrov, an assistant professor at California State University, San Francisco. A phone number is included."

"So you think Petrov is involved somehow?" said Remington.

Without saying anything, Glance reached across the table, picked up a stack of eight-by-ten photographs, and handed them to Remington. Remington thumbed through the six photographs of Willie Radcliff standing over a tiger with a bolt-action, high-powered rifle in his hands.

"Did you notice anything?" said Glance.

"What? The incredible size of the tiger?"

"Besides that. Look closely at the last photograph."

"I see a tall, thin man in the background. His hand is covering his face. Apparently, he didn't want his picture taken."

"Do you see what he's wearing?"

"It looks like a green parka with a purple sweatshirt underneath."

"What color is the lettering on the sweatshirt?"

"It appears to be gold."

"Take this magnifying glass and tell me what letters you're able to make out," said Glance.

"Most of them are covered by the coat," said Remington, deep in thought. "San Francisco State!" he blurted.

"What do you want to bet that's Professor Petrov in the picture?" said Glance.

"Do you think he's still at San Francisco State?" said Remington.

"He is, and he recently received a full professorship. I called the university administration office this morning and talked to a student intern named Betty. Betty said Professor Petrov teaches Russian History and a class called International Studies. She's actually taken his International Studies class. Apparently, Professor Petrov is quite popular with the coeds."

"What else did Betty tell you?" said Remington.

"Petrov's office is in Building 4, in the northeast quadrant of the university. His office hours are from 1:00 p.m. to 2:30 p.m., Monday, Wednesday, and Friday—no appointment necessary."

"When would you like to pay the good professor a visit?" said Remington.

"How 'bout this Friday?"

"Sounds good."

"Hank, I dropped off the keys and checked on Radcliff's arraignments this morning," said Mayberry.

"How did that go, Jack?"

"As expected, he pled not guilty to the battery charge from yesterday morning and the assault charge from yesterday evening."

"That figures."

"Since I was already at the courthouse, I decided to sit in on the arraignment. Eric Shaw, Radcliff's attorney, asked if the charges could be combined. When the deputy DA agreed, Shaw requested a jury trial. That's when things got interesting."

"What happened?" said Glance.

"Judge Graves said the jury-trial calendar for the next several months was full and the first open date was December 5. Shaw said that would be fine, expecting his client to be released on his own recognizance. 'Not so fast,' said the judge. 'These are serious charges, involving two different acts of violence against a peace officer. Your client will have to sit it out in jail until his trial date comes up.'"

"Did Shaw go into his act?" said Glance.

"You should have seen it. He whined and carried on for ten minutes until Judge Graves was notified by the court clerk that a jury trial scheduled for September 20 had been settled with a plea bargain. Shaw snatched it up like a chicken on a grasshopper. Radcliff's assault-and-battery trial is now set for next Thursday at 10:00. Will Freeman told me to tell you he wants a formal report and a list of witnesses ASAP."

"I'll make sure he gets it," said Glance. "Jack, I really appreciate your checking on this for me."

"No problem, Hank. Will I be receiving a subpoena?"

"Yes. I think the three of us will be able to handle it. I'd rather not involve Heath Marsden if we don't have to. Kurt, you and I better head for Sacramento."

THIRTY

U.S. FISH AND WILDLIFE SPECIAL AGENT Kurt Remington's undercover van pulled into the visitors' parking lot at California State University, San Francisco, at 12:30 p.m., Friday, September 14, 1973. Dressed in casual civilian clothing, Glance and Remington beat a path across campus to Building 4, Northeast Quadrant.

Reaching Building 4, Glance suggested to Remington that they check the directory near the entrance to find out where Professor Petrov's office was located. "It's down the hall where all those people are lined up," said a passing student.

"I guess we'd better get in line," said Remington. "Maybe we should have called and made an appointment."

"I kinda like the idea of surprising him," said Glance.

"Let me guess," said Remington. "So you can determine how guilty the man is by the frightened look on his face?"

"It's worked pretty well in the past."

The last student walked out of Petrov's office at 2:10. A tall, slender man with shoulder-length, light-brown hair poked his head out the door. "Anyone else?"

"Just us," said Remington.

"Come on in and have a seat. I only have twenty minutes before my next class."

Since the investigation Glance and Remington were conducting was a federal case, Glance had insisted that Remington do most of the talking. Remington had reluctantly agreed.

Petrov plopped down in a rolling chair, leaned back, and propped his feet on the desk. Remington took a chair in front of Petrov's desk, while Glance remained standing.

"You're welcome to sit down," said Petrov, looking up at Glance.

"That's all right," said Glance. "Standing feels good after the long drive."

"Long drive?" said Petrov. "Come to think of it, I don't recall seeing either of you in any of my classes."

"That's because we're not students," said Remington, pausing while Glance pulled up a chair and sat down. "I'm U.S. Fish and Wildlife Special Agent Kurt Remington, and this is California Fish and Game Warden Hank Glance."

Petrov removed his feet from the desk and sat up. His jaw dropped, and a look of terror spread across his face. "What's this about?" he said.

"We're here to talk about your Russian hunting trip with a man named Willie Radcliff," said Remington. He and Glance flipped open their identification folders and displayed them for the professor.

Petrov sat motionless, as if in a daze.

"Professor Petrov, we have a lot of questions to ask you," said Remington. "Would you like us to come back after your next class?"

Petrov stood up, walked to the window, and looked out at the passing students. "I knew it was too good to be true."

"What's too good to be true?" said Remington.

"I was just awarded a full professorship here at San Francisco State, I'm engaged to be married, and next month I'm on track to become a U.S. citizen."

Convinced that Petrov was the man in the photograph with Willie Radcliff and the dead tiger, Glance said, "Professor Petrov, you're not in custody, but we feel it's in everyone's best interests to advise you of your rights. You have the right to remain silent. Anything you say—"

"I know all about Miranda," said Petrov, sitting down at his desk. "I refer to that case in the lesson plans for one of my classes. With your permission, I'd like to give this some serious thought, talk to my fiancé, and consider whether or not I should consult with an attorney."

"That's probably a good idea," said Remington. "How much time do you think you'll need?"

"Is a week too much?"

"A week will work, as long as you're sincere and not stringing us along. Warden Glance and I will not be going away, so you'll have to deal with this matter sooner or later."

"I understand," said Petrov.

"We can arrange to meet someplace a little more private, if you'd like," said Remington.

"Yes, I'd prefer not to meet here at work, with students knocking on my door and coming in and out."

"Would you have any objection to driving to Sacramento? I can arrange for us to meet at the U.S. Fish and Wildlife Service office next Saturday. The office is closed on weekends, so we'll have the whole building to ourselves."

"I believe that would work."

"How does 1:00 sound? The address is here on my card."

"That would be fine."

"You're welcome to bring an attorney," said Glance.

"Thank you," said Petrov. "I guess I'll see you gentlemen next Saturday."

"We can't promise you anything," said Remington, standing and following Glance to the door, "but Warden Glance and I will be happy to impress upon the prosecutor how cooperative you've been."

"Thank you," said Petrov.

"Do you think we were too easy on him?" said Remington, as he and Glance walked back through the campus.

Glance gave Remington's question careful thought before answering. "Not in this case, I don't."

"Why do you say that?"

"Petrov all but admitted he was our man without being asked a single question."

"He did appear frightened, didn't he?"

"Petrified is more like it! I think the good professor has a lot more weighing heavily on his mind than a dead tiger. If we're going to crack this can of worms, we may have to take it slow and easy."

THIRTY-ONE

DURING THE DRIVE HOME FROM SAN Francisco State University, Agent Remington revisited the question of who should play the lead role in what had become known as the Radcliff Investigation. Remington agreed with Glance that it was a federal case but disagreed with the idea of his being in charge just because he happened to be a federal agent. "I wouldn't have known that Willie Radcliff or Adrian Petrov even existed, had it not been for your investigative skills, your people skills, and your incredible tenacity," said Remington. "I'm happy to act as a front man for any issue that requires a federal badge, but make no mistake about it, Hank, you're the officer in charge of this investigation."

"ASSISTANT U.S. ATTORNEY MARSDEN'S OFFICE."

"Hello, this is Fish and Game Warden Hank Glance. May I please speak to Mr. Marsden?"

"He's on the phone right now. Would you like to wait, or shall I have him call you?"

Marsden returned Glance's call in fewer than five minutes. "Hank, how is our investigation going?"

"It's going well, Heath. Kurt and I contacted a key figure last Friday, in San Francisco. His name is Adrian Petrov. We have a formal interview set up for this coming Saturday, at the U.S. Fish and Wildlife office in Sacramento. Are you available?"

"What time?"

"We asked him to be there at 1:00. He may bring an attorney, so having you there would put us in a position to make concessions, if necessary. Kurt and I are ninety-nine percent sure that Petrov was involved in the killing of that endangered Siberian tiger. We have a photograph to prove it. Based on Petrov's reaction when we identified ourselves and asked about his association with Willie Radcliff, that tiger isn't all he's worried about."

"I may show up wearing my golfing clothes, but I'll be there," said Marsden. "How did Radcliff's arraignment turn out?"

"There were actually two arraignments. One was last Tuesday, three hours after he elbowed me in the face. The other was twenty-four hours later, after he took a swing at me the evening we conducted the search."

"I witnessed the swing," said Marsden.

"Which brings me to this question: How busy is your schedule this Thursday, September 20?"

"I'm in the middle of a trial and will be in court all day."

"That makes it easy. I won't give the deputy DA your name, and you won't receive a subpoena."

"Thanks, Hank. I appreciate that. By the way, what did you find out from the doctor about the side of your face?"

"He said there appeared to be a hairline fracture but didn't think surgery was necessary."

"What else did he say?"

"He recommended I stay away from the person who did it to me. I told him I was safe for now because the man who did it is in jail."

"Let's hope the trial goes well and he stays there. I'll see you next Saturday."

WILLIE RADCLIFF'S JURY TRIAL BEGAN RIGHT on schedule. Wardens Glance, Calloway, and Mayberry testified as to what had actually happened. Deputy DA Will Freeman presented a photograph of Glance's black-and-blue face and a copy of the doctor's diagnosis.

Radcliff's defense for the charge of elbowing Glance in the face was as expected: "I was minding my own business, on my own property, when this game warden grabbed me by the collar. Fearing for my safety, I wheeled around and accidentally brushed him with my elbow."

Radcliff's defense for the charge of trying to punch Glance in the face was also predictable: "I told them to get off my property, but I never tried to hit anyone. It's all a pack of lies, made up by those three game wardens over there."

The jury found Radcliff guilty on both counts.

"Mr. Radcliff, do you remember what I said to you the last time you appeared in my courtroom?" said Judge Ronald Graves before sentencing.

Radcliff shook his head.

"Let me refresh your memory. You had been arrested the night before for hitting your wife. She had chosen not to press charges, so I had no choice but to let you go. As you were leaving, I called you up to the bench and advised you to consider yourself warned."

"I don't remember that, either," said Radcliff.

"That's because you only hear what you want to hear," said Judge Graves. "I'm going to give you some time to improve your listening skills. Taking into consideration the nine days you've already served, I'm sentencing you to serve eleven months and twenty-one days in the Butte County Jail, commencing now. Bailiff, take this man away."

Saturday afternoon found Warden Glance and Agent Remington at the U.S. Fish and Wildlife office in Sacramento. They had arrived at 12:15, giving them time to prepare the conference room and set up the tape recorder.

"Do you think he'll show?" said Remington.

"He'll show," said Glance, shifting chairs around.

"How can you be so sure?"

"Because he has too much to lose if he doesn't—the possibility of becoming a U.S. citizen, his professorship at San Francisco State, and maybe even his future wife."

"That makes sense. What time is Heath Marsden supposed to be here?"

"I told him the meeting was set for 1:00. He said he had a golf date this morning and may be late."

Glance and Remington heard tapping on the glass door at the front of the building. "That may be Heath now," said Glance.

Marsden arrived dressed in tan-colored slacks and a blue-and-white, collared golf shirt. "We're so glad you made it," said Glance, pushing the door open and shaking Marsden's hand. "How was your golf game?"

"Not so good. My mind was on this meeting instead of my follow-through. When I shanked the ball on the sixteenth hole, I told the other three to carry on without me."

"I hope this meeting didn't cause you any problems with your golfing buddies."

"They were still laughing when I left. My ball had bounced off an oak tree and rolled down the bank, into the American River."

Glance laughed and led Marsden down the hallway to the conference room.

"How'd Radcliff's jury trial go?" said Marsden.

"He was found guilty on both counts and sentenced to serve eleven months and twenty-one days in the Butte County Jail."

"That's great! When you and Kurt complete this investigation, we'll know right where to find him."

"Couldn't happen to a nicer guy," said Remington, returning from the coffee room. "Heath, would you like a cup? I know Hank doesn't want one."

"Sure," said Marsden. "I see you have a tape recorder set up."

"Yes," said Glance. "Would you mind being the operator and guiding us through the proceedings?"

"I think I can manage that," said Marsden, taking a chair at the conference table, next to the recorder. "Is your boy going to show?"

"Somebody's knocking at the front door right now," said Glance, leaving the conference room.

Glance returned with Adrian Petrov, a beautiful young woman, and a thirty-plus-year-old gentleman wearing a dress shirt and tie.

"Professor Petrov," said Glance, "you've already met Agent Remington. This is Assistant U.S. Attorney Heath Marsden. Please introduce the young lady and the gentleman you brought with you."

"Thank you, Warden Glance. This is my fiancé, Kristina Blum, and my attorney for today, Aaron Bauman. Professor Bauman teaches constitutional law at San Francisco State and has agreed to sit in on the meeting."

"Would any of you like coffee?" said Remington.

"I'll take a cup," said Bauman.

When everyone had settled in, Marsden turned on the tape recorder and said, "For the benefit of the tape recording, those present are Professor

Adrian Petrov, Attorney Aaron Bauman, Kristina Blum, California Fish and Game Warden Henry Glance, U.S. Fish and Wildlife Special Agent Kurt Remington, and Assistant U.S. Attorney Heathcliff Marsden. The date is September 22, 1973. The time is 1:05 p.m."

"Before we begin, I'd like your assurance that anything Professor Petrov says during this meeting will not be used against him," said Bauman.

"How do you officers feel about that?" said Marsden, addressing Glance and Remington.

"I would agree on two conditions," said Glance. "One, we may use evidence we already have against Professor Petrov if he fails to fully cooperate. Two, Professor Petrov must agree to testify against Willie Radcliff, should Radcliff's case come to trial."

"Agent Remington," said Marsden, "what about you?"

"I believe Warden Glance has sufficiently addressed my concerns."

"Please excuse us for a few minutes," said Bauman.

Petrov and Bauman left the room to discuss the conditions brought up by Glance. Marsden turned off the tape recorder. He turned the tape recorder back on when Bauman and Petrov returned to the room a few minutes later.

"I accept the conditions brought up by Warden Glance and agree to answer any questions that are asked," said Petrov.

"Warden Glance, why don't you begin the questioning," said Marsden.

"Thank you," said Glance. "Professor Petrov, are you still associated with Nicolas Cantor?" Glance had learned about Cantor by painstakingly examining everything in Willie Radcliff's journal. He suspected that Radcliff and Cantor may have engaged in a criminal conspiracy.

"No. I severed my relationship with Mr. Cantor on March 16 of this year and haven't seen or heard from him since," said Petrov.

"Please tell us how you happened to be in the Primorsky Krai region of the Soviet Union with Willie Radcliff on March 12, 1973," said Glance.

"It's a long story. Do you want to hear it from the beginning?" said Petrov.

"Yes," said Glance. "We may interrupt you with questions as we go along."

"Very well. I originally came to the United States six years ago, on a student visa which has since been extended. Three years of graduate work and living expenses in the San Francisco Bay Area required a bank balance way beyond my means. I grew up in one of those ten-story Soviet government apartment buildings you see on American TV; you can imagine how difficult it would have been for me to come up with that kind of money."

"Are you saying that you needed a sponsor?" said Remington.

"Yes. Nic Cantor could be described as my unofficial sponsor."

"Why did you refer to him as your *unofficial* sponsor?" said Glance.

"Because he provided the money but had nothing to do with my acquiring a student visa or being admitted to UC Berkeley. Mr. Cantor is quite secretive, as you'll learn from my statement."

"How did Mr. Cantor's apparent generosity come about?" said Marsden.

"While I was attending the University in Khabarovsk, I worked as a part-time hunting and fishing guide for the outfitting business owned and operated by Nic Cantor and Leonid Grekov. I hadn't actually met Mr. Cantor until I was introduced to him by Mr. Grekov."

"Where is this outfitting business located?" said Glance.

"Most of the clients come from the United States. The actual hunting and fishing takes place in Far Eastern Russia. When I say Far Eastern Russia, I'm talking about the Soviet Union."

"Thanks for making that clear," said Marsden. "Please continue."

"Mr. Cantor was impressed with my people skills and how well I spoke English. He asked me to become one of his associates in the United States. Based on our agreement, Nic Cantor would pay my educational expenses and I would accompany wealthy Americans on expensive hunting and fishing trips to Far Eastern Russia four times a year."

"What, exactly, did you do on these trips?" said Glance.

"I carried the necessary papers, dealt with any Soviet officials we encountered, and made sure our clients stayed out of trouble."

"Does Nic Cantor now live in Sausalito, California?" said Glance, increasingly interested in Cantor as a possible suspect.

"The last time I saw Nic, he was still living at 196 Ocean View Terrace, Sausalito. By the way, the name he was born with is Alexey Nikolaev. He goes by Nic Cantor here in America."

"Please tell us about your association with Willie Radcliff," said Remington.

"The first time I met Willie Radcliff was in September 1972. I accompanied him on a taimen-fishing trip into the wilderness north of Komsomolsk."

"Did he discuss anything with you during this trip?" said Glance.

"Plenty!" said Petrov. "During the commercial flight from San Francisco to Seoul, South Korea, Radcliff bragged to me about all the animals he'd killed for the trophy room in his mansion. He seemed particularly proud of what he called his kitty collection."

"His kitty collection?" said Marsden.

"Yes. He described killing a number of big cats, including African lions, a leopard, a jaguar, and a mountain lion."

"What else do you remember about the fishing trip?" said Glance.

"During the drive from Khabarovsk to Komsomolsk, a tiger crossed the road in front of us. For the next several days, all Radcliff talked about was adding a Siberian tiger to his kitty collection. He said he was willing to spend a fortune to make that happen."

"You and Radcliff must have gotten along well if he spoke so openly in front of you," said Glance.

"I don't think he liked me at all. You must understand that Willie Radcliff is the quintessential braggart. He loves boasting about the big game he's killed."

"What else happened on the drive to Komsomolsk?" said Remington.

"After the tiger had disappeared into the woods, our driver, Oleg Kozlov, told me a story about an old school chum he'd run into in a Khabarovsk bar. Kozlov spoke limited English, so he told me the story in Russian."

"Are you saying that Radcliff didn't understand what was being said?" said Marsden.

"Not a word. Kozlov's school chum was a trapper named Igor Popov. While Kozlov and Popov bought each other drinks, Popov bragged about how he and his cousin, Yegor Vasiliev, had killed a mother tiger and her cub. Popov pulled a photograph out of his handbag. The photograph showed Igor Popov standing over the mother tiger and her cub with an AK-47 rifle in his hand. The date stamped on the photograph read November 5, 1971. I wrote all of this on the back of my hand while Oleg was telling the story."

"Did he see you doing that?" said Remington.

"No. I was sitting in the back seat, and he was busy driving through some pretty rough country."

"Why did you write down what he was telling you?" said Glance.

"Because it made me angry at the time and I thought about turning the information over to a Soviet game inspector . . . if I could find one."

"Did you ever find one?" said Glance.

"No, but I asked Oleg what his friend had done with the two tigers he'd killed. Oleg said Popov and Vasiliev sold the tigers to a Chinese business-man from Mudanjiang. For those of you not familiar with Far Eastern Russia, Mudanjiang is north of Vladivostok, about an hour inside the Chinese border."

"I'm surprised that you're able to remember all of this," said Marsden.

"As I said, I wrote the names of the two trappers and any important details on the back of my hand. You must understand that lawlessness in the Soviet Union is rampant, particularly when it comes to poaching wild-life. There are high-ranking officials and public figures who poach at will and seldom suffer any consequences. People like the two trappers I just told you about don't respect wildlife laws. They think they should be able to trap and kill anything they want. Very few wildlife officers like you exist in the Soviet Union. Those who do are paid almost nothing."

"How do you know all this?" said Marsden.

"While doing graduate work at UC Berkeley, I wrote a research paper on the subject."

THIRTY-TWO

Being the consummate investigator, Warden Henry Glance steadfastly kept his own counsel, played his cards close to his chest, and refrained from displaying his personal feelings during the course of an investigation. That practice proved increasingly difficult as the questioning of Adrian Petrov continued. The more Petrov talked about the Russian trappers who'd killed the mother tiger and her cub, the more animosity boiled up inside Glance's gut. Igor Popov and Yegor Vasiliev were going to have to pay for their unspeakable crimes, and somehow, someway, Henry was determined to see that they did.

"Professor," said Glance, "did Popov and Vasiliev have anything to do with Willie Radcliff eventually killing a tiger?"

"Yes," said Petrov.

"Thank you," said Glance. "Please tell us what happened during the flight back to San Francisco after the 1972 taimen-fishing trip."

"During the flight back to San Francisco, Willie Radcliff complained continually about not catching any fish. He insisted that Nic Cantor compensate him."

"Was Radcliff implying that Cantor should arrange a tiger hunt, or did he actually say it?" said Glance.

"He implied it to me, but three weeks later, he came right out and said it to Nic Cantor."

"Can you elaborate?" said Remington.

"On September 30, 1972, Nic Cantor met with Willie Radcliff on Cantor's boat moored in Sausalito Yacht Harbor. I knew about the meeting at the time, but Nic didn't tell me what was said until March 9, 1973."

"What did Cantor tell you about the meeting?" said Glance.

"He said he and Radcliff had come to a business agreement. Radcliff would pay him a quarter million dollars to set up a Siberian-tiger hunt in the Primorsky Krai region of Soviet Russia. I was to accompany Radcliff and keep him out of trouble, like I'd done during the taimen-fishing trip."

"How much of that quarter million were you supposed to receive?" said Marsden.

"Twenty-five thousand."

"How did you react when Cantor said you were going back to Russia and again would be charged with keeping Radcliff out of trouble?" said Remington.

"I protested vehemently, but Nic said Radcliff had already paid him part of the money and Grekov, Nic's business partner in the Soviet Union, had already located a tiger. I found the part about Grekov already locating a tiger hard to believe."

"Why was the part about Grekov already locating a tiger hard for you to believe?" said Glance.

"Tigers don't stand still. I figured they must have trapped it somehow. Leonid Grekov and his crew have pulled that same trick with bear-hunting clients."

"Please elaborate," said Glance.

"Kamchatka bear hunts provide the majority of outfitting profits Nic Cantor and Leonid Grekov make every year. On occasions when bears are scarce, they sometimes bait them in and capture them in a culvert trap."

"Go on," said Glance.

"They lead the client to a spot near the location where the trap is hidden. When the client is in position, someone releases the bear, and the client shoots it."

"Is this without the client knowing that the bear has just been released from a trap?" said Remington.

"Yes," said Petrov. "The clients are so excited about killing one of those mammoth bears, they don't ask where it came from."

Glance shook his head. "You said you vehemently opposed the idea of assisting Radcliff on the tiger hunt. What, exactly, did you say to Cantor?"

"I said Willie Radcliff was the most despicable man I'd ever met and I wanted nothing more to do with him."

"Were there any other reasons you refused to go?" said Glance.

"Yes. There are fewer than a hundred and fifty wild Siberian tigers left on Earth. The idea of killing one repulsed me. I expressed my feelings to Radcliff several times during the previous September's fishing trip."

"But you went anyway," said Remington. "What changed your mind?"

"If you knew Nic Cantor, you'd know the answer to that question. He's a very persuasive man, and he didn't get to be as wealthy and successful as he is by forgiving people's debts."

"Did you take the twenty-five thousand?" said Glance.

"I accepted half of it before the trip but refused to accept the other half when I returned. After you hear the rest of my story, you'll understand why."

Glance motioned with his hand for Petrov to continue.

"Leonid Grekov and Mikhail Pasternak picked up Radcliff and me at the airport in Vladivostok. Pasternak is Grekov's right-hand man and an expert skinner."

"What does Grekov look like?" said Remington.

"He's short and stout, with bushy, gray hair and a Joseph Stalin mustache."

"Do you remember the date you arrived in Russia?" said Glance.

"The day everything happened was March 12, 1973, so the day we arrived in the Primorsky Krai had to be March 11."

"Was this a commercial flight?" said Remington.

"Not all of it. We flew on a commercial airplane from San Francisco to Seoul, South Korea, and by cargo plane from Seoul to Vladivostok. It was the same World War II-era cargo plane we had flown to Khabarovsk the previous September. Nic Cantor owns a significant share of the company."

"You must have been tired by the time you arrived," said Marsden.

"We were exhausted. Grekov invited us to spend the night at his home near Shkotovo. Early the next morning, we drove for almost four hours to the area where the tiger was supposed to be. On the way, I questioned Grekov about it. We both spoke in Russian so Radcliff wouldn't understand.

Grekov said he had asked Oleg Kozlov, one of our drivers, if he knew any-body who could find us a tiger. Oleg introduced him to Igor Popov."

"Is this the same Igor Popov who'd killed the mother tiger and her cub?" said Glance.

"Yes. According to Grekov, Popov was working on the loading docks in Nakhodka the day he talked to him."

"What day was that?" said Remington.

"Grekov didn't tell me the exact date. He said it was in early October 1972. He offered Popov forty thousand rubles if he could find a live, full-grown Siberian tiger for his client. Popov said it might take some time, but he was pretty sure he and his cousin could do it."

"And Grekov told you all this?" said Glance.

"Yes. He also told me about Igor Popov and Yegor Vasiliev inheriting a large tract of land in the mountains of the Primorsky Krai. For the previ-ous ten years, the two cousins had spent their winters trapping and hunt-ing out of a shack on the property."

"What mountains are you talking about?" said Glance.

"The Sikhote-Alin Mountain Range—one of the few places on Earth where wild Siberian tigers still exist."

"So it wasn't a miracle that these two trappers were able to find Grekov a tiger?" said Marsden.

"Extremely unlikely, but not necessarily a miracle. Sometime during the first week of March 1973, the two trappers found fresh tiger tracks in the snow near their shack. Popov called Grekov from the store in Lazo. Grekov and Pasternak brought in a culvert trap and set it near the spot where the tracks were found."

"How did they do that?" said Marsden.

"The trap was mounted on a trailer."

"What did they bait it with?" said Glance.

"They baited the trap with a freshly killed deer Popov shot for the occa-sion. Popov and Vasiliev were the type I described earlier—they didn't believe game laws applied to them. Two nights after baiting and setting the trap, they found it occupied by a full-grown, male Siberian tiger."

"Please tell us more about the trip to the trappers' property," said Glance.

"We drove through miles of scenic countryside before coming to a locked gate on the east side of the road. I looked at a map this week in preparation for our meeting. As near as I can figure, the gate is about ten miles north of the village of Lazo."

"That's very helpful," said Glance.

Remington motioned Marsden to turn off the tape recorder. Marsden nodded.

"Excuse me," said Remington, "would anyone like more coffee?" Bauman and Marsden declined. Blum said she'd like a cup.

"Professor Petrov, please continue," said Marsden, turning the tape recorder back on.

"Grekov handed me the key to the gate and said to make sure I locked it after we went through. We splashed our way in and out of mud puddles for two miles before coming to a barn and a rundown shack. About fifteen meters from the barn was the steel culvert trap Grekov had told me about. I suspected the tiger was inside."

"Were Popov and Vasiliev there when you arrived?" said Glance.

"Yes. They came out of the shack to greet us."

"What type of weapon did Radcliff use on the tiger hunt?" said Remington.

"He used his own .30-06 rifle. Nic Cantor smuggled it into the country for him."

"How was Cantor able to get the rifle through Soviet security?" said Glance.

"Nic Cantor's primary business is shipping. Outfitting for rich hunters and fishermen is a sideline. You must understand that the Soviet government is infested with opportunistic larcenists. Nic Cantor has been able to smuggle just about anything in or out of the Soviet Union by utilizing the myriad contacts he's developed and financially nurtured over the years."

"You mentioned that Cantor owns interest in a cargo plane," said Glance. "What else is he invested in?"

"Nic owns a fleet of trucks in Oakland and a fleet of trucks in Alaska. He's part owner of a cargo ship, and he's the major stockholder of an Anchorage bank."

"Do you happen to know the name of the bank?" said Remington.

"Gold Rush Savings and Loan. There's one in Anchorage, one in Fairbanks, and one in Juneau."

"Let's cut to the chase," said Glance. "Did Radcliff shoot the tiger?"

"Yes."

"Did he shoot it while it was still inside the trap?" said Marsden.

"No. As heartless as I knew Willie Radcliff to be, he refused to shoot the tiger while it was still inside the trap."

"So what happened?" said Remington.

Kristina Blum began to whimper softly and covered her face with a scarf.

"Was it something I said?" said Remington. "I hope she's all right."

"Kristina, would you like to wait outside in the car?" said Petrov.

"No. I'll be all right. Just give me a minute."

"I'm sorry, gentlemen," said Petrov. "We've lost sleep over what I'm about to tell you, but Kristina and Aaron both agreed that I should come clean and tell the whole story."

Marsden stopped the tape recorder and suggested they take a ten-minute break. During the break, Marsden used Agent Campbell's office phone to call his wife.

"My wife and I had made plans for this evening," Marsden said to Glance and Remington. "I just called to tell her I was going to be late."

"How did she take it?" said Glance.

"She knows it goes with the territory."

"I wish I had a dollar for every time I've called Anne to tell her I was going to be late," said Glance.

"You'd be a millionaire?" said Remington. "By the way, I have a feeling you were right."

"Right about what?" said Glance.

"When you told me you thought the good professor had more weighing heavily on his mind than a dead tiger."

"I believe that now more than ever."

THIRTY-THREE

"I'D LIKE TO KNOW A LITTLE more about the two trappers, Igor Popov and Yegor Vasiliev," said Glance, when everyone had returned to the conference room.

"Popov and Vasiliev were in their forties," said Petrov. "Popov was short and a little on the chubby side. Vasiliev was a big, unsophisticated lout with a thick, gray beard. Based on what I witnessed, the two of them lived a primitive lifestyle."

"You seem to be describing them in the past tense," said Glance. "Is there something we should know?"

Blum let out with a muffled squeal.

"If you'll permit me to continue my story," said Petrov, looking over at his fiancé, "everything will become perfectly clear."

"Then please proceed," said Glance.

"The skinner, Mikhail Pasternak, was standing on top of the culvert trap. His job was to lift the trap door and set the tiger free. Popov and Vasiliev were standing off to our right, halfway between the trap and their shack. Radcliff was about twelve meters from the trap, directly facing the trap door. Grekov and I were standing three meters behind Radcliff, with our backs against the barn. The Russian carryall was backed against the barn, about three meters to our left."

"What happened next?" said Glance.

"When Radcliff said he was ready, Grekov shouted out to Pasternak and told him to free the tiger. The higher Pasternak lifted the trap door, the more the sunlight poured in, exposing the frightened animal."

"Frightened?" said Remington. "Didn't he come out right away?"

"No. I can't tell you how badly I felt, seeing that magnificent creature cowering at the back of the culvert."

"Cowering?" said Marsden.

"Yes, cowering. Instead of charging out of the culvert, like we expected him to do, he was crouched on his haunches, with his ears folded back. I saw him flash his teeth once or twice, but he never growled or displayed any signs of aggression."

"What was Radcliff doing while this was going on?" said Glance.

"He kept saying, 'When's he gonna come out? When's he gonna come out?' That went on for about ten minutes, until Grekov shouted, 'Shut the hell up, you whining fool!' Grekov's gruff voice must have spooked the tiger, because out he came, bounding straight for us."

"How did you react?" said Marsden.

"Grekov and I were running for the carryall, when we heard a rifle shot, followed by a loud clang. Radcliff had panicked and jerked the trigger. His bullet ricocheted off the trailer, causing the tiger to bolt left, in the direction of the two trappers."

"What did the trappers do?" said Marsden.

"They just stood there like deer in the headlights. Neither of them knew which way to turn. I remember Grekov shouting, 'Run, you dumb sonsabitches, run!'"

"In Russian or English?" said Glance.

"In Russian. Neither Popov nor Vasiliev spoke a word of English. Vasiliev was in such a panic, he knocked his cousin down and trampled him while trying to make it to the safety of the shack. Popov was climbing to his feet, when the six-hundred-pound tiger pounced on his back, drove him to the ground, and plunged his canines into the trapper's neck. The tiger's powerful jaws were still gripped around Popov's neck when Vasiliev came running back, wielding a shovel. He raised his arms over his head and was about to strike the tiger, when Radcliff fired his second shot."

"Was that the shot that killed the tiger?" said Glance.

"No. That was the shot that killed Vasiliev."

A hush swept over the room. Remington looked across the table at Glance, made eye contact, and nodded that Glance's hunch had been correct. Petrov's fiancé again began to whimper.

"Shall I continue?" said Petrov.

"By all means!" said Glance. "Please tell us what happened next."

"Radcliff missed the tiger and hit Vasiliev right between the eyes. Vasiliev fell backwards into a mud puddle and never moved again. The rifle blast caused the tiger to drop Popov and race across the meadow for the distant hills."

"How did Radcliff react to having shot Vasiliev?" said Glance.

"I don't think it bothered him at all. Especially with Grekov shouting in his ear, 'He's getting away, he's getting away!'"

"Let me get this straight," said Marsden. "Two humans have been killed and Radcliff and Grekov are more concerned about the tiger getting away?"

"I know this is hard to believe," said Petrov, "but that's exactly what happened."

"What did *you* do?" said Glance.

"I was furious and started shouting, 'Enough! Enough!'"

"Did Radcliff respond to that?"

"No," said Petrov, his fiancé weeping heavily. "Instead of putting down his rifle and ending this fiasco, Radcliff stepped over to the carryall and rested his left arm across the hood. 'All cats are the same,' he said. 'This one will stop for a breather, and that's when I'll take him.'"

"Did the tiger stop?" said Remington.

"I prayed he wouldn't, but the tiger did exactly what Radcliff had predicted. He reached a point about seventy-five meters out in the meadow, slowed to a stop, and looked back over his shoulder. I can still hear Radcliff's rifle going off and see that magnificent beast's legs give way beneath him."

"How did Radcliff react?" said Glance.

"He was jumping around like a damn fool, shouting, 'I got him! I got him!'"

"What happened next?" said Remington.

"Grekov told Radcliff to bring his rifle and follow him and Pasternak out to where the tiger's body lay. After confirming that the tiger was dead, Pasternak walked back to the carryall to gather his skinning equipment and Radcliff walked back to get his camera."

"Was anything at all said about the dead trappers?" said Marsden.

"Not a word. I ran over to see if Popov had a pulse. He looked like he'd been run through a meat grinder. Vasiliev was lying on his back in the puddle with a bullet hole where the bridge of his nose had been. His eyes were wide open, staring up at the sky."

"What did you do next?" said Glance.

"I walked into the shack in hopes of finding something I could use to cover their bodies."

"I don't suppose the trappers had a phone?" said Marsden.

Petrov smirked. "Unless you count the primitive hand pump at the kitchen sink, they didn't even have indoor plumbing. The stench of rotting flesh was so strong inside the shack, I had to unzip my coat and cover my face with the tail end of my sweatshirt."

"Rotting flesh?" said Marsden.

"Yes, rotting flesh. The inside of the shack was stacked floor to ceiling with stretched animal hides."

"Were you able to find anything to cover the trappers' bodies?" said Glance.

"I found a couple raggedy blankets in the bedroom, along with this photograph that was tacked to the wall." Petrov handed the photo to Glance.

"This must be the same photo Popov showed Kozlov in the Khabarovsk bar," said Glance. "It shows the dead tigress and her cub lying in the snow and that poaching miscreant standing over them with a rifle in his hand."

Marsden cleared his throat and pointed toward the tape recorder.

"Sorry," mumbled Glance.

"That poaching miscreant was Igor Popov," said Petrov. "I'm sorry if I sound callous, but I find it fitting that a tiger had given that disgusting little man the punishment he deserved."

"Poetic justice?" mumbled Glance.

Again, Marsden cleared his throat and pointed to the tape recorder. "Please continue," he said.

"I walked outside and was about to cover the two trappers with the blankets I'd found, when I looked up to find Grekov and Radcliff watching me."

"Why do you think they were watching you?" said Remington.

"They both knew how I felt about killing the tiger, not to mention what had happened to the two trappers. Had I even hinted about contacting the authorities, there would have been three bodies lying in the mud instead of two."

"Are you sure about that?" said Marsden.

"I'm positive. Leonid Grekov is a cold-blooded killer. He was a sniper in the Soviet Army during World War II, and just like many of the Soviet leaders, places no value on human life. I don't have to tell you what a heartless sonofabitch Willie Radcliff is."

"What happened next?" said Glance.

"I had just finished covering the bodies, when Grekov shouted, 'We need your help out here.'"

"What did he want?" said Remington.

"I wasn't sure, but I figured I'd better do what he said if I wanted to keep on living. I had almost reached their location when I looked up to find Grekov snapping photographs of Radcliff standing over his trophy. I asked him to stop until I was out of view, but he kept right on clicking the shutter."

"Do you think that was deliberate?" said Glance.

"Of course it was deliberate. In Grekov's twisted mind, it was a way of solidifying my participation in the crime and preventing me from telling anyone about it."

"What did they end up doing with the trappers' bodies?" said Glance.

"While Pasternak skinned the tiger, Grekov and Radcliff walked back across the meadow to the dead trappers. Grekov fished through Popov's pockets, then grabbed him by the arms and dragged him into the shack. Radcliff grabbed Vasiliev by the legs and dragged him inside. He apparently couldn't stand the smell, because he came running back out. Grekov remained inside the shack for another twenty minutes."

"What do you think he was doing?" said Glance.

"I know exactly what he was doing—he was searching for the forty thousand rubles he'd paid Popov for finding the tiger. When Grekov finally did come out, he joined Radcliff and Pasternak in the meadow."

"Skinning that tiger must have taken some real skill," said Marsden.

"As I said, Mikhail Pasternak is an expert. It was approaching 4:00 p.m. when he finally finished the job. Leaving the bloody, skinned-out carcass behind, Pasternak and Radcliff carried the hide back to the carryall and secured it in a large ice chest. Then Pasternak climbed into the driver's seat, and Radcliff climbed in back with me."

"Where was Grekov while this was going on?" said Glance.

"Grekov was in the barn. I watched through the back window as he carried a fuel can to the shack and went inside. A few minutes later, he came running out of the shack and carried the same fuel can back to the barn. Emerging from the barn, he ran to the carryall and said, 'Let's get the hell out of here.'"

"Are you saying that Grekov set fire to the shack?" said Glance.

"Yes. As we drove away, I looked back and saw smoke billowing from the half-open front window."

"Where did you spend the night?" said Remington.

"We spent the night at Grekov's home. From the time we arrived until the time Radcliff and I were dropped off at the cargo section of the Vladivostok Airport, not a word was said about the two trappers. Just before Radcliff and I boarded the cargo plane for Seoul, Grekov reminded Radcliff to pay Cantor the second $125,000 when his mounted trophy arrived. Radcliff complained about having originally paid Cantor a $50,000 security deposit in cash and wanted credit for it. Grekov said he'd have to take that up with Cantor."

"Did Grekov say anything to you?" said Glance.

"Yes, and he said it in English so Radcliff would understand. 'If you value your life, you'll forget this trip ever happened.'"

"You mean he threatened you right in front of Radcliff?" said Marsden.

"Yes. I think it was Grekov's way of telling Radcliff not to tell anyone about what happened on the trip or the same thing would happen to him."

"Did Radcliff express any remorse at all about having killed Vasiliev?" said Glance.

"None that I saw. The man doesn't have a conscience. I don't think Willie Radcliff is capable of feeling guilty about anything."

THIRTY-FOUR

"**W**HAT HAPPENED WHEN YOU RETURNED TO San Francisco from Vladivostok?" said Glance, as the bell in the church steeple down the street struck 5:00. "Did you or Willie Radcliff talk to Nic Cantor?"

"It was 1:00 in the morning when we arrived at Nic's home in Sausalito," said Petrov. "Radcliff grabbed his gear from the van and drove off in his Cadillac. He did not enter the house, and he did not talk to Cantor. I saw a light on in Nic's living room, so I decided to go inside and tell him, once and for all, that we were through."

"Had he heard from Grekov about the dead trappers?" said Glance.

"He must have because he was drinking heavily and his mind was a million miles away."

"What did you say to him?" said Glance.

"I said I didn't want anything more to do with him or his business."

"How did Cantor react to that?" said Remington.

"I expected him to try to talk me out of it, but he shrugged his shoulders, made himself another drink, and flopped back down in his easy chair."

"Did Cantor say anything at all?" said Marsden.

"Not until I started to leave. That's when he pointed to an envelope on the table and said, 'That's for you.'"

"What did you do?" said Marsden.

"I told him what he could do with his money and walked out the door."

"Has Cantor tried to contact you since then?" said Glance.

"No. It's been six months and I've had absolutely no contact with Nic Cantor."

"Have you told this story to anyone other than the people in this room?" said Glance.

"No. Until you and Agent Remington showed up at my office door, I had taken Leonid Grekov's advice and tried to forget the trip had ever happened."

"How did that work out?" said Glance.

"Not very well. Every time I was reminded of those two trappers lying in the mud or being set on fire, I got sick to my stomach. More than once, I excused myself from the classroom so I could run down the hall and throw up. Fear of being arrested even caused me to stop watching crime shows on TV."

"Professor Petrov has been open and forthright throughout the interview, and he's told you gentlemen the entire story," said Petrov's attorney Aaron Bauman. "I suggest we call it a day."

When Petrov and his entourage had left, and Agent Remington had locked the office door behind them, Glance, Remington, and Marsden gathered at the conference table for a meeting of the minds.

"Where do we go from here?" said Glance.

"Considering the witness statement we just heard and the mountain of evidence you seized from Radcliff's home, you and Agent Remington have developed a reasonably good case against Willie Radcliff and Nic Cantor," said Marsden. "I'd go so far as to say we have the makings of a felony criminal conspiracy."

"I detect some reservation in the tone of your voice," said Glance. "You don't seem as excited as I thought you'd be."

"You're very perceptive, Hank. The problem I see is this. A man as wealthy as Willie Radcliff is going to hire a cadre of experienced defense attorneys. They'll attempt to quash the search-and-seizure warrant and suppress the physical evidence. If they're successful, all we have available to us here in the United States is Petrov's word against Radcliff's and possibly Cantor's."

"How can they quash the search warrant?" said Remington. "We did everything by the book and had two eyewitnesses as to what was inside

Radcliff's home. The way I see it, we had all the probable cause in the world."

"I hope you're right," said Marsden, "but I've seen iron-clad cases thrown out of court because of one nitpicky technicality and a sympathetic judge who somehow ended up presiding over the trial. I don't think they'll be able to make it stand, but you can be sure Radcliff's attorneys will say Rebeca Radcliff had no right to open her husband's safe and use the key inside to enter his private trophy room."

"We didn't use the key inside the safe to open the trophy room," said Glance. "We used the key on Radcliff's key ring."

"That's right," said Marsden. "I remember now."

"In order to make a case like that, wouldn't Rebecca have had to be operating as our agent?" said Glance. "She and Martin Fletcher went inside that trophy room long before Kurt and I even knew they existed. We didn't put them up to it."

"I understand," said Marsden, "but we're still walking on thin ice. If we had a way to corroborate Petrov's story, this case would be a slam dunk."

"I'd be happy to travel to Far Eastern Russia," said Glance, "but if I were to ask my captain for permission, it might finally send him off the deep end."

Marsden and Remington laughed.

"What if we're able to turn Nic Cantor?" said Remington. "Instead of being a defendant, he'd be a witness."

"First, we'll have to find him," said Glance. "I'm guessing Nic Cantor is long gone by now."

"What makes you think that?" said Marsden.

"It's been six months since Petrov has seen or heard from his former boss. He said Cantor was drinking heavily and didn't say two words to him the night he returned from the Russian tiger hunt. I think that's because Cantor had already heard about the two dead trappers and was worried sick. What would either of you have done if you had been in Cantor's shoes?"

"If I had been in Cantor's shoes and I had his money, I'd be safe and sound, drinking margaritas on some island," said Remington.

"I suppose I would too," said Marsden. "What are the odds of no one finding out about the two dead trappers?"

"We just did," said Glance.

"Thank you, Hank," said Marsden, chuckling. "I rest my case."

"Maybe someone should find out if Cantor is still living in Sausalito," said Remington.

"I know just the person," said Glance. "He's a warden friend of mine who works the San Francisco area. I'll give him a call the minute I get home."

"Meanwhile, I have another idea," said Marsden. "I've been doing some research and making a few phone calls since we served that search warrant the other night. There's a federal prosecutor in the U.S. Department of Justice who's made a name for himself prosecuting wildlife trafficking cases. He works out of a special division of the Attorney General's Office in Washington, D.C."

"What's his name?" said Remington.

"His name is Gavin Skerrett."

"I read about him in one of my conservation-group magazines," said Glance. "He successfully prosecuted a huge case involving elephant ivory and rhino horns."

"That's the man," said Marsden. "Another case Gavin prosecuted involved an Amur leopard pelt that was smuggled into the country. Amur leopards are even rarer than Siberian tigers, and most of them come from the same place in Far Eastern Russia."

"How can Skerrett improve our case?" said Remington.

"He may know something about dealing with the Russians that we don't. I talked to Gavin last Friday. He said to send him everything we have about the case and he'll take a look at it. By the end of the workday on Tuesday, I'd like you gentlemen to provide me with a transcribed copy of Petrov's recorded statement and a detailed report of everything that's happened since this investigation began."

"I'll have Petrov's statement transcribed by one of the stenographers in our office," said Remington. "Hank, since you've been working this investigation longer than anyone, would you like to write the report?"

"Absolutely!"

SAN FRANCISCO WARDEN MARK WILCOX'S PHONE rang at 7:40 Saturday evening, two hours after Warden Glance had left the U.S. Fish and Wildlife office in Sacramento.

"The man's name is Nic Cantor, and his Sausalito address is 196 Ocean View Terrace," said Glance.

"I've been on Ocean View Terrace a few times," said Wilcox. "It's on a hillside overlooking the harbor. Cantor must be loaded if he lives in that neighborhood."

"My informant says he keeps his boat down at the Sausalito Yacht Harbor. That's probably a good indication of how wealthy he is."

"Then the boat marina will be the first place I'll look if he's no longer living on Ocean View Terrace," said Wilcox.

"YOUR HUNCH WAS RIGHT, HANK," SAID Wilcox over the phone on Sunday evening, after checking out Nic Cantor's Sausalito address. "Cantor moved out June 18. A seven-foot professional basketball player now lives at 196 Ocean View Terrace."

"I wonder why Cantor waited until June to leave," mumbled Glance.

"What was that?"

"I'm thinking out loud, Mark. Even a wealthy man like Cantor isn't going to run out on seventy-five thousand dollars. The mounted tiger was delivered to Radcliff's home on June 16, so it makes sense that Cantor received the money a day or two later. Cantor was probably packed and ready to go when the delivery was made."

"All is not lost," said Wilcox. "I have a clue as to where Mr. Cantor might have gone."

"Mark, I had a feeling you were going to say that."

"One of my snitches answers the phone on weekends in the harbor-master's office. He scrubs algae off boat hulls the rest of the week. It just so happens that Nic Cantor was one of his regular customers. He told me I was the second person to ask about Cantor's disappearance in the last three months."

"Interesting!" said Glance. "Who was the first?"

"The first was a man claiming to be an insurance investigator. He was reportedly dressed like an Eastern European tourist when he knocked on the glass door of the harbormaster's office several Sundays ago."

"How does an Eastern European tourist dress?"

"Plaid Bermuda shorts, Hawaiian shirt, wingtip shoes, and argyle socks."

Glance laughed. "What did your snitch tell him?"

"He told him Cantor had sailed away in his sloop back in June and no one had seen him since. Then the guy asked if Joy Patrick was around."

"Who's Joy Patrick?"

"Apparently, it was no secret that Joy Patrick worked at the harbormaster's office on weekends and that she and Nic Cantor were more than just tennis partners. Someone must have given that information to this phony insurance investigator."

"What makes you think he was a phony?"

"Joy was on vacation at the time this guy showed up. My snitch was about to close the door on him when the phone rang. While my snitch was talking on the phone, he looked back to find this guy standing at Joy's desk with a postcard in his hand. He'd removed the postcard from Joy's bulletin board and was photographing it, front and back, with a pocket-sized camera. 'Hey, what the hell are you doing?' shouted my snitch. The guy dropped the postcard and ran out the door."

"Did your snitch try to stop him?"

"He said the man jumped into a gray Chevy sedan that had pulled up in front of the office. They were gone before my snitch could hang up the phone and run to the door."

"Do you have any idea what was on the postcard?"

"I'm looking at it right now. On the front is a photograph of the beach at Puerto Escondido, Mexico. Handwritten on the back are the words, 'Wish you were here.' It's postmarked July 24, 1973, and signed 'Nic.' My snitch said Joy never returned from vacation, so his boss told him to clean out her desk. He did, and, luckily for you, he kept the postcard. Would you like me to mail it to you?"

"That would be great, Mark. Please photograph the front and back, in case the card gets lost in the mail. I can't tell you how much I appreciate all your help."

THIRTY-FIVE

A FEW WEEKS AFTER THE SEPTEMBER INTERVIEW with Adrian Petrov, Assistant U.S. Attorney Heath Marsden telephoned Glance and Remington, requesting a meeting in his Sacramento office. The meeting took place on October 16, 1973. Present were Assistant U.S. Attorney Gavin Skerrett, Assistant U.S. Attorney Heath Marsden, California Fish and Game Warden Henry Glance, and U.S. Fish and Wildlife Special Agent Kurt Remington.

Skerrett was in his late thirties, slightly built, with sandy-colored hair trimmed just below his ears. He had flown all the way from Washington, D.C., leading Glance and Remington to believe they were about to hear something important.

After introductions, Marsden closed the office door. "Hank," he said, "I'm eager to hear what you've learned about Nic Cantor's whereabouts."

"Cantor moved out of his home in Sausalito June 18, 1973," said Glance. "He was last seen sailing his fifty-seven-foot sloop out of Sausalito Yacht Harbor."

"Any idea where he might have gone?" said Skerrett.

"Puerto Escondido, Mexico."

Skerrett looked over at Marsden and nodded.

"Is there something Kurt and I have missed?" said Glance.

"You'll understand by the time Gavin finishes his briefing," said Marsden, gesturing for Skerrett to begin.

"In early September of this year, the Soviet Union's ambassador to the United States contacted our State Department and requested an urgent meeting. One of our top diplomats in Washington met with the ambassador the following day. The ambassador lambasted our diplomat with a complaint about one of the Soviet Union's most cherished animals, a Siberian tiger, being illegally killed by a wealthy American named Willie Radcliff. He went on to say that the grandsons of Konstantin Popov, a prominent former member of the Soviet Union's Communist Party Central Committee, had been murdered during the commission of the crime. According to the ambassador, the bodies of the two grandsons had been set on fire in an effort to destroy the evidence."

"Heath, it sounds like the Soviet ambassador may have given us the corroboration you asked for," said Glance.

Marsden nodded. "Wait until you hear the rest of the story," he said.

"According to the Soviet ambassador, the story about the tiger being poached and Popov's grandsons being murdered had spread throughout the USSR and their citizenry was outraged," said Skerrett.

"Since when does the Soviet government care what its citizenry thinks?" said Glance.

"I said the same thing when I heard this story," said Skerrett.

"What did this Soviet ambassador want from us?" said Remington.

"He insisted that the American who had committed this heinous crime be put on trial and punished in the Soviet Union."

"How did our diplomat respond to that?" said Glance.

"He believed it was just another story made up by the Soviet government to stir hate and discontent toward the United States. Without revealing his true feelings, he told the ambassador we would look into it and get back to him."

"Did we look into it?" said Glance.

"A letter detailing the Soviet ambassador's claims was sent from the U.S. State Department to the U.S. Department of Justice. The letter suggested that this was nothing more than the usual anti-American propaganda but requested that the matter be investigated. Copies of the letter were distributed through channels, and one of them found its way to my inbox. I read it and put it aside, believing, as the author of the letter did, that it was more anti-American bullshit spread by the Soviet government."

"Had you seen our report when you read this letter?" said Glance.

"No. I didn't receive your report until a couple weeks later. I was reading Adrian Petrov's transcribed witness statement, when it suddenly dawned on me that the Soviet ambassador's complaint might have contained a shred of legitimacy."

"What did you do?" said Remington.

"I walked down the hall to my supervisor's office. He began making phone calls up the chain of command until he reached the deputy attorney general. The deputy attorney general, acting on instructions from the attorney general, scheduled a meeting with the State Department. The State Department set up another meeting with the Soviet ambassador."

"Now I understand why Heath shut the door," said Remington.

"On October 4, 1973, a high-ranking representative from the U.S. State Department, the deputy attorney general, and I met with the Soviet ambassador," said Skerrett. "Inside my briefcase were three copies of Warden Glance's report and Adrian Petrov's transcribed witness statement. The three of us compared everything the ambassador told us that day with what was written in those documents. The Soviets had inserted a few of the usual bald-faced lies, but for all practical purposes, the stories matched."

"I'm curious as to how the Soviet government learned about the tiger incident," said Glance.

"They learned about it the same way most serious crimes are revealed," said Skerrett.

"Somebody couldn't keep his big mouth shut?"

"You guessed it, Warden Glance. In this case, it was Mikhail Pasternak, the man Petrov described as the expert skinner. He reportedly bragged to his girlfriend after receiving the equivalent of twenty-five thousand American dollars for his part in the crime. His girlfriend gossiped to someone, and, soon thereafter, Pasternak received a visit from the Soviet authorities."

"What did Pasternak tell them?" said Glance.

"As you might expect, the Soviet authorities were quite persuasive. Pasternak led them to the scene of the crime, where they found the tiger skeleton and the skeletons and desiccated flesh of Popov's grandsons. Apparently it had rained the night of the incident, extinguishing the fire and leaving enough of the shack intact to prevent scavengers from drag-ging the bodies off."

"You sound as if you've seen some of the evidence," said Glance. "Did the ambassador provide photographs?"

"Yes, he showed us photos of the tiger's remains, the burned shack, and the larger grandson's skull. The photo showed a bullet hole between what would have been his eyes."

"Did Pasternak reveal the names of others involved?" said Glance.

"As I said, the Soviet police were quite persuasive. Before they were finished with Pasternak, he'd given them Willie Radcliff, Leonid Grekov, and Alexey Nikolaev—whom you know as Nic Cantor. Everyone except Radcliff is now in Soviet custody."

"How did Cantor, I mean Nikolaev, end up in Soviet custody?" said Glance.

"The Soviet ambassador refused to tell us, but our own intelligence agencies have provided what we believe is the answer to your question."

"I can't wait to hear it," said Glance.

"On Tuesday afternoon, September 4, 1973, the crew of a Mexican navy patrol boat spotted a woman running around and acting strangely on the deck of a large sailboat."

"What do you mean, she was acting strangely?" said Remington.

"She was completely naked, gagged, and her hands were cuffed behind her back."

"Where did this happen?" said Glance.

"Off the coast of Playa Santa Cruz, Mexico. The woman was identified as forty-nine-year-old Joy Patrick from Sausalito, California. Uncuffed and provided with clothing, Miss Patrick told the following story to naval lieutenant Juan Alverez. What I'm about to read is from the lieutenant's translated report.

> Miss Joy Patrick and her boyfriend, Nic Cantor, had left Puerto Escondido, Mexico, on what was to be a two-day sail. They anchored a half mile off the coast of Playa Santa Cruz for the evening. Just before daylight the next morn-ing, Patrick heard footsteps on the deck above the cabin where she and Cantor were sleeping. Five men, wearing

what appeared to be sailors' uniforms, burst into the cabin. Three of them dragged Cantor, kicking and screaming, up on deck; he was completely naked. The other two men gagged Patrick and cuffed her arms behind her back with plastic flex cuffs. Patrick stated that she was told, in broken English, not to move for at least an hour or she and her companion would be killed."

"Wow!" said Remington. "This is like one of those TV movies."

"That's not all," said Skerrett. "Our own intelligence detected an unidentified submarine off Mexico's southern coast at the time this incident occurred."

"With Nic Cantor in Soviet custody, where does that leave our case against Willie Radcliff?" said Glance.

"Nowhere," said Marsden.

"Nowhere?" said Glance. "You mean we're not going to prosecute him?"

"Tell them, Gavin."

"Alexey Nikolaev, the man you know as Nic Cantor, has reportedly provided the Soviet authorities with a detailed account of how Willie Radcliff talked him into arranging the tiger hunt. He claimed to have been dead set against it until Radcliff offered him a quarter million dollars."

"What about Grekov and Pasternak?" said Glance. "What did they have to say?"

"Grekov and Pasternak claimed to have been against the whole idea from the start, but the amount of money they were offered was more than they could turn down. They said Radcliff was so eager to kill the tiger, he shot and killed Yegor Vasiliev in the process."

"Are the three of them getting off scot-free?" said Remington.

"Not entirely. If we can believe what the Soviet ambassador told us, Grekov and Pasternak will likely be sentenced to five years in a Soviet prison in return for their testimony against Radcliff."

"What about Cantor, I mean Nikolaev?" said Glance.

"Nikolaev is a horse of a different color. He's incredibly wealthy and has connections all the way to the Kremlin. Knowing the Russians, they'll play this for all it's worth and use Nikolaev to their advantage."

"How will they do that?" said Remington.

"Isn't Radcliff a multimillionaire?" said Skerrett. "The possibilities are endless."

"How can they extort Radcliff when he's here in the United States?" said Glance.

"The Soviet government wants Willie Radcliff so badly, they've offered us a trade," said Skerrett.

"A trade for what?" said Remington.

"Two American CIA agents—one male and one female—who've been locked in the Soviet prison system since 1970."

"Are we going to accept the trade?" said Glance.

"We already have. Willie Radcliff's future is now in the hands of the U.S. State Department. Before daylight on Sunday morning, October 21—five days from today—he will be removed from the Butte County Jail by U.S. marshals, driven to Beale Air Force Base, and flown to an undisclosed location. The transfer will take place soon thereafter."

THIRTY-SIX

"**R**ADCLIFF, WAKE UP," SHOUTED BUTTE COUNTY Deputy Sheriff Ray Swanson.

"Go away and leave me alone."

"You have a visitor."

"Who is it?"

"I'm not your secretary. Get your ass out of that bunk and come see for yourself."

"What day is it?"

"It's Friday, October 19, 1973. Anything else, your highness?"

"Who's the visitor?"

"He didn't give his name, but he said he knows you."

"Tell him I can't be disturbed."

"Are you sure you want me to do that? Your attorney is the only visitor you've had since you've been in here."

Radcliff climbed from his bunk, donned his orange jumpsuit, and followed Swanson down the hallway to the visiting stations.

"You've got twenty minutes," said Swanson. "If you finish before then, push the buzzer."

"Hello, Willie. Do you remember me?" said the reed-thin, ninety-two-year-old gentleman on the other side of the glass.

"Those gold-rimmed glasses look familiar, but I can't say that I do."

"The last time we met, you and some other kid were throwing rocks at salmon up in Bidwell Park."

"I'll be damned! You're that pesky game warden who used to follow me around. Jed Sutton, wasn't it?"

"That's right, Willie. If you'd only listened to me back then, you wouldn't be in here right now." During his forty years on the job, Sutton had earned the reputation for being willing to arrest his own mother if he caught her doing something wrong. He'd reluctantly retired but softened a bit since then. The sight of his one-time nemesis on the other side of the glass had brought a glimmer of moisture to Sutton's tired old eyes.

"You woke me up to tell me that?" said Radcliff.

"I guess I did, Willie. Do you remember what I said to you?"

"No, and I don't care."

"I said one of these days, you were going to get yourself into real trouble and your rich daddy wasn't going to be around to get you out."

Radcliff pushed the buzzer.

"I heard a couple deputies whispering about your being moved soon. Where are they sending you—to Folsom?"

"Radcliff, stop pushing that buzzer!" said Deputy Swanson, opening the door and escorting the prisoner back to his cell.

"What's this about me being moved?"

"Where'd you hear that?"

"From that crazy old man."

"Don't believe everything you hear, Willie. That's how rumors get started."

Just before daylight on Sunday, October 21, 1973, four U.S. marshals swept into the Butte County Jail and snatched Willie Radcliff from his cell. They anchored him in the back of a caged corrections van and headed south toward Marysville. Three hours later, an unscheduled military transport jet lifted off from Beale Air Force Base and headed northwest.

THIRTY-SEVEN

WILLIE RADCLIFF NEARLY FROZE TO DEATH in a Vladivostok jail cell for the rest of October and all of November before being assigned a defense attorney who spoke English but displayed nothing but contempt for his client. Jury trials were unheard of in the Soviet Union at the time, so a court trial was set for December 4, 1973.

William Lawson Radcliff was charged with actions that caused the death of Yegor Vasiliev, actions that caused the death of Igor Popov, and the killing a of a fully protected Siberian tiger. Witnesses testifying for the prosecution included Alexey Nikolaev (also known as Nicolas Cantor and Gerardo Calderon), Leonid Grekov, and Mikhail Pasternak. There were no witnesses for the defense.

The Soviet judge found Radcliff guilty on all counts and sentenced him to serve fifteen years in a 1913-era penal institution near Khabarovsk. Radcliff didn't know it at the time, but two weeks earlier, the man he knew as Nic Cantor had been sentenced to serve two years in the same prison. Considering Cantor's political connections, it came as no surprise that he'd been incarcerated fewer than ten miles from the home of his sister, Sasha—the same home where Willie Radcliff had once chased her around the living room.

"THE PLAN IS SIMPLE," SAID CANTOR, meeting with Radcliff in the corner of the prison's exercise yard. "When the time is right, you'll be picked up and transported from the day's work site to Petropavlovsk-Kamchatsky, on the eastern shore of the Kamchatka Peninsula."

"When will the time be right?" said Radcliff.

"In July, when the weather warms and the land isn't covered with snow and ice."

"What happens when I get there?"

"You'll be pirated aboard a Russian cargo ship. Somewhere between Petropavlovsk-Kamchatsky and the Aleutian Islands, the cargo ship will encounter an American freighter. At that point, you'll be lowered into an inflatable life raft and the freighter will pick you up."

"I'm still not sure I can trust you," said Radcliff, "especially after you testified against me."

"What did you expect me to do, Willie? If I had refused to testify against you, my sentence would have been fifteen years instead of two. You and that crazy idea of killing a Siberian tiger are the reason I'm not in Sausalito right now, playing tennis with my girlfriend."

"Don't give me that," said Radcliff. "When I offered you a quarter million dollars, your eyes got as big as saucers."

"I give up, Willie! If you don't accept my offer and convince your wife to wire the money, you can stay here and take your chances. Considering how unpopular you are, I'll give you six months before one of these murderous thugs sticks a shiv in your gut."

"All right, I'll go along with it."

"That's the first wise decision I've ever known you to make."

On April 11, 1974, Rebecca Radcliff found a tattered, brown envelope stuffed in the mailbox next to her front door. Her first name was handwritten in large letters across the front. Inside, Rebecca found a letter penned in what she recognized as her estranged husband's handwriting.

> Rebecca:
> I desperately need your help. I'm imprisoned in the Soviet
> Union and expect to be murdered at any time unless I'm
> able to escape. Please wire one million dollars to Gold
> Rush Savings and Loan, Anchorage, Alaska. It is to be
> deposited in the account of Nicolas Cantor, account

number 264-390-876.

If you have any doubt about the authenticity of this
letter, remember the last term paper you wrote for me
at the UC College of Agriculture in Davis? It was titled
"Noxious Weeds of the Sacramento Valley."
My life is in your hands,
Willie

Rebecca seriously considered the possibility that Willie had been
coerced into writing the letter, but her overpowering sense of responsibil-
ity compelled her to follow his instructions.

EARLY ON THE MORNING OF JULY 8, 1974, Willie Radcliff and Nic Cantor
held a clandestine meeting on the way to their assigned workstations—
Cantor would keep books and perform clerical tasks at the prison
headquarters while Radcliff cut brush and moved rocks on one of the
hard-labor crews.

"Tell me again what happens when I'm picked up by the American
freighter," said Radcliff.

"The captain of the freighter is a trusted employee of mine," said Cantor.
"He may put you to work on the ship, but a month from now, you'll be back
in California, counting your money. Do you remember Oleg Kozlov?"

"Yeah, I remember him."

"He'll be the one driving the getaway vehicle."

"That makes me feel a little better," said Radcliff, his stomach churning,
"but how do I know the guards won't shoot me in the back?"

"The colonel in charge of the prison, the foreman in charge of today's
work detail, and the guards assigned to today's work detail have all been
paid handsomely. Just stick to the plan and everything will go smoothly."

"Tell me again where the getaway vehicle is going to be."

"Oleg will be parked behind the abandoned shack. The shack is about
a hundred meters north of the road where you'll be working today. The
guards don't want the other prisoners to suspect anything, so don't make
your intentions too obvious. I suggest you go about your regular business,
cutting brush, then slowly edge your way toward the shack. When you get
there, Oleg will swing around from behind and pick you up. It's all arranged.

Oleg will even bring clothes for you to change into. Any more questions?"

"I guess not."

"Good! After today, I never want to see you again."

Not a word was spoken during the forty-five-minute drive to an isolated country road near the village of Nagornoe. With rifles in hand, six uniformed guards watched as twelve prisoners were unchained by the driver and ordered off the truck. Flanked by the guards, the prisoners picked up their cutting tools and spread out along the abandoned road.

Everything progressed routinely for the first hour. Radcliff cut brush while trying to summon enough courage to make the break. Every time he turned and edged in the direction of the rickety old shack, he spotted one of the guards watching him. It was half past 9:00 when the guard watching Radcliff reached into his shirt pocket, turned his back to the wind, and lit up a cigarette. Seizing the moment, Radcliff quietly placed his cutting tool on the ground and shuffled toward the collapsing building with the boarded-up windows. When he'd gone thirty yards without incident, he quickened his pace to a fast walk. When the frightened fugitive from Soviet justice had made it halfway to his destination without causing a commotion, he threw caution to the wind and started to run.

Radcliff was approaching the shack's splintered front porch when exhaustion and an excruciating pain in his left side forced him to stop, grasp his knees, and gasp for air. Beginning to catch his breath, Radcliff peered back over his left shoulder to find six AK-47 rifles pointed straight at him.

"The big American is escaping," shouted the crew foreman, in Russian. "Kill him!"

A bullet whizzed over Radcliff's head and punched a hole in the shack's front door.

"I knew I couldn't trust him," said Radcliff, standing and facing his captors with his hands in the air. "He cheated me out of a million dollars, and now I'm gonna die out here in this field."

When a second bullet skipped past Radcliff's right foot, he shouted, "Don't shoot, you double-crossing Russki bastards! I surrender."

No sooner had Radcliff surrendered, when an army-green Russian carryall roared from behind the shack and stopped in front of him. "Get in," shouted Kozlov, just before the right-rear window was blown out.

Radcliff dove into the front passenger seat as the carryall fishtailed back around the building and sped out of sight.

"I thought I was a goner," said Radcliff. "Why are you laughing?"

"Guards not shooting at you. They fire rifles to fool other prisoners. Sit back and relax. Long journey ahead of us."

EPILOGUE

THE TELEPHONE WAS RINGING AT THE Chico, California, home of Rebecca Radcliff.

"Hello."

"Hello, this is Commander Neil Comstock, at the U.S. Coast Guard Air Station in Kodiak, Alaska. May I please speak to Mrs. Rebecca Radcliff?"

"This is she."

"Mrs. Radcliff, I'm afraid I have some bad news for you . . . Mrs. Radcliff, are you there?"

"Yes, I'm here."

"We found a man who identified himself as Willie Radcliff floating in the Bering Sea, about fifty miles east of St. Paul Island. He was incoherent and suffering from hypothermia, but he gave our rescue crew your name and phone number before he went into cardiac arrest."

"Are you saying that my husband is dead?"

"I'm afraid so. We have no idea how long he'd been floating around out there in the open ocean. Are you able to shed any light on why Mr. Radcliff's life ended that way?"

Rebecca thought for a minute before answering. "Commander Comstock, do you believe in karma?"

REBECCA ARRANGED FOR THE RETURN OF her estranged husband's body and for his burial in the Radcliff family plot, next to the mother who'd coddled him from the day he was born until the day she died. When Rebecca had taken care of what she felt were her personal responsibilities, she set about to rectify all the harm her husband had done.

All plans for further excavation and development of Radcliff property adjacent to Radcliff Mansion were canceled. Warden Henry Glance introduced Rebecca to a relatively new method of saving wildlands and open space called a conservation easement. Under the conservation easement, all 1,700 acres of undeveloped Radcliff property along the Sacramento River would remain pristine riparian forest until such time as it and Radcliff Mansion could be donated to the California State Park system.

Rebecca offered former Radcliff Farms president Bob Masterson a three-year contract to run the renamed Sacramento River Resort. Masterson would retire at the end of his three-year agreement and live off the handsome pension Rebecca had set up for him.

Rebecca offered her son, William Radcliff Junior, the position of assistant manager of the Sacramento River Resort, provided he attend college part time and earn a degree in business. Butch had developed a noticeable change of attitude after his humbling experience of being chased down, arrested, and booked into the Butte County Jail by Warden Henry Glance. Unlike his father, Butch worked well under Bob Masterson's supervision. Rebecca's plan was for her son to take over as manager of Sacramento River Resort upon Masterson's retirement.

Using funds from the sale of Radcliff Farms and its properties, Rebecca arranged generous pensions for all of the former Radcliff Farms employees who had worked for the company twenty years or longer.

Rebecca placed the remaining Radcliff Farms fortune—over sixty-three million dollars—in a nonprofit, charitable organization established to honor the memories of Preston and Molly Radcliff. The organization's mission was to preserve wildlands and open space, preserve agricultural lands, and provide scholarships and educational opportunities for the residents of Butte, Glenn, and Colusa counties.

Martin Fletcher and Rebecca Radcliff were married in the spring of 1975. Over a hundred and fifty guests, including Henry and Anne Glance, Kurt and Joyce Remington, Tad and Rose Calloway, Heath and Susan Marsden, Jack and Maggie Mayberry, Bob and June Masterson, and most of the former Radcliff Farms employees and their spouses, showed up at Sacramento River Resort. In the shade of one of California's oldest and most majestic valley oaks, they celebrated with the happy couple. Entertainment for the reception was provided by a recently revived singing group called the Martin Fletcher Trio. The group featured Martin Fletcher on banjo, Butch Radcliff on guitar, and Henry Glance on guitar. By popular request, their first number was a Gordon Lightfoot favorite titled "Did She Mention My Name?"

STEVEN T. CALLAN IS THE AWARD-WINNING author of *The Case of the Missing Game Warden*, a 2022 "Best First Novel" award finalist in the Next Generation Indie Book Awards. Callan's first two books, both non-fiction, earned excellent reviews. *Badges, Bears, and Eagles* was a 2013 "Book of the Year" award finalist (*Foreword Reviews*). *The Game Warden's Son* was named "Best Outdoor Book of 2016" by the Outdoor Writers Association of California. Callan received the 2014, 2015, and 2016 "Best Outdoor Magazine Column" awards from the Outdoor Writers Association of California.

Steve grew up in the Northern California farm town of Orland, spending his high-school years playing baseball, basketball, hunting, and fishing. With an insatiable interest in wildlife, he never missed an opportunity to ride on patrol with his father, a California Fish and Game warden. Steve graduated from CSU, Chico, and attended graduate school at CSU, Sacramento. Hired by the California Department of Fish and Game in 1974, he began his career as a game warden near the Colorado River, promoted to patrol lieutenant in the Riverside/San Bernardino area, and spent the remainder of his thirty-year enforcement career in Shasta County. Steve and his wife, Kathy, live in the Redding area.

Learn more about the author and his books at steventcallan.com.

Favorite quote: "*My love of nature is what drives my writing. I include a conservation message in everything I write.*"